PRELUDE TO TRUST

Desire was beginning to relax in Cetán's company but she was still on her guard. As the sun lowered, Cetán looked across the fire at her and smiled. "I will comb out your hair for you," he said, and moved closer to her, as though in invitation.

"I can comb out my hair myself," Desire said, rising.

"I am aware that you can comb your own hair, Wacin. I would like to do this for you. Come." He held out his hand and she moved closer, powerless to resist him, and bent to sit in the space Cetán had made for her between his powerful thighs.

As he lifted the comb to run it through her hair, the scent of wildflowers assaulted his senses. Her silken hair shimmered in the moonlight.

As he combed her lovely hair, Cetán murmured to her. He could feel her body relax against his. Aching to run his fingers over the shapely curves, he forced himself to look away from her perfection.

As he looked up at the night sky, Cetán murmured a prayer to Wakán Tanka. "Hurry the day, oh Great One, when my woman will fully open her heart to me."

Desire thought she heard Cetán say something else, but she was too tired to try and make out his words. With a soft sigh, she leaned closer to him and closed her eyes in sleep.

BOOK YOUR PLACE ON OUR WEBSITE AND MAKE THE READING CONNECTION!

We've created a customized website just for our very special readers, where you can get the inside scoop on everything that's going on with Zebra, Pinnacle and Kensington books.

When you come online, you'll have the exciting opportunity to:

- View covers of upcoming books

- Read sample chapters

- Learn about our future publishing schedule (listed by publication month *and author*)

- Find out when your favorite authors will be visiting a city near you

- Search for and order backlist books from our online catalog

- Check out author bios and background information

- Send e-mail to your favorite authors

- Meet the Kensington staff online

- Join us in weekly chats with authors, readers and other guests

- Get writing guidelines

- AND MUCH MORE!

**Visit our website at
http://www.zebrabooks.com**

LEGEND OF DESIRE

Kathleen Drymon

Zebra Books
Kensington Publishing Corp.
http://www.zebrabooks.com

ZEBRA BOOKS are published by

Kensington Publishing Corp.
850 Third Avenue
New York, NY 10022

Zebra and the Z logo Reg. U.S. Pat. & TM Off.

First Printing: July, 1998
10 9 8 7 6 5 4 3 2 1

Printed in the United States of America

For Carolyn Drymon

Thanks for introducing me to the world of romance novels. You changed my life forever.

Prologue

The ancient storyteller sat cross-legged upon Mother Earth before the ceremonial center fire. Sparks showered upward against the backdrop of a velvet night sky. Talking Woodpecker, the greatest storyteller the Sioux had ever known, had traveled many days to reach the Lakota summer valley. Earlier in the afternoon, he had traded the goods in his packs with the people. This first evening of his arrival, the entire village had turned out to listen to his storytelling.

The village children sat closest to Talking Woodpecker; the adults sat in groups, close enough to hear every word the old man spoke. Besides bringing news and gossip from other villages, Talking Woodpecker was famous for holding his audience's attention.

Making himself comfortable, and making sure all eyes were upon him, Talking Woodpecker began. "I tell you, my children, it was many summers past, after the winter when the snow blizzard covered the land and the buffalo calves died standing in their tracks, that a great chief among the Sioux left his village with a band of braves.

"It was during the moon when the ponies shed.

"The One Above sent Chief Gray Owl to the Pahá Sápa: The Black Hills, Dakota Territory."

And so he began his tale . . .

* * *

The fertile valley lay in early morning silence. Curling fingers of wood-smoke escaped the chimney, denying the cabin's appearance of isolation. Remaining in their hiding places, the band of twelve Sioux braves studied the cabin and nearby surroundings. The wasichu, white men, had been told several moons past not to remain here in the sacred Black Hills of the Sioux people. The Pahá Sápa was the home of the mighty wakinyan—thunderbird. Every inch of this land was sacred. The wasichu trespassers must be punished!

As the sun broke through the pre-dawn sky, three men made their way outside the cabin. Each carried a rifle over his shoulder. As two of the sturdy pioneers gathered axes and picks, the other took the single mule from the corral. After placing a collar and headstall on the animal, he fastened the harness and reins. With an affectionate pat to the beast, he guided the mule into the encircling forest. Already the sharp thwack of axe hitting tree trunk could be heard resounding through the valley beyond.

A cock crowed. Behind the cabin a milk cow bellowed for attention.

More life appeared around the cabin as the door opened and a dark-haired woman wearing a white cotton blouse tucked into a coarse brown skirt and a cotton apron took a few steps outside. She made clucking sounds as she scattered cracked corn over the ground for her prized rooster and four hens.

The familiar sights and sounds of early morning greeted her senses as she breathed deeply of the fresh air, lingering an extra moment to look over the valley that she, her husband, and his two brothers claimed as their own.

"Indians!" The shout broke over the brittle morning air. For a stunned moment the woman remained still, her hand freezing in midair as she reached for a handful of feed. She stared in the direction of the forest; the noises made by her husband and brothers-in-law as they cleared trees for fertile planting ground had suddenly halted.

Rifle shots brought a sudden reaction; her features paled as she watched Ben, her husband, and Samuel, his younger brother, break through the edge of the forest and run toward the cabin. The feed in her apron fell to the ground; clucking fowl rushed about her feet as they greedily devoured the feast.

"Run, Sarah, run!" The shout filled the valley, but the woman was frozen before the cabin in a stupor of disbelief as she watched Ben and Samuel try to outrun the painted Indians whose war cries and blood-curdling shouts mingled and converged, shattering the peacefulness of the beautiful valley.

A noise from inside the cabin broke through the woman's horror. At the same time she witnessed Samuel fall facedown, a tomahawk buried in the center of his back. She gasped, the sound turning to a scream as Ben suddenly fell a few feet away from his brother! Giving no thought to her actions, knowing only that she had to reach her husband's side, she began to run, her terror magnifying tenfold as she was circled by a band of Sioux warriors.

"We were wrong, Ben! We should have listened! We should have gone somewhere else! Back to St. Louis, anywhere but here!" Tears streamed down her face as she bent over her husband, her quivering fingers wrapping around the rifle still clutched in his hand. As she saw Ben's eyes close for the last time, she drew the weapon up and aimed. Pulling the trigger, the recoil sent her reeling backward against Ben's chest. As an arrow pierced her chest, she gained a second's satisfaction as she saw one of the Indians fall to the ground.

The leader of the band, Gray Owl, was the first to enter the cabin. Sounds from across the interior drew him further into the structure. Peering down into a small wooden box next to the hearth, his dark eyes widened as he looked upon the infant within.

Arriving back at their village, the victorious warriors were greeted warmly. Gray Owl did not linger among his people; instead he directed his pony toward his lodge.

Entering his tepee, Gray Owl's gaze immediately went to the woman sitting next to the center fire. As her eyes rose to his, he saw the depth of sorrow that still lingered there. His own grief over the loss of their first child had been the reason he had gathered his warriors for the raid in the Pahá Sápa.

"Wakán Tanka, God, has blessed us, wife." A small smile settled over his lips as he felt the tiny bundle in his arms squirm.

"How can you say such words, husband, when my soul is walking with the spirit people?"

"I can say these words because no longer will your soul walk with those who have gone on to join the sky people. Your soul will be reborn." Gray Owl bent near the fire and, stretching out his arm, uncovered the bundle.

Pretty Dove looked at the infant with stunned surprise.

"She is yours. The Great Spirit knows of our loss and pain. He has set the child upon our life path."

Pretty Dove took the bundle bearing the child. Clutching the babe to her bosom, she wept openly, her tears falling lightly upon the tiny, dark head. As she looked down into the heart-shaped face, the child's eyes opened to reveal stunning gold. Pretty Dove softly murmured, "Wacin un mitáwa wicánte—Desire of my heart."

One

The Great Plains, 1829

Mother Earth trembled with the vibration of thundering hooves. As the earth churned and dust settled throughout the Oglala Sioux village, everyone hurried to the entrance flaps of their lodges. Looking outside, the people glimpsed two bold warriors coming from either end of the village, clutching horsehair lead ropes bearing many fine Indian ponies.

The villagers called loudly in greeting to the warriors, many faces wreathed in smiles, for the people knew the intent of the young men. As the warriors drew closer to their destination, young and old alike followed their progress.

Approaching the largest lodge in the center of the village, both young braves halted their mounts, dark eyes hardening with the realization that each had arrived at Chief Gray Owl's lodge with the same intention.

The noise from outside drew Gray Owl away from the warmth of his center fire. After a quick glance from the entrance flap, Gray Owl turned back into his lodge. He spoke to his wife and daughter in low tones. A young maiden of eighteen summers stepped through the entrance flap and stood at her father's side as Gray Owl greeted the two warriors.

Her name was Desire and her beauty was unrivaled throughout the plains tribes. A bleached, fringed, and beaded doe hide dress covered her womanly shape. Her long legs were encased in fringed leggings, her small feet graced with quilled and beaded moccasins. Her waist-length, midnight hair was braided in plump lengths over her shoulders, vermillion-dyed leather strippings with delicate singing bells twined throughout the braids. Her smooth forehead was blessed with fine, dark-winged brows; lush jet lashes guarded her exotic gold-brown flecked eyes. Her cheekbones were high, a rose blush staining their curve. Her full lips held the power to draw the male eye, and in their depths lay the promise of paradise.

For a full minute, neither warrior spoke as they looked from the graying chief of the village to the young woman standing at his side.

It was Thunder Hawk, known among the Sioux as Cetán, The Hawk, a war chief of a Lakota Sioux tribe, who was first to break the silence. "I bring these fine ponies to you, Gray Owl. I ask that you consider them a bride price for your daughter, Wacin—Desire." As the warrior spoke, he did not hold his gaze upon the elder chief; his dark eyes warmed with hidden lights as he studied Desire's facial features. With the conclusion of his words, he watched her slender fingers reach down to caress the head of the large silver wolf that was never far from her side. With each movement, the sound of her singing bells softly filled his ears.

Gray Owl nodded silently. Looking at his daughter, he could read none of her thoughts. Her features did not reveal her feelings toward the warrior. As renowned as Wacin was for her beauty, Cetán was legendary for his strength in combat against the enemy. Gray Owl was honored that such a brave warrior desired the hand of his only child.

Appearing cool and calm, Desire felt the inner trembling of her heart. This breathless excitement overtook her only

when she was in Cetán's presence. Now his words washed
over her with an impact that was hard to ignore.

As Cetán had studied her earlier, her brilliant gaze could
see the power of his lithe body, even as he sat upon his
beautiful gray stallion. He was by far the most handsome
warrior Desire had ever seen. She forced herself not to
stare at his sculpted features for fear that her own face
would reveal more than she wished any to know. Instead,
she drew her gaze over the intricately crafted headdress he
had donned for this occasion. The headpiece contained
some seventy feathers from the tails of immature golden
eagles, each tipped with yellow horsehair and white gyp-
sum. The carefully prepared feathers had been laced to a
red tradecloth base surmounted by a skullcap supporting
a circle of feathers. A beaded brow band and an extension
of feathers reaching Cetán's waist accented the war bonnet
and covered much of the ebony hair that fell in silky rivulets
down his muscular back. Secured around his throat was a
necklace of dentalium shells and brass studs. A fully beaded
vest boasting his sacred sign of the hawk opened down his
chest to reveal the strength of his upper torso. The beadwork of his leggings matched that on his vest, with an ex-
panse of bronzed thigh exposed below his leather
breechcloth.

For a few fleeting seconds, Desire's gaze went over
the flanks of Cetán's prancing, high-strung mount. She
had heard many tales about this stallion who was called
Whirling-Warrior's-Ghost by his owner. It was told around
the campfires of the people that Cetán's mighty stallion
fought as fiercely as his master when the pair came up
against the enemy.

Sensing and resenting the attention being given to
Cetán, the second warrior boldly stated his own intention
to pursue the hand of Gray Owl's daughter.

"I seek the maiden Wacin, to join her life path with my

own. I also bring a bride price of many fine horses for you, Gray Owl."

It was not often that two such fine warriors pursued the same maiden for their lodge, Gray Owl reflected. But, wisely, he knew that his daughter was different from the other young maidens of his village. She was already known as a healer. At an early age she had been gifted with an uncommon ability to comfort and cure humans and animals. Either one of these warriors would be a fit match for his daughter.

Desire's gaze turned away from her perusal of Cetán. A nervous smile settled over her lips as she looked upon Panther Stalks. There was an easy familiarity between the two. Panther Stalks was a war chief from her own village, and often visited her father's lodge. She admitted, though, that she'd given no thought to the prospect of his becoming her husband—that is, until now.

Panther Stalks was not as large nor as handsome as Cetán, and Desire felt none of the inner trembling which overcame her every time she was in Cetán's presence.

Her smile silently faded as her glance took in Panther Stalks' appearance. He also had dressed in finery for this occasion. But, in Desire's eyes, he appeared lacking next to Cetán. His war bonnet was not as beautiful or as carefully crafted; his upper torso was covered by a buckskin shirt that had been painted and decorated with quill work and tufts of human hair. His moccasins and leggings had been painted with the same design as the shirt.

As Desire's glance took in his mount, even here she found some disappointment. He sat upon a fine war pony, but the animal lacked the high-spirited will of Whirling-Warrior's-Ghost.

Panther Stalks gloried in the warm smile he received from Desire. His gaze rose from the crown of her head, and as his black eyes sparkled with bravado, he stared boldly into Cetán's features.

Cetán's expression did not change, the only sign of his anger toward the other warrior the open display of his hand moving to the weapon at his side. Never far from his reach, the deadly weapon was secured with a beaded sash over Cetán's shoulder. A large Spanish cutlass embedded in the stock of a rifle, the blade curved to twelve inches wide and one inch thick, lay easily against Cetán's left thigh. At one end of the dangerous-looking weapon was a metal tomahawk, at the opposite end dangled the scalplock of an enemy. And, at this moment, Cetán knew that Panther Stalks was his enemy; he would not be averse to securing a piece of the warrior's hair with that on the end of his weapon.

Gray Owl was wise enough to feel the instant friction between the two warriors. Trying to calm the moment, he spoke loudly, so everyone could hear his words. "I am honored this day to have two such brave warriors coming before me with worthy horses as a bride price for my beloved daughter. I know that either of you would be a good provider for Wacin. I could ask for no more than this for my precious child." What he did not say was that he would never force his daughter to join with a warrior not to her liking. Pretty Dove and he had agreed, two summers past, that Wacin was not like other maidens, that the choice of a husband should be left entirely up to her.

As he finished his words, Gray Owl looked at his daughter. She did not betray her thoughts by the slightest facial expression. As her gaze locked with her father's, her head shook slightly. Turning around, she stepped back through the entrance flap of Gray Owl's lodge, her pet wolf closely following.

With the simplest movement of her body, the wind seemed to delicately lift the small bells twined in her hair and in the fringe at the bottom of her dress. Cetán's breath lay captured in his lungs as he watched the interplay be-

tween daughter and father. As she shook her head, he did
not feel rejection, but his heart swelled with even greater
determination. Her pride was considerable; he had sensed
this about Wacin the moment he had first laid eyes on her
two summers past. As she turned away to reenter her father's lodge, Cetán was able to breathe once more in a
regular fashion.

"Wacin is but eighteen summers," Gray Owl stated, as
though by way of an explanation for his daughter's actions.
"I would give her more time to make her choice." His
word was final on the subject of his daughter, even though
he well knew that most Indian maidens were already joined
and raising children at his daughter's age. In truth, he felt
some relief, now that the moment of his daughter's decision had passed. It would be a hard choice between these
two warriors, especially if he had been the one forced to
make such a decision.

Panther Stalks felt some slight that Wacin had not chosen
him. Both Gray Owl and his daughter had to realize that
by choosing him, she would stay here in her father's village,
near her friends and all that was familiar. These things
meant much to a young woman, and Panther Stalks knew
that he held the upper hand between himself and Cetán
as rivals for the fair Wacin.

"I will return," Cetán promised as he dropped the
leadrope tethering his horses at Gray Owl's feet. With a
movement of his thigh, Whirling-Warrior's-Ghost turned
on his hind legs, and, for a few seconds, paused. Then he
leaped into a gallop and raced out of the village.

Panther Stalks was not unaware of the imposing appearance of Cetán and his war-trained horse. Still, in his heart,
he kept the belief that he held the upper hand and would
one day soon claim Wacin for his own. He also dropped
his leadrope of ponies. Before turning away from Gray Owl,
though, he stated, "I wish to court your daughter in the
custom of the people, Gray Owl."

"That is also up to Wacin, Panther Stalks. Come this night to my fire and you will learn of my daughter's decision."

Two

The tattooed teardrop beneath Medicine Woman's right eye held the power to capture her audience's attention. The teardrop stood out starkly on the aged bronzed flesh as the old woman stared across her center fire, her bent fingers methodically crushing the yarrow plant in her medicine bowl until it became powder. "I remember the time long past when I went with my husband to a Hunkpapa village. A warrior was very sick, and my husband, Medicine Bear, was the only healer with the right medicine for his illness." Setting aside the bowl, the small woman reached out to place a braided length of sweetgrass on her fire. After the end of the grass ignited, she brought it to the bowl of her pipe and leisurely drew upon the mouthpiece; the fragrant scent of kinnikinnick—Indian tobacco made from willow bark—circled the lodge.

Desire nodded absently. Watching Medicine Woman and hearing her words, her heart was not in the conversation that was customarily shared between the two.

The old woman noticed Desire's lack of enthusiasm. Continuing her story, she hoped to spark some interest. "We traveled for four suns to reach this village where the warrior lay sick. Medicine Bear would not go on this journey without me." Again, she drew deeply on the pipe.

"When we reached the village the people were glad to see us. The warrior lay in his lodge, rolling back and forth upon his sleeping pallet. He had been kicked in the head

by a horse, and between his eyes there was a large purple
lump. He could not see, nor could he speak.

"Right away my husband knew what must be done. The
entire village helped to ready the warrior for the ceremony
of healing. He was brought into the center of the village,
while Medicine Bear readied himself. Around the warrior,
the people made a circle of sacred sage, and within this
circle was another of sweet grass. The sweet grass was set
afire and it gave off an aromatic scent.

"Medicine Bear did not keep the people waiting long.
He was a compassionate man and did not wish anyone to
linger in pain. I will always remember the minute he entered the circle of sacred grasses. The people gasped in
surprise, their sounds mingling with that of Medicine
Bear's rattles and the beating of the medicine drums. Medicine Bear entered the circle in a crouch position, his body
appearing to move in slow motion. He was a large man
and could not hide his size. He was covered from head to
foot by the hide from a red grizzly bear. The head of the
bear served as a mask, the huge legs and claws dangled
against his wrists and ankles.

"In one hand, he clutched a rawhide rattle with a complete eagle head on the handle, the mouth of the eagle
open to reveal the gourd that called out its noise to the
spirits. In his other hand, he clutched his medicine spear,
which was adorned with medicine pouches and love
charms. As a hush settled over the assembled onlookers,
Medicine Bear chanted, calling on his spirit helpers.

"This portion of the ceremony took some time. When
Medicine Bear felt the moment was right, he directed two
braves to help the warrior into a sitting position. Bending
over the warrior, my husband pressed his mouth to the
back of the warrior's head. With a large grunt of noise,
Medicine Bear sucked out the evil spirits from the warrior's
head; he spat a mouthful of foul matter on the ground
outside the sacred circle. The warrior was once again laid

down upon his mat, and for the first time in many days, he slept a peaceful sleep."

With the conclusion of her story, Medicine Woman held her gaze upon the young woman sitting across her fire. She now glimpsed some interest in the golden eyes.

"Did you never wish to join with another warrior after Medicine Bear passed over?" Medicine Woman had still been a young woman when her husband had been killed by a Crow warrior.

A gnarled finger reached up and traced the tear-drop tattoo. "This is a reminder of my sorrow. You know this well, Wacin. What makes you ask questions when you already know the answer?"

"But, I wonder why you never joined with another after Medicine Bear? Did you not enjoy being joined? Have you been content to live your life alone here in your lodge?"

"I joined my life path with Medicine Bear's because my father instructed me to," the old medicine woman confessed. "At first, I was not sure of my place in my husband's lodge, because he had another wife. Moon Woman became my friend, and I became my husband's helper. I missed Medicine Bear when he passed, but even in those days, I would rather have lived alone. Warriors can be difficult, and I am set in my ways."

For the first time this morning, Desire revealed a breathtaking smile. "I feel the same way you do, Medicine Woman." Appearing more relaxed, she snapped off the tough green stem of the medicine plant called long-billed curlew. The stems would be used to make baskets in which to carry meat; the roots were fed to horses when they appeared sluggish and tired.

For a long minute the lodge remained quiet. Medicine Woman silently drew on her pipe as she watched the young woman. Her dark eyes twinkled with knowledge as she lowered the pipe and questioned, "Are you having a hard time deciding your future, Wacin?" Medicine Woman, like everyone else in the village, had heard about the two braves approaching Gray Owl's lodge.

Desire's dark head nodded as she kept her eyes turned to the plants in her lap. Since she was twelve summers old, she had been coming to Medicine Woman's lodge. The old woman was as close to her as her own mother. In fact, there had been times when she had been able to confess things to Medicine Woman that she had been unable to tell her mother. "I do not wish to join myself with any warrior. I wish to be like you, Medicine Woman. I wish to live alone and take care of those that are sick."

Medicine Woman was not surprised by this confession. Desire had always been different in her ways. But now Desire was speaking of things she did not know. "When the right warrior comes into your life circle, you will wish to go to his lodge as his woman. You can still take care of the sick, Wacin. You are already a fine healer. Every day you learn more about medicine, and no one would take this special gift away from you."

"But how will I know when I meet the right warrior? You did not know when you met Medicine Bear that he was the right one. Your father arranged your joining." Desire had many inner fears about leaving her father's lodge to go to a warrior's. She felt alone with these fears, because the other maidens of the village did not appear to have the same worries about joining themselves for the rest of their lives. Each time she thought about the things that went on between a man and woman, she began to tremble with anxiousness.

"Do you not find Panther Stalks or Cetán appealing?" Medicine Woman noticed the slight shiver that overtook Desire as she asked this question. If she could, she would help to calm those fears.

Desire's head jerked up, her brilliant eyes widening with the realization that she had no secrets in this village. "Panther Stalks has been coming to my father's lodge every evening since the day he first brought horses there."

"Do you not care for him a little? Is he not the one that could help you set your fears aside?"

She could not hide her uneasiness about going to a warrior's pallet. "He is a friend, Medicine Woman. How do I know if he is the one? Why should I have to choose a warrior anyway? Why can I not just live as I wish?" Desire enjoyed talking with Panther Stalks about the everyday matters of the tribe, but she grew uncomfortable whenever his dark eyes stayed upon her for too long, or when, upon occasion, their hands made contact or their bodies brushed against each other.

"And what of the one called Cetán? You say nothing of him?"

Again Desire's gaze lowered to the plants. A flush of heat traveled over her face and down her slender throat. "What does Cetán matter? He is from another village. I will never agree to leave my family and friends."

Medicine Woman knew, in that minute, that in her heart Desire had already chosen the one known as Cetán. All that had to come to pass now was bringing her mind and her heart to an agreement. "And what of children, Wacin? Do you not wish to have a child one day? It is a lonely life without a daughter to see to your comfort in your old age."

Desire shook her head adamantly. She had helped Medicine Woman with too many birthings to willingly want to subject her body to such torture. "I will make do in my old age just as you do now," she bravely stated.

The old woman's laughter rang out. "You are far too beautiful not to share who you are, and all that you have to offer, with another. One day, you will look back to the time we spoke of such things next to my fire, and you will smile."

"That day will never come!" the dark-haired beauty swore as she placed the roots in the basket next to her.

...

"You will see, Medicine Woman. I will forever be content with my animals and my healing gift. These things will be enough for me."

Chief Gray Owl's lodge was one of the largest in the Sioux village. The structure was made from the buffalo skins of twenty animals, each hide cut and sewn skillfully to produce a semicircular cover. The hides had been drawn together at the front of the lodge with lacing pins. There were some twenty poles, each twenty-five feet in height, which rose out of the smoke flaphole. The lower edges of the tepee were secured with heavy hardwood pegs, which had been driven through holes in the buffalo hide. The aged skins had been painted vermillion and yellow, the artwork depicting Gray Owl's vision signs and his greatness in battle.

After dinner, Desire and Pretty Dove sat upon a pile of furs as they listened to Gray Owl and Panther Stalks talking next to the lodge fire. The women busied themselves with their sewing. Stretched out next to Desire was Elkhunter, and with her every movement, the great wolf's yellow eyes followed the sound of her singing bells as her slender fingers deftly pushed a bone needle through the doe hide draped over her lap.

As he had on previous evenings, Panther Stalks had brought the string of ponies to Gray Owl's lodge. The warrior had arrived shortly after dinner. The two men sat and smoked Gray Owl's pipe and companionably spoke about the events that had taken place in the village that day.

Often, Desire felt Panther Stalks' gaze leaving the fire, seeking her out where she sat next to her mother. Though she felt the heat of his dark gaze, she did not lift her head from her task. She knew what was expected of a maiden being courted by a brave, but this evening she was in no mood for politeness. She did not enjoy this courting, and she was finished with pretending that she did.

"I wonder if I could speak with your daughter alone for a few minutes, Gray Owl?" Panther Stalks had at last built up the courage to ask to be allowed this small intimacy. He had not dared to be so bold in the past, but two weeks had passed and each evening he came to Gray Owl's lodge, and each evening he left feeling more frustrated than he had felt the day before. Desire's beauty seemed to grow daily, and he ached to hear the sweet sound of her voice. He longed to touch the back of her hand and feel the softness of her flesh. Usually, a young couple was not allowed the privilege of being alone this early in a courtship, but Panther Stalks knew he could not wait any longer to tell her of the things which filled his heart.

Gray Owl leaned back against his backrest, his dark eyes turning toward the women. Glimpsing his daughter's grim expression this evening, he was not so sure it would be a good idea to grant permission to this young man to be alone with Wacin. "Perhaps it would be best if you seek Wacin out tomorrow, Panther Stalks. She has had a busy day helping Medicine Woman heal a sick child. This evening she wishes to remain at her mother's side." The old chief knew that his daughter was not enjoying this brave's pursuit, but he held the hope that she would begin to respond to Panther Stalks.

Panther Stalks' gaze stayed upon the two women, and for a few seconds anger clouded his vision. Gray Owl was too easy on his daughter. If the old man did not always give Desire whatever she wanted, she would be forced to look at him with more favor. Any other maiden of their village would be honored to have him come to her father's lodge nightly to court her in the tradition of the people. Drawing in a deep breath, Panther Stalks fought to get a tight grip on his emotions. He could not confront his chief on this matter, for to do so, he knew, would only make the gap between himself and Wacin much larger. No . . . he would take his time in courting her. The prize would be well worth all of his efforts one day!

Desire did not raise her head from the work in her lap until she heard Panther Stalks leave her father's lodge. As he exited the entrance flap, she breathed a sigh of relief. Pretty Dove looked at her daughter with questioning eyes. It was beyond her why Wacin did not find Panther Stalks appealing. He was a war chief and had many fine horses. He would make any young woman a fine husband. Her daughter was lucky that such a warrior wished to court her.

Three

Long after Gray Owl's lodge-fire dimmed and the heavy breathing of sleep came from the direction of the chief's sleeping pallet, Desire turned restlessly upon her bed of furs. Now and then, Elkhunter lifted his head from his paws, searching out his mistress's mood.

The haunting sounds of flute music invaded Desire's peace as she lay fully awake. For some time, she had worried with thoughts of Panther Stalks, and just as she made the decision that tomorrow she would seek the brave out to try and explain that she had no desire to join herself with him or any other warrior, the stirring melody from the flute settled over the night air. Strangely, the music held the power to capture Desire's senses. She could find no means of escaping the sounds that invaded her father's lodge—and her thoughts.

Taking a deep breath, Desire swung her legs to the earthen floor and silently pulled on her hide dress. She would only gain the quiet she needed by approaching the flute player and requesting that he continue his concert at a decent hour. Elkhunter rose to his feet to follow his mistress outside, but was halted by a soft command to stay put.

A warm night breeze lifted Desire's hair away from her shoulders. The music from her bells blended with the melody of the flute, the only sounds heard throughout the village at this late hour.

Needing no assistance to find the source of the music,

Desire's steps were drawn toward a stand of cottonwood trees some distance behind her father's lodge. A full moon rode high in a dark velvet sky, surrounded by thousands of twinkling stars. Desire easily made out the form of a lone warrior sitting at the foot of a tree, a long piece of wood in his hands, its mouthpiece captured by his lips.

The warrior did not set the flute aside with her advance; if anything, the music had a quality of welcome. For a few seconds, Desire halted as she tried to discern the warrior's identity, fearing it could be Panther Stalks and she might be caught in one of his courting traps.

Her patience had worn thin where Panther Stalks was concerned, and if he was disturbing her sleep, she would set him straight immediately. Her steps took her closer to the cottonwood tree, and even though she stood only a few feet away from the warrior, Desire still could not make out his features. She dared not advance any closer, but stood, hands on hips, waiting for him to put down his flute so she could request that he stop his foolishness for the night.

The warrior appeared content to play his music for a few more minutes, his dark gaze keenly observing her.

Desire opened her mouth to demand that he stop playing just as the warrior placed the instrument at his side.

"I have been waiting for you, Wacin. Come and join me here beneath the tree. I have many things to share with you. Things that fill my heart and wait only for your presence."

Desire stared at the man in total confusion. Silently she shook her head, even though her heart hammered heavily in her chest. She felt the familiar rush of gooseflesh course over her arms as the husky voice wrapped around her senses. "You!" she was at last able to gasp, the sweet sounds of bells softening the accusation in her tone.

Cetán heard the surprise and trace of accusation in her voice. One question had the power to stoke his anger fully to life. "Did you leave your father's lodge with the hope of finding Panther Stalks out here in the night playing his siyotanka for you, Wacin?" He could not stop himself from asking the question though his tone held no trace of the anger he was feeling.

"Of course not! I came out here to ask whoever was playing the music to wait until morning. I cannot sleep!" The outrage in her voice softened with her words.

Cetán's lips drew back into a wide smile. "The courting flute has been known to have such effects on maidens. The music of my heart escapes the end of the flute, and sends its melody to your father's lodge, Wacin." Cetán was pleased with her reaction to the accusation that she'd hoped he'd be Panther Stalks. His friend Slender Quiver had told him that Wacin was not responding well to Panther Stalks' courtship, but he had been unsure of the truth of that until this moment. Still, in the back of his mind, he worried that she would choose the other warrior over him. He had seen the smile she had bestowed upon Panther Stalks the day he had gone to Gray Owl's lodge with his horses.

Desire felt her face flush, and was silently glad that darkness shaded her features.

"Come and sit here upon Mother Earth next to me, Wacin." Once again, Cetán's bronzed hand lightly touched the grass next to him.

All Desire was capable of was a slight shaking of her head. She would never have left her father's lodge if she had thought Cetán was out here waiting for her. She could have faced Panther Stalks and demanded that he stop playing his flute, but Cetán had some strange power over her senses, and she dared not allow herself to be drawn any closer to him. She could not lose control of her thoughts— or her plans for her future.

"Come." The hand that had caressed Mother Earth seconds ago was now held out in her direction, the long fingers tantalizing her senses with the promise of caressing her flesh.

Desire stared at the large hand, mesmerized by its strength and its gentleness.

Several seconds passed . . . a long, ragged sigh escaped Cetán. If she would not come to him, he would send his words of adoration upon the night wind, he told himself, and without a second thought, he began to speak. "Your name, Wacin, fills my heart as sweetly as your singing bells. Wacin . . . Desire to look upon your beauty day and night fills my heart. Wacin . . . Desire to hold you, to know that you are mine throughout this life and all eternity, clouds my thoughts. Wacin . . . Desire as strong as any warrior can bear, rages throughout my blood and pulses deeply in my chest. My days are not my own, Wacin . . . Desire for you has robbed me of my breath, my heart, my very reason for being."

"Why do you say these things to me?" Desire was trembling, her knees beginning to buckle. How could any woman endure such words? Did he think she was made of stone? Did he not know that he was the only man who could make her feel confused and dazed by the simple sound of his voice?

From where he sat, Cetán easily saw Desire tremble. Before she could fall, he was at her side, his strong arms around her as he held her against his powerful chest. "I say only that which fills my heart, Wacin. I do not mean to upset you."

Upset her? Didn't he realize he was slowly killing her? In his arms she felt the death of all that she believed. The need to stand alone without a man at her side, the wish to remain with family and friends, to fill her days with her work of healing . . . all that she was seemed so small compared to the feelings that overtook her as she stood there wrapped in Cetán's embrace. From somewhere in the depths of her soul she fought to resist the temptation, telling herself to flee his embrace and turn her back on the aching need that held her there.

The earthy scent of wildflowers and herbs ensnared him. The trembling of her body set the tiny bells to shimmering musically as Cetán's hand lightly caressed her forearms. "You are mine, Wacin. From the first moment when I looked upon you, and our eyes touched, I knew that you were the woman who was to share my life path."

Desire attempted to refute him, but she could not force the necessary words from her constricted throat, nor could she move her head in denial. Her senses were consumed by his closeness. All of her declarations about not desiring a man deserted her before the flame of his dark, sensual gaze.

"Make no mistake, Wacin, Panther Stalks will never claim you as his own." With this heartfelt declaration, he dipped his head toward her, his full lips covering Desire's.

Desire had never experienced this joining of lips with a warrior. For a few seconds, her head spun and she felt giddy and weak. Her slender fingers splayed over his naked chest as though to steady herself, his strong arms holding her upright. As his tongue pressed between her lips and began mating with her tongue, she knew she should pull back, but all she could do was melt against him as small sounds of pleasure escaped the back of her throat. With a will of their own, her hands moved over his chest then circled his neck, her slender fingers twining in the strands of midnight hair lying down his back.

Cetán would have liked nothing more than to sample fully the incredible pleasure that this woman he claimed in his heart was willing at this moment to offer. But, wisely, he held the raging fury of his desires in check. He had no wish to frighten her with the searing heat of his need. His intent had been to leave her with the memory of the blending of their lips. He desired her to burn with the longing for what could be, if only she were willing to accept him.

With a valiant warrior's will, Cetán forced himself to pull away from her delicious honey taste. His heart vibrated as though a herd of tatanka stampeded recklessly in his chest, his breathing escaping in ragged breaths as his jet eyes looked down into her beautiful features. A long, bronze finger trailed a path from her cheek to her kiss-swollen lips. "I am the warrior who will ignite the fire within your body, Wacin. No other will ever claim you!"

Cetán's words were a declaration that Desire would never forget, but at the moment, all she wanted was to taste the cool fullness of his mouth against her own. Her tawny-gold eyes stared at his lips, hearing but not hearing his vow. She would have pulled his head back down to her, but before she could, he took a step backward, forcing her hands to drop to her sides.

"The next time I come to your father's lodge, be ready to step upon the path of your future at my side."

Desire stared at Cetán's back as he strode away from her toward the stand of cottonwoods. The second she lost sight of him, she released her pent-up breath. Her heartbeat trembled harshly as she tried to regain her senses by drawing large gulps of night air into her strained lungs. Hands shaking, she brought them to her mouth and tried to wipe away any remembrance of the kiss so recently shared. Cetán was out of his mind if he believed she would ever agree to become his bride!

Four

The next time I come to your father's lodge, be ready to step upon the path of your future at my side." These words rang over and over through Cetán's mind as he mounted Whirling-Warrior's-Ghost and began the long ride back to his own village.

Cetán knew he had been overly bold with Wacin, but he also knew that boldness would remain far longer in her mind. Tomorrow and the following day, she would remember his lips joining with hers, and his words that she would be his and no other's.

He pushed thoughts of Panther Stalks out of his mind. For now, he wanted to savor the memory of holding Wacin in his arms. He relived the thrill of feeling her slender fingers traveling over his chest, then at the back of his neck. The tiny bells had sung wondrously as she'd molded her womanly form against his torso.

Cetán expelled a deep breath. Whirling-Warrior's-Ghost snorted aloud, recognizing a change in his master.

The warrior's large hand reached out and lightly patted the stallion's neck. "You are right, brother. A woman such as Wacin holds the power to turn a warrior's thoughts to things besides the dangers awaiting him in the forest. For now, I will concentrate on the trail before us. I pray only that Wakán Tanka takes pity upon me and will give me the means to claim Wacin as my own." Cetán's words were offered in prayer as he looked up at the night sky, his gaze filling with the splendor of a full orange moon and thousands of glittering stars.

If anything, the encounter with Cetán reinforced Desire's need to avoid the warrior at all cost. Those moments when she had stood within his embrace, and had lost all sense of time and herself, had verified her belief that Cetán seriously threatened her peace of mind.

Desire awoke later than usual the next morning. After her return to her father's lodge, she had not found sleep until the early hours. Each time she shut her eyes, Cetán strode boldly into her thoughts. Lying naked upon her sleeping couch beneath her cover of furs, she keenly felt the pressure upon her nipples as she had in Cetán's arms with her breasts pressed against his bare chest. As her fingers innocently touched her lips, again she could feel Cetán's mouth against her own. A simmering heat began to build in the pit of her belly and spread downward to the very center of her woman's need.

Pretty Dove allowed her daughter to sleep late. She had heard Wacin leave the lodge late last night; she had also heard the melody of the courting flute. She had supposed the flute player to be Panther Stalks, and was not surprised that her daughter did not return quickly to her father's lodge. Many young Sioux women had been lured by the music of the courting flute, and thereafter had realized their hearts. Pretty Dove could only hope that after last night, Wacin would agree to join with Panther Stalks and settle into her place in the village as all maidens eventually do.

As Pretty Dove began to prepare the morning meal, she smiled thoughtfully as her dark gaze went to where her daughter slept. It would be hard to imagine Wacin conforming to the life of other Sioux maidens. She had always been different from the children she had grown up with.

Admittedly, Pretty Dove and Gray Owl had not discouraged her, but had allowed her to become the maiden that she was today. While the other children of the village had romped and played, Wacin had spent much of her time in the company of the elder women or had been out in the forest picking her healing plants and herbs. She had preferred the company of her father's horses to that of the other maidens.

Pretty Dove was very proud of the young maiden that Wacin had become. The villagers respected her daughter. She had healed many sick children and adults with her special medicine root, and many warriors sought her aid for cures for sick horses. Gray Owl boasted of his daughter's prowess as a healer as he sat next to the village fire late at night with the elders of the tribe.

Now, all that was needed was for Wacin to join her steps along the path of a warrior's, such as Panther Stalks, and Pretty Dove's job as a good mother would be complete.

Desire awoke to the smell of cooking food. Realizing the lateness of the morning hour, she rose from bed and dressed. By this time of the day, she had usually gone to the river for water and wood for the lodge's daily use. Looking at her mother, she saw no censorship upon Pretty Dove's brow. Elkhunter was no longer in the lodge; Desire imagined that he had exited at the same time as her father, and, more than likely, the great wolf was chasing a rabbit for his morning meal.

"I am sorry to have lingered so long upon my sleeping mat this morning, Mother. I don't know why I am so tired." Desire did not look at her mother as she spoke the lie. Instead, she straightened her bedding and began to braid her hair, taking the time to twine the bells attached to strips of trade cloth throughout its thick length.

Pretty Dove nodded silently as she watched Desire from her seat next to the fire. She had hoped her daughter would announce her feelings toward Panther Stalks this morning. Perhaps she would feel like confiding once she had something to eat. "We had water from yesterday, Wacin. After you eat, you can go to the river. There is no harm in sleeping late now and then."

"I am not hungry, Iná. I will go to the river now. I promised Medicine Woman I would help her this afternoon, and I would like to bathe before starting the day."

Pretty Dove knew by her daughter's words that she would not be confiding in her about last night, nor about the brave who had been playing the flute. She watched Desire gather the water pouches before leaving the lodge.

A long, pent-up breath escaped Desire as she stepped outside the lodge. She had felt her mother's curiosity and was glad she was able to escape. Somehow, Desire knew that Pretty Dove was aware of what had taken place last night. Her mother was too light a sleeper not to have heard her leave the lodge. The thing that Pretty Dove didn't know, though, and Desire had no intention of telling anyone, was that Cetán had been the flute player, and the two of them had shared a breathtaking moment when the bold warrior held her in his arms and gave her her first kiss.

Desire shook her head to clear away all thoughts of Cetán. A breathtaking moment, indeed! The whole ordeal had been disgusting . . . horrible . . . one of the worst moments in her entire life! Cetán was a beastly warrior, and she hoped never to see him again!

Before she had been so rash as to leave her father's lodge last night, and find Cetán sitting beneath the cottonwood tree, she had decided to put a halt to Panther Stalks' courtship, but this morning she was not so sure that was a good idea. Maybe she had been too hasty. Maybe she should spend more time in Panther Stalks' company. She did not feel her senses slipping while she was in his presence. She could not remember a time when she had felt faint from just the sound of his voice. She had always been in complete control while in Panther Stalks' company, and that was exactly how she wanted things to remain!

Reaching the riverbank, Desire found Elkhunter jumping in and out of the cool water as the large beast playfully chased a fat bullfrog. Seeing his mistress, he gave her a yip of greeting before splashing after his playmate once again.

Most of the village women had gathered wood and filled their water bags by this late hour of the morning. Desire found the quiet of the river suited her mood; walking down the river's edge a short distance, she shed her dress and moccasins to take her morning swim.

Normally, Desire shared her morning bath with the other women of the village. And usually, Elkhunter joined the women in the middle of the river. This morning, however, Desire did not call the wolf to join her. She swam in the cool, circling depths for a few minutes, then floated back to shore. Her thoughts were plagued with images of Cetán. His too-handsome . . . too-virile features haunted her mind relentlessly. With an inward groan, Desire knew she would find no peace at the river. The only way to drive thoughts of Cetán from her mind would be by keeping herself busy.

After dressing and filling the water skins, Desire called Elkhunter before starting up the path that would lead them back to the village. With the great wolf at her side, she gathered an armload of firewood for her mother.

She and Elkhunter had gone only a short distance down the path when Panther Stalks appeared a few feet ahead. Elkhunter instantly bristled, the silver hair on his neck rising as a low growl started deep in the back of his throat.

Desire's hand lightly touched the wolf's large head. The cautious yellow eyes looked up at his mistress, then toward the man in front of them. Softly, Desire spoke to the beast, "It is Panther Stalks—he is our friend." It amazed her that Elkhunter always reacted toward Panther Stalks in this manner. One would think he would have grown accustomed to the warrior over the past weeks.

"I had hoped to find you here, Wacin." Panther Stalks was as wary of the animal at the young woman's side as the beast was of him. "May I carry your wood for you?"

Desire's first reaction was to refuse. A warrior did not carry wood; this was a woman's job, but remembering her earlier thoughts, she relented. "Thank you, Panther Stalks."

The brave seemed pleased that she had so willingly agreed to allow him this small favor. "May I walk back to the village with you, Wacin?" he asked, pushing his luck a bit farther.

Desire smiled invitingly up at the brave, the singing bells adorning her body musically accompanying her movements, lending her a mystical quality. "I would be pleased to have you accompany me, Panther Stalks." Desire's brilliant eyes gleamed with curiosity as she studied the warrior's features, her gaze settling on his lips. *I wonder if his kisses are as wonderful as Cetán's.*

Panther Stalks could hardly believe that this was the same young woman he had been courting for the past few weeks. She appeared warm and receptive this morning. Her thick, dark lashes fluttered against her cheeks in a flirtatious manner as she looked up at him, stealing his very breath with her beauty. Forcing himself to reach out, he took the wood from her; his fingers lightly caressed the soft flesh of her lower arm, and instantly his breath grew ragged.

The simple touch of his hand against her arm quickly brought back memories of Cetán caressing her upper forearms the night before. Panther Stalks' touch caused no wild trembling of her heart, nor did her flesh tingle in expectation, as had been the case last night. Perhaps if she allowed Panther Stalks to hold her and kiss her as Cetán had, she would be able to chase thoughts of Cetán out of her mind for once and for all!

"Panther Stalks?" Desire's tone was low with nervousness, but determined to follow through with her thoughts, she proceeded. "Do . . . do you think you would like to join your lips with mine?"

For one crazy minute, Panther Stalks thought he had heard Wacin ask him to kiss her! He stood in front of her along the path, staring at her, the sound of his heartbeat rushing through his bloodstream and inside his head.

Desire knew she was taking unfair advantage of the brave as she batted her thick lashes at him. But she was determined to find out if this warrior's kisses could make her feel as she had in Cetán's arms. She had witnessed other maidens flirting and teasing with warriors; what harm could there be if she practiced the game? "If you . . . do not wish to . . . kiss me, I will understand." Her words washed over him in a singsong tone, which she hoped held enough sultry appeal to earn her what she desired.

"Yes, I wish to join my lips with yours, Wacin." Panther Stalks said as he pushed the words out of his tight throat. He had never seen Wacin as a seductress; she played the part so well, she robbed him of his senses as well as his breath.

When Panther Stalks took a step closer, Elkhunter raised his head, teeth gleaming as he brandished them in feral warning.

Desire's hand caressed the beast's large head. "Remain still, Elkhunter." She spoke softly, and as Panther Stalks took another step toward her, she took one toward him.

The wolf did as he was bid, though he was not pleased when the brave set the armload of wood down and stood close to his mistress.

Desire took a deep, calming breath. This was the moment that would tell all, she thought as she waited for Panther Stalks to take her into his arms and sweep all thoughts of Cetán from her mind. Inadvertently, she had already decided she would join with Panther Stalks or another warrior from her village. She needed only to find the warrior who could stir her senses as Cetán had done last night.

Panther Stalks sighed raggedly as he drew Wacin into his embrace. Her beauty entranced him as he stared down into her heart-shaped face. Her sparkling eyes were closed, the dark-lush lashes feathering delicately against smooth cheeks. He peered down at the rose-petal lips one second before his head lowered, his mouth covering hers hungrily.

But Desire experienced none of the all-consuming rapture of the night before. Her only feeling was that of being suffocated! Panther Stalks' mouth not only covered her lips but also the lower portion of her nose! Her nostrils being covered, her hands began to push against him desperately as Desire tried to turn her head away for a breath of air.

Panther Stalks was unaware of her discomfort. All he was feeling was the perfect woman's shape pressed tightly against his own body. Wacin's taste was like that of a meadow after a first spring rain, fresh and sweet. He drank of her like a man thirsting for the nectar of survival. He did not notice her futile attempts to escape as he pressed tighter against her shapely curves. Feeling his manhood throbbing with desire, the hunger in his soul for this woman grew beyond the physical bonds of restraint. He would take her here and now, and from this moment on, she would be his!

Desire felt herself growing dizzy; her hands stopped trying to push Panther Stalks away as her knees began to buckle.

She awoke a few seconds later, lying on the ground with Elkhunter standing over her. The great wolf's threatening growls warned Panther Stalks to keep his distance.

"What . . . what happened?" Desire softly questioned with confusion, one delicate hand reaching up to brush dark strands of hair away from her face as she stared up at him.

"Joining my lips to yours caused you to faint, Wacin."
Panther Stalks' tone was filled with pride; he believed he
had overpowered her.

In a rush, everything flooded back into Desire's mind.
Looking up at Panther Stalks, she groaned softly. His kiss
had been little to her liking; indeed, he had smothered
her! What was she to do now, she asked herself. Was she
to seek out all unjoined warriors in the village to sample
their kisses? Was it possible she could survive such an ordeal?

Five

Unlike Desire, Cetán's lustful thoughts had been stoked into a frenzy that night beneath the cottonwood tree—thoughts he did not wish to forget. On the contrary, he brought their kiss to mind as often as possible.

As he lay in camp with his band of braves stretched out on their trade blankets next to the campfire, Cetán stared up at the night sky and his thoughts drifted to Wacin. A westerly breeze stirred the canopy of trees, rustling leaves as he recalled the shimmering softness of Wacin's singing bells. He found himself comparing the brilliance of the star-bright night to that of gold-sparkling eyes and curling-dark tresses, and in his mind, the night display came up wanting.

Wacin. The name fit the woman, for he desired her above all in this life. Desire robbed him of rational thought, leaving him with one obsession—to make Wacin his own!

Because of his desire, he had put together this raiding party, joining powers of stealth and warfare with that of the bravest warriors from his village. He was the lead war chief of this band of Sioux, and he had made a vow before leaving his village: he would not return until he had obtained the means to stand before Chief Gray Owl to claim Wacin for his woman!

The braves who rode with him knew of his plight and determination, and had agreed to help him. Over the past week, they had been making raids upon their enemy, the

Crow. Today they had captured a small herd of horses. Yesterday, they had fought with a raiding band of Crow and had captured many fine pelts and several rifles. Late this afternoon, Cetán and his band had picked up the trail of an overland mule pack-train. Seeing the wheel tracks bogged down deep in the earth, Cetán knew that the wagons were weighted down with goods. Knowing they were probably heading for a rendezvous, Cetán silently made his plans for the day ahead.

He had sent out a scout early in the afternoon, and the brave had returned to camp after dark. The report was that there was a total of seven wagons, each with a driver and another man riding as guard. It would be a simple matter to overtake the overburdened wagons, but Cetán made his plans carefully, not wishing to lose any of his braves.

Long before daylight the band of Sioux broke camp.

As the first fingers of dawn touched Mother Earth, the trappers and mule drivers began to stir. When a shout of warning echoed through the camp, the men instantly reached for their rifles.

"What the hell's going on here?" one of the trappers cried sharply, finding his rifle missing from where he had laid it next to his blanket the night before.

"Where's me gawd-damned rifle?" another shouted, pulling himself from his sleeping roll as one hand absently scratched at his groin.

"Was that young Henry shouting?" a mule driver questioned as the entire camp awakened. Finding their weapons missing, they rose to their feet in alarm.

"If that green-horn punk has taken off with me rifle, I'll skin the hide clear off his mangy backside!" a grizzled trapper said as he spat a wad of tobacco on the ground. Pulling on his boots, he chewed off another chunk and then stuffed it back into his shirt pocket.

As a group, the trappers and mule drivers stumbled toward the rear wagon, where they had heard the youngest of their team shouting. The camp appeared to be in order, the only thing wrong being the missing weapons.

"I'll bet ye young Henry's pulling one of his pranks again!" said a mule driver sporting a full gray beard and spectacles riding low on the bridge of his nose. "I'm going along with Amos this time! The lad needs to be taken down a peg or two, even if he is the boss's nephew!"

As the group rounded the double wagon, each man halted still in his tracks. There before them was young Henry, gagged and staked out spread-eagle on the ground. The young man's eyes were wide with terror as he looked up at his mates.

"What the hell is going on?" a trapper questioned as he looked around and was given no indication of who had treated young Henry this way.

The rest of the men turned warily in every direction, trying to see their enemy, sensing that whoever it was who had stolen into their camp, attacked young Henry, and stolen their rifles, was nearer than they thought. As the rough trapper who had sworn he would skin the hide off of Henry's backside pulled his large hunting knife from the leather sheath at his side, the other men began to do likewise.

"Who the hell done this to ya, boy?" The trapper stepped to young Henry's side, and bending down, he started to cut the young man's bindings. Before his sharp blade made contact with the strip of leather tied around young Henry's wrists, a rifle shot sounded. The bullet hit the ground only inches from the trapper's boots, warning him away from young Henry.

"Keep your distance, waichu!"

The trappers and mule drivers stared with a mixture of terror and surprise at the Sioux warrior sitting atop a large, gray stallion, who seemingly had appeared out of nowhere before them. The sun rising over the mountains behind the Indian made him seem even more menacing with his war shield held loosely over one arm, war paint on his face and running down his arms, and a rifle clutched in one hand.

The trapper who had been about to cut away young Henry's bindings and appeared to be the leader of the group spoke. "Lookey here, Injun, ye ain't got no business in our camp. If'n ye gots any brains in yer thick skull ye'll be gittin' yer stinkin' hide on outta here!"

"Be careful, Amos. He looks pretty dang mean to me!" One of the mule drivers spoke low, giving his friend some advice. The Injun was even larger than Amos, who was the largest man in their group. The way he sat upon his prancing horse and held the rifle pointed at them was indication enough that they had best go easy in their dealings with him.

"Shit on that!" Amos spat a stream of tobacco juice on the ground. "He might be able to capture the kid and tie him up, but the redskin can't git us all! There's only one of him and twelve of us!"

"Yeah, but he's got our rifles, don't ferget, and he's got one of 'em aimed at us right now!"

"And he can speak English, so he's smarter than most of his kind," another trapper added.

"Like I said, Injun, ye done made a mistake by comin' into our camp. Me and the boys won't be botherin' ye none, if'n ye get on out now, while ye still have the chance!" Amos reasoned that showing fear in front of an Injun would get a white man nowhere! At all times, a man should stand up to one of these heathens, no matter the odds.

Cetán indeed knew the English language. His blood brother Spirit Walker had taught him the wasichu words when he had been just a boy. "Do not be stupid, wasichu." The rifle in Cetán's hand turned directly toward the large trapper. "You might think I am foolish enough to come into your camp alone, but you will see—I am not as stupid as the wasichu, who dare to cross our lands and kill our buffalo without permission!" Another shot was fired, this time into the air. Within seconds, several Sioux warriors on horseback came up behind Cetán. The canvas covering on the last wagon was flung aside and a dozen more braves brandished rifles at their enemies as they let loose a round of war whoops.

"Oh me gawd, me day of reckonin' has finally come!" One trapper grabbed at his chest as though his heart were going to fail him before he could be murdered and scalped by the warriors.

"Throw down your weapons," Cetán ordered, and without hesitation, all of the men slung their knives to the ground.

Amos couldn't believe they had been overcome without even a struggle. These were the most cunning savages he had ever come up against. Amos knew that the Sioux were dangerous, but this warrior leader was far superior to any Injun he'd heard about. "What is it yer wantin' from us, Injun?" Amos believed that the only thing men such as these respected was strength and bravery, and his speaking out might well save his hair.

The Indians in the wagon jumped to the ground. Pushing the white men aside, they picked up their weapons. With their war-painted features and each carrying a brace of weapons, the Indians were more than a little threatening; several of the trappers and mule drivers fell to their knees as they awaited fate's final stroke.

"We gots some whiskey, if'n that's what yer after," Amos volunteered, seeing the fear on his mates' features. "You can take all you want, and there's some pretty beads fer yer women in one of the wagons."

"We will take it all!" Cetán announced in a clear, commanding tone.

"Ye'll do *what?*" Amos stared hard at the regal-looking

Indian, admiration in his eyes for the warrior's powerful build and intelligence, but his tone bristling with objection to the Indian's words.

"If you wish to see the sun set, do as I say, wasichu," Cetán ordered briskly. He believed the white men stupid to allow themselves to be so lulled with their own sense of power that they would sleep soundly enough for his braves and himself to sneak into their camp and steal their weapons. "You and your men can sit there on the ground next to your friend." Cetán's dark gaze swept over young Henry, who was still bound and gagged.

"Ye can't be meanin' to tie us and leave us out here in this gawdforsaken country! Why, ye might as well jest put a bullet in our heads now and get it over with!" Amos tried his best to sway the savage as he sat down with the rest of his group next to young Henry.

"Do not tempt me, wasichu!" Cetán again pointed the rifle at Amos. Relenting, he offered, "Your bonds will be loose enough for you to break free before the sun lowers." Cetán spoke contemptuously to the white man as he nodded his head toward the warriors, who were waiting to see if they would tie the trappers or if Cetán would just shoot them.

My gawd, it was only daybreak, Amos thought, but this time he thought better of voicing his objections. For a minute there he had feared the Injun was going to shoot the lot of them and add a piece of their hair to that deadly weapon secured over his shoulder. The sharp blade embedded in the rifle stock looked as though it could easily sever a man's head with a single blow! And from the looks of this warrior, he knew it would only take one swing from that powerful arm!

Two of the warriors tied the white men together in pairs, back to back. As the trappers and mule drivers were secured, Cetán and the rest of his band hitched a team of six mules to each double wagon.

Within a short time, there was little sign of Indians, mules, or wagons in the camp. The trappers and drivers spat out curses and vows of vengeance as they worked to untie their wrists.

Throughout the day, Cetán and his braves drove the wagons in a westerly direction. That night after making camp, the wagons were thoroughly searched. One of the double wagons was filled with the booty to be shared by each brave. The wagons, mules, horses, and goods they had captured during the days of their raiding would all go with Cetán to Chief Gray Owl's village.

Six

Sioux legend claims that many of their greatest medicine men and women learned secret skills from animals. He-Who-Sees-the Spirits claimed that an antelope told him the right medicine to use in order to stop the bleeding of a bad wound. In a vision, an eagle carried Medicine Crow up to the clouds, and there, the eagle showed him the remedy for snow blindness, headaches, and stomach aches. Desire had been but twelve summers when a matóhota showed her where to find her healing medicine root.

Elkhunter had been just a pup the spring day when Desire went into the forest to pick wild strawberries. Already, at a young age, she had developed an interest in the art of tribal medicine. Her only weapon when she came face-to-face with a large grizzly bear was a short stick with a flat edge, which she used for digging plants and herbs.

Elkhunter had instantly halted his play, the hair on his neck standing on end, his puppy yips turning into low growls. Terror was Desire's first reaction as she stared at the great beast, but as the brown flecks circling her gold eyes darkened with emotion, her fear slowly began to abate. Communication passed between the two as Desire's gaze locked with that of the bear's. The bear let out a low grunt. He was close enough for Desire to feel the heat of his breath, but she knew in that minute that the great beast posed no threat to her or Elkhunter.

Desire reached down and laid her hand upon Elkhunter's head. "He is a friend," she whispered, her eyes still locked with the bear's.

The large animal turned away from where he had been feeding on the berries. Something in his manner spoke to Desire. She knew that he had been waiting for her. Without hesitation, she began to follow him through the forest.

Some distance from her village, the bear left the cover of the forest and near the river where Mother Earth was moist and warm, he began to dig with his sharp, three-inch-long claws. As his mighty paws pulled forth an oblong root, his gaze went to Desire.

That one look spoke volumes. Desire understood that the matóhota was very sick. As she stared at him, she gained an inner knowledge that the great beast did not have much longer to live. She nodded in understanding. The grizzly bear left the root upon the mound of earth and turned back into the forest.

Desire took the root and placed it in her basket. Without being told, she knew it had special healing properties.

The next day, when she and Elkhunter returned to pick strawberries, Desire found the matóhota dead on the forest trail. With the help of Medicine Woman, Desire made herself a medicine pouch from the hide of the bear's right foreleg. She also made a medicine necklace from the bear claws; a sacred ebony stone pendant, which Medicine Woman had given Desire, swung from a leather tie in the center of the claw necklace.

Cutting shavings from the medicine root and placing them in the parfleche, or hide bag, of water suspended from a deer antler, Desire began to place glowing lime-rocks from the lodge's center fire into the parfleche. She wiped away the beads of sweat from her brow as she heard the sizzling made by the water. The aromatic scent of her medicine root filled the lodge, and with it, Desire began the silent count of passing time before she would pour the tea into her medicine bowl.

The lodge was quiet as she performed her task—only the heavy breathing of the injured child lying on his pallet disturbed the silence. Yellow Doe had sought Desire out in her father's lodge before Wi had touched Mother Earth with the first traces of dawn. The mother anxiously sat next to her son as Desire prepared the medicine; she prayed to the Great Spirit that Wacin could help her son, Little-Bird-Boy.

The child had become sick from a fever caused by a broken leg. Three days earlier, Desire had been called to his side and had splinted the injured limb. Little-Bird-Boy had fallen from his father's war pony. The bone in his lower leg had snapped like a dry twig, the sharp edges breaking through the skin below the knee. Desire had worked over the child for hours. Knowing how important it was for the leg to be set properly, she made a splint in the fashion she had been taught by Medicine Woman, who in turn had been taught by her husband, Medicine Bear. That day she had cautioned Yellow Doe to watch carefully for infection or fever. Little-Bird-Boy had been well until the early hours of this morning.

Filling her medicine bowl, Desire returned to the child's side. Looking down at the small figure, she noticed his flushed features. Her fingers automatically traced the bear claws on her medicine necklace. As she bent over the child, she clutched the sacred ebony pendant tightly as she began to chant her prayers aloud. She called forth the power of the matóhota to help the child recover.

As Yellow Doe helped her son sit in an upright position, Desire placed the medicine bowl to his lips and eased the contents into his mouth. This was a long and painstaking process, for the child cried to be released, his parched throat aching as the hot liquid filled his belly.

Within minutes after drinking the medicine tea, the boy's breathing seemed to ease. Yellow Doe settled him back upon his pallet as Desire finished her prayers and began to replace the articles she had used for this healing in her medicine bundle, which she then placed inside her medicine pouch.

"I will return this evening, Yellow Doe. Little-Bird-Boy should have this medicine one more time, to make certain that the fever does not return and to ensure that all the infection in his leg disappears." Desire watched the child for an extra moment; even as she stood over him, his skin took on a healthier color.

Yellow Doe could not thank Desire enough. She willingly gave her one of her finest blankets and her best trade pot.

"This is not necessary," Desire said and tried to return the items. She had not helped the child with the hope of receiving anything. Yellow Doe had little enough to spare, and Desire felt guilty taking anything. "This is too much, Yellow Doe," she protested.

"Silver Fox and I have only this one child. Little-Bird-Boy means everything to us. You have already helped him, Wacin. I have no other way to thank you. We will replace these things, but Little Bird Boy can never be replaced."

Desire smiled warmly, understanding the mother's gratitude. She took the blanket, trade pot, and her medicine pouch and left the lodge.

Desire absently rubbed the back of her neck with her free hand. She admitted only to herself that she was tired and would welcome the cool interior of her parents' lodge. Of late, sleep had been hard-won for her. But it was becoming easier to accept the images of Cetán that stole into her thoughts and disturbed her peace. The past few nights she had even been able to get a few hours rest. Any evening now, perhaps, she would return to her old sleeping habits.

She noticed a group of people making their way toward the center of the village, and with a weary eye, she made certain that Panther Stalks was not among the group before she ventured any further.

Avoiding Panther Stalks had become Desire's daily goal

of late. After the shared kiss when Panther Stalks had caused her to faint, she was again determined not to join her life path with his. Each morning, she went to the river in the company of other women, not wishing to be alone on the path once again and find Panther Stalks waiting for her. The warrior had returned to her father's lodge several times after the incident, but Desire would not speak to him nor would she look in his direction.

Desire had found some small relief in the fact that Panther Stalks had not come to her father's lodge in the last two days. She hoped that he had lost interest or perhaps had found another maiden to court.

Since that evening when Cetán had joined his lips with hers, Desire had come to the realization that she was not so averse to the idea of joining herself to a warrior as she had at first believed. After several days of thinking upon this subject, she had discarded the idea of Panther Stalks as a possible husband but she had been looking over the other braves from her village.

The ideal husband, in Desire's mind, would be a brave from her own village who could kiss her in the same breathless fashion as Cetán had. She needed a warrior who would not interfere with her work. She must be allowed to practice her medicine, to spend time helping her people and animals. Her husband would hunt and boast as all warriors do, she assumed, but the best part about this imagined joining would be that whenever she desired it, her husband would kiss her. It would be pleasant to have her own lodge and be able to look across her fire at her handsome husband, knowing that any time she desired, he would accommodate her with kissing lessons.

With such planned-out determination and the fact that Panther Stalks appeared to be leaving her in peace, all that Desire had to deal with was her constant dreams of Cetán. But even these dreams did not have the effect that they'd had at the beginning. She would soon be able to forget all about Cetán just as soon as she found the warrior that could kiss her as well, if not better, than she had been kissed that evening beneath the cottonwood tree.

More and more villagers appeared to be heading in the same direction as Desire. Absently, she wondered what could be the cause of such a stir throughout the village, so early in the day. As her father's lodge came into view, she saw that more villagers were standing before his tepee. Her heart suddenly skipped a beat as her steps quickened. Had something happened to her mother or father? Her father was going to break some of his horses today; she prayed nothing was wrong as she began to run, pushing her way through the crowd.

Desire was caught up short as she saw who was standing before her father's lodge. As bold as life, with arms crossed over his powerful chest, Cetán stood next to Gray Owl; the elder chief appeared to be listening intently to every word the warrior spoke.

Desire felt the usual racing of her heart from just the sight of the mighty warrior, but as she glimpsed the seriousness on her parent's features, she also experienced a sudden inner fear. What on earth was the handsome brave telling her father? Was he telling him that it had been he, Cetán, who had been playing the courting flute that night? That he had kissed his daughter and had now come to claim her? Desire's face flushed with such thoughts, gooseflesh coursing over both arms as her body tingled with trepidation. Trying to gain a grip on the emotions that suddenly washed over her, Desire took a step toward the two men. Before she could shorten the distance between herself and her father, she noticed the wagons and mules. Warriors were unloading boxes and crates of goods, setting them on the ground outside her father's lodge.

It was Cetán who sensed, rather than saw, Desire's presence behind him. Turning, he faced her. Taking a step backward, he glanced at Gray Owl before speaking loudly, so everyone could hear his words. "I honor your daughter Wacin above all in my heart, Gray Owl. I give you all that you now see—horses, mules, and wagons filled with goods as a bride price." His dark eyes turned back to Desire, his heart pounding madly in his chest as the sound of her singing bells filled his ears.

Clutching her medicine pouch and the gifts that Yellow Doe had given her, Desire was unable to convey to the bold warrior and villagers her rejection of Cetán. She wanted to place her hands on her hips and shake her head in denial, but her hands were full as she shook her head. She would have grinned if she dared, because she felt assured that her father would honor her feelings as he always had in the past, and at last she would be able to get even with Cetán for that damn kiss!

But never before had Gray Owl been so overwhelmed with so many fine gifts! There were at least fifty horses, all stout and of fine blood. The wagons and mules he would find a use for later. Perhaps he would trade them at a trading post for items that were hard for his people to find. It was the goods that the warriors were unloading and setting out on display before him, though, that captured his full attention and made it hard to honor Desire's wishes.

There were sacks of sugar, flour, coffee beans and dried beans being piled high. Shovels, picks, traps, trade pots and pans, beads, blankets, knives, everything openly displayed. Wasichu shirts, hats, boots, jackets, trousers, and women's dresses were being taken out of another wagon. Rolls of pigtail tobacco were visible, as were boxes packed with jars of pickled eggs, peaches, and pears. What caught all eyes were the rifles and ammunition on the ground not far from where Gray Owl stood.

The bounty was far too hard for any man to resist, especially a man who was the chief of a large village, who knew the worth of what he was looking upon. His village would be rich with all these goods. There would be no cold women and children this coming winter. There would be no empty bellies with such a supply of rifles and ammunition. Looking directly at Desire, Gray Owl's eyes saddened. He knew that he could not honor her wishes in this matter of joining herself with a warrior any longer. Slowly he nodded his head in acceptance to Cetán.

Panther Stalks had made his way to the center lodge with the rest of the villagers. Shoving through the crowd in order to see what was taking place, anger instantly leaped to the surface as he saw Cetán and his braves. Before Gray Owl could speak the words that would seal his daughter's fate, he stepped boldly forward.

Panther Stalks' gaze was riveted directly upon Cetán. "I claim Wacin for my own! I challenge Cetán in combat!"

The people stirred, gasps of surprise escaping their lips. Gray Owl looked at Panther Stalks, then at his daughter. He would be loath to lose Cetán's gifts, but his own honor was at stake here. He saw the instant sparkle of hope that filled Desire's eyes, and knew that a man could not live without honor. She would have this last chance to stay here in her own village.

Desire felt dizzy with relief. She had read in her father's features that he had been about to agree with Cetán that he could claim her as wife. Panther Stalks was now her only hope to stay among her own people. Though she did not wish him for her husband, she told herself she would make herself forget that kiss they had shared. She would join with him, if she had to—she would do anything to stay here in her village! Her honey-gold eyes gazed at the warrior with hope.

Glimpsing the glitter in her eyes as Desire looked upon Panther Stalks, Cetán felt anger ignite in the pit of his belly. "I accept the challenge!" he stated boldly, drawing Desire's full attention. And in the ebony eyes that rested so fully upon her, Desire read the promise that Cetán would not be defeated!

Seven

The choice of weapons and the means of combat was solely chief Gray Owl's decision. With the slender hope that neither warrior would meet with death, Gray Owl called for war clubs and a length of horsehair rope, each end having a slip circle that would be placed over the warriors' wrists.

As the villagers watched, a large circle was drawn upon the ground not far from Gray Owl's lodge. The combatants would have to remain within the circle for the duration of the fight.

Desire's first thought was to take flight. She did not want to stand with the group of villagers to watch the two braves fight. Especially since she knew that the winner would claim her for his bride. This whole affair was outrageous, and if she dared, she would tell her father this to his face. But she dared not approach Gray Owl. Her father was watching the preparations, resolve etched upon his features, and Desire realized there could be no changing what had been decreed.

Feeling the glances cast in her direction, Desire tried to still the inner trembling of her heart. Like the others, she waited for the moment when her father would deem the fighting to begin.

Earlier, Desire had grudgingly admired Cetán's clothing. He was wearing a hide shirt painted green with zigzag lines of dark blue, which indicated lightning. These zigzag lines infused power and speed into the wearer's body. The arms were fringed with human hairlocks, with porcupine quilled bands painted orange on the sleeves and shoulders. His leggings had also been painted green; the legging strips were beaded in a geometric design, which matched his moccasins. Now Cetán wore only his leather breechcloth, his physical strength apparent for all to see.

Panther Stalks also awaited the command from Gray Owl. Wearing only a breechcloth, his muscular physique was not as powerful as Cetán's, but his limbs were fit, sinewy, and lithe with hidden strength.

Gray Owl presented the war clubs. Similar in appearance, they were eighteen inches long with stone heads and leather bands that had been dyed blue. Cetán and Panther Stalks tried the weight in their hands before nodding acceptance.

Each warrior slipped his hand through the end of the horsehair rope as they entered the fighting area. Cetán's glance strayed one last time to where he had seen Desire standing earlier. She was as fair to the eye as he remembered. He imagined he could hear her singing bells over the noise the villagers were making. As her gaze turned to meet his, he read the fear in her eyes and wondered which warrior she worried over. His anger peaked as his grip on the war club tightened. He had come too far in this quest for Wacin to allow negative thoughts to hinder him now. This would be the final step before he could claim her as his own!

During these few seconds, Panther Stalks silently watched his opponent for any sign of weakness which could be turned to his advantage. Cetán looked as hard and formidable as any warrior he had come against in the past— perhaps more dangerous, because of his size and strength. He saw where the other warrior looked and a slow grin twisted his lips. Wacin was Cetán's weakness. He saw the uncertainty in Cetán's dark eyes and the anger that followed. Wacin had the power to make a warrior worry. She did not realize how she affected a man. But after this day she would know the effect she had on him. She would be his! Once they were joined, he would slake his lust upon her beautiful body as often as he desired. He imagined her crying out his name, knowing that she belonged to him and no other!

The second that Gray Owl dropped his raised hand, the two combatants came together in a clash of chests, war clubs striking out, but neither hitting their target.

For a moment they struggled, taking the measure of each other's strength. Panther Stalks grunted as he pushed against Cetán's brute force. "Wacin is mine! Her purrs of satisfaction will only be heard by my ears!"

Cetán slung Panther Stalks away from him, his war club brandished high overhead as the warrior's words circled his mind and his fury reached a raging high.

Panther Stalks grinned, knowing his taunt had hit his mark. The first lesson any brave learned was to keep a grip on his emotions. Cetán wore his weakness like a badge. With one movement, he charged Cetán, his body rolling on the ground, his war club coming up at an angle as he once again taunted, "Wacin's lips taste of the sweetest honey. When I hold her in my arms, her sighs of pleasure fill my ears!" His club met its target, grazing Cetán's midsection.

A gasp went through the crowd with the first sight of a club hitting flesh. Desire clutched the folds of her dress, her teeth biting into her lower lip. Gray Owl stood next to her, his palm upon her forearm, keeping her from rushing forward to try and halt this insanity. She could not stand by and watch Cetán being harmed! As she glimpsed blood beginning to flow from the wound, her features paled and she turned her face into her father's shoulder. She could watch no more!

Cetán did not feel pain; Panther Stalks' words drummed

through his mind as an animal-like growl left his lips. His fingers touched the wound, turning red like the crimson rage that stormed through his body.

Panther Stalks stood back with a bold grin. He would best the mighty Cetán and savor the victory!

With a twist of his wrist, Cetán caught the rope in his hand and began to pull his opponent toward him. As Panther Stalks was jerked forward, Cetán rushed in, his mighty fist catching the warrior full on the chin. Cetán's war club hit his opponent's shoulder, but was too far off its mark to do serious damage.

Caught by surprise, Panther Stalks hit the ground, regaining his senses just in time to twist away from the full downward assault of the war club. He regained his feet, but before he could draw a full breath, Cetán was on top of him once again!

The two warriors fought, war clubs clashing, fists flying, bodies straining with unleashed power. Panther Stalks looked for an opening, but Cetán did not appear to be tiring, nor was there a weak spot to be found.

"The next time I hold Wacin in my arms, I will think of you, Cetán. I will think of this day when I defeated the mighty Cetán, and I will take pleasure in the fact that you will never know the paradise I will know nightly!"

These words were Panther Stalks' undoing. Cetán rushed him, his body bending low as he lifted Panther Stalks from the ground for a few seconds before he slung him back to Mother Earth and quickly straddled him. His war club came down hard against the side of Panther Stalks' head.

Panther Stalks lay still, his breathing shallow as Cetán rose to his feet. Untying the rope at his wrist, Cetán drew in deep breaths of air as his dark eyes searched the crowd for Wacin. His anger did not lessen as he watched the beautiful young woman lean against her father. Had she turned her face from the fighting because she could not bear to watch her lover being harmed?

From the noise made by the villagers, Desire knew the fighting was at an end. The only thing she was not sure of was who was the victor. Taking a deep breath and dreading what she would see, she silently turned away from her father's shoulder. The first sight to meet her eyes was Cetán, looking directly at her. Her heart leaped with joy. When Desire had seen Panther Stalks wound Cetán, in her heart she had known she would die a slow death every hour of every day if Cetán did not survive! Her only concern now was that Cetán was unharmed! Giddy relief washed over her. She did not understand these feelings at all but for now, it was enough that Cetán was the victor.

A few breathless seconds passed as man and woman stared into each other's eyes. Desire broke the contact first as she gazed beyond Cetán, glimpsing Panther Stalks lying on the ground. Instantly, her need to help those who were suffering assailed her. Without a second thought, she stepped through the crowd to Panther Stalks' side.

For a moment, Cetán had been lost to all but the glittering gold of Desire's eyes. This woman was his, he thought triumphantly. As she stepped away from her father's side and began to make her way toward him, for an instant his heart began to hammer wildly. She knew he was the victor and was bringing him his due!

Desire would have stepped around Cetán to assure herself that Panther Stalks was not mortally wounded, but the warrior's hand reached out, his fingers circling her arm in a vise-like grip which held her at his side.

"You are mine, Wacin." Cetán pushed the words out between clenched teeth, his anger intensified by the knowledge that she was not coming to him but was, instead, hurrying to her lover's side!

Desire would have pushed his hand away but her father appeared at their side.

Sensing Cetán's anger, Desire refused to look at him until he released her. It was to her father that she spoke. "I would see that Panther Stalks' wounds are tended."

Gray Owl shook his head. "He will be taken to Medicine Woman's lodge, daughter."

"At least, let me make sure he can be moved." Desire felt guilty that Panther Stalks lay wounded because he had attempted to save her from becoming Cetán's bride. As she felt the sting of his fingers biting into her flesh, Desire wondered if she should be so glad that Cetán had won the fight.

Gray Owl shook his head. "Go to our lodge, Wacin. We will speak later."

Desire would have argued, but she glimpsed the hard tilt of her father's chin and knew it would not help. Turning her heated gaze upon Cetán, she said, "Release me!"

Cetán did not oblige her immediately. He wanted to pull her into his embrace and force her to accept the fact that she now belonged to him. Amethyst shards of light sparkled in the golden eyes, silently proclaiming her anger, and Cetán knew better than to attempt to quell her temper before her father and the villagers. His fingers eased their hold as his thumb lightly caressed the underside of her arm. It was enough to know that she belonged to him and no other. All that was left was for him to claim the prize. Turning toward Gray Owl, he spoke firmly. "I will return to your village with the next full moon. The joining ceremony will take place then."

The next full moon was only two weeks away! Desire gasped. She would have preferred more time in order to get to know Cetán better before being forced to become his wife and leave her family and village.

Before she could get the words out, her father took hold of her other arm and responded. "Wacin will be ready to become your wife, Cetán. When you return to our village, you and she shall be joined by the pipe."

Eight

Desire awoke with a blissful smile. Contentment washed over her as she stretched her shapely limbs. In a state of half-sleep, half-wakefulness, she felt comfortably secure lying upon her sleeping couch.

But reality quickly assailed her. This was the day that Cetán had vowed he would return to the village. This very evening, she and the warrior would be joined together as one, as was the custom of her people. An inward groan trembled over her lips. Elkhunter raised his head, his pale eyes appearing to comprehend his mistress's thoughts.

Pretty Dove did not disturb her daughter. This would be the last day on which Wacin would awaken in her parents' lodge, the last morning that her mother would prepare the morning meal and the two women would share the dawn of a new day. Pretty Dove's thoughts centered around the day when Gray Owl had first brought Wacin to their lodge. The One Above had blessed them with a fine daughter, and now the day had arrived when this same daughter would join herself with a warrior.

Pretty Dove had always known that this day would arrive for her and Gray Owl. She had hoped that their daughter would remain here in their village so she would be able to share Wacin's daily life.

It was the way of the people to believe that their steps were led by an unseen force; Pretty Dove had long ago accepted this fact. From that first moment when she had looked down into Wacin's beautiful face, she had known that Desire's life would be different from the other children. To Pretty Dove, her daughter's joining with a warrior from another village was part of the plan that the Great Spirit had created for Wacin.

Desire had not accepted her fate so easily. Several times she had approached her father, hoping to convince him to put a halt to this insanity that swirled around her. Desire had even suggested that she join with a different warrior, any warrior; her father could even choose the one that would please him, from their own village. Gray Owl had adamantly refused to discuss the topic of his daughter's joining with Cetán. He pointedly told her that Cetán had proven himself strong and brave, and he would make her a good husband. There was nothing left to say on the matter. His pride and honor were at stake—he would not go back on his given word.

Desire knew her father's honor was at stake, but what good was such honor if his only daughter would be miserable for the rest of her life?

The morning hours passed in silence on Desire's part. Pretty Dove tried to lure her daughter out of her dark mood, but after sharing the morning meal, the older woman gave up and silently began her beadwork.

Desire remained within the security of her parents' lodge throughout the long morning, not wishing to go to the river with the other women because she could not bear to hear their excited chatter about the preparations taking place in the village for the ceremony that evening. The Sioux people loved to celebrate, and the joining of their chief's daughter' to a great warrior-chief such as Cetán was reason enough for the entire tribe to work together in preparation for the ceremony and feasting which would follow.

It was still early afternoon when several village women arrived at Gray Owl's lodge. As they were invited into the cool interior, Desire was quickly surrounded by the bevy of women; amidst shoving and giggling she was pulled out of the lodge and hurried down the path that led to the river.

As was the nature of the Sioux people, when a special event was about to take place, a sweat-lodge was constructed along the banks of the river. The women had worked all morning, fashioning the sweat-lodge in the sacred custom of the people. It had been constructed with sixteen willow sticks, each one resilient and easy to bend. The sticks had been shaped into a beehive-shaped dome. Two buffalo hides were stretched over the framework, allowing a small entrance flap. The entire floor of the sweat-lodge was covered with sage. In the center, a circular pit had been dug to receive the burning wood, which would be topped with rocks. Wood was also piled outside the lodge to make sure the fire remained hot throughout the ceremony. After the fire burned down to coals, white lime rocks would be placed in the center pit. The lime rocks had been gathered from the sacred hills; those with green moss on their smooth surface were believed to be etched with secret spirit writing. The dirt from within the center pit was piled in a small mound outside the lodge. This dirt represented Unci, Mother-Earth. A sacred prayer had been said by Medicine Woman as the mound of earth was piled. Outside the entrance flap, a buffalo skull altar had been set up with tobacco ties fastened to the skull's horns.

Desire had not even considered that the village women, including Medicine Woman, would set up a sweat-lodge for her. "You should not have done this," she began in protest. If left alone, Desire would have hidden in her father's lodge for the remainder of the day.

"Of course this is all necessary, Wacin." Medicine Woman stepped before Desire, her smile warm, her dark eyes sparkling brilliantly. "Your friends wish to participate in a sweating ceremony with you. After this evening, your path will turn differently from the paths of your sisters. We wish to call upon the Great One Above to guide you in your decisions, to help you in your new life, and to allow your knowledge of healing the sick to grow.''

There was nothing Desire could say to Medicine Woman to refute such a statement. Dancing Moon and Eagle Woman took hold of her arms and began to pull her along toward the sweat-lodge. Outside, the women disrobed before bending to enter. Medicine Woman was designated the sacred leader of this medicine rite; she entered the lodge first with her sacred pipe. As the eight women watched from the entrance, the old medicine woman placed pinches of tobacco at the four corners of the center pit. Silently, Medicine Woman began to burn sweet grass, rubbing her entire body and pipe with the smoke to drive all evil things from the lodge. With this completed, she offered pinches of tobacco to all the visible and invisible powers that ruled their lives. As the village women stepped back, Medicine Woman left the lodge and placed her pipe on the mound of earth outside the lodge. The bowl of the pipe was placed on the west side, the stem slanting to the east.

Now, all of the village women participating in the ceremony entered the sweat-lodge. Within the dim interior, they moved sunwise around the lodge, then sat on a ring of sacred sage. As the women settled in their places, silence reigned, each remembering the Great Spirit's goodness toward them and their families.

Medicine Woman's pipe was passed back into the lodge by Buffalo-Spirit Woman, who had been chosen as the sacred leader's helper. Medicine Woman drew deeply on the pipe, then began to chant a prayer to evoke the spirits' presence during this ceremony. The pipe was passed to each woman in turn, who, after inhaling deeply, called forth their own prayers and spirit helpers.

As the pipe was passed to Desire, her hand automatically reached for the smooth stone pendant in the center of her medicine necklace. She called on the mighty matóhota to help now in her hour of need. Her spirit bear was the only power that could save her from the joining ceremony that was to take place that evening.

As the sacred leader's helper, Buffalo-Spirit Woman was also the fire-tender. As she pushed aside the entrance flap, she carried a heated lime rock in the fork of a deer antler, which was transferred into the center fire pit. As rock after rock was transferred in the same manner, Medicine Woman touched each with the bowl of her pipe.

Without instruction, the fire-tender sprinkled the rocks with green cedar. Taking up a gourd of cool, fresh water, she slowly poured a small amount of the liquid over the white-hot rocks. The air instantly filled with an aromatic odor as steam hissed over the rocks, filling the lodge with a moist haze.

As the haze began to clear somewhat, Medicine Woman bent forward and silently studied the lime rocks with their secret spirit writing etched over their surfaces. "We women of the Sioux are the heart of our nation. We tend the fires of our husbands' lodges, we give birth to those who will one day take our places here on Mother Earth, we teach the ancient traditions of our grandmothers to our children and our grandchildren."

The women nodded agreement with the healing woman's words. They were already beginning to feel light of mind and body; the heat in the lodge had a languid effect on their senses. Medicine Woman's soothing voice seemed to envelop them.

"It is this great circle of life that the One Above has planned for His children. Wakán Tanka is pleased that we come together as sisters in the tradition of those who have gone on to join the sky people. For the people to be reborn and open their minds and hearts, they must be purified from without as well as within."

Desire's limbs seemed to turn liquid. She leaned back,

the tiny bells in her hair singing softly with every movement. As she listened to Medicine Woman's words, her fingers never left the cool stone at the base of her necklace.
Everything around her seemed hot and heavy, but the
stone remained cool; matóhota's spirit of earth and water
filled her.

Minutes turned into an hour; once again, the fire-tender
drew back the flap and poured more cool water on the
red-glowing rocks. Immediately, there was a hissing noise
as more steam filtered throughout the lodge interior.

A few of the women groaned aloud from the intense
heat, but with an inner will, they remained seated, none
daring to disregard tradition to flee from their discomfort.

"The Great Spirit desires us to see with the eye of the
heart as well. Within the heart lies the message that He
wishes to impart to His children." Medicine Woman's
words took on a singsong quality as she leaned forward to
study the sacred rock writing.

*Within the heart . . . See with the eye of the heart . . . Within
the heart . . . The message lies within the heart.* Desire lost herself in the spell of Medicine Woman's words. In her inner
vision, she saw the image of the great grizzly bear she had
followed through the forest years before. The matóhota
called out silent words to her, as he had that day when she
was but twelve summers. He imparted the answers to her
inner questions in the depths of his dark stare; she had but
to look. She envisioned taking a step closer toward him,
wishing to see this message that was waiting for her.

Standing only a step away from the large beast, slender
threads of fear slowly traveled over her body. His great,
furry arms surrounded her in an embrace. She felt she was
being suffocated—the grizzly bear was squeezing the life
out of her! Suddenly, the bear's image changed into that
of a man. Staring into the dark eyes before her, she saw
herself lying upon a sleeping couch, her body entangled
with that of a warrior's. As she watched, the warrior's fea-

tures were lost to her; only the image of his naked body seared her imagination. His body was bronzed and hard with muscles, his jet-colored hair unbound and twining with hers upon the bed of furs.

Try as she would, Desire could not make out the warrior's face. Her own body hindered her view. She watched herself as a moan escaped from the back of her throat and the two bodies merged, coming together. Desire's body flushed with heat as she saw the open floodgates of desire reflected in her own face. Her lips parted as moans of sheer carnal pleasure filled her ears.

The fire-tender again poured water from the gourd over the rocks, but Desire was beyond the world of beings. She was in the spirit realm, that place where the great matóhota had led her.

In her vision, the warrior's body glowed from the touch of Wi, his muscles rippling with physical strength as his body covered her. His large hands reached out with great gentleness as he stroked her limbs. She rose to meet his every touch, welcoming the pleasure that he stoked to life within her body. Desire felt herself being renewed, brought to full life for the first time, but a portion of her heart drew back from such a powerful vision. The woman on the sleeping couch appeared more seductress then maiden. Her silken body lay in anticipated welcome, receiving the rapture that the warrior showered upon her. Desire tried to make out his features, but his face was obscured within the shadows of her inner sight.

As suddenly as the vision had come to Desire, it began to fade. The man and woman upon the sleeping couch began to pale. "No!" Desire gasped aloud. "I must know who he is!"

Medicine Woman drew deeply on her pipe, her dark eyes misted with knowledge as she looked at Desire, knowing that the young woman had received a strong vision. As the fire-tender turned aside the entrance flap and secured it tightly against the side of the lodge, the women inhaled deep breaths of fresh air. The ceremony was finished—daylight shone brightly within the lodge.

Desire felt the women around her stirring; trying to regain her composure, she attempted to shake away the languid, dream-like feeling that still seemed to have a grip on her. As seconds passed, she silently questioned, *what on earth had happened?* What kind of insane vision had she received? Going over all that she had seen, she felt even more confused. Who was the warrior who had held such command over her body and senses? She wondered if it was Cetán. Had the great matóhota tried to tell her that her vision would be her fate after this night? Silently, Desire rejected the thought. She would never give herself over so fully to any warrior! In her heart, Desire knew that to do such a thing would be the end of all her beliefs. She would no longer be the same woman; her mind and soul would be lost to another's keeping. Desire would never allow such a thing to happen! She had to remain the woman she was— it was all she had to hold on to! Perhaps the vision had been a warning, showing her a side of her nature that she should guard against. Feeling Medicine Woman's steady gaze, Desire rose and left the sweat lodge with the other women. But even as she dove into the cool, refreshing river, she made a vow: her fate would not be like that of the woman in her vision!

Nine

From the moment the village women pulled Desire out of her parents' lodge, she felt all control over her life slip away. After the sweat-lodge ceremony, the women dove into the river, washing away the impurities of mind and body which had been drawn out by the sweating. Desire had almost been able to forget that this day would see the changing of her life forever as she swam and frolicked in the refreshing water with these women who had been her lifelong friends.

After a swim in the river, Desire usually returned to her father's lodge alone and went about her daily life, but this day was far different. The women walked with her to the lodge she had grown up in, and amidst gossip and laughter they set about helping to ready her for the joining ceremony that would take place as soon as Wi lowered in the sky.

Each woman, young and old alike, seemed to have a special talent or suggestion to contribute. After swimming in the river, the women had wrapped Desire in a buffalo robe. They now stripped the robe away as several pairs of hands reached out to help dry her body and hair. After this, they applied a soothing ointment over every inch of her body; the scent of wildflowers filled the lodge instantly.

At first Desire attempted to push away the hands rubbing the lotion into her flesh, but Medicine Woman's gentle words stilled her protests. "These women are your sisters,

Wacin. This will be the last time they can assist you. After the joining ceremony tonight, your steps will lead you down a different path. Enjoy this time with your sisters—allow them to share in this day."

Looking at the women standing around her and understanding Medicine Woman's words, Desire no longer attempted to push the women away. Medicine Woman was right. These women were her sisters. None in her village had ever pointed out the fact that she had been born a white woman, though all knew the circumstances under which she came to the people. Everyone accepted her as Gray Owl's daughter, and now that her life had taken a direction that she did not care for, she could not hurt those who wished to share in what should have been the happiest day of her life.

The massaging completed, two women began to work on Desire's hair. Leading her to the side of the lodge fire, they combed the long, dark tresses until they dried in shimmering waves, the firelight reflecting brilliant auburn highlights. Entwining slender braids at each side of her head, the women bound the lengths with strips of white ermine, the bottom fringe decorated with tiny silver bells. The braids fell over Desire's shoulders as the women swept back the rest of the cloud of shimmering curls and allowed the length to flow over her shoulders and down her back. Over her brow, they placed a slender headband beaded in clear-blue crystal.

Desire's joining dress, which Pretty Dove had painstakingly made from the hides of two doe deer, had been bleached to a brilliant white. Ermine fringe had been attached to the hem and along the upper sleeves, forming a yoke around the neckline. Crystal-blue beads and silver bells had been stitched with a patient hand along each border of ermine. The fringed design had also been sewn on the bleached-hide leggings that were pulled over her calves. After Desire stepped into a pair of blue-beaded moc-casins, Pretty Dove stood before her daughter.

With tear-filled eyes, Pretty Dove reached out to place a delicate necklace of slender bone beads around Desire's neck. "You have been a good daughter, Wacin, and this day your mother's heart sings with happiness."

Mother and daughter were allowed only a minute to clutch each other tightly before the other women pulled Desire away, and, with much excitement, admired their handiwork. All agreed they had never seen a more beautiful maiden before her joining ceremony.

Desire was barely allowed a deep breath before the women were pulling her out of the lodge; they headed toward the area where a large ceremonial fire had been built. Many villagers were already singing and dancing around the circle of flames.

Desire looked around in desperation as the women left her standing alone before the ceremonial fire. Panic claimed her as thoughts of taking flight skittered through her mind. She turned, thinking of trying to disappear into the crowd, but before she could take one step, her father approached. The people quieted, standing back and watching father and daughter as they silently stood before the great fire.

Desire tried to calm the wild racing of her heart. She felt trapped, clinging only to the hope that for some reason Cetán would not arrive for the joining ceremony. Her hopes depended upon this one last reprieve. So far, she had not heard any announcement that Cetán had appeared. With luck, he might have been detained, or, if fate saw to it, never arrive in her village at all! Many things could happen to a lone warrior on the trail. As soon as this thought struck, her compassionate inner spirit took hold. Well, perhaps he would decide that he did not wish to take a bride who did not wish to join with him!

Such hopes were not to be realized. Shortly after Medi-

cine Knife, the ancient wicasa wakán, or holy man of the
village, stepped before Gray Owl and his daughter, a disturbance parted the crowd.

Cetán strode into the midst of the villagers circling the
large ceremonial fire; his bearing that was overwhelmingly
proud. His searching gaze sought out, and found, the
woman he wished to claim as his own; with sure steps, he
drew nearer.

Magnificent was the only word that came to mind as Desire's breath caught in the back of her throat, her golden
gaze riveted on Cetán. This man was a warrior chieftain,
and at the moment, he looked every bit the part!

Cetán had chosen his apparel carefully. In his heart, his
life-path joining with that of Wacin's was the most signifi-
cant occasion in his life. He had dressed in his prized coup
shirt and leggings, boldly displaying his courage and
strength. The collar and upper sleeves of his shirt were
decorated with bone pipes and fringed with ermine, signifying his leadership on raid expeditions. The undersleeves,
leggings, and bottom portion of the shirt were heavily
beaded in horizontal lines, indicating his bravery in war.
Atop his head he wore an impressive buffalo horn bonnet.
The fur at the crown of the headdress had been taken from
a bobcat. Around the fur was a quilled ring and many dyed
eagle breath feathers. The side and horn feathers had been
taken from the hawk. A long plume at the back of the
bonnet attested to the fact that Cetán had participated in
the sundance ceremony one or more times. The headdress
also boasted a long, trailing double tail of golden eagle
feathers.

In Cetán's right hand he held the reins of a spirited black
mare. She wore a Spanish saddle made from tooled Mo-
roccan leather, decorated with shiny silver discs and silver
braidwork. The fine animal also wore an elaborate horse
mask, heavily fringed and beaded, and a matching martin-
gale.

As Cetán's dark eyes traveled over Desire's body, her own gaze filled with the splendor of the warrior approaching her. Suddenly, her legs felt wobbly and her breathing grew erratic. A shudder laced a path down her back and gradually encompassed her entire body. Gray Owl felt the trembling of her slender frame; his hand lightly encircled her arm, allowing her to lean against his larger frame. This man held the power to steal her thoughts . . . her control . . . her inner self! Desire's thoughts whirled as they interwove with the remembrance of the vision she had had in the sweat-lodge. She had not seen the warrior's features, but looking at Cetán now, she knew it had to be him. She would have turned around and run, if not for her father holding tightly to her arm. Her mind cried out that she could not go through with the ceremony, no matter the cost to her father's honor!

Speaking in low tones to the mare, Cetán dropped the reins. The animal stood quietly as Cetán took the few steps to Desire's side. Gray Owl silently removed his hand and stepped back to the front of the crowd.

Standing so close, Desire could hardly breathe; her heart began to flutter crazily in her chest as trembling beset her limbs. She was held there by the sheer force of Cetán's jet eyes as he looked down into her pale features. Within the depths of his gaze, Desire could see a storm of emotions. Desire . . . strength . . . and even anger were openly visible. She was powerless to turn away, even as the warning sounded in her mind that she should escape before it was too late!

Medicine Knife broke the spell that had been cast around the couple by stepping in front of the blazing ceremonial fire. As all eyes turned toward him, the holy man drew forth a piece of braided sweet grass and ignited it in the flames. As soon as the fringed edge of the grass caught fire, he fanned the smoke with an eagle feather above his medicine bundle. Completing this, he turned away the

folded edges of the medicine bundle to reveal an ancient
tribal pipe, which rested upon a vermillion-dyed blanket.
Silently, the holy man fanned the smoke over the pipe and
blanket, his dark stare penetrating the distance as he gazed
upon the couple in silent appraisal.

An eternity passed in those few seconds as Desire was
forced to endure the slow perusal of the holy man. His
look was measured and meaningful, as though he wished
to seek out her hidden thoughts. After studying Cetán in
the same fashion, he softly grunted out his satisfaction.
Taking up the pipe in reverent hands, he brought the sweet
grass to the bowl, and igniting the Indian tobacco within,
he softly drew upon the mouthpiece.

"I call upon all the powers of life to guide the steps of
these two that stand before their people," Medicine Knife
loudly stated after blowing smoke in the direction of the
four powers. "I call upon Wakán Tanka to bless this joining
ceremony and to give each of you the strength for that
which lies ahead. You will know hardship, you will know
loss; I see this in the smoke. But still, it is the will of the
One Above that your steps be joined down one path."

With the completion of the smoking of the pipe and the
blessings being called forth, Medicine Knife pulled the
blanket from his medicine bundle. With the pipe in one
hand and the blanket in the other, he draped the blanket
over Desire and Cetán's shoulders, the cover drawing them
closer together. Holding out the sacred tribal pipe, he instructed each to lay a hand upon the stem.

Cetán did not hesitate but Desire could not force herself
to reach out to the pipe. She stared at Cetán's large hand
as though it were an alien thing to her, his long bronzed
fingers wrapped around the pipe stem in a confident manner. As though she fully expected, even at this late moment,
to find the means to end this madness, Desire lifted her
gaze and silently looked around the crowd of villagers.

Cetán knew that Desire was hesitant to join with him.

He felt the slight trembling of her body as she stood next to him beneath the blanket, but his determination to claim this woman was far stronger than any inner fears for the future. Without a second thought, he reached down and captured her hand and drew it up to the pipe. He did not release his gentle hold until she wrapped her slender fingers around the pipe stem next to his own.

Medicine Knife nodded his gray head in satisfaction. Bending down to his medicine bundle, he pulled forth a piece of red tradecloth. Murmuring a prayer to the Great Spirit, he bound the two hands, making them one with the pipe as they would now be one throughout their life-paths.

Taking up the eagle feather once again, Medicine Knife drew the piece of burning sweet grass close and fanned the smoke over the tied hands and down the length of the pipe.

Even now, Desire had thoughts of snatching her hand away, and perhaps she would have attempted such an act, but as Medicine Knife fanned the smoke over their hands on the pipe-stem, a surge of power coursed through the pipe, up her arm, and through her body. Cetán felt the energy also; his dark eyes locked with Desire's of brilliant gold and were as wonder-filled as the woman's looking up at him. His heart hammered wildly as the unleashed current of power coursed through his body.

Medicine Knife chanted an ancient prayer of thanksgiving, he also having felt the power. He thanked the spirits for their presence at this joining ceremony. "The spirits are pleased with this joining," he loudly announced as he untied the tradecloth strip that bound the couple's hands, then pulled the blanket from over their shoulders. "Wakán Tanka is watching and is happy that His children have joined their lives with the pipe, as is the ancient way of the people."

Desire felt totally numb, inside and out. The ceremony was finished, she and Cetán were joined, the villagers were happy, her father was happy. She forced a smile as hearty congratulations were called out. She would force herself to go through the motions and appear the part of the happy bride, but inside, where no one could see, she was trembling with an inner fear of what was to come later this evening—and all the tomorrows that would follow.

Not daring to look at her husband lest she see in his eyes that he could discern her inner feelings, Desire felt a wash of relief as Cetán stepped away from her side. Medicine Woman approached while she stood alone, and holding out a hide-covered bundle, she lightly caressed Desire's smooth cheek.

"You have been the daughter I never knew, Wacin. I wish to give you this gift so you will long remember our days of working with plants and making medicine." She unwrapped the hide covering and held forth an ancient medicine rattle. The handle was wrapped in ermine skin and there was a gourd at the top, decorated in different designs of Desire's spirit bear; a dangler of cut deer claws was secured at the base of the handle. "This was my husband's, Wacin. Medicine Bear was given this when he was a young man. It has been in the possession of the people's greatest healers, and has much power."

Desire brushed at the tears that fell down her cheeks. As she reached to the gift, she dared not attempt to express her appreciation to this kind woman for fear that if she tried to speak, she would cry aloud that she had never wished to be joined with Cetán; all she had ever wanted was to remain here with her own people in her own village.

"I also have a gift for my bride," Cetán announced, sparing Desire the need to speak. Glimpsing the tears on her cheeks, Cetán longed to reach out and wipe them away. He restrained the impulse. Stepping before her, his hand held the reins to the horse he had walked into the village. "Star is my joining gift to you, mitáwicu, my wife."

The mare was extremely beautiful, and as the villagers

admired her sleek black coat and well-built limbs, Desire tentatively reached out and accepted the reins from her husband. "I am afraid I have no such fine gift for you, Cetán." Desire was unable to force the word *husband* out of her mouth.

"I have already received the only gift that has ever mattered to me, Wacin. You are now my wife." Cetán spoke softly, his words heard only by Desire and Medicine Woman. The old woman smiled with pleasure at the warrior's words. Desire felt instant flame rise to her cheeks.

The couple stood before the ceremonial fire as the villagers offered their well-wishes amidst the celebrating. As time passed and the feasting and dancing continued, Cetán caught Desire's hand within his own. "You should tell your parents good-by now, Wacin. The hour grows late, and I would leave the village this night."

"What?" Desire tried to draw back, but Cetán would not loosen his hold. "But why should we leave this night? I thought we would stay here with my mother and father for a few days before making the trip to your village." She desperately tried to gain more time before being forced to be alone with this man who was now her husband.

Her features visibly paled, her eyes enlarged, and Cetán knew that, unlike himself, his bride was not anxious for them to be alone together. With a soft sigh, he controlled the flare of irritation that settled over him. He spoke softly but firmly. "It will be two days of hard travel to reach my village, Wacin. I would leave as quickly as possible in order for you to become accustomed to me and my people." The longer they put off leaving this village, the harder it was going to be on her.

"But I still have to pack my belongings." Desire had forgotten about this chore in all the confusion that had spun around her for the last few days. "I surely cannot be made to leave my plants and medicines!" She grabbed onto any excuse that would help her remain even for a few more hours.

"Your mother has already packed your things, Wacin. I spoke to her earlier. She and Gray Owl are at their lodge waiting for us. They wish to tell their daughter good-by in private." Cetán understood her hesitation about leaving those she had known all her life, but silently he reassured himself that soon she would learn that happiness could be found among his people. Once in his village, she would learn that her fears had been groundless. She would be happy as his wife—he would make sure that she had no regrets!

There was nothing Desire could say or do that would sway Cetán's plans. It was obvious he was not the type of man who would easily yield a decision once he had made it.

The couple left the area of celebrating in silence. Desire clutched the hide-covered medicine rattle tightly in her hands as Cetán took up Star's reins once again. As they approached the large lodge, Gray Owl was waiting outside for them.

"I would speak with my daughter for a few minutes, Cetán," Gray Owl stated in a friendly manner. Taking hold of his daughter's elbow before turning toward the path leading to the river, he added, "Pretty Dove has finished packing. We know that you wish to leave soon, Cetán. The parfleches should be ready to load."

Leading Desire away from the lodge, daughter and father did not speak for a few minutes. The night wind whistled a pleasant tune throughout the valley, as pine boughs swayed overhead and the warm evening breeze rustled through the treetops.

"I wish you to know, Wacin, that I would never have agreed to your joining with Cetán if I did not feel in my heart that this was the right path to follow. The bride price brought to our village would have been turned away if I

believed that Cetán was not the warrior who should walk
at your side in your life circle. I have known for many winters, that the warrior to join his life with yours would need
to possess much strength to see that you remain safe. Cetán
proved this by defeating Panther Stalks in battle." Gray
Owl had waited until this moment after the joining ceremony to speak these words to his daughter, for fear he
would weaken and give in to her desire not to join with
Cetán. In his heart, he knew that Cetán was the warrior
who would protect and love her. He had prayed to the One
Above and had sought out Medicine Knife's advice several
times about his daughter's joining with a warrior from another village. Always, his answers had been positive, Medicine Knife asserting that Wacin would need strength at her
side in the days that would come.

Desire felt totally defeated. She had hoped that somehow, even at this last minute, her father would offer her a
reprieve. "I do not wish to leave my village," she got out
on a strangled breath.

Gray Owl's heart felt the great pain his daughter was
suffering. Gently, he drew her into his embrace. "It is now
a long time in the past since that day I lifted you out of
the box the wasichu had placed you in. You have been a
good daughter to me and your mother, Wacin, but we have
always known that The One Above would lead you in different steps from the other maidens of the village. You will
one day be known as a great healer among your people,
Wacin. You will find happiness and harmony with Cetán
because, daughter, deep in your heart, you are Sioux."

Desire silently brushed at the tears dampening Gray
Owl's hide shirt. He was offering her words of comfort,
which he believed would help her be strong. It was too late
for anyone to change what had occurred this evening. Her
life path was now joined with that of Cetán's. She could
either bear herself up with the pride of her people, or she
could fall to weeping out her misery and fear of the un-

known. Drawing strength within the loving arms of her father, a long sigh escaped her lips. She had never been the type of woman who easily bemoaned that which she could not change; she would force herself not to do so now.

Returning his daughter to her husband, Pretty Dove and Desire hugged each other tightly. With the finish of their good-bys, Cetán led Desire to Star and reached out to help her mount. Looking around for Elkhunter, Desire eyed her husband to gauge his reaction as she stated, "Elkhunter must accompany me—he has been at my side since he was a pup."

Cetán nodded his head thoughtfully. He had no wish to deprive his wife of her animals. After he'd lifted her up to take her seat in the Spanish saddle, Cetán mounted Whirling-Warrior's-Ghost.

As the couple left, with Elkhunter chasing after them, a lone warrior stared in their direction from beneath a cottonwood tree not far from Gray Owl's lodge. "You will be mine one day, Wacin. I swear this on my life!" Panther Stalks' angry gaze watched the man and woman until they rode out of sight.

Ten

Night shadows along the path of the forest were illuminated through the canopy of trees overhead by the cast of the full moon riding high in the velvet-dark sky. Cetán no longer wore the headdress and coup outfit—he wore only a hide breechcloth and leggings, his dark hair held back by a beaded headband. Over his shoulder rested the beaded sash secured to his rifle-stock weapon, the cool steel of the blade caressing his muscular thigh as Whirling-Warrior's-Ghost made his way through the woods of tall pines and thick underbrush.

Elkhunter ran ahead of the couple. Following Cetán's lead, Desire had no fear of the elements of nature around her. Her fear was an inner dread that had taken root in her soul and was directed toward that moment when her husband would halt his gray stallion and declare his intent to make camp. As they left the village and started along the forest trail, inner apprehensions had begun to overwhelm Desire. She knew very little about this man with whom she had left her home. She had heard stories of his mighty powers as a great war chief, but little else did she know about him. How could she be expected to give her body to her husband, as a bride was supposed to do on their joining night, when she knew so little about him? Desire could not shake thoughts of impending doom, nor could she forget the vision she had had in the sweat-lodge.

The couple had been traveling in silence for over three

hours when Cetán suddenly directed Whirling-Warrior's-Ghost off the forest path. Tentatively, Desire followed. She would have dared to call out to question his motives, but her throat was too dry. She could only pray to The One Above that her husband had not decided to find a spot to rest. She was more than willing to ride throughout the rest of the night!

If he'd been alone, Cetán would have traveled on with little thought of tiredness. But, this night of all nights, he needed no reminder that he was not alone. He had desired to put distance between Desire's village and themselves; he now deemed the distance far enough. "We will make camp here, Wacin. The moon is already lowering and tomorrow will be another day of travel." As the animals halted, he dismounted and going to Star's side, reached up to help his bride dismount.

Desire stiffened at his touch. Cetán felt her body's reaction to his hands around her waist and once again remembered that he would have to use all his patience in order to gain his wife's trust. "I will start a small fire, Wacin. If you are hungry, there is food in my parfleche." As always, when speaking to Wacin, his tone gentled.

Desire quickly moved away from his reach, her singing bells sounding musical as their sound was caught up on the night breeze. Elkhunter ran around the area, sniffing out a rabbit in the underbrush, but feeling his mistress's tension, he returned often to her side.

Desire took in deep breaths in order to steady her emotions. Her voice was barely loud enough for Cetán to hear as he took a step away from her. "I . . . I . . . am not hungry, Cetán." Food was the farthest thing from her mind at this minute. Her fear of what would take place now that they had stopped drove all other thoughts from her mind.

Turning back to her, Cetán's warm gaze searched Desire's pale features beneath the moonlight. He noticed the way her lips trembled, her golden eyes glancing everywhere except directly at him. He sensed her apprehension as though it were a living thing. She looked like a frightened bird caught in a snare. Her distrust would ease in time, he told himself. Once she realized he would never harm her, she would begin to trust. With a soft smile, he reached out a hand and with his forefinger, lifted her chin so she looked directly at him. "I am not hungry either, Wacin."

At Desire's side, Elkhunter growled low in his throat, warning the warrior who dared touch his mistress.

"Iwástegla—be at ease," Cetán commanded, his tone firm but with that gentle masculine timbre that caused Desire to feel out of breath.

Elkhunter instantly obeyed the softly spoken command. His growling ceased; the silver ridge of neck fur which had stiffened when he saw the warrior lay a hand upon his mistress instantly smoothed.

Desire was amazed at the great wolf's response to her husband. Since he'd been a pup, the beast had obeyed only her; even her father complained that Elkhunter had a mind of his own when it came to protecting his mistress.

Seeing surprise on Desire's features, Cetán chose to ignore her reaction. "I will ready a fire, Wacin, while you spread out our sleeping blankets." His dark gaze did not waver when he noticed the instant flush spreading over her cheeks. He did not await her response, but began to take the gear off the horses.

Her senses cleared as soon as Cetán turned away. Desire looked at the parfleches he was placing next to a tree. As he began to gather wood for a fire, she silently picked up the blankets that were lying next to the parfleches. Attempting to keep a tight grip on her emotions, she spread her blanket on one side of the fire, and Cetán's on the opposite side.

After he'd coaxed a small fire to life amongst the twigs and sticks he had placed in a shallow pit, Cetán stood back and eyed the sleeping arrangements his wife had made. A small smile played over his lips as his dark eyes sought Desire out. She sat on a fallen log, brushing her dark tresses, and for a few minutes Cetán was unable to speak. He drank in her beauty. In his heart, he understood that he had waited a lifetime to see this sight. When she replaced the porcupine quill comb back in her parfleche, he spoke. "It will be safer if we sleep side by side, Wacin." His gaze went to the sleeping blankets on opposite sides of the fire.

"I feel very safe, Cetán." Desire felt her heartbeat stir and her hands shake as she took out a less decorative hide dress from one of her bags. She had not had time to change out of her joining outfit before leaving the village.

Looking at her standing near the tree with the hide dress clutched to her bosom as though she needed a barrier of protection, Cetán did not have the heart to push the matter of their sleeping arrangements any further. He would need to win her trust. Silently, he watched her step into the shadows of the forest to change her clothes. With an effort he forced himself not to try and seek out his wife's shapely curves. He had realized that day when he had brought the wagons full of supplies to her father for a bride price and had witnessed her shaking her head against the prospect of becoming his wife that the cost to him would be much dearer than the bride-gift. But whatever the cost, he was certain that the prize would ultimately be worth it all!

"When I was a boy, I would look up into the night sky for long periods of time, thinking that the stars were reflections of the sky people, and that they were trying to speak out to me." Cetán's masculine voice settled over Desire. The night was quiet; he was lying on his blanket across the fire from where Desire lay upon hers.

She smiled, trying to envision this large, seemingly invincible warrior as a child looking up to the sky, waiting for the stars to speak to him. She did not reply, but allowed the husky tremor of his voice to lull her into a peaceful place somewhere between wakefulness and slumber.

"There, high in the sky, is the spirit trail of our people, Wacin." Cetán pointed out the Milky Way. "Long ago the people believed that the night sky was like a vast lake of water, and the spirit trail, the bridge that had to be crossed to gain the plentiful hunting grounds, where the people no longer worry about having enough meat to eat and water to quench their thirst. On this bridge, the people believe, an ancient grandmother sits and waits. When one of the people sets out upon this bridge she meets them and asks to see their tattoo. If the one trying to cross over cannot show the grandmother a tattoo, she pushes them off the bridge and they drown in the big lake. Those with a tattoo are allowed to pass on and join the sky people."

Desire remembered this legend from her earliest childhood. "And what do you believe, Cetán?" she softly questioned her husband. "Do you believe that there is an old grandmother on the spirit trail, waiting to push those off the bridge who do not have a tattoo?" It was rather strange, but Desire felt comfortable lying there next to the warm fire, asking her husband questions.

Cetán's husky laughter touched her ears. "I do not know if the legend is true or not, Wacin, but I would not chance being pushed off the bridge. When I climb the spirit trail and I meet the old grandmother of the bridge, I will show her the tiny mark on my forehead that will allow me to pass by freely to the hunting grounds."

"You have a tattoo?" Desire turned sleepily on her side so she faced Cetán across the fire.

"It is but a tiny mark, given to me by an old wicasa wakán after my first sundance. I believe Medicine Crow believed the legend. Each brave that he helped during the sundance ceremony received this same mark."

Desire smiled warmly. She was so tired from the long day and the ride from her village she could barely keep her eyes open. "Perhaps I will also get a tattoo," she responded sleepily, telling herself that this first night as wife to Cetán had passed comfortably. With that thought, her eyes shut and she fell into slumber.

Cetán lay awake looking at the woman across his fire. Silently, he studied the beauty of her heart-shaped face, his gaze gently touching the soft curls that feathered against her cheeks and twined around her shapely body. He remembered the first time he had looked upon her two summers past, and also remembered the promise he had made that he would one day claim the beautiful Wacin as his own. This day they had joined their life-paths together, but wisely he knew that like the wild bird of the forest, he could never claim his wife's inner spirit. He would have to allow her time to learn his heart; then, perhaps, she would be willing to open herself freely to him. An image of Panther Stalks intruded upon his thoughts, and he harshly pushed it aside. He would not dwell on what had been between the other warrior and his wife. All that mattered was that he had been given the chance to win her heart.

The next day, travel was slow. Cetán did not push the horses; stopping at times, he pulled Whirling-Warrior's-Ghost to a halt along a lush creek bank swollen with snow-melt. In a blur of cascading beauty, the rushing stream angled through a colonnade of towering red cedars and lodgepole pines, the underbrush vibrant green with a tapestry of oak ferns. As the couple on horseback watched, a doe and her fawn fed on the summer berries growing along the creekbank. When the deer stepped back into the safety of the forest, Cetán helped Desire to dismount. In a companionable manner, the couple picked the berries and ate them with a piece of pemmican for their noon meal.

In the early afternoon, Cetán directed Whirling-Warrior's-Ghost off the forest trail, leaving the coolness of dense foliage and trees. They traveled a short way before he once again halted his mount. They sat atop a crest which overlooked a meadow surrounded on two sides by vast mountain tops, their peaks shimmering with snow beneath the afternoon sunlight.

Desire was allowed only a few minutes to draw in the picturesque beauty before Cetán set his horse into motion, directing him down into the meadow. Scarlet Indian paint-brush, white yarrow, and purple daisies covered the crest, overflowing in abundance throughout the meadow. Horsemint blossoms and blooms of bear grass spiraled up-ward from tall stalks which dotted the scenery. Following Cetán's lead, Desire found they had cut across the meadow to arrive at the point where the creek they had been fol-lowing throughout most of the day ended.

In a dramatic display, the water from the creek rushed down a stairway of rocks, cascading in a shimmering de-scent where it was captured within the crystalline depths of a large lake. "This place is wonderful," Desire whispered as she gazed from the colorful meadow to the beauty of the water falling into the lake.

Cetán was pleased with her reaction and also happy with his own decision, which had been made the previous night while he had watched his bride in her sleep, to prolong their arrival in his village for at least another day. Seeing his wife's delight with her surroundings, he smiled warmly as he stated, "We will make camp here next to the lake."

Desire would have remembered that there was still trav-eling time before the sun set, but her husband's close pe-rusal left her feeling rather over-heated. Elkhunter saved the moment as he sprinted through the tall grass and flushed out a rabbit. Cetán's attention was drawn away from her for the time, and Desire was able to pull her emotions in order.

As Cetán began to unpack the horses, freeing them to graze on the lush meadow grass, Desire wondered at his reasons for setting up camp so early in the afternoon. Though she was not anxious to reach his village, she nervously pondered the situation before her. Would this be the night that her husband would approach her and force her to accept him on her sleeping blanket? Her fingers lightly touched the soft curve of her lower lip, and with the movement, she was vividly reminded of the night when Cetán had kissed her. Images from her vision filled her mind and Desire tried to force her thoughts in a different direction. She would go mad if she kept thinking about that!

Cetán's dark eyes kindled with lights of his own silent reflections as he watched his bride. An aura of sadness appeared about her, as though she were unsure in which direction she should turn. Being a man who always tried to be true to his inner self, Cetán admitted he was not entirely lost to the cause of her distress. He knew well that she had been against their joining their life-paths together. The image of Panther Stalks again intruded in his thoughts, and he was reminded that he was unsure of the relationship that had been shared between the two. Perhaps his bride already missed her lover! A blinding pang of jealousy caught him unaware, and it took all his effort not to react to the twisting blade of anger that filled his chest!

A harsh sigh escaped his throat as Cetán finished setting the last of the parfleches in a dry place and loosed the horses. If only his wife would turn to him for comfort, he would gladly open his arms to her and help her get beyond the hurt that filled her heart. He wisely knew that Wacin would reject any offer on his part to ease her plight. She was a proud woman, and she would have to work out her feelings. Soon she would forget about Panther Stalks and realize that he wished only to make her happy, and to complete their lives as one. "If you would like to refresh yourself by swimming in the lake, Wacin, I will join Elkhunter and find fresh game for our evening meal."

Cetán's words startled Desire out of her reflections. A swim . . . it was certainly a tempting idea. It would be sheer heaven to be able to strip away her clothing and take a long, leisurely swim. She did not voice this response; instead, she watched silently as Cetán gathered his bow and quiver and set off on foot through the meadow.

Once Cetán was out of sight, Desire was at last able to breathe easy. She quickly set about gathering wood for a fire and refilling the water parfleches. With this completed, she turned the idea of a swim over in her mind once again. The water looked inviting. As she walked back down to the edge of the lake, she could no longer hesitate. Looking around one last time to be sure Cetán was nowhere in sight, she stripped away her hide dress, leggings, and moccasins. Enjoying the feel of the afternoon sun caressing her naked flesh, she dove into the cool, refreshing depths.

The water was invigorating, clearing Desire's senses and leaving her, for the first time in days, feeling somewhat relaxed. For a time she swam, running her fingers through her long hair as she washed away the day's travel from her body. This was the first real enjoyment she had known in some time, and even with the finish of bathing, she was loath to leave the water. Believing that she still had plenty of time before Cetán returned to camp, she floated on her back for a while, allowing the rays from the late afternoon sun to warm her body. As she did so, the coolness of the silken liquid surrounded her and she lost all sense of time and place. Desire shut her eyes as she drifted in and out of a far-distant realm of forgetfulness. She regathered her inner strength, trying to come to terms with the events that had so quickly and drastically changed her life.

As this moment of calm filled her, she attempted to deal with her fears one at a time. Though she had not wished to join her life-path with Cetán's and leave her village, the act had already taken place!

You can make the choice to deal with this fact, or you can suffer in misery because of it! she said to herself.

But how can I accept that which I do not wish? Her inner

thoughts were no longer angry and rebellious, she sought answers by questioning herself. *Do you truly know what you want? Why is it that you cannot share this part of yourself with another? Have you even attempted to give Cetán the chance to know that portion of yourself that you wish to guard? Have you made any effort to learn anything about this man you are joined with?*

Thoughts of the kiss shared between herself and Cetán floated in and out of her mind. Does a warrior truly care to know a woman's heart? she silently questioned.

Eleven

Upon his return to camp, Cetán's dark gaze scanned the area around the lake. Spying Desire's clothes lying on the ground next to a bush at the lake's edge, he made his way on silent feet to where she had stacked the wood earlier. Within minutes he built a small pit fire, then skinning and gutting the plump rabbit he had killed, he skewered the meat over the glowing coals.

His task completed, Cetán took a deep, steadying breath, his steps taking him to the lake, where his gaze silently sought out his bride. Standing immobile, he hungrily took in each delicate curve.

As Desire lay floating atop the crystal water, the smooth texture of her skin sparkled in the sun. The silken threads of her glorious hair were spread out across the surface with a gentle motion due to the flow of the water. The darkened budding peaks of her full breasts undulated temptingly in and out of the clear surface, as did the flattened contour of her belly, smoothly rounded hips, and long, slender legs.

Without a will to stop his own actions, his hands unbound the leather tie that held his breechcloth about his hips. He then slipped his leggings down his muscular legs. Thus far undetected by his bride, Cetán dove into the swirling depths.

Surprise and instant awareness of her surroundings swept over Desire the second she heard the loud splash. Without hesitation, she lowered her body under the water.

A strangled gasp escaped as she watched Cetán's dark head rise from the surface. "What . . . what are you doing here?" she sputtered, her hands automatically crossing over her breasts.

Disappointment instantly filled Cetán when his wife lowered her beautiful body beneath the water. He covered his feelings well with a lazy smile. "The day has been long, Wacin, the trail dusty. I also wish to swim in the lake."

"But you can't!"

Cetán turned his head as though looking in each direction, shimmering droplets of water flying from the long strands of his ebony hair. "Who is here that would tell me I cannot swim with my wife?"

"You . . . you are my husband, Cetán," Desire relented, but in the next breath stated, "but, I do not know you well enough to . . . to . . ." She was unable to finish her response, feeling her face flaming from embarrassment as he watched her closely.

Cetán's smile reflected gentle understanding as he glimpsed the upset that had overtaken his bride. "Ease your fear, mitáwicu. I will do nothing to cause you hurt. I know that you have not had time to learn the ways of your husband." Cetán wished to remedy this as quickly as possible, but the only way to do so was for Desire to get used to him. He desired her trust, and then, eventually, her heart.

Desire saw no sign of an ulterior motive on Cetán's features, but still, she was nervous about being in the water with him, particularly because she was naked. Her head nodded silently, as she was unable to find any reason why he could not swim in the lake. But even though she consented, her golden eyes remained guarded, watching her husband's movements.

Cetán's heart thundered with joy at this first budding sign of trust, even though he was not lost to the anxious look in his wife's eyes as she looked across the water at him. Without warning, he dove into the swirling crystal depths.

Desire cautiously watched the spot where he had disappeared; as seconds passed, her alarm grew steadily. Taken totally unaware, a gasp escaped her lips as she felt strong fingers encircle her ankle, and a second later she was pulled off balance. She fell backwards in the water, making a loud splash.

Cetán rose out of the water, the bronzed beauty of his broad chest gleaming beneath the afternoon sunlight, as his hearty laughter filled the area. Desire surfaced, gasping aloud and spitting water. "As a child did you not play with the other children in the water, Wacin?"

"Of course I did!" she spat out as soon as she was able to catch her breath.

"Then why do you not relax, and remember those days of youth? I wish only to be your friend. Why can we not play here in the lake as you did as a child? In so doing, we can learn of each other's ways."

This man is offering you the chance to get to know him better. Why do you hesitate, when earlier you were wishing for this very opportunity? Because you play here in the water with Cetán does not mean you must give anything of yourself that you do not wish to give. Desire's inner mind chided her before she could refuse her husband's offer. "It is true that the children of my village, both boys and girls, play together in the river," she confessed.

Her words came out so softly, Cetán had to strain to hear them. His smile returned. Desire was not turning his offer of friendship aside. He had never expected their first few days as husband and wife to be easy for either of them. He was more than willing to become her friend, to encourage her to look deep in her heart to find that which she could share with him. She was his wife, and nothing could change that. He was more than willing to give her the time she needed. "In my village it is the same, Wacin. The children laugh and play together. We can do the same here, away from prying eyes." Cetán cupped his hands together and a spray of water spiraled out and hit Desire full in the face.

This time, laughter followed her gasp of surprise, and the next instant Desire was diving beneath the water.

Cetán waited for some form of retaliation, and was only slightly taken off guard when he felt his wife's hands grabbing his leg from behind. Going along with her attempt to offset him, Cetán fell face first. Turning around beneath the water, he glimpsed the full outline of her naked beauty. As his head rose, he caught sight of a shapely hip and buttock. Her laughter again filled his ears as she swam a small distance away. The instant tightening in Cetán's groin cautioned him to go easy. He did not wish to frighten her—he hoped only to find a way in which she could relax in his company. But if the slightest glimpse of his wife's nakedness was able to set his hot blood coursing throughout his veins, he was not so sure that swimming here in the lake with her was such a good idea.

"I'll race you to the rocks!" Desire called over her shoulder as she turned and started swimming toward the opposite bank.

The tantalizing shape of Desire's buttocks greeted Cetán's eyes as she swam away from him, and with an inward groan he began to swim after her.

Desire was a strong swimmer, having always loved the water. As she swam away from Cetán she felt much of her earlier nervousness disappearing. It had been some time since she had felt so carefree.

Cetán followed at a safe distance as he attempted to force some kind of control over his body. He was no callow youth feeling the first flush of desire, he warned himself. He was a man with a mission: to make his bride fall in love with him!

Desire's laughter filled the area where the rushing water cascaded over the rocks and boulders. "I always won the swimming races when I was a child, too," she called out to Cetán.

His grin widened in enjoyment as he watched the happiness on her face. "You are indeed a strong swimmer," he called back, slowly drawing closer, believing his passions at last in check.

Desire would have liked nothing better than to climb up on the rocks and dive into the water, as she would have done as a child. Good sense prevailed; she was no longer a child, but a grown woman, and a naked one at that! She swam beneath the rushing water, allowing the spray to shower over her head and shoulders. "This is a wonderful place, Cetán," she said and laughed aloud as she attempted to grab the sparkling burst of droplets that the sun shimmered upon, causing multicolored gems to shower around her.

Only a few feet away, Cetán agreed fully with her statement as his dark eyes drank in her beauty. "I agree, Wacin. It is a beautiful sight." Not wishing her to glimpse his inner thoughts because he knew she would read his desire there, without warning Cetán grabbed her slender leg and pulled her from beneath the showering water.

Catching her breath just in time, Desire went under, kicking her legs to free herself. At the same time, she pushed against her husband's chest and sent him backward. She hurriedly swam away, her thoughts still confused by his close contact. Perhaps she should swim to the opposite bank, retrieve her clothes, and go back to camp. This childish fun suddenly seemed very dangerous. *Why is it that you cannot allow yourself to enjoy these few moments of pleasure with Cetán? After all, the man is your husband, and only wishes your friendship. He acts as though your nakedness does not affect him in any way, so why does it bother you so much?*

Cetán discerned Desire's intentions as she swam toward the opposite bank. For a time, she had seemed able to let down her guard and enjoy his company; he had hoped to be given a little more time in order to win over her trust. Slowly, he began to swim after her. She was as determined as ever to keep him at a distance!

With some surprise Cetán noticed Desire veer away from her original destination and then disappear underwater. When she resurfaced, she was on the other side of him, laughter tinkling upon the afternoon breeze when she saw the confusion on his handsome face.

All thoughts of right or wrong fled, as did modesty, as Cetán dove after the comely beauty. Desire squealed with delight as the bold warrior pulled her underwater, then splashed her mercilessly when she resurfaced. His husky laughter mingled with her musical sound, enhancing the mood of carefree abandon.

Desire gave no more thought to keeping her distance, allowing that bolder side of her nature to take over. After all, she was this man's wife, and thus far he had done nothing out of the way. Why should she not enjoy this play here in the lake?

Only a short time later, when Cetán caught her and their bodies were drawn tightly together, did the full realization return that they were both entirely nude! At first contact with his hard, muscular body, she was horrified, and again had thoughts of leaving the water, but Cetán did not give her another moment to dwell upon their nudity. He acted as though it were the most natural thing, the two of them swimming and playing together. For a time, Desire almost forgot that nothing prevented their flesh from touching. As his hands reached out to her and carelessly caressed a full breast or lightly ran over a rounded buttock, he made light of the gesture, keeping their frolic playful and innocent.

As the sun began to lower, Elkhunter joined the couple after returning to camp and hearing the laughter and splashing coming from the lake. The great wolf was a distraction for Cetán. For a while, his mind was not fully centered upon his wife's bountiful charms as the pair took turns throwing a branch out into the water while Elkhunter swam after it.

A short time later, Cetán called the fun to a halt. With a wide grin, he stated warmly, "I am worn out, Wacin. Let us go back to camp and eat the rabbit I left cooking over the fire."

Desire was also feeling the full force of her hunger. It had been some time since she had played so hard. She was tired, but felt entirely exhilarated.

"Come," Cetán stood up in the water, his body glistening as he held out his hand for her to take.

Looking at his hand, Desire was reminded once again that she was naked. The water had covered her for the most part, and enjoying herself as she was, she had given little thought to those parts that had been exposed throughout the afternoon. But looking at the proffered hand, she knew she could not reach out to him and simply step out of the water, retrieve her clothes, and act as though this were the most natural thing for her to do. "You . . . go ahead. You . . . go first, Cetán."

Cetán had known that this courtship would not be an easy matter, but he took heart in the fact that this afternoon had opened a pathway for their relationship to grow. Not allowing himself to grow discouraged, he smiled warmly. "Do not linger, Wacin. The rabbit must be well done by now." With this, he turned and made his way to shore.

A soft sigh escaped Desire as she watched Cetán's back. She had feared for a few seconds that he would try and force her to leave the water with him. But she was swiftly learning that her husband was not the type of man who would force her to do that which she did not wish. Any other warrior would not have been so kind! Fleeting images of Panther Stalks weaved throughout her mind. She pushed them aside as her golden eyes widened to stare at her husband's naked body. He was not facing her, but this did not diminish the full power of his muscular manliness. His back rippled with corded muscles, tapering to a narrow waist and firm buttocks. His thighs bulged with bronzed strength. Desire fought for a breath of air; as she looked away, her mind filled with images of the sweat-lodge vision once again.

After donning his breechcloth, Cetán looked across the few feet that separated him from the woman of his heart. Her back was turned to him in maidenly shyness, and he regretted that the pleasant afternoon had drawn to a close. His heart was light, though, with the prospect of the coming night. Perhaps he would be able to further their friendship after enjoying this day.

Very cautiously, Desire turned back around, and finding Cetán gone from the riverbank, she and Elkhunter made their way to shore.

"I have never met a man such as this warrior who is now my husband," she said softly, sharing her thoughts with the great wolf at her side. "I fear, though, the power he could so easily claim over me," she added, as though trying to sort out her inner thoughts. She did not state aloud, even to the animal, that she also feared her body's reaction to Cetán's slightest touch—or the heat that infused her, starting deep in the pit of her belly, when she looked upon his nakedness. Trying to control such potent images, Desire slowly began to dress. When she finally approached camp, the smell of cooked rabbit drew her closer to her husband's side.

Looking up from where he was bent over the small campfire, Cetán grinned. "I am afraid our meal is a little overdone." He looked down at the burnt rabbit and his husky laughter broke the tension that so easily could have descended upon them now that they were in camp.

Sitting down on the piece of fur that Cetán had laid out near the fire for her use, Desire found her mood improved as she looked at Cetán's handsome profile. Taking a bite of the well-done on the outside, juicy on the inside, piece of meat that he handed her, she smiled back. "I have never tasted finer rabbit, Cetán."

Cetán delighted in watching her movements as she ate the simple fare. Watching a bit of the juice from the meat running down her chin, he forced himself to restrain the impulse to bend toward her and kiss away the moisture. She was indeed very beautiful sitting there with her damp hair and sparkling eyes. With much gusto, he began to eat his own portion of the game. "I agree, mitáwicu. Either we have gone too long without food, or this rabbit is good."

The meal became as carefree as their afternoon swim. Desire was slowly beginning to relax in this man's company, and Cetán felt his pulses heighten each time his wife bestowed a small smile upon him.

With the completion of the meal and the lowering of the sun, Cetán looked across the fire at Desire and suggested, "I will comb out your hair so it can dry free of tangles." He moved to the side of the piece of fur he was sitting on, as though in invitation.

Distrust was instantly reflected in Desire's features. "I can comb out my hair myself." She rose and went to the parfleches to retrieve her comb. Silently, she stood on the other side of the camp and began to comb her long, dark hair.

"I am aware that you can comb your own hair, Wacin," Cetán said, his voice intruding upon the quiet that had settled around their camp. "I would like to do this for you. You do not fear your husband, do you?"

Desire's hand stilled where the comb rested in her thick tresses. Should she tell this imposing warrior, yes, she did indeed fear him? Or should she tell the truth, that she feared her own reaction to his presence?

"Come," he said and held out his hand once again as he had earlier at the lake. She began to move in his direction, powerless to resist. Cetán's eyes of darkest ebony locked with his wife's of sherry gold and seemed to have the power to soothe any resistance she might offer. With no release from his burning gaze, Desire bent to sit in the space Cetán had made for her between his thighs. With his body encircling her, a slight trembling was set off within her; her heart fluttered wildly as her breathing became ragged.

Cetán's reaction to this closeness was not much different from Desire's. He felt his pulse take flight as his heart began to hammer heavily beneath his ribs. As he drew in a deep breath and began to run the comb through her hair, the scent of wildflowers assaulted his senses. He felt the slight trembling of his hand as the comb ran from the crown of her head to the small of her back. As his gaze followed the movement, he silently marveled at such beauty. Unlike his own hair, hers curled and twined, the silken strands shimmering with a warm, rich hue as though the rays of Wi were reflected there.

Neither spoke as the warmth of the fire and Cetán's attentions slowly dried Desire's hair. A soft yawn escaped her lips, and her limbs slowly relaxed. Unconscious of her actions, Desire leaned back against the sturdy strength of her husband's chest.

"Do you regret greatly that you are joined with me, Wacin?" Cetán's words were gentle next to her ear, his warm breath stealing across her soft cheek.

Desire would have attempted some kind of coherent response if she had had the ability, but deep in the languid spell of his presence, she could only moan a soft reply, "Mmmmm."

"Why did you refuse me when I came to your father with the bride price?" He had hopes that by talking about these things and trying to confront that which still lay between them, she would finally begin to trust him.

Desire was very tired, but Cetán was just as persistent. Drawing out of the warmth of his embrace, reality hit Desire full force. A small gasp escaped her as she jerked herself upright, then out of his arms completely. Gaining her feet and stepping around the campfire, she confessed aloud, "I did not wish to join myself with you because I did not wish to leave my people." She could not tell him the rest of her fears—she did not wish to give him any more power over her than he already had. She was amazed that she had been so easily pulled into the web of tranquility he had so effortlessly spun. As she looked past the firelight at his handsome features, Desire knew she would have to stay on guard against the seductive power that her husband seemed capable of wielding over her.

Cetán carefully watched each emotion pass over her face. He had known that she did not wish to leave her village, but he was wise enough to know that there was more to her reasons for not wishing to join her life-path with his. If her fear had been only that of not wishing to leave her village, then why had she not agreed to join with another warrior? Why had she also refused Panther Stalks?

Twelve

From atop the crest leading down into the meadow, four Crow warriors watched the couple playing and swimming in the lake below. Their glances took in the large beast chasing after a tossed stick, but they discounted the animal as any threat. With interest, their eyes returned again and again to the woman whose carefree laughter carried over the meadow upon the late afternoon breeze. They sat, watching the scene at the lake, quiet cloaking their surprise at finding the warrior and woman here where they also had planned to spend the night.

The leader of the small hunting party was first to speak. "We will go back into the forest and wait for darkness. A lone warrior will be easy to overtake, and the woman will help us pass the night."

The other braves grinned enthusiastically at their leader's comments. Silently, they turned their ponies back into the shelter of the forest. From this distance to the lake, it was difficult to fully make out the woman's features, but it was obvious that she was young and shapely and that was all that mattered! "We will feast on more than elk this night," another warrior boasted as he threw one last look over his shoulder.

Desire spread out her blanket on the opposite side of the fire from Cetán's. Again, he offered her the safety of lying at his side. "I will make room for you here, Wacin."

"I am comfortable here, thank you," Desire responded. They had said little to each other since she had sat before him and Cetán had combed her hair. His questions had reminded her that he had caused her life to be turn totally upside down. She warned herself to stay on guard, or she would soon find herself losing her will to him once again!

"I think only of your safety, Wacin."

The coaxing sound of his husky voice tempted Desire, but with an inner determination not to allow him to affect her so strongly, she rolled away from the fire to her side. "Elkhunter will give us warning if there is danger." She shut her eyes, willing sleep to come.

Cetán studied her back for some time. Perhaps he should not have allowed her to bring along her great wolf, he thought a bit belatedly. He had gained a small portion of her trust, but he desired more. He would have her trust him with her protection as well as her friendship. His dark gaze roamed at will over the curling threads of her long hair where it lay uncovered by the blanket. He ached to run his fingers through its thickness, and as his gaze roamed over the shapely curve of her hip, he forced himself to look away. As he gazed up at the night sky, he murmured a prayer to Wakán Tanka. "Hurry the day, oh Great One, when my wife will open her heart to me."

Desire thought she heard Cetán say something else, but she was too tired to try and make out his words; with a soft sigh, she fell asleep.

It seemed to Desire that she had just dozed off when she was awakened by the pressure of a hand covering her mouth. "Do not move from where you are," Cetán whispered next to her ear as he slipped the bone handle of his large hunting knife into her hand. As Elkhunter jerked his head up and started to rise, he was ordered in low tones, *"Eñajin,* stay where you are!"

As the hand drew away from her mouth, Desire asked anxiously, "What is wrong, Cetán?"

"Warriors approach our camp. Pretend you still sleep."

Hardly daring to breathe, Desire noticed that the moon was now high in the heavens and their campfire had burned down to dim embers. She could hear nothing as she strained to hear the approach of steps coming in their direction. Her hand rested atop Elkhunter's head, the animal's yellow eyes passing over the dark shadows that encircled the encampment. He and his mistress stayed still as they had been ordered.

They did not have long to wait. From out of the darkness, war cries erupted as their camp was attacked. Jerking her head up, unable to remain still, Desire saw that Cetán's blanket looked as though he was still lying in it. As the first warrior rushed into the dim light of the campfire, Elkhunter sprang to his feet. Growling fiercely, he charged the warrior who was brandishing a war axe high overhead.

Before the wolf reached the intruder, the warrior fell to his knees, his eyes staring wide with disbelief as a gurgling sound spilled from his lips; Cetán's arrow was embedded deep in the center of his chest.

Elkhunter watched the warrior fall facedown. Without hesitation, he vaulted toward the next warrior racing out of the darkness. With tomahawk and gleaming hunting knife swinging widely, the Crow brave attempted to fight off the vicious beast as it lunged toward him. Elkhunter's sharp, deadly teeth snapped cruelly as the great wolf sought his opponent's throat, reaching his goal before the warrior had a chance to strike out at him.

Cetán's rifle-stock weapon whistled upon the night breeze as he boldly presented himself before the two remaining Crow warriors; his large instrument of destruction sang out with a murderous threat as Cetán expertly whirled it overhead. In the depths of his dark eyes, Cetán held no mercy for the invaders. At the same moment as his fierce war cry broke from his lips, his body powerfully supple, Cetán attacked the two warriors. Charging, Cetán dodged both opponents' attack by throwing his body on the ground between them; a second later, he sprang to his feet. The blade of his weapon caught one enemy in the shoulder, all but severing the upper portion of his body from the lower. With a practiced movement of his wrist, Cetán freed the blade, and the other warrior was greeted with the same swift taste of death, but from the opposite end of the weapon, the tomahawk bluntly striking the attacker's head and crushing his skull.

The swiftness of Cetán's killing was astonishing. The four Crow warriors lay lifeless upon Mother Earth. Elkhunter left the prone body of his victim upon hearing Cetán call him to his side. As quickly as the enemy had approached, they had been vanquished!

Amongst her people, Desire had grown up with the ever-present threat of attack from the enemy, but as she stood clutching Cetán's knife tightly in her palm, she could not remember a time when such a threat had appeared so real. Her features were pale, her gaze wide and filled with terror as she watched the bold, powerful strength that Cetán unleashed upon his attackers. As the last of the enemy fell, she drew in a steadying breath, and with some effort, she tried to subdue the trembling that had taken hold of her limbs.

As the adrenaline began to ease from his body, Cetán's first thought was for his wife. Elkhunter at his side, he turned and looked toward the campfire. Beneath the moonlight Wacin appeared pale and terrified. Without another second's hesitation Cetán went to her, welcoming her into his strong embrace. As she stepped within his arms, he felt the trembling of her body pressed against his own. He lovingly placed a kiss on the crown of her head. "It is over now, Wacin. I am here to protect you—no harm will come to you." His words were softly spoken as he tried to ease away her fears.

Desire buried her face in the warmth of her husband's chest, the heavy thunder of his heartbeat surrounding her, giving testimony to the words he whispered against her hair.

For a few minutes the couple stood thus, clutched tightly together. Everything had happened so swiftly, it all seemed like a blur in Desire's mind. One minute she had been sleeping, then the terrible screams, the fighting and death. Another shudder coursed her length as the horrible thought swept over her: if Cetán had not been the victor, he could have been lying there upon the ground in a pool of blood. The fleeting images of what the three warriors would have done to her without Cetán here to protect her were too terrible to think about!

Cetán tightened his hold upon her, allowing her a few more minutes to pull her emotions into order. Slowly, he began to feel the warmth returning throughout her body and he could hear the ease of her breathing.

"If you had not awakened, Cetán," Desire murmured against his chest, as the thought washed over her that the enemy had approached their camp so silently, Elkhunter had not been disturbed as he lay next to her blanket. Another shudder swept over her. Even though she knew the answer, she still questioned, "Were they Crow?" Hearing her husband's response, she knew that if the assault had turned out any differently, their enemy would have had no mercy upon her, or this man who was now giving her comfort.

"Come over to the fire, Wacin." Cetán led her to his blanket and as she sat, he pulled her blanket over her shoulders. Leaning forward, he placed a few pieces of dried wood on the campfire. "Sit here and warm yourself." From here, she would not be able to watch as he carried the warriors' bodies out of sight of the camp. Before leaving her side, he lightly traced a finger over her soft brow. "I have always been a light sleeper, Wacin. With my need to protect you, the Great Spirit has sharpened my senses and blessed my strength this night. Do not think about anything except the fact that you are safe and your husband will always protect you." With this, he left her side and set about ridding the camp area of the bodies.

Elkhunter did not remain long in camp after the battle was won. After watching Cetán settle his mistress on the blanket, he turned toward the forest. Earlier in the evening, he had heard the lone call of a wolf, and now, his energy level high, he set off in search of more action before this night ended.

Cetán made quick work of cleaning the camp. Going to the lake, he washed away any traces of the other warriors' blood from his arms and chest. Desire sat next to the fire where he had left her. She appeared to be quietly studying the flames in the fire-pit. As he approached, her head jerked around in his direction. Cetán glimpsed the lingering traces of fear still in the depths of her brilliant eyes.

Cetán was unsure how to go about helping Desire get beyond this fear. He was a warrior who had practiced the art of war since his youth. If she had been a young brave, he would have reminded her that people survived only because of their strength and power over their enemies. In his lifetime, he had comforted mothers who had lost sons in battle, and he had made certain that grandmothers in his village did not go lacking for food or warm hides. But this woman of his heart, who was displaying the first traces of her vulnerable nature, left him feeling inadequate because of his fear that he would not say or do the right thing to help her. Had she already given him her heart and accepted his, he would have gone to her and held her throughout the rest of the night, his body and love words helping to chase away any lingering thoughts of the enemy and their attack. But this was not to be—not tonight, he reminded himself as he stood next to her and looked down at the small covered form, her golden eyes watching him closely.

"Are you warm now, Wacin?" he questioned. Not knowing anything else to do, he placed a small log on the fire.

Desire silently nodded, her eyes tracing the sculpted handsome lines of her husband's features as the firelight illuminated his face. As his large hand withdrew from placing the log on the flames, she envisioned that same hand swinging his deadly weapon.

Remaining only a foot away from his bride, Cetán squatted next to the fire, his dark gaze upon Desire. "There has been little time for us to learn of each other, Wacin. I understand it is hard for a maiden to leave everything and follow a warrior." He did not mention that it was still harder for a maiden who had boldly refused that warrior. "I only ask that you try and trust in my words when I say I will always protect you."

How could she not trust in such words? Had he not already proven that he wielded greater strength than any warrior she had ever seen? She knew he wanted to ease her fears, and looking at the warmth in his gaze as he watched her intently, awaiting her reply, she felt a rush of heat travel up from her breasts to her cheeks. "I believe in these words that you say, Cetán," she softly confessed, and feeling warmed through, she lowered the blanket from her shoulders.

With that movement, the soft sighing of bells on her dress mingled with her words. Cetán saw the flush on her features and knew that she was no longer chilled. His tension felt eased as he told himself that soon she would learn to trust him with all her needs and cares. She would one day learn to trust her heart into his keeping. This thought set his inner spirit to flight, but wisely, he tempered his excitement. To win all that he desired would take time; he would never rush her into giving up more than she was willing. "We should get some rest, Wacin. We will leave this place tomorrow."

Desire had not missed the relief in his expression as she told him that she trusted in his protection. With his reminder that it was still the middle of the night and they should try to sleep, her gaze left him and traveled to the other side of the fire. Do . . . do . . . you mind If I sleep here tonight, Cetán?" Her words formed a hesitant question, but she could not bear the thought of sleeping alone after what had occurred.

Without a word in reply, Cetán straightened his blanket and lying down next to his wife, he pulled the other blanket over their bodies. His entire being was attuned to the woman lying next to him. He could smell her wildflower scent, his ears filling with her ragged breathing as she rolled to her side facing the fire, her body touching his harder contours. Where her shapely curves touched him, Cetán felt his flesh burn. This night, she had stepped into his embrace and welcomed his comfort. She admitted that she trusted his protection, and now, she lay next to him on his blanket. Perhaps to some, these were small victories, but to Cetán, each step drew him closer to the goal of gaining his wife's heart!

Thirteen

In his youth Cetán had been taught by the holy man of his village that for the people there is just the pipe, Mother Earth which he sits upon, and the boundless, open sky. The spirit is everywhere one chose to look. As a warrior draws upon his pipe and smoke goes straight up to the spirit world, power also flows through that same smoke and fills the warrior's body.

Cetán greeted the morning star standing alone upon the rocks that were washed continually by the stream's water rushing into the lake. Before starting his morning prayers of thanksgiving, he lightly ran his fingers over the cool pipe-stone that made up the bowl of his pipe. Having filled the bowl earlier with kinnickinnick, he lit the tobacco with the piece of ignited sweet grass he held in his opposite hand. Drawing upon the mouthpiece, the smoke swirled around his head, and he fanned it over his naked body.

This pipe had belonged to his father and his father before him. The power of his ancestors flowed through the bowl and stem, traveling up his arm, circling his heart with the need to cry aloud to the powers that ruled his life.

Looking out upon a pre-dawn sky lightly tinged with pink and purple, he drew deeply, allowing the smoke to travel upward as he greeted the morning star at Mother Earth's edge and in so doing, welcoming this new day. He requested Wi to guide him through this day, and teach him those things it would offer.

Turning his entire body toward the south, he again drew upon the mouthpiece as he beseeched the mighty south power to impart its energy into his life and into his prayers. In his mind, he reviewed those things that took life from the south powers, as the summer days brought plant life and abundant food to his people.

Turning once again, he faced the west and placed the pipe to his lips, the smoke traveling upward. The west winds brought the power of life to his people. He thanked this power for the lifegiving rains and refreshing winds.

Turning to the north, the smoke from his pipe continued to rise. Cetán called out his thanks for those powers which cleansed Mother Earth and allowed her to rest beneath a white blanket. The snowmelt traveling downward from the mountains held the power to cleanse and purify.

Bending, Cetán touched the ancient pipe-bowl upon Mother Earth, thanking her for the life-giving nurturing which expands from the center of her being.

With his prayers to the powers at a finish, he turned back to face the morning star and held his pipe upward, reaching for father sky; he thanked The One Above for all things good in his life-path. "Wakán Tanka, hear my cry, oh Great One! Guide this warrior's steps upon this life path that can so easily twist and turn. Grant me the strength to help those in need, and to protect and provide for my family and the people of my tribe. I ask also that You allow my wife to learn her heart."

Turning upon the blanket and seeking out the bulwark of warmth whose heat had warmed her throughout the night, Desire slowly awoke with the realization that the heat she was seeking had been her husband's body, and he was no longer lying next to her.

Looking around camp, she saw no sight of Cetán or Elk-hunter. As she pulled herself from the blanket, she brushed at the wrinkles that creased her dress. Heading toward the

lake, she thought to have a morning swim before the start
of this new day.

Caught by surprise, Desire stood transfixed there along
the riverbank, her golden eyes filling with the magnificent
image of her husband. He stood with arms upraised, his
husky voice settling over the area, and holding the power
to cause gooseflesh to travel down the length of Desire's
arms. For a few breathless seconds, she could not force
herself to move, let alone breathe.

The morning dawn appeared to break full upon Cetán's
form, capturing his bold, muscular maleness. The gold of
Desire's eyes shimmered brightly. Her gaze drew downward
from the pipe he held in his hands to the water swirling
around his parted feet, where he stood upon the rocks.
Truly, Cetán's body was the most magnificent Desire had
ever seen. Besides the naked man of her vision, Cetán's
body was the *only* male body she had ever seen! He looked
like a fearless, god-like warrior from legend of old who had
come to life by stepping from the depths of Mother Earth.
He stood straight and proud, not an ounce of wasted flesh
covering the muscular contours of his splendid bronze
torso. Glittering droplets of water shone within the damp
midnight strands of his hair, which reached to the center
of his broad back. His upper arms and chest were sculpted
with powerful, restrained strength; his midriff, a washboard
of rippling muscles, hips and buttocks firmly tight. His
hard, power-filled thighs and legs strained with energy
braced apart on *Inyan,* the rock. But what drew Desire's
gaze back up his legs and caused her heartbeat to thunder
wildly within her chest was the turgid length of his great
lance which jutted upward from the junction of his legs.
For a spellbound second, she stared in awe as the imprint
of his image was seared forever in her mind. A wave of
dizziness washed over her. Her pulses raced as heat traveled
over her entire body. As Desire heard her own name being
called aloud in Cetán's prayers, she drew upon all her inner

resources. Turning away from the sight of him, she hurried back to camp.

Not until she reached the campsite was she able to regain her normal breathing. She felt flushed, her legs wobbly. Never had Desire thought it possible that a man could cause such a disturbance of her emotions.

He is a warrior among warriors! And he is your husband! Desire's mind's workings attempted to help her sort out her feelings. *That wondrous body is all yours to look at! Remember his kisses—they as well are yours! You have but to let Cetán know of your wish to feel his mouth pressed against your own once again. You have but to look again and you can fill your vision with his manly beauty!*

"No!" Desire gasped aloud, rebuking these crazy thoughts for daring to tempt her so wickedly. She would not think about the image she had seen at the lake! She would push all thoughts of Cetán's kisses out of her mind! Attempting to busy herself before Cetán returned to camp, and feeling flushed and confused, Desire began to fold up the sleeping blankets, readying everything for the moment when they would start the trek that would lead them to his village.

As she folded the blankets, she was reminded of the previous night, and how she had pressed herself up against her husband's chest to steal some of his warmth. Now, it all seemed like some faraway dream. She had known even in the depths of sleep that it had been Cetán she had been pressed up to, but even then, it had seemed somehow right. Clutching the blanket to her chest, Cetán's manly scent swept over her, triggering her senses into reaffirming the image of him which lingered in her mind.

Was she going mad? She pressed her hands to the sides of her head as though she could command such images from her thoughts.

When Cetán returned to camp, he found Wacin sitting

next to the fire, their gear packed in the parfleches and waiting to be tied on the horses' saddles.

Watching him enter the small camp area, Desire offered, "If you are hungry, Cetán, I have left out some pemmican for you." Next to the fire, where she sat, was the food she offered her husband for his morning meal.

Cetán seemed pleased with life in general this morning. His dark gaze swept over his bride as he remembered the feel of her bountiful curves pressed against his body throughout the night. In sleep, her body had succumbed to the closeness he desired between them; awake she watched him through guarded, half-closed lids. "Did you rest well last night, Wacin?" He said nothing about the attack on their camp. Hoping not to see fear in her eyes once again, his gaze warmed as he awaited her reply.

Desire wished for no reminders of sleeping next to him. Instead she posed a question of her own: "How much longer will it take to reach your village, Cetán?"

"The village of my people is not too far away from this place, Wacin. With the passing of half this day, we will arrive there." A slight flush stained her cheeks, put there by his question about her sleep, so Cetán did not press for an answer. She needed to feel that it was a natural thing for a wife to sleep upon her husband's sleeping pallet; to press her now would push her further away.

"If your village is so close, why did we not go on yesterday afternoon?" Surely they would have been safer in his village, Desire thought, reminded of the attack on their camp and wondering about his reasons.

"I wished us to have some time alone before arriving in my village, Wacin. It is hard for two people to learn of each other with others always around." Cetán watched the way she turned her head at his words. He still had a long way to go before she could truly trust and give her heart to him.

"Elkhunter has not returned to camp yet." Desire attempted to change the subject from anything personal.

"If he has not returned when we leave, he will follow our tracks and shortly catch up." Cetán had much confidence in the great wolf.

As her husband ate his portion of the pemmican, Desire fought her mind's images of him. With some relief, she mounted Star and once again, they made their way into the forest, traveling down an invisible path which Whirling-Warrior's-Ghost appeared to know without guidance.

Later in the morning, Elkhunter caught up with the pair, his boundless energy sending every rabbit and bird along the trail fleeing for cover.

Throughout the rest of the morning, the couple rode in silence, each seemingly lost in thought. It was when Wi was straight up in the early afternoon sky that Cetán led his horse out of the forest. Halting, he waited for Desire to come abreast of him and his mount. Silently, the couple stared down into the valley that stretched spectacularly before them. They sat upon horseback, overlooking a lush green valley and the picturesque scene of over a thousand conical-shaped dwellings along the dark depths of a wide river which slashed, like a streak of lightning, across the valley floor. Beyond the tepees, vast herds of horses grazed on the knee-high grasses.

"It is truly a beautiful sight, Cetán," Desire said in breathless anticipation. Looking down into the valley, she remembered when her own tribe had come to this valley for a sundance ceremony a few years past. She had been filled with girlish excitement by the prospect of several different tribes coming together for the ceremonial days. It had been a time to become reacquainted with old friends, for the people to relax and enjoy themselves. Now, looking down upon the valley floor, Desire knew that those childish days were forever gone. Still, some of that same excitement remained. The women of this village had treated her kindly, and the old medicine man had taken the time to listen to her questions; he had even told her which plants to use for snakebite.

Looking at his bride, Cetán's chest filled with pride. He never tired of viewing the valley from this summit. "During the early summer months my people move higher into the mountains. This valley protects them from the full force of the winter winds." Cetán's tribe had recently moved from the mountains to the valley, and he was pleased that Wacin's first view of his village, as his wife, was from this summit.

As Elkhunter raced ahead, Cetán kicked his stallion's flanks to begin the ride downward. As Desire followed her husband's lead, she marveled at the primitive beauty before her. Her own people's village, in contrast, was not as large nor as richly displayed. As they rode down into the valley and drew closer to the lodges, she gazed at the tall dwellings with lodgepoles reaching up through smoke flaps. The outer hides of the tepees were artfully decorated with brilliant colors, each having been painted and decorated with the emblems of the dwellers' visions and dreams; many were replete with religious symbolism. Such pageantry filled her heart with excitement. Many of the tribe's people smiled and called out a welcome as the villagers stood or sat near outside fires. Many of the women were preparing the evening meal, their blackened trade pots resting next to glowing coals.

Desire recognized many of these women, and when they called to her in greeting, the fear of arriving in her husband's village disappeared. These were the faces of her people; though not her own tribe, they were her people.

Cetán led his bride toward the inner circle of the village, and there, before a large lodge replete in design with his vision-sign hawk, were many battle scenes painted on the lower portion of the tepee. "I hope you will be pleased with your new home, Wacin." He spoke softly as he dismounted, going to her side to help her off Star's back.

The lodge was as large as her father's, and Desire assumed the inside would be similar. As Cetán's large hands encircled her waist and he set her to her feet, her small smile trembled slightly as she attempted to show a brave face.

"I will unpack the horses and bring our things inside." Cetán was allowing his wife time to go and look around at her new home.

Elkhunter entered the lodge at Desire's side, but quickly lost interest, exiting the flap in order to explore the new village. He had already asserted his authority over the village dogs, who had greeted his presence with growls of warning, then barks and yips of retreat.

The interior of Cetán's lodge resembled that of her own family. As Desire's gaze swept over the central fire-pit, the fur-draped sleeping couch, and Cetán's weapons secured with leather ties against one wall, she noticed the lack of a woman's touch. Her parents' lodge had been warm and cozy due to Pretty Dove and Desire's willow baskets containing beads and sewing implements, herbs and flowers drying in a corner, a pot of stew simmering over the fire. Looking around, Desire knew that her husband's lodge could have the same appeal. It would only take a little effort on her part, and strangely, Desire was eager to make her husband's lodge a home.

Before Cetán entered, Desire heard a female voice call; without waiting for a response, a beautiful, flame-haired woman entered the entrance flap. "I wish to welcome you, Wacin. I have brought you and Cetán a portion of my evening stew." The woman was obviously a wasicun winyan, a white woman. Desire was to learn that her name was Ptanyetu Anpo, Autumn Dawn.

Desire had seen this woman before, and knew that she was wife to the legendary Spirit Walker. "Thank you," Desire replied as she studied the woman who bent to the fire-pit with the pot of stew.

"I was sure you would be hungry when you arrived. My husband tells me often that I worry too much about others, but I remember my own nervousness when I came here with Spirit Walker." Autumn Dawn's gaze warmed as she looked upon the other young woman. She hoped they could become friends. Her husband and Cetán were close, and knowing some of Desire's past, Autumn Dawn believed they could have much in common.

Desire searched her mind for bits of information about this woman who had become one of the people, and who now recorded the winter counts of her husband's village. "It is kind of you to think of us, Autumn Dawn." Desire noticed the other woman was far along with child, and softly ventured, "I am known as a healing woman among my own people. If there is anything I can do to help you when your time draws nearer, I would be pleased if you would call on me."

Autumn Dawn's face lit up. She nodded eagerly. "I have heard that you are very talented with your healing art, Wacin. I will keep your offer close to my heart."

Desire's smile was genuine as she listened to the other woman speak of the two children she and Spirit Walker already had, and how they were all excitedly awaiting this new child.

When it was time for Autumn Dawn to return to her own lodge, Desire went with her. Spirit Walker and Cetán were waiting for the women. Desire could not help but notice the loving manner in which Autumn Dawn's husband drew her against his side as the couple said their good-bys to Cetán and herself. They were very much in love—it was obvious for anyone to see.

Standing next to Desire as they watched their company walk away, Cetán softly stated, "There goes proof that the

Great Spirit can straighten the twisted pathways that lead to one's heart."

Cetán's friend Spirit Walker had fought valiantly for Autumn Dawn's love; Cetán was just as determined that he would do no less for the woman of his own heart!

Fourteen

"I have thought many times about that night outside your father's lodge when I played the courting flute for you, Wacin." Cetán was sitting against his willow backrest. The warmth radiating from the fire-pit relaxed him as his eyes took in the beauty of his wife. She sat across the fire, her attention focused upon the piece of fur she was beading.

After Autumn Dawn and Spirit Walker had left, Desire and Cetán had put away the things from their packs and had silently eaten the food Autumn Dawn had left. Desire felt more comfortable in her husband's lodge with her belongings around her. As he spoke, her eyes rose from the work in her lap.

The curiosity in her golden gaze spurred Cetán on. "That night I offered you the very secrets of my heart."

Desire easily recalled the things he had spoken of. He had claimed she was his, even though she refused to join with him. He had also stated that he would be the warrior to ignite the fire within her body. A slow burn of heat suffused her face at the memory.

"I remember also that after telling these feelings of my heart, our lips joined. It is this joining of our lips that I have often thought about, Wacin."

He spoke so easily about this thing that they had shared. He appeared at ease sitting against his backrest, Desire thought, her sewing totally forgotten with the simple mention of that kiss!

"Do you also remember that which I speak of, Wacin?"

Could any woman have forgotten that which her husband was speaking about? It had been that kiss that had changed her mind about joining her life-path with that of a warrior's. It had been that kiss that had tempted her into accepting Panther Stalks' kiss that day at the river! She nodded silently, not sure she could speak as easily as her husband about that night.

"Did the joining of our lips please you, Wacin?" Cetán remembered the feel of her slender hands around his neck, her shapely form melting against him, and the small sounds of pleasure that had escaped from the back of her throat.

Why do you not confess the truth, Wacin? Tell him you have thought often about the kiss you shared with him. Is this not what you had hoped your joining with a warrior would be? Did you not envision yourself being kissed by your husband whenever you wished? Desire had not believed her husband would be Cetán when she'd had such thoughts! She'd tried to bring reason to her runaway senses, even as she felt the continued searching gaze of her husband's dark eyes.

But you desired a warrior who would kiss you like Cetán. You wanted to be held against a broad chest, and to lose yourself to the strength of your husband's arms! Speak the words aloud now, Wacin, and once again feel Cetán's hard body pressed against your own, that same body you looked upon this very morning at the lake!

Desire blushed furiously as she felt Cetán's dark gaze watching her for an answer. "I . . . I . . ." She could not lie, claiming she was displeased with the joining of their lips together, but neither could she state that she had been pleased; such a confession would be giving away too much of her inner self!

An understanding smile settled over Cetán's lips as he

watched her conflicting emotions. With a soft sigh, he relented. Rising to his feet in a supple motion, he looked down at his bride and as he stretched out a hand. "Join me for a walk along the riverbank, Wacin."

As she hesitated, somewhat confused by this sudden turn, Cetán added softly, "I am restless this evening. A walk will help me to turn aside these thoughts that will not release themselves from my mind."

A reprieve . . . he was offering her a gentle reprieve from his questioning. Setting her sewing aside, Desire rose from the pallet of soft fur. He seemed intent upon her taking his hand, so she silently slipped her slender fingers into his warm palm.

The night air was cool against Desire's flushed skin as the couple walked, hand in hand, along the edge of the river. For a time neither spoke, but then, as though the husky tremor of his voice were part of the dark night, Cetán turned. His hand released Desire's as he gently pulled her into his embrace. "A walk at night chases away unwanted thoughts, Wacin, but the thoughts in my mind are very much wanted."

Desire trembled at his touch, reliving the kiss they had shared, her vision from the sweat-lodge, and the memory of Cetán standing unclothed as he called forth his prayers. Her heart-shaped face turned upward as she waited for what was to happen next. As his head began a slow descent, she exhaled a second before his lips brushed against her mouth.

As though unwilling to push his bride into doing something against her will, Cetán held himself back, lightly pressing his mouth over her own. His senses were keenly aware of every curve of her body as he waited for her to push him away or draw back. When she did not resist, the slight quivering of her limbs testifying to her innocence, Cetán intensified the kiss. His lips parted slightly, slanting more fully; his arms pulled her closer against his chest as her shapely curves became more fully defined. The power of this woman was the true elixir of life! His caution waned; at first he drank slowly of her sweet bounty, then more fully.

Had Desire ever known such true pleasure? Was this not what she had desired from a husband? Her hands rose up and of their own will, they glided over his muscle-hard chest, lightly settling over his shoulders as her fingers brushed against his hair and twined in the silken strands. Her heartbeat danced a wild tempo, her body melting against his chest. A scorching heat began to grow deep in the depths of her belly and slowly spread into the very center of her womanhood. She could not force herself to pull back from the storm of Cetán's kisses!

Though her mind was not aware that she truly belonged to him, her heart knew! Cetán welcomed this knowledge as her body responded to his own with a need that could not be quenched by the simple joining of lips. Slowly his fingers gently wound within the soft nest of her hair. He drew her head closer, to accept the searing heat of his plundering tongue. He pushed through the slight resistance of her teeth to feast fully upon the incredible honey-taste of her inner depths; his hungry need conveyed its meaning into Desire's body.

She rose on tiptoe to mold herself against her husband's powerful body. Her mouth opened to receive his searing tongue. A soft moan escaped her as she felt a simmering heat igniting in the very depths of her being.

Cetán's ears delighted in the soft sounds coming from deep within her throat. He crushed her against him as his lips left her mouth to taste the softness of her cheek, the fragile curve of her jaw, the slim line of her throat. As he placed moist kisses along the upper edge of her dress, he felt the straining fullness of her breasts. His hands followed the path of his kisses, until his fingers rested upon the upper swell of her bosom. With a deft motion, he lightly pushed aside the lacings which held the upper portion of her dress together. Lowering his lips, he placed feathery kisses between the valley of her breasts as his fingers brushed against the hardened buds.

Nothing in Desire's life had ever prepared her for such an erotic assault upon her senses. She had heard the maidens of her village speak of certain warriors and their prowess as lovers, and her mother had shyly informed her, in a roundabout way, what she could expect out of the joining couch, but no one had ever told her of the wanton pleasure to be found in the arms of a warrior such as Cetán! Her breasts pressed against the heat of his searching fingers; she wanted to feel all he was willing to give her! His kisses scorched a path back up her throat to recapture her lips.

Cetán drew upon his willpower to pull his mouth away from the delicious taste of Desire. He held her tightly against his frame as he whispered against her flower-scented hair, "My heart beats with desire for you, Wacin. The taste of your lips, your breasts, your soft flesh beneath my hands leaves me wanting more."

His words tantalized her, sending her senses spiraling. Breathlessly, she drew her head from his chest to look into his handsome sculpted features. "Why do you speak? Kiss me again."

With a groan that was a mixture of pain and consuming pleasure, Cetán pulled her tightly up against his chest. "You are an innocent to that of which I speak. But soon, my heart, soon you will learn about the power you hold over me. The power of the heart is stronger than any power Wakán Tanka has ever gifted to a human."

"And is this power that you speak of that which makes your kisses so wonderful?" Indeed, Desire was an innocent. A more experienced woman would have accepted this offer of power to further her appeal.

"The joining of our lips is just as wondrous to me," Cetán softly confessed.

Desire turned this over in her mind. "Have you not kissed other maidens as you now kiss me?"

This talk about kissing was almost as tormenting as the act itself, Cetán thought as he looked down into his wife's beautiful features. "Yes, Wacin, I have kissed other maidens." He would not lie to her about his past.

"Then where is the difference, Cetán, if you join your lips with mine, or another's?" Even as Desire asked the question, she knew the answer. Had she not allowed Panther Stalks to kiss her and hold her in his arms? The outcome of that experience had certainly been far different than what she encountered when Cetán held her in his arms.

"Why do we not return to our lodge? Near the warmth of the fire, we can continue this talk of kissing." His bride appeared unaware of the effect she was having on his body as she stood pressed fully against him. Cetán was made fully aware as hot blood surged to fill his manhood. He needed a few minutes to control his emotions. The heady inducement of the balmy night breeze and the sparkling stars held the power to weave a seductive spell around them. He wanted his wife, there was no denying this fact, but he wanted her to want the moment as much as he. Looking down at her, he knew the moment was not right. Her thoughts were still innocently focused on kissing, his were on more pleasurable acts of passion. Without saying another word, Cetán scooped his bride up in his arms and began the walk back to his lodge.

Desire should have been outraged that this bold warrior dared to lift her off her feet to carry her to his lodge. But her senses were foggy, and she had little strength to resist him. With her breasts pressed against his chest, her chin tucked into the curve of his shoulder, her slender arms rose up to slip her hands around his neck. A soft sigh escaped her lips.

Her arms around his shoulders and the movement of

her body pressing closer against his own all but undid Cetán. His steps quickened. His strength of will was weakening. The minute they entered the lodge, Cetán set his wife on her feet.

"Thank you, Cetán. I rather enjoyed being carried," Desire said without guile. Cetán wanted to pull her back into his arms. Instead, he took her hand and led her to the center fire.

Here in the lodge, with the fire shedding light throughout the interior, some of Desire's senses quickly returned. She sat stiffly before the fire, keeping some distance between herself and her husband.

Leaning back against the backrest, Cetán's dark gaze traveled over the blushing features of his bride. "While we talk, I will comb your hair, Wacin." He remembered sitting before another fire and combing her hair, and how pleasurable those moments had been.

Desire hesitated. With her returning reason, her caution also returned. "I am tired, Cetán," she said, using the first excuse that came to mind, hoping to avoid being close to that magnificent body and falling prey to the spell which Cetán was capable of weaving around her.

In a fluid motion, Cetan rose from the backrest and left the fire. He retrieved the porcupine quill comb from the parfleche and swiftly returned. "I will take the bells from your hair, then comb it for you before you go to bed." He eased his large frame back down against the beaded-willow backrest. Spreading his thighs, he made room for his bride to sit close. "Besides, Wacin, we have not finished this talk about kissing."

Desire could easily have foregone any more discussion about kissing! She knew the danger that could result from such a subject. Outside beneath the moonlight, in Cetán's arms, she had not been able to think clearly. Now in the tepee with the fire spreading its light, she knew better than to venture forth into the unknown. Suddenly, her inner thoughts filled with her sweat-lodge vision, and heeding the potent warning, she softly said, "I will comb my hair, Cetán."

Stretching forth his hand, Cetán took hold of her arm and easily pulled her toward him. "Come, wife. It will give your husband pleasure to do this for you." He would allow her no leeway, knowing that the sooner this distrust she had for him was out of the way, the sooner they could become the people that The One Above wished them to be.

Having no choice, Desire silently relented. As she sat upon the mat of his backrest, she did her best to avoid touching any part of his body.

Cetán did not seem to mind her stiffness. As he reached up to begin to unbraid her hair, the tiny bells sang out softly beneath his hand. "You asked me about the difference in kissing another maiden and kissing you, Wacin, and I would now answer your question."

She would have spoken out and told him not to bother himself, but she could not get the words out. It was all she could to to sit near him, drawing in one ragged breath after another.

Setting the strips of leather decorated with tiny bells aside, Cetán gently eased the comb through his wife's long, curling tresses. "In the past, I gave only slight thought to the act of joining my lips with another. There is something lacking in the act if the heart is not wholly involved. When I join my lips with yours, Wacin, my heart sings because you are that portion of my spirit that was separated, but now is joined. My heart beats with the sound of your name when I hold you close in my arms."

Her blood seemed to slow within her veins. She felt liquid, her heartbeat skipping wildly. She silently relaxed against the warmth of his body. Cetán's thighs pressed close against her own, his hand lightly drawing the comb through her hair.

"Everything about you is a miracle in my eyes, Wacin.

The Great Spirit blessed me above all other warriors when he provided the way for me to claim you as my own. At times I look upon you, and within my body there is a sweet aching need that fills my depths because I know that I am the one that you are joined with. I am a patient man. I can wait for you to experience these same feelings. It is enough for now that you find pleasure in the joining of our lips. More will follow when the time is right."

What more could he want from her? His presence totally consumed her senses. His kisses were so potent they intoxicated her, leaving her clinging, wanting the moment never to end. As his words flowed over her like passion-laced honey, she fought to keep her senses clear. She had to keep him at a distance, for in so doing, she could retain her self-will!

"One day you will trust me with all the inner secrets of your heart. When that day comes, that is when you will know true joy. When we see with the sight of the inner heart and look beyond that which our mind tells us, we can truly be the person that we have been destined to be from the first moment of creation."

Had ever another warrior spoken such words to another maiden? Had ever another maiden been so overwhelmed by the heady assault to the senses she was now being forced to endure? She was drowning in a great gulf of passion. Unable to break away from the seduction of his softly spoken words and the presence of his body encircling her, his words twined in her mind with those spoken by Medicine Woman in the sweat-lodge: *"See with the eye of the heart"*. Unaware of the potency of the spell he was casting, her body moved before him with a will of its own.

With the slight movement of her body upon the mat, Cetán felt the pressure of her breasts against his chest as her honey-gold eyes looked fully into his. Time spun and hung suspended as the couple stared at one another, locked in the rapturous spell.

With a soft sigh, Desire's hand moved toward her husband. As Cetán's lips met hers, Desire's mouth opened to receive his heated tongue, shyly tasting his essence. As her own tongue pressed between his teeth, he gently suckled as Desire's body pressed fully against his.

Cetán plied a subtle seduction. A soft caress here, the slight shifting of a leg, his heated breath along the slender curve of her neck. Nothing threatening, nothing overtly applied. She kissed him as generously as he could desire, and in return, Cetán warmed to the challenge of winning his wife's favor.

Desire came up for a breath after the fiercely intense kissing. "You are very good at this joining of the lips, Cetán."

"I am happy I please you, wife." Cetán nibbled lightly on the slender undercurve of her jaw. His fingers toyed with the ties of her dress. Just before his lips recaptured hers, he breathed against her smooth cheek, "Why do you not take off your dress, Wacin?"

His words were like a blast of ice cold water. Her lips stiffened beneath his own and her hands began to push against his chest as Desire fought to right herself upon the mat. Kissing her husband was one thing. She admitted that she had been eager to experience this joining of their lips once again, but taking off her clothes for him was another matter entirely! She was not ready to take such a step, and was unsure if she ever would be! Her mind filled with her sweat-lodge vision; she vividly glimpsed her naked body joined with the faceless warrior's upon the sleeping couch. The image did nothing to calm the inner turmoil that had suddenly beset her!

As soon as the words had left Cetán's mouth, he wished he could call them back. Feeling her pushing away from him, the moment of their shared closeness now totally destroyed, he tried to explain. "I meant nothing more than to say that you would be far more comfortable sleeping without your dress on, Wacin. I would not rush you into anything more than you wish to give.''

She was out of his arms and already a good distance from him. ''You need not worry about my comfort, Cetán.'' Elk-hunter rose from his position near Cetán's sleeping couch as he heard the tone of his mistress' voice. As Desire's hand rested upon the great wolf's head, her calm returned. ''I am very comfortable sleeping in the manner which I have these past two nights.''

Cetán cursed his tongue as he watched his bride move to the sleeping couch. Lying down, she stiffly turned her body away from him. He could still taste her sweetness. With a silent groan, Cetán knew that this night would be longer in passing than any other he had ever endured. Clothed or not, the temptation of Wacin lying next to him upon their bed of furs, and being unable to touch her, was beyond any test of strength he had ever known.

Fifteen

The next several days in the Lakota valley swept by with much similarity to life in the Indian village Desire had grown up in. Each morning, Autumn Dawn and her two children met Desire, and together, they gathered with the other women of the village to swim and gather firewood. Many of the women spoke to Desire of ailments they or their family members were suffering from, and a great portion of her time was given over to mixing plants for medicines, then distributing them.

Autumn Dawn and Desire became fast friends. Each afternoon Desire went to the other woman's lodge where the two would visit and work on their sewing. Desire enjoyed these times of companionship, for in the past, she had few close friends near her own age. She also found enjoyment in Autumn Dawn and Spirit Walker's children. The little girl, age seven, and the boy, age five, were very intelligent and highly active. The women laughed constantly over their antics.

The second day Desire had visited Autumn Dawn's lodge, the other young woman enthusiastically volunteered to teach Desire to speak English. Autumn Dawn seemed so eager, Desire did not have the heart to explain that she had never had any desire to learn the tongue of the wasichu. But in the interest of friendship, she repeated the strange-sounding words and then stated their meaning in the familiar tongue of the Sioux.

Desire found her nights here in her husband's village did not pass as easily as her days. Since that first evening, there had been no more kissing lessons, but the sensual tension that filled the lodge each evening was more than Desire could bear. With but the slightest look from Cetán, Desire felt her body's reaction. Heat traveled to her cheeks from the very points of her breasts. With the sound of his husky voice, her heartbeat accelerated and her limbs began to tremble. A double torment blessed her; they slept, side by side, upon his sleeping couch; she was fully clothed, he lay naked, covered only by a piece of fur.

Thoughts of Cetán plagued Desire one day as she held Star's reins and led her out into the river. Halting when the water reached the mare's knees, Desire crooned softly to the animal.

This had been the first afternoon in which Desire had found the time to get acquainted with the horse she had been given as a bride gift from her husband. Finding the usual gathering place for the women and children next to the riverbank deserted, she led the mare a short distance downriver and out of sight of the village.

Having taken off her moccasins and dress before leading Star out into the water, Desire dampened her dress in the cooling water and lightly ran the soft hide material over the mare's flanks, allowing her the time to take in her mistress's scent, as well as her voice.

The mare responded as she threw back her head then brought it down to lightly nudge Desire's shoulder.

Running the dampened dress over the horse's sleek neck and finely sculpted front flanks, Desire laughed aloud. "Indeed, you are a rare beauty, Star. You and I will become good friends."

The mare appeared to understand the words and snorted a response.

Desire's tinkling laughter echoed along the riverbank as

she continued to dip the dress into the water and allowed the refreshing droplets to flow over Star's back.

Never in Cetán's life had he seen such a wondrous sight as he now looked upon from the shrubbery and tall pines growing along the river's edge. Sitting atop Whirling-Warrior's-Ghost, rider and horse were immobile, neither sound nor movement revealing their presence.

Cetán was transfixed as his dark gaze watched his bride standing in thigh-deep water at Star's side. The late afternoon sun broke through the trees that grew in abundance along this portion of the river. Desire's dark tresses dipped into the swirling water rushing around her body, the sun glistening off her curls. Droplets from the shimmering liquid produced an iridescent sheen over her pearl-satin skin. She stood naked before his gaze, her slim figure delicately outlined. She held her hide dress, and bending to the water, dipped the dress then with gentle strokes rubbed the sodden gown along the animal's neck, over her face and down her back. The animal responded fondly to her mistress's ministrations, and the sound of Desire's laughing and crooning filled Cetán's ears.

This temptation was by far too hard for any man to resist. with a slight movement of his heels to Whirling-Warrior's-Ghost's sides, Cetán directed the large stallion down the slight incline of the riverbank and into the water.

A gasp of surprise escaped Desire as she heard the sound of splashing behind her, and turning, she spied Cetán and his war-horse coming directly toward her and Star. She had no time to protest the disturbance of her privacy. Even before Cetán halted the stallion, he was slipping into the water to stand next to her, his dark gaze upon her with such intensity that all protest fled.

The only sound was from Whirling-Warrior's-Ghost as he snorted loudly and stepped to Star's opposite side. The mare whinnied, her finely shaped legs moving in the water as she stepped away from her mistress and drew closer to the gray stallion.

"Traitor!" Desire hissed before her sherry-gold eyes were ensnared by Cetán's dark regard.

"Star is wise enough to follow her heart."

The husky allure of Cetán's voice suffused Desire's senses and stirred her deep in the pit of her belly.

"And what of you, wife? Do you still deny your heart?" Cetán did not expect an answer. He took a step closer, his eyes lowering to Desire's full breasts. A searing hunger raced through him as he slowly appraised the water-glistened twin globes, their dusty buds swelling to hardened points.

The water surrounding the couple was cool, but did not cause the gooseflesh that coursed over Desire's skin. A slight trembling beset her as the heat of his gaze seared her flesh, and her heartbeat began to quicken.

His dark eyes rose again to capture those of honey-gold. "Your beauty astounds me, Wacin. I would teach you to accept from me what you offer your horse." He reached out, his palm cupping a handful of water, and allowed the liquid to flow slowly over Desire's shoulder. "I would teach you my touch, the sound of my voice, my scent." As his other hand lifted water and in a slow, deliberate manner he turned his palm, the water slipped over her hair and ran down her slender back.

Desire felt trapped. Her breathing became shallow as her eyes shut against the power of sensual delight. She endured the slow attention he lavished upon her, because to do otherwise at the moment would be unthinkable. The tiny bells twined within her hair sang softly on the afternoon breeze as her body moved closer to his hands. She felt the cool water flowing over her back, his large hand following its path over the curve of her shoulderblade, down her spine, traveling the softness of a rounded hip and lightly capturing the fullness of her buttock.

As his other hand followed this same tempting path, Desire's head tilted back, her lips parting as if to draw more air into her starving lungs.

Cetán had expected resistance. Caught unaware, he had to use all of his will to keep his raging need at bay. His hands cupped water and slowly allowed it to fall over her shapely curves, his searching fingers traveling over the satin texture of her flesh, lingering over the perfect curve of her collarbone, over the slant of her ribs to the smallness of her waist, then back up to her full breasts. Hungrily, he took in her closed eyes, her slightly tilted head, lips openly parted. No strength remained to resist the invitation. His dark head lowered, lips pressing gently at first over hers, then more urgently.

Thinking of nothing more than the intense pleasure she was receiving, Desire allowed herself to be totally consumed. Her senses were lost to the rapture of the moment—not just by the power of his kisses, but also by his body. One of his hands lightly pushed against her back, pressing her closer to his chest. The slow rub and press against his torso gave Desire the oddest feeling, as her breasts were caressed and massaged by turns. The other hand cupped beneath the full curve of her soft buttock, lifting her until his hard bulge was settled directly at the heart of her womanhood. She felt totally assaulted on every front, overwhelmed by the glorious sensations. As though this were not enough, his tongue made a deep, erotic foray into her mouth, completely destroying any lingering resistance.

Cetán was completely caught up in the storm of his own creation. His body was attuned to every curve of her slender form, the heat of her need burning through his breechcloth. With the full realization that she wanted him as much as he wanted her, boiling blood rushed into his groin, creating a throbbing to match the pounding beat of his heart.

A slight noise made by the horses stole into Cetán's

thoughts, reminding him that this was not the place to initiate his bride into the joys to be had by the joining of their bodies. The downy comfort of a soft pallet of furs would be more pleasurable for her to remember in years to come. He wanted a lifetime of such enjoyable moments. He would not greedily devour her offering now, but would savor fully this bounty that would soon be his by being even more patient. Forcing himself to relax, he rained kisses over her eyelids and her soft cheeks to the delicate slant of her jaw. "I must go back to our lodge now, Wacin. I came only to tell you of my kill this day."

"What?" Desire questioned a bit dazedly.

"I went hunting with Spirit Walker, remember? I killed an elk buck and now must return to clean and dress the meat." Her eyes were still half lowered, her appearance tousled. She was a woman in the throes of passion, a woman ready to be made love to. Cetán groaned inwardly, not allowing himself to give in to the moment's sweet pleasure. "I will leave you to finish working with Star." He forced the words out of his throat.

In seconds, Desire was once again standing alone in the thigh-deep water. But now, as her passion-clouded eyes watched her husband mount and leave the river, she ached with a fierce, unknown need deep in the center of her womanhood. Clutching Star's long, silky mane to keep from falling, Desire questioned softly, "What is this man doing to me?"

By the time Desire returned to the lodge, Cetán had butchered the large bull elk. Much of the meat would be given to those of the village who were in need. The rest was set aside for Desire to place strips upon a drying rack plus a portion to be cut up to roast and make stews.

Cetán's smile was a warm invitation as he saw his bride

entering the lodge. "I have started a pot of stew, Wacin. I hope your afternoon was pleasant."

The flavorful odors of cooking meat, wild onions, and turnips filled the lodge and mingled with her husband's greeting. Desire could only nod in acknowledgement. Did this man not know how he was affecting her? She went across the lodge to pick up her sewing. She glanced to where he was sitting next to the fire, Elkhunter stretched out next to him in companionable silence. Cetán's skilled hands were working a slender shaft of wood back and forth through a tubular groove in the center of two pieces of sandstone. After this smoothing procedure the shaft would undergo more work before becoming an arrow.

Cetán enjoyed this work with his hands. Several weeks past he had cut a pile of twenty such sticks, tied them in a bundle, wrapped them with a hide cover, and hung them at the top of his lodge where they would be smoked by the lodge fire. Thus, the shafts would be seasoned and also freed from any insects. This afternoon he had retrieved the bundle of sticks and had begun the procedure that would make them into arrows. As his fingers deftly worked the first shaft through the sandstone, he wondered about his wife's thoughts. Was she, like he, thinking of their encounter down at the river? Would she again welcome his advances, now that they were here in his lodge? He felt himself beginning to harden. His bride was driving him mad with the wanting of her, whether she realized it or not!

"I want to thank you again for Star, Cetán. She is a wonderful animal." Desire felt the increased tension and hoped her words would ease the mood.

"If it is your wish, we can put her and Whirling-Warrior's-Ghost together when she comes into season. The two of them will have fine, strong offspring."

This conversation centering around horseflesh seemed to be safe ground for the couple. "In my father's village,

I of ten helped him with the breaking of his horses," Desire offered, silently hoping Cetán would consider allowing her to do the same with his animals.

Cetán did not speak right away. He lifted the shaft of wood he was holding up near the light of the fire. Carefully, he inspected for a curve or crook. Finding one, he rubbed the section with buffalo fat and allowed it to heat over the flames. With his arrow-making tools spread out next to him, Cetán placed the slender stick through the two holes in the ram's horn used for this purpose, then applied enough pressure on the wood to straighten the curve. His glance once again went to where his wife was sitting near their sleeping couch. "I have many horses, Wacin, and could use your help when you have time. Curly Bear and Flying Fox often help with the taming of my new horses. I am sure they would appreciate your help also." Cetán was wise enough to realize that his wife had many talents, and he was not the type of man to see that wasted. He had watched her handling Star this afternoon at the river, and only a stupid man would turn her offer aside.

Desire was surprised by how quickly Cetán agreed to her offer. Her father had allowed her to help break his horses, but many of the younger braves of the tribe had taken her abilities as an affront to their manhood. She had heard them talk, when they thought she could not hear them, expressing their thoughts about a woman's place being in the lodge, tending their fires and their children. Her husband did not appear to have this same fear. A slow curve touched her lips as she smiled softly in Cetán's direction. She was learning quickly enough that her husband was unlike any other warrior she had ever known.

Her smile was not lost upon Cetán, and with its blessing, he felt his inner being burst with joy. He would agree to anything she desired in order to see such radiance. She had but to ask, and whatever she wished would be granted.

"Perhaps tomorrow you would like to go and look my herd over?"

"I would love to, Cetán. I have tried to keep myself busy, and I do love visiting with Autumn Dawn, but I have never enjoyed staying inside a lodge all day. Besides working with my medicine plants and helping the sick, I love being around horses. I have a keen ability to spot an animal that is lagging in spirit and strength. Perhaps I will be able to make up some medicines for those horses in need of such treatment." Desire's excitement at the prospect of helping her husband was evident in her tone.

The rest of the evening passed in this same pleasant mood. After the meal, Desire sat across the fire and watched as Cetán continued the work on his arrows.

"In my father's village, there is an old man called Straight Arrow who makes bows and arrows for many of the warriors of the tribe. My own father many times traded him fine buffalo robes for his handiwork." This evening was pleasurable for Desire, with the prospect of going with her husband to look over his herd in the morning, and watching Cetán work so skillfully on the slender reeds.

With his sharp hunting knife, Cetán carefully cut away a U-shaped nock of wood at one end of the arrow for his sinew bowstring. The nock was cut deeply in the wood, and when completed, the fingers of his drawing hand would hook around the bowstring with the arrow held between two of his fingers. The sinew bowstring would then be drawn back, the arrow pinched between Cetán's two fingers. "In my village, there are those who are expert at making such weapons, and many of the warriors use their talents. I enjoy making my own weapons. With the completion of each arrow, I pray to The One Above that it will be straight and fleet, hitting its target without mishap."

Desire's golden eyes warmed as they followed the movement of her husband's hands. At the opposite end of the wood shaft, Cetán cut a thin slit, about three quarters of an inch deep. This would be the head of the arrow shaft, where Cetán would insert an arrowhead. Once the arrowhead was in place in the slit, it would be secured with glue and a binding of sinew. Before Cetán would place the arrowhead and feathers, he would make his personal groove sign, which would run the length of the arrow.

Picking up an ancient, sharp stone stylus, Cetán's obsidian eyes turned back to Desire. "Come, Wacin, sit closer. I will show you how I make my sign upon my arrows." He parted his legs, making room for her to sit before him on the mat of his backrest.

Most warriors believed that women had their own power, and were capable of drawing power out of a man's weapons if they handled them. Desire was surprised by her husband's offer for her to draw nearer to his weapons. Her first reaction was to refuse when memory of those shared moments this afternoon assailed her. But, as her gaze fastened upon his strong hands, those same memories caused her to move from her position across the fire to the beaded mat of his backrest. He was entirely too difficult to resist! All evening she had been watching his hands, imagining their feel upon her body.

As she sat between his thighs, Cetán tried to steady his breathing. His arms encircled Desire as he brought the stone stylus and reed together. "The grooves on my arrows are always shallow—I run them in a wavy pattern down the length of the wood. These marks will make my arrows fly through the air like lightning in the sky and will prevent warping." He leaned his body forward, his chest pressing against her back. Her scent flooded his senses as his husky voice patiently explained what he was doing and his hands expertly ran the stylus down the length of the shaft.

Desire's eyes glowed brighter as she felt his strong arms enclosing her. She forgot everything except the need to have his hands caressing her flesh as they were caressing the piece of wood. Without thought, her hands reached out and covered his. Her fingers began to caress the backs of his hands, his knuckles, his long, bronzed fingers.

Cetán inhaled sharply, all of his senses attuned to the touch of her hands. "Tomorrow, these arrows will be crested with my identifying bands of color. The final step will be when I glue, and fasten with sinew, the turkey feathers at the shaft of the arrow. Each will be set at an equal distance around the shaft. When released from my bowstring, the arrow will have a twisting or spinning motion, similar to that of a bullet leaving the barrel of the wasichu's fire stick." Cetán forced his tone to remain even, explaining each step of his arrow-making as though his bride were totally unschooled in the procedure. The last thing in the world he wanted to do was cause her to stop her exploration of his hands. As he finished making the last groove, he still held the stylus and arrow. Instead of drawing her hands away, Desire silently moved her fingers up his forearms, then over the bulging strength of his upper arms. Hardly daring to draw breath, his arrow and tools now totally forgotten, Cetán awaited his wife's next move.

Sixteen

There was no reason to the madness that beset Desire. She could not take her hands away from the exploration of her husband. His warm, sun-kissed flesh enticed the soft skin of her palms. Her fingers traced a path up his wrists and over his muscular forearms. Lingering over the splendid strength of his upper arms, a soft breath hissed from the back of her throat. She shifted in his embrace, her fingers stroking his shoulders and the curve of his collarbone. In the back of Desire's mind, she remembered receiving like touches from her husband this afternoon at the river when he had poured water from his cupped hands over her shoulders and then run his hands over the same path. Her body shuddered in remembrance.

"I love your touch, mitáwicu." Cetán said softly.

"As I love yours, higná." Desire knew the implication of these words, but once they were spoken she was powerless to recall them. She ached with a fierce desire to feel Cetán's hands upon her flesh. She yearned with a maddening need for him to set aside his tool and arrow, to touch her as he had today at the river.

This was the first time that Wacin had called him *husband*, and Cetán's heartbeat tripped with unrestrained joy. His tool and arrow lay next to the fire, totally forgotten. Turning on the mat, his finger lifted her face to meet the warmth of his loving gaze. He glimpsed the invitation he had been longing for. The brilliance of the moon and sun shone from the swirling depths of her eyes; her full, petal-soft lips opened slightly as they beckoned to join with his.

Cetán's head lowered, Desire's rose; their mouths met, blending their senses, erasing all thought. Only this close-ness, only this shared passion beneath the surface that flamed to life every time they were in each other's pres-ence, was real. Desire clutched the silken strands of his midnight hair. Cetán's embrace tightened as he drew her closer. There was no stemming the raging ardor that drew them together.

The kiss was like no other before it. Where their lips touched they burned, the fire igniting, their hunger inten-sified beyond all boundaries of caution.

Desire welcomed Cetán's tongue into her mouth with a deep hunger of her own. She devoured his taste, her tongue mating with his in a heady, passionate dance. Thoughts of remaining the woman she feared would some-how be changed if she let down her guard fled her mind. All that mattered was this moment, and the incredible plea-sure she received in Cetán's arms. As she was kissed, and kissed him in return, her hands roamed over her husband's body. Releasing her grip on his hair, her fingers traced a path over his broad shoulders, committing to memory the feel of the smooth, hard planes and the muscular contours of his upper arms and chest.

Her sweet ambrosia taste inflamed Cetán's senses, stok-ing a cauldron of emotions. He knew he had to go slowly and not frighten her. He wanted to guide her to that path which would bring her to the door of her heart, and therein allow her to understand the rightness of their union. These thoughts assailed him as he fought an inner battle to keep a grip on the firestorm of passion surging within his loins. The battle was lost before it was started. Hot, molten need raced from the heart of his groin to fill his manhood with aching desire. As Desire began to touch him, her buttocks shifted closer against him on the mat, and an animal-like groan escaped the back of his throat.

The satin-smooth flesh beneath his fingers shimmered like gold in the firelight. Cetán's lips feathered kisses across her brow, over her eyes, and down the profile of perfection to her chin. Lightly, his fingers traveled along the slender curve of her throat as she leaned her head backward to increase his touch. His fingers stroked the sweeping contour of her collarbone, ran down the length of her upper arms, rising again to linger at the valley where the tie of her dress guarded her full upper beauty from his caress.

Desire's own touching never ceased. Her fingers drank of his sun-bronzed skin, the same as his were now partaking of her flesh. Her breathing sharpened as he brushed aside the dress ties. He bared her bosom to the burning penetration of his gaze. She had no thought of covering her upper body. Instead, her woman's pride grew as she drank in his appraisal. Never had she been made so aware of her own beauty. She rejoiced, proud that her husband found favor with her body.

Esteemed . . . exalted . . . glorious . . . these were just a few of the words that flew through Cetán's head as he looked upon the magnificent beauty of his bride's breasts. Today at the river, he had not fully appreciated their exquisiteness. Now, as she sat before him and the firm mounds of flesh with rose-dusted tips strained outward for his touch, he marveled at such sublime creation.

For a second, Cetán's onyx eyes left the splendid globes and rose upward to look fully at Desire. She felt blessed by the obvious worship he had for her.

"You make it hard for that part of me that wishes to resist to do so, Cetán," Desire stated breathlessly.

"Why is that, mitáwicu?" Cetán questioned softly, not breaking the spell.

"You look upon me as no other ever has. Where your

eyes touch, I feel alive and warm, as though I have been born only for this moment.''

Looking at his bride, Cetán knew she spoke from the heart. ''Look further into your heart, Wacin. Accept the fact that you and I have always been one. From the dawn of creation, we have traveled the paths of the past, together. This is what is between us, this heat of the sun that touches our souls and awakens long-dormant feelings from the past. Throughout all eternities, you and I shall rediscover what has always been.''

''I look into your eyes, and know the truth of what you speak, but I am afraid.''

''Then let me help you.'' With his eyes locked upon hers, Cetán stood up and stretched his hand downward.

She could not resist. On trembling legs, she stood before him.

Gently, Cetán pulled the upper portion of the hide dress down Desire's arms; the material floated into a puddle around her ankles. ''The One Above made your body to be admired by my eyes.'' As he had silently worshiped her breasts, his obsidian gaze slowly took in the perfect outline of her form. She bore not the slightest imperfection. His gaze wandered over the beautiful breasts, then down her trim ribcage to the tiny indent of her navel. His eyes absorbed the womanly flare of shapely hips and long, slender legs, then caressed her delicate ankles and slim feet. He was filled with burning desire as he boldly looked upon the feathering of dark curls at the junction of her legs.

An uncontrollable shiver of passion raced down Desire's spine. She stood spellbound, seeing her own beauty reflected in her husband's appreciation. As Cetán's gaze rose to lock with her own, she felt the escalating rampage of her heartbeat. Her husband desired her above anything else in this life; she rejoiced in her woman's power. Cetán had mentioned this power that she would one day feel, and now she understood. It was a wisdom as old as time, as powerful as any force upon Mother Earth. This mighty warrior could bend or stand tall before her; the choice was hers. Reaching out, she lightly took hold of the leather tie that secured his breech-cloth. The material fell from his hips to the lodge floor; the choice had been made!

Cetán's heart sang. As the bright gold eyes broke away from his, he felt the heat of her appraisal, but forced himself to stand before her, allowing the imprint of his body to be branded in her mind forever.

The flashing gold of Desire's gaze swirled with hidden lights as they moved slowly over his long midnight hair and caressed his tanned, muscled shoulders. His forearms and broad chest exuded raw power. Hard slabs of muscle-corded flesh covered his ribs and tapered down to a narrow waist and slim hips. The tight contours of his buttocks and powerful thighs then drew her notice until her full attention was trapped by the giant lance protruding from the junction of his legs. Thick and long, his swollen shaft rose up, throbbing with need! Desire gasped aloud, her gaze rising to meet Cetán's. In the depths of his dark eyed she was captured by a firestorm of passion that threatened to engulf her.

Cetán heard her gasp and saw the moment's fear in her eyes. Not hesitating, he pulled her into his arms, her ragged breathing conquered by his lips. The kiss was languorously overlong as Cetán's heated tongue probed and plundered, swirling around her moist tongue, leaving her clutching his shoulders for support.

Honey-sweet nectar filled Cetán's mouth as the kiss was prolonged; all fear was chased away. Desire's lush curves pressed against his body, the contact increasing the sensual pull. His hands traced a path down her slender back to the soft curve of her buttocks. As he pressed her tighter against him, a moan of sheer carnal desire escaped the back of his throat.

Desire was too swept up in the moment to back away.

His heat drew her closer. She clung to him, the fire of his love searing her belly. As he drew her even closer, he lifted her to meet him. The flame touched the very bud of her woman's heart; a small cry escaped her parted lips with the contact.

"Not yet, mitá wicánte. Let me love your body as I have longed to do since the first time I saw you." It took all of Cetán's willpower not to take her, not to claim her as that part of him that longed to be rejoined. His arms encircled her, drawing her into his arms, the pounding of their heartbeats joining as her breasts pressed against his chest. His mouth slanted over hers as her fingers twined within the dark strands of his hair.

Carrying her to the pallet of soft furs, he placed her in the center as though she were a precious jewel. His dark gaze seduced her very breath as it traveled slowly over her, then captured her glance. As they stared into one another's eyes, Cetán lowered his body down upon the sleeping couch next to his wife. His hard body brushed against her woman's soft curves, and with the contact of naked flesh touching naked flesh, the fire of their passions burst forth.

Cetán's head bent to her, his mouth descending as large, gentle hands reached out in exploration. "You are all that I shall ever need in this life path, Wacin. You give unto me a most wondrous gift. Your body . . . your heart . . . your beauty, are treasures without price. This warrior is humbled before your offering." His mouth covered the soft petals of her lips, gently sampling their lushness.

His softly spoken words stoked the irresistible pull of pleasure's sweet promise. At this moment, Desire was unsure who was the one more humbled. She had promised herself that her life as wife to Cetán would not come to this moment, but she had been powerless to resist him. Cetán was right; what was between them had been fated from the beginning of time. A soft moan of delight escaped her as Cetán's mouth and hands began an exploration of her body. He showered her with fevered kisses, his mouth and teeth nibbling as his tongue partook of her flesh. As her hands reached up to draw him closer, he ravished both breasts, his teeth caressing the soft underflesh, his actions driving her mad with a need that only he could satisfy.

The attention of his mouth and tongue slowly wound downward, over the inviting line of her ribcage, across the indent of her belly to the curve of her hip. The honey-taste of her tender flesh and the feel of her satin-smooth body seduced Cetán's senses. His hands circled the smallness of her waist, drawing her hips closer to the assault of his lips. His moist, searing tongue caused flames of desire to ricochet throughout the lower portion of Desire's body as Cetán laved the insides of her thighs.

The assault captured all of Desire's senses where his mouth kissed and licked. Her body jerked in passionate surprise as his mouth brushed against the bud of her woman's jewel. Her breathing all but stopped and her hands clutched tighter in his hair, even as her inner consciousness responded. Her legs parted to welcome this new assault of sweet, forbidden pleasure.

Desire's heart hammered wickedly as his fingers gently opened her. With a circular motion of his tongue, he delved into the very heart of her woman's passion. His action cast Desire headlong into a torrent of boundless rapture as the seductive movements of his tongue filled her, again and again, with waves of heat.

Riding high upon the outer edges of a swirling vortex of unbelievable feelings, exquisite pleasure raced through Desire's entire body. Scalding shards of desire ignited deep within the center of her womb. Riding out the raging torrent of passion, hot flames of molten desire pulsated wantonly within the depths of her womanhood. A cry of intense pleasure burst from her lips, her body shaking out of control as the flames erupted.

Merciless in his desire to bring her total fulfillment,

Cetán's tongue delved deeper into her moist, sweet depths, then lingered over the sensitive nub at the fountain of her womanhood as shudder after shudder carried her onward.

Slowly, the trembling that gripped her body subsided. Desire's fingers loosened their grip in his hair, and though her breathing had not, as yet, returned to normal, her senses cleared enough for her to marvel over what had just taken place.

Rising from his position between her thighs, Cetán rained branding kisses over her body as he once again pressed his full length against her. "You are my heart, Wacin, my love, my wife. This night I will chase away all thoughts of Panther Stalks from your mind forever!"

Her woman's knowledge told Desire that her husband was not totally finished with his lovemaking. He rose over her, their bodies fitting perfectly, his throbbing, blood-engorged lance pressing heatedly between them. He sought out the place where only seconds past, his lips and tongue had left her trembling in the grips of passion, and she heard his words over the harsh pounding of her heart. *Why would her husband be speaking about Panther Stalks now?* Then, with the covering of her mouth by Cetán's, she totally forgot anything except the incredible things he was doing to her body.

As Cetán pressed between her thighs, she opened to him. Never in her life had she ever experienced such wondrous feelings of wanton bliss. His simple touch ignited a thirst within her depths that only this man could quench!

As Cetán's tongue plunged within her mouth, his pulsing, blood-thickened lance began a slow descent, the sculpted marble head pressed gently against the moist opening of her sweet passion. As he entered her just an inch, the velvet warmth of her tight passage enclosed him; another inch, and he felt the soft trembling of her inner sanctum. A low rumbling came from deep within Cetán's chest, filling the lodge with his animal-like groan.

At the same time, a small cry reverberated as Desire's maidenhead was pierced. Cetán stilled, his raging desire stemmed for the moment as he was caught by surprise. Not once had he considered that this woman of his heart was a virgin. Her refusal to join with him, the smile he had seen her bestow upon Panther Stalks, and the warrior's taunting remarks when they had fought had all led Cetán to believe that she and Panther Stalks had been lovers. It had truly not mattered to Cetán that his bride came to him after she had lain with Panther Stalks; all that had ever mattered in his heart was that Wacin belong to him. Now, as he looked down into her face and glimpsed the pain etched upon her lovely features, he felt blessed beyond his dreams.

"You hurt me, Cetán." The accusation was childishly soft as Desire's golden gaze looked at him with a mixture of disbelief and fear.

Cetán lovingly wiped away the tear that rolled down her cheek. "Ah, my heart, had I known, I would have prepared you better for my entry. It is always thus this first time, these first few seconds."

"I don't want to do this anymore." Desire had had enough. Everything until this minute had been so beautiful; she should have known something terrible was about to happen. This was her punishment for letting down her guard. She had been paid a cruel reminder that she could not afford to lose herself to her husband's passion.

Cetán's smile was tender as he remained where he was above her and lightly caressed her cheek. "The pain will pass, Wacin, and never again will it return. Often, this is the way of things. Pain is the threshold to the greatest pleasure." His determination to make this woman his own had been the cause of his own pain—the pain of his heart had been unmerciful after her refusal to join with him, but now, now his joy was boundless!

"Trust me, Wacin, as I lead you through the doorway to

incredible pleasure." He did not await her response, but lowered his head toward her, his lips settling over hers in a breathless assault upon her senses.

This kiss was by far the tenderest Desire had ever received. All of Cetán's feelings of love and adoration were conveyed to her with the touch of his mouth. The kiss told of regret over the pain she suffered, of his need for her to trust him, and of the promise of all their tomorrows.

As he released her lips, she was lost within the depths of his dark eyes, his tenderness surrounding her, holding her in a spell of wonder. Her mind centered upon the fullness between her legs; the pain had already diminished as Cetán had promised it would. As her tawny-gold eyes stared into his darkest jet, she shifted her buttocks, testing the slender traces of lingering fear.

Cetán felt her slight movement against him and rejoiced as he glimpsed the gold of her eyes take on a more brilliant sheen. It was hard for her to trust, and harder still for her to release her will into another's keeping. Perhaps these traits were a part of the reason that he was so drawn to her. She did not do things in half measure. When he gained her trust, it would be entirely; this would be how she would give her heart. "You will only know pleasure from my touch from this moment forth," he softly promised, right before his mouth captured hers. Cetán began a gentle lulling upon her senses, which he hoped would bring their passions back to those earlier moments.

Desire held back as long as she was able, her body remaining tense, as though she expected the pain to return. When it didn't, she began to respond to his gentle wooing. She moved slowly at first. She experienced only the feeling of fullness, so she moved more vigorously against him, as though she sought out that elusive delight which they had shared moments past.

Her movements stoked their passions to full wakefulness. Cetán's kisses slowly grew to a deep hunger. All thoughts of holding back began to wane. Desire's passion built and increased. In a few short moments, she capitulated completely to her husband's masterful touch. He plied her with his skillful seduction, his body moving in a slow rhythm, not yet allowing the full thrust of his massive size to claim her, keeping in mind to have a care for her virgin's body. His manhood slowly moved deeper, then withdrew to the lips of her moist opening. Desire's hands clutched his back, her head thrown back in mindless ecstasy as the fullness in her loins drove her toward a frenzy of desire. Each time his fiery lance drove into her hidden regions, then returned to the tightness of her opening, her body moved closer, searching for total fullness. Her legs slowly rose as she sought to capture the entire length of him within her sleek, trembling sheath.

The vein-ribbed, throbbing length of him continued to fill her and then ease from her hot depths, the motion creating a glorious sensation which grew in the very center of her womb, causing a shuddering action in her depths which traveled the length of his swollen manhood. As her velvet-warm depths tightened deliciously around him, Cetán drew in deep breaths, willing himself to maintain control and not release the full fury of his raging passions!

Shudders of unbelievable pleasure gripped Desire's body, and centered fully upon the scorching heat of Cetán's probing shaft. Spasm after rippling spasm coursed through her body and pulsed within the depths of her woman's passion. As her movements stroked and tightened around the swollen length of him, she slipped beyond the limits of control. Her body thrashed about wildly, hips jerking convulsively as she spiraled toward the spinning vortex of true satisfaction.

All of Cetán's senses were attuned to the power of the climax which gripped his wife. For a time longer, he fought the aching desire that possessed him to give vent to the fiery need that raced through his loins and threatened to overcome him. He watched her passion-filled features, climactic moans escaping her throat and filling his ears. Each thrust given was torture-laced as he fought off his own aching need for fulfillment. Only at the point when he sensed her climax was receding did Cetán allow himself the pleasure of giving total vent to his own desires. His lips caught hers as he plunged a fraction deeper into her soft velvety depths; a firestorm of pleasure burst from the very center of his being and showered upward, racing heatedly through his powerful shaft to erupt in her womb.

Seventeen

So this is what it was all really about! Desire felt like laughing aloud, so great was her happiness. Her fear of the unknown had been wasted, and as she felt her husband's heartbeat thumping against her breasts, she marveled that the act of joining could be so beautiful! "You should have told me how it would be, Cetán." She could not prevent a small giggle. "Perhaps I would have been the one bringing you a bride price."

Cetán's husky laughter filled the lodge as he rolled over with his bride still joined with his body. "Would you have believed me, Wacin?" His dark eyes twinkled with happiness as he searched her glowing face.

"Maybe, if you had explained what pleasure was to be had by lying on your sleeping couch without my clothes on."

Cetán's arms tightened. She was direct, and though he had not expected this light banter from her, he was happy that she had not turned shy and innocent after what they had just shared. "Now that you know, I hope you will spare your clothes some of the wrinkles they have endured."

Desire wriggled her bottom gently against his groin, still feeling him deep within her. "I think I could get used to this, husband," she lightly purred against the side of his throat. It was not this act of joining with a warrior which had the power to change her from the woman she was. It was the man himself, and with this knowledge, she cautioned herself to guard her heart closely. There was nothing wrong with enjoying the pleasures that her husband's body could give her—it was the feelings of the heart that she had to guard against!

Cetán lovingly brushed the hair back from her cheeks, enjoying the feel of her soft curves lying unclad atop his body. "I think we should take things easy at first, Wacin." One large hand laid against her bottom to halt her squirming against him. He felt the tightening in his groin as his manhood began to respond to her movement.

"Why is that, Cetán?" This act of joining was a new-found delight, and Desire saw no reason why they should not do it as often as they wanted.

Cetán grinned, and with an iron will, fought temptation. Remembering that her body had been untouched until only a short time ago, he was also reminded of the things which he believed had taken place between her and Panther Stalks. "Your mind may wish to share this pleasure once again, Wacin, but your body is like a tender bud and must be treated with care. Tomorrow you will be sore. I do not wish you to suffer needlessly. In a couple of days, when your body adjusts to the newness of joining with mine, there will be no limit to our pleasure."

Desire would have argued, assuring her husband she would be fine in the morning. She had always been hale and hearty, but there was something very comforting about the manner in which Cetán was cradling her, and determining the care of her body.

The couple lay upon the downy softness of the furs, each drawing comfort from the other as they silently reflected over what they had shared moments ago, and the closeness that now bound them together.

Settling his bride back against the soft furs, Cetán rose, in all of his naked splendor, and made his way to the center fire. With sparkling eyes, Desire watched his every movement as he placed several heated rocks in a rawhide water parfleche. The gentle sound of hissing filled the lodge as the glowing rocks hit water. Once the water was heated, Cetán poured a bowl of the warmed liquid and returned to Desire's side.

Holding a piece of tradecloth in one hand and the warmed water in the other, Cetán bent down next to the sleeping couch. His dark eyes glittered with passion as he drew the piece of fur away from his wife's body and began to gently wipe the dampened cloth over her bountiful curves.

Desire sighed softly as she lay still beneath her husband's tender ministrations. As Cetán lovingly wiped away the flecks of virgin's blood from her thighs, she marveled at his gentleness. Had ever a warrior, so bold and so strong, been this loving to another maiden? She could not imagine other men being so attentive to their wives. She was reminded of Panther Stalks, knowing with a certainty that if she had joined with the warrior, she would have received no such gentle treatment. Thinking of him, she was reminded also of earlier when her husband had spoken his name aloud. She wondered why Cetán would mention the other warrior at such a time. As he finished the washing of her body, she softly questioned, feeling somewhat shy as she remembered the exact moment when Cetán had mentioned Panther Stalks. "Why did you mention Panther Stalks earlier?"

There was no need to elaborate her question. Cetán's dark eyes met Desire's, and for a few seconds, he lost himself within their brilliant depths. Setting aside the bowl, Cetán cautioned himself about the answer he would give. A woman would not take kindly that her husband believed her capable of lying with another warrior. "I confess, I believed there was more between you and Panther Stalks than there truly was, Wacin." There was no easy way to make this confession.

"You mean . . . you thought . . . Panther Stalks and I . . .

you thought . . . we . . . we did this?" Desire could not continue. She stared at Cetán incredulously. Seeing the concern on her husband's features, a smile eventually settled over her lips, and then the giggles began. Desire was soon rolling upon the sleeping couch. "You really thought that Panther Stalks and I had . . . had . . . oh, you know what I mean!" she managed to say between peals of laughter.

Cetán wondered what was so funny as he watched his bride's reaction. "Well, any warrior would think the same, Wacin. When I brought the bride price to your father, you did not smile at me like you did at Panther Stalks."

Cetán was serious. Desire forced herself to calm the laughter that still threatened to spill from her lips. "I only smiled at Panther Stalks because I was nervous, Cetán. I knew him because he is from my father's village. I did not know you, Cetán." She did not reveal that all she knew about him was that one glance at him could cause her body to tremble and her heartbeat to race.

Cetán gave his belief one last defense. "Panther Stalks taunted me that day when we fought, saying that you and he were more than friends." Cetán could still hear the other warrior's voice in the back of his mind. It still had the power to stoke his anger. *Wacin's lips taste of the sweetest honey. When I hold her in my arms, her sighs of pleasure fill my ears!*"

"He taunted you? You mean that Panther Stalks told you . . . that . . . he and I . . . ?" Desire's humor faded to anger. How dare Panther Stalks insinuate that something had taken place between herself and him. How dare he let anyone think that she . . . she . . . would have joined herself with a warrior before being joined in the tradition of the people. "The only thing that ever happened between Panther Stalks and myself is that he caused me to faint one day near the river!"

"What did he do to you, Wacin?" Cetán's fingers gently closed around her forearm. His dark eyes filled with ven-

geance as he questioned his bride about the treatment she
had received from the other warrior. He should have killed
Panther Stalks when they had fought and he had had the
opportunity in front of Wacin's people! If Desire told him
that the warrior had harmed her, he swore silently, he
would leave the village in the morning and face Panther
Stalks in mortal combat!

"Why, he smothered me!" Teasing lights of laughter
again filled Desire's honey-gold eyes.

"What do you mean, he smothered you?" Had the warrior tried to steal her, and somehow covered her face with
something causing her to faint?

"He kissed me, Cetán. It was the morning after I left my
father's lodge and found you playing the *siyotanka* beneath
the cottonwood tree. I wanted to discover if another warrior's kisses had the power that yours did." Her face began
to warm, and unable to look her husband in the face, she
stared at his broad chest, her eyes upon the faint scars
above his nipples.

"Panther Stalks kissed you, Wacin? But you say that he
smothered you?"

Did she have to fully explain everything to this man?
"Yes, he did smother me. When he joined his lips with
mine, he also covered my nose!"

It took Cetán another few seconds to fully understand
what had taken place that morning near the river. "His
kiss made you faint?" Then Cetán could not stop his own
laughter.

Now that Desire had explained, she no longer thought
the ordeal as funny as she had moments earlier. "He could
have killed me!" She pushed Cetán's hands away from her
arms.

"Killed you by smothering you with a kiss?" Cetán forced
himself to stifle his humor. His grin spread, but the husky
laughter stopped. "I've have never heard of a maiden dying
in such a way, Wacin."

"Well, if not for Elkhunter, there would be no telling what could have happened that day! When I came to, Elkhunter was standing guard over me. Panther Stalks acted as though I had fainted because of the power he had by joining his lips over mine!" She should never have told Cetán about Panther Stalks! She should have allowed him to believe what he wanted!

Stretching out upon the sleeping couch next to her, Cetán pulled his bride's reluctant form tightly against his own. She was hurt by his reaction to her revelation, but his relief was so great that nothing more had taken place between her and Panther Stalks, he was hard pressed to contain his happiness. "You are right, Wacin. I am glad that Elkhunter was there." The reality of what else Panther Stalks might have tried to force upon Wacin took seed in Cetán's mind. His grip upon her tightened with his thoughts of her lying defenseless, at Panther Stalks' mercy!

Desire's anger slowly eased, her body fitting against her husband's in a manner which set her pulse to racing. "After that morning, I didn't have the heart to experiment any more with joining my lips with any other warriors in the village!"

Cetán's laughter rumbled in his chest, but this time, he kept a tight leash on his humor. "I could have told you that night, under the cottonwood tree, that such experimenting would be wasted. The joining of our lips together is meant to be, Wacin. The feelings that exist when we come together could only exist between you and I." He turned her fully against his chest, his hand reaching down to tilt her chin upward. "When I join my lips to yours there is an awakening in my body."

"It is the same for me, Cetán," Desire softly confessed, and was greeted warmly by her husband's loving smile.

"This awakening that begins in the center of our bodies and spreads upward to the joining of our lips is the same when our bodies join. It is meant that you are mine, and

I am yours." His lips softly slanted against hers. "I have waited forever for this night, Wacin." Cetán pressed Desire's head against his chest, not allowing his passion for her to spring to life. Her body was too newly exposed to the bliss that could be had with their joining. "You are the blending of my tomorrows, my past, and this minute. My heart beats only because yours beats against it."

Desire sleepily listened to his words of adoration, content to be held tightly in his embrace, and to feel his heart beating against her breasts. She had never dreamed that being joined with a warrior could be so wonderful. She knew she had to guard against losing her heart to Cetán, and in so doing, she would not have to worry about losing that portion of herself that she had always fought so hard to retain. She would be like Medicine Woman. The old woman had joined with a warrior, but still remained the woman she wished to be. She would do the same. In order to accomplish this, she would keep herself from falling in love with her husband; as sleep ensnared her, her last thought was that this should be an easy task to accomplish!

Eighteen

Awakening as the first shafts of sunlight stole into the lodge, Cetán's first thoughts were centered upon the woman wrapped trustingly in his embrace. Turning his head to gain a better view of her beauty, he drew in a deep, steadying breath.

It was right that he should awaken to find his wife sleeping snugly against his side. His world was almost complete. Wacin had given her trust over to him completely, and their joining had proven more glorious than he had ever imagined. Now, all that remained in order to totally fulfill their destiny was for him to win his bride's love. In his heart, Cetán had no doubt that he would succeed. There was but a slender barrier standing in the way of that which he desired most. Being a man who did not waver easily, Cetán was sure he would soon woo the words he longed to hear from her lips: her vow that her love for him was as great as his for her!

Even in sleep, Wacin touched his heart with her innocent loveliness. For a few quiet moments, Cetán studied her. Her thick, dark curls twined around his forearm, filling his nostrils with the scent of wildflowers. Her heart-shaped face was tilted toward him, and he lovingly traced each precious feature. The lush sweep of lashes delicately dusting her rose-hued cheeks sent a fierce pang of desire stealing through him. He fought off the urge to gather her tightly in his arms and kiss those closed lids until she awakened and he could once again gaze into the sparkling-gold depths. Restraining the impulse, he continued watching her. In sleep, her lips appeared to pout in the most provocative fashion. Her small, firm chin lay trustingly against a piece of soft fur. Viewing her without hindrance, Cetán knew that if he were to ease away the fur, he would find incredible perfection. Never had his senses been so overwhelmed. This completeness that she brought to him was a new thing which seemed to capture him totally.

With a small, sleepy sigh, Desire snuggled closer against her husband's warmth, her body stretching against him with her inner feeling of well-being. As she slowly came out of her sleepy state, she smiled as she remembered the previous night.

Cetán could have easily spent the rest of his life lying here upon the bed of furs looking at his bride. But with her wakening, he was just as pleased as her copper eyes brightened softly. "I love to awaken to the warm rays of your beautiful eyes, mitáwicu," Cetán declared softly before his lips gently settled over hers in a morning greeting.

"Mmmmm, I thought I was dreaming." Desire enjoyed the feel of her naked body rubbing against her husband's.

"No dream could compare to what we have shared, mitá wicánte, my heart." Cetán's manhood stirred against the soft flesh of Desire's thigh, and with the tightening in his groin, he softly questioned, "Are you well this morning, Wacin?"

"You will learn that I rarely feel ill, Cetán. There is no need for you to worry about my health so much." Remembering his concern the night before, Desire hoped her husband was not one who tended to be preoccupied with her health.

Leaning over her, Cetán drew both of Desire's hands up and over her head, and held them there with one of his hands. "I do not worry about sickness now, Wacin. I speak of the soreness that you might feel."

Desire blushed. Her tawny eyes turned away as Cetán stared down at her, awaiting a reply. "I am fine, Cetán," she softly confessed. In fact, Desire had never felt better! Her senses were completely attuned to this man's magnificent body! He pressed against her, setting off a trembling that slowly began to spread through her limbs.

"You are to tell me what you feel, Wacin." Cetán wanted to explore the depths of his bride's passions as he had last night, but she was a novice. He did not wish to cause her undue pain; he wanted only to bring her pleasure. His kiss was gentle, his swirling tongue awakening temptations of the flesh that were wonderfully new to Desire.

As his kisses caressed the corner of her lip and began to make a warm path down her chin, Desire attempted to draw her arms from the hand that held them over her head. "I want to touch you, Cetán," she whispered against his cheek.

"Not yet. Tell me what you feel." Cetán's moist lips drew downward along the slender column of her throat, nibbling delicately against the curve of her collarbone to the upper fullness of her breasts.

A deep breath was inhaled as Cetán's tongue glided around the tempting rose crown at the point of one full breast. Desire's body moved closer, her breasts straining toward the moist heat of his swirling tongue. Again, the tip of his tongue traveled in a circular motion as it rotated and licked the taut peak. "Don't tease me so, Cetán." Again, Desire attempted to free her hands, wishing to allow them to roam over the muscular contours of her husband's body.

"What do you want, Wacin?"

"I want to feel you," Desire gasped as Cetán's lips gently tugged upon one delicate rose crest.

"What do you feel, Wacin?"

As his mouth opened to cover the tempting bud, Desire felt a burning heat quickening in the lower depths of her womanhood. As he drew the fullness farther into his mouth and began to suckle, the quickening became an aching throb. "I ache, Cetán. I want . . ." Caught up in the erotic assault of her husband's play, Desire cried aloud as his manhood brushed the moist cleft at the entrance of her woman's fountain. She positioned her lower body closer, seeking the fullness that she yearned for. But there was no satisfying her torment; Cetán held back still.

"What do you want, my heart?" Cetán wanted to hear her need expressed aloud. As he held the marble head of his fiery lance at the very doors of paradise, he endured the same burning need as she, but was determined that he would teach her the freedom to be shared in their relationship. He wanted her to tell him what she desired, as he would tell his own needs aloud to her.

"I want you, Cetán!"

"You want me to do what, Wacin?"

Desire pressed full against him, welcoming the feel of him between her legs, needing him to fill her, to ease the ache growing out of control by slow, burning degrees. This was so new to Desire, she was not sure what he wanted her to say. She knew only her need to feel her husband moving inside her, to have him quench the raging fires of her passions! "Join with me, Cetán. Fill me . . . put an end to this . . ." She'd said what he wanted to hear, not caring that she was responding entirely to his will.

Cetán released her hands, his swollen shaft slipping into her warm, tight sheath. Desire was consumed by the sensations clamoring inside her, the sheer pleasure of his touch, his weight upon her, his manhood filling her!

Buried deeply, his rigid manhood clasped tightly within her satiny depths, Cetán was instantly drawn into an eddy of exotic pleasure. As he moved with her in a steady, rhythmic motion, her moans were lost in his searing kiss.

Desire met the hard crush of his mouth with her own, her lips parting to accept the urgent thrust of his tongue. He kissed her over and over, his probing delving deeper and deeper into her tantalizing sweetness as he plunged his staff into her velvet heat.

Cetán fought an inner battle to remember to go slowly, not to fully partake of his wife's lush body, but the effort was more than any man could withstand. As her nails lightly raked his back and her buttocks rose to meet each thrust, he felt new fire stirring in his loins. Burning hotter and hotter with each thrust, he was mindless except for the need to bring her to pleasure and then experience his own release.

Faster and harder he plunged, driven on by a passionate, all-consuming fury. The muscles of her femininity contracted violently around the rigid length of his shaft, squeezing, holding, embracing the swollen organ as she rode upon the ecstasy of his manhood. Her body became a savage blending of pure rapture and wild torment as his deep stroking inside her inflamed her senses.

Their joining raced out of control when Cetán's hand slid between their bodies to find the secret button of passion hidden in the folds of her soft flesh. Intensifying her pleasure, his thumb and forefinger gently rubbed against the swollen nub. Her senses spinning out of control, Desire was lost to the incredible sensations his actions evoked throughout her body. Her mind whirled over the brink of delicious agony, then spun wildly out of control as a shuddering took hold of her inner depths, capturing his lance and racing headlong to the sweet, total satisfaction.

Cetán was pulled into the vortex of her climax, his own body surging in unison with the shuddering that had beset his bride, his seed erupting in an explosion of release.

They descended slowly, drifting contentedly as reality was slowly regained. Cetán could not seem to get enough of the feel of her tender flesh. He caressed her body, his senses breathing in her scent as his mind centered upon the uniqueness of their joining. Never had a woman so pleased him. Everything about Wacin drew him, enticed him!

Desire shifted slightly against Cetán; his dark gaze immediately drew over her, in concern. Silently, he rebuked himself for the greed his lust had provoked. He should have more control over his passions, not allowing the full brunt of his need to overtake his good sense.

"If you ask me once more if I am sore, I will scream, Cetán!" Desire grinned, seeing the concern in her husband's eyes. Rubbing her breasts seductively against his broad chest and feeling the tingling of her nipples, Desire softly assured him, "Surely I know my own body, Cetán. I feel wonderful! This is an excellent way to start a morning!"

Cetán groaned softly. The bold seductress that his wife was becoming could prove more tempting than he had ever imagined. Attempting to take his mind away from the tantalizing movements of her body brushing against his own, he pushed the fur cover away and started to leave the bed. "I will start a fire to take the chill out of the lodge before you rise, Wacin."

Desire did not respond with words. She rose on her elbows and pressed herself fully against her husband's bare chest, slanting her lips over his. The kiss was a sweet thank-you. Not only was Cetán offering to warm the lodge, as Desire usually did each morning, but he had chased away her fears she had about joining with her husband. No other could have introduced her into this world of pleasure so wondrously as Cetán!

His joy with this woman knew no bounds. This was the first kiss that Wacin had initiated, and he delighted in her. He had to use an iron-clad will, though, not to crush her to him and again partake of the sweet bounty of her body. Drawing in a deep breath with the release of her lips against his own, Cetán stared down into her fathomless gold eyes and had to fight off the beckoning he read in their depths. Clutching at anything that would distract him from the instant leap of fire in his loins, Cetán offered, "After we eat, we shall go and look at my horses."

Desire had totally forgotten about the promised outing. With the prospect of spending the day at her husband's side, her world suddenly seemed much brighter.

With the completion of breakfast, the couple set out hand in hand, to look over Cetán's herd. The morning was chilled with the first breath of winter air, and Cetán wrapped a softly tanned buffalo hide over his shoulders. As the pair made their way to the center of the valley where vast herds of horses were grazing, Cetán pulled Desire tightly against his side to share the warmth of the buffalo robe.

The river which ran through the Lakota valley, and the mountains on three sides, made a natural enclosure for the hundreds of horses that roamed over the valley floor. Many of the lead mares had been hobbled with twisted lengths of rawhide. Most warriors kept their best buffalo and war ponies tied or staked next to their lodges, fearing an attack by the enemy and the loss of prized animals. Cetán had no such fear where Whirling-Warrior's-Ghost was concerned. The large gray stallion would let no one approach him but Cetán. He would not hesitate to rise up on his back legs, teeth bared, at anything coming near him.

Cetán waved to several of the young boys watching over the horses this morning. Standing on a grass knoll, he proudly pointed out his herd. "Over there, those are my lead mares."

Desire heard the pride in her husband's tone. As her eyes went over the fine animals, she caught sight of Star and Whirling-Warrior's-Ghost. "I can see that you take good care of your horses, Cetán." The fine condition of his animals told much about the man. Cetán was protective of those things that belonged to him.

Cetán squeezed Desire lightly around the waist. "Would you like to ride down into the valley and take a closer look at the horses?"

"Of course," came Desire's instant reply.

Without hesitating, Cetán gave a sharp whistle that could be heard over the valley floor. Whirling-Warrior's-Ghost's ears perked; throwing back his long, gray mane, the stallion trotted in their direction, Star following closely at his heels.

"It would appear that Star has found herself the male of her choice and isn't about to let him out of her sight." Desire laughed aloud as she watched the fleet-footed little mare chasing after the larger animal.

"Upon occasion, animals are wiser than we humans; they do not linger over their decisions when it comes to choosing a mate." Cetán's huskily-voiced statement caressed her ears as the horses drew closer.

Admiring the large gray's beauty and size, Desire reached out to rub his nose.

Grabbing hold of her hand before it came into contact with Whirling-Warrior's-Ghost's deadly-sharp teeth, Cetán sternly admonished her. "He tolerates no one's touch but my own, Wacin." Fear filled Cetán as he imagined the damage the stallion could have done to his bride's delicate hand.

"Nonsense," Desire said, bristling at her husband's worry. "I have a way with animals. My father says it is a gift. Animals know I am no threat—I care only about their well being." Before Cetán could stop her, her free hand reached out and began to caress the light and dark gray silken strands of Whirling-Warrior's-Ghost's mane.

Cetán's heartbeat tripped several breathless beats until he realized that the mighty war horse was standing easy beneath Wacin's touch. "This is amazing! Never have I seen him so relaxed around anyone but myself." The great beast was moving closer to the hand caressing him, his large head pushing gently against her arm as though wishing for her to continue the attention.

"As you said, Cetán, sometimes animals are much wiser than humans." Desire smiled as she glimpsed the admiration in her husband's eyes.

Cetán did not allow her to ride Star. Instead, he lifted her up before him on Whirling-Warrior's-Ghost's back. At first, the animal snorted and sidestepped, letting his master know he was not used to the extra weight on his back. But Desire softly spoke to him in reassurance, and soon the animal's tension eased.

Star followed closely as Cetán led Whirling-Warrior's-Ghost down into the valley. Desire pressed her back as close as possible to Cetán's chest, enjoying the feel of the motion of the horse, the warmth of the robe, and her husband's body encircling her.

As Cetán pointed out a stallion or mare and told Desire something about their merits, she realized that her husband practiced horse breeding to a remarkable degree. He was breeding his animals for size, task, swiftness, and colors, the most prominent being the pinto. On an average, they stood fourteen hands, having strong features; the Indian ponies' heads were somewhat larger in proportion to their bodies. These animals were much swifter and more durable, due to their rigorous life on the plains, than the larger horses of the wasichu.

Desire listened attentively as Cetán told her of his plans for his animals, and pointed out the buffalo and war ponies that he worked with frequently. These horses were especially prized by the Plains Indians, for their lives greatly depended upon them. Cetán's ponies were coveted by members of his tribe, and even those of other villages. He had gained much wealth in trade, because of his ability to teach buffalo and war ponies how to react swiftly and with assurance.

As the morning passed, Desire's admiration for her husband grew. Not only was Cetán a great war chief, he also planned wisely for the future.

It was early afternoon when the couple left the valley on horseback and slowly made their way along the winding river. "Would you like to swim for a while, Wacin?" Cetán questioned. As the sun had warmed them, the buffalo robe had been folded and settled on Whirling-Warrior's-Ghost's back.

"A swim would be wonderful, Cetán." Their swim this day would be far different from those in the past. A new-found relationship had sprung up between the couple since last night, and admittedly, Desire was filled with anticipation for the afternoon ahead.

Nineteen

A gasp of surprise escaped Desire, but was lost within the cover of Cetán's mouth as he plied her with ravishing kisses. Here at this isolated portion of the river, the couple swam together for some time, their play turning more serious. The temptation was more than either wished to resist. The cause of Desire's surprise: the rush of cool water entering her warm depths as she prepared to receive her husband's passion.

Gently, Cetán brought her legs up and wrapped them around his hips, his legs braced apart to carry their full weight as his manhood filled her, his lips covering hers hungrily.

The water intensified Desire's sensitivity. She felt each curve and muscle of Cetán's body; her breasts pressing against the hard contours of his chest stirred the dusty rose-buds to hard nubs. The contact of his hands caressing her buttocks, gathering her legs and setting them against his hips, took her breath away as she felt his hands upon her thighs gently easing her downward. As she felt the velvet smoothness of his lance touch the core of her passion, her heart seemed to stop; with the feel of him sliding into her, she expelled her breath with a gasp, an uncontrollable shudder traveling over her body. She felt the water circling her, filling her, a small amount of the coolness traveling before the heat of Cetán's powerful shaft, showering into the depths of her womb. Desire felt herself rocking back and forth upon his manhood. She was on fire and being quenched at the same time.

Cetán was lost upon the surging tide of passion. He felt every movement of her body as she pressed against him. The tightness of her sheath moving back and forth on his love-tool became the very center of his existence. He felt the flaming cauldron of white-hot passion in his loins, and when Desire cried his name aloud, her head thrown back, eyes tightly closed, Cetán met her release with a storming climax, his seed expelling as he clutched her tightly against his heart.

For a time, the couple could not move nor dare to breathe as their bodies slowly calmed. The fire-laced passion that had so fiercely claimed them waned by slow degrees as their lips joined in a tender kiss.

Desire was absolutely amazed! It did not seem possible that every time they joined, it was better than the last! Her golden gaze traveled over Cetán's handsome face, his eyes questioning as they met hers. He wondered if her thoughts were similar to his own.

"Surely no two people upon Mother Earth have ever experienced these feelings that you and I have shared, mitá wástélakapi, my love." Cetán's forefinger lightly traced the delicate outline of her face, drinking in her beauty.

"I was thinking the same thing, Cetán. Will this joining between us always be like this?" Desire wondered if she were up to such potent feelings, if each time the act was more glorious than the last.

Cetán understood her thoughts. A hearty chuckle escaped his throat. "For us, mitá wicántc, passion will only grow, as will the feelings of our hearts. It is fated by the will of The One Above!"

His words reminded Desire to stand guard against the treachery of the heart, not to allow herself to be lulled by such statements. But, in Cetán's arms, the cool water surrounding them, their wondrous passion still in the forefront of her mind, the effort was too much for Desire. She pushed the need to guard her heart aside. She would remain the person she had always been! Did she not deserve this moment? What harm could there be if she enjoyed her husband's attentions, his words of love filling her ears? Tomorrow, she would think about protecting herself against Cetán's masculine charm . . . tomorrow she would worry . . . today she would enjoy her happiness.

The winter months slowly passed in the Lakota valley, and for Desire, they were a time of awakening to her woman's awareness. She enjoyed her husband's attentions, thriving on the closeness developing between them and often daydreaming about Cetán at the oddest times. Many times, while sitting with Autumn Dawn and some of the other village women, sewing and sharing everyday matters, Desire found herself lost to the conversation. Her sweatlodge vision and the reality of what she and Cetán shared each night upon their sleeping couch filled her inner vision with passionate reminders of the heated words of love and searing caresses which Cetán had showered upon her the night before.

Desire had never been happier. When she left Cetán's lodge she could not wait to return. When Cetán was away hunting or raiding, she counted the hours until his return. As the days passed, she did not allow herself to look too closely at this new-found relationship. It was enough that she was happy. She didn't want anything to intrude upon her world. She was being selfish, but she didn't care. Nothing mattered except the feelings she experienced when Cetán was nearby. Many times, when her passion for her husband's body had cooled, she would attempt to fully explore her feelings for Cetán. But, instead of waning, her desire for him seemed to grow more out of control with each passing day.

This evening, Spirit Walker joined Cetán before his fire while Desire worked on the hair-pipe bone breastplate she was making for her husband. Now and then, she looked up from her work, her gaze going to the center fire to rest upon Cetán. Early evenings were a peaceful time after a long day, and often some of the warriors would come to visit and smoke their pipes with Cetán. Their talk was mostly about hunting and raiding, but these days with the snows heavy in the mountains, there were few braves daring enough to venture very far from the village.

The breastplate that Desire was fashioning for Cetán had beaded leather ties which would join behind the neck. There was a beautiful quilled ornament that dangled in the center of the breast, and brass beads were fashioned in two rows down the middle. An eagle talon dangled at the bottom of the center beadwork, and vermillion-dyed leather fringe decorated both sides. Desire would make a matching armband and a headband in a similar pattern. She was anxious to finish her task and admire her handiwork on her husband's body.

Cetán looked toward the sleeping couch he shared with Wacin, and a tender smile parted his lips. Desire looked across the center fire at that same instant, and a quick flush of heat caught her unaware. It seemed incredible that even after these weeks of sharing her husband's sleeping couch, he could make her feel so warm inside by just the simplest look. She lowered her gaze back to her work, glad she had something to occupy her thoughts besides what would take place later in the evening upon this same bed of furs.

"It is good that my blood-brother is content here in his lodge on these cold nights." Spirit Walker had not missed the smile that Cetán had bestowed upon his bride.

Cetán nodded his dark head in agreement. "I am a happy man, my friend. Now I understand why you often declined my offer of going on the hunt so often in the past."

Spirit Walker laughed softly. "I admit I am a man bewitched by my wife, brother. I am content to sit and look upon Autumn Dawn's beauty and allow my days to pass. Even great with my child in her belly, she is the most beautiful of women."

Cetán agreed. It was true that Autumn Dawn, with her copper colored hair and large, blue eyes, even with her abdomen swollen, was incredibly beautiful. "We are both lucky men." Cetán looked toward Wacin, the dark lights in the depths of his eyes reflecting his admiration of his wife's fair beauty.

"I will leave you to pursue a more pleasant ending to your evening than sitting here and speaking of combats long past." Spirit Walker rose to his feet.

Cetán felt guilty, not wishing to appear inhospitable, but Spirit Walker quickly put his mind at ease.

"Autumn Dawn has not felt well throughout this afternoon. I would not have left my lodge for the short time I already have, except that she was complaining that I was driving her mad with my worry over her every movement."

Desire heard this last portion of the conversation, and immediately set her work aside. "Is it time for the babe?"

Spirit Walker nodded solemnly. "Each time Autumn Dawn carries my child, I worry that she remains safe. I helped her when she delivered my daughter. That day I witnessed the great pain which a woman must endure to bring a life into the world."

Desire was surprised at this warrior's answer. It was rare that a Sioux warrior assisted in a birthing. Most men believed that a woman's blood held power that could contaminate them. Spirit Walker was a wiser man than many, and the fact that his wife was a wasicun winyan probably was part of the reason he had helped her with their first child's birthing. "Send for me, Spirit Walker, when Autumn Dawn needs me," Desire reminded her friend's husband.

The tall warrior smiled his thanks. "Autumn Dawn claims she will have no other to help her with this babe. When her time comes, I will come and sit here by my brother's fire."

With Spirit Walker's leave-taking, Desire quickly put away the breastplate. With one glance she made sure that her medicine bundle was in its usual place, in case she was needed later in the evening.

"Spirit Walker is a happy man," Cetán reflected, his dark eyes roaming over his bride.

Desire did not reply, but instead straightened the furs on their bed.

"I also look forward to the day when you and I will bring another life into our lodge." He could only imagine the beauty of a child that would be nurtured by Wacin's body.

"I thought you were happy with me, Cetán." This was his first mention of children, and Desire felt somewhat uncomfortable with the conversation. "Is it not enough that you and I are happy with one another? Why should we need anyone else in our lodge?" Desire thoroughly agreed with Spirit Walker's words: a woman's pain was far too great in order to bring a baby into the world.

"It is because of what we share, that I wish to share what we have with a child made from our bodies, created by our love." Cetán was taken by surprise with her words. He would never have thought that Wacin would not wish to have children right away. She was so loving and generous of heart that he believed she would feel the same as he and wish a baby as soon as possible.

"But I am not sure of these feelings I have. Everything is so new. Why do we have to rush things? Why can't we go on as we have been for these past few weeks?"

Cetán glimpsed the paleness of Wacin's features from across the lodge. Rising from his backrest, he went to her. His arms encircled her and drew her against his body. He had no intention of pushing her into anything. Everything they had between them was new, and at times frightening to her, and he had no thoughts of making her accept anything she was not ready for, even talk of babies. "I am happy to hold you, Wacin. I am content in my lodge, and able to look across my fire at your beauty. This is enough for me." His head descended to place a gentle kiss upon her soft lips.

"Will you be content forever like this, Cetán?" Desire could not help pressing herself to his warmth, her senses spinning out of control because of her husband's nearness.

"As long as you are mine, I am content, Wacin. Nothing else matters." His large hands ran down the length of her arms, marveling at the softness of her flesh. It was true; he would be forever content, as long as she was at his side. He could live the rest of his life without anyone else, but he could not live without Wacin!

Small pinpricks of guilt settled over Desire as Cetán's dusky gaze traveled over her face. Perhaps she should confide her fears in him, she told herself, but before she could get the words out that would make him understand, a call from outside the lodge disturbed the moment.

It was Spirit Walker bringing the news that Wacin was needed at the birthing hut, set up near the river. Autumn Dawn had already gone to the hut with two of the village women; they waited for Wacin to join them to help with the ordeal ahead.

All thoughts about her own fears of having children fled as Desire hurriedly began to gather the things she would need for the birthing. With her medicine bundle clutched in her hand, she took a moment to give Spirit Walker ease. "Do not fear, Spirit Walker. I will allow nothing to happen to Autumn Dawn. She has become a dear friend, and I have much knowledge of birthings."

Cetán gave her one last smile of encouragement before Desire hurried from the lodge and made her way to the birthing hut.

The interior of the hut was small, half the size of a normal lodge. By the time Desire arrived, Water-Spirit-Woman and Falling Leaves had started a fire, and Autumn Dawn was lying upon a pallet of thick furs. Desire was greeted warmly by all three women as she pushed aside the entrance flap and entered the hut.

"I hoped that you would arrive soon." Autumn Dawn attempted a small smile, but a sharp pain made the effort look more like a grimace.

"I came as soon as Spirit Walker arrived at my lodge." Desire immediately began to pull items out of her medicine pouch. A parfleche of water was hanging from a deer antler near the fire. Desire handed the eldest woman of the group, Fallen Leaves, a small horn vial containing the crushed roots of the western sagebrush plant, which when made into a tea would help a woman deliver her child easier.

As Falling Leaves did as she was instructed, Water-Spirit-Woman placed several braided strips of sweet grass on the flames. Instantly an aromatic odor filled the hut.

Autumn Dawn lay back against the furs, the scents assailing her to give her renewed strength.

Going to the laboring woman's side, Desire spread out the rest of her supplies at the foot of the fur pallet. Opening another horn vial, she poured a small amount of lotion into her palm. The lotion was made from pine seeds and rose hips, the fragrant odor filling the space around the pallet. "Relax, Autumn Dawn. I will massage your stomach to bring you ease," Desire offered. Medicine Woman had mixed the lotion, and Desire had watched her use it many times in the past. There was also a soothing herb mixed in the lotion with properties for numbing the flesh.

"You have been in labor most of the day," Desire reaffirmed as her hands lightly massaged the rounded mound of Autumn Dawn's abdomen. "You should not have too much longer before the babe comes." After checking for the position of the babe and insuring that all would go well with the delivery, Desire said, "Relax for a few minutes and then I will help you into a sitting position."

Before Autumn Dawn was helped from the pallet, Falling Leaves brought the warmed tea, and as instructed, Autumn Dawn drank down the contents of the medicine bowl.

"The baby will come soon now." Desire helped Autumn Dawn to rise, and going to the prepared place in the hut, she clutched the stake that had been driven into the ground, and bore down as Desire coaxed her between contractions.

Trying to take Autumn Dawn's mind off the labor, Desire questioned her about what Spirit Walker had mentioned this evening about his helping her deliver their first child. Autumn Dawn enthusiastically told Desire about how she and Spirit Walker had met, stating that she had been attacked by a large grizzly bear in a meadow and Spirit Walker had bravely charged the dangerous animal, leading him off into the forest in order for her to escape his deadly claws. She had also told Desire about being stolen from her husband by her stepfather and the man he had auctioned her off to at a rendezvous. The two men had held her captive in a whorehouse in St. Louis. She had been pregnant with their daughter Crystal Heart at the time, and after being rescued by Spirit Walker, she had gone into labor on the trail returning to her husband's village.

Desire had never realized how strong a woman Autumn Dawn was until this moment. Her admiration only grew as the woman's labor increased. Rarely did the beautiful white woman complain as unbearable pain ripped through her body. She spoke with pride about her children and her husband, adding that she and Spirit Walker wished to have more children. They believed that their joining had been destined, that their children would be strong, healthy warriors and maidens.

Autumn Dawn's labor was not as long and hard as many

Desire had witnessed. The tea did its work quickly, and with the passing of another hour, a healthy baby boy was lying on the piece of fur placed in the small dugout to catch the infant the moment it left its mother's body.

Desire's features were aglow as she looked the baby over, then finished with the necessary work before helping Autumn Dawn lie back upon the fur pallet. As the women washed the infant and wrapped him in a soft piece of fur, Desire took out the small piece of her medicine root that was wrapped tightly in her medicine bundle. There was very little left. She would need to go to the forest near her father's village for more as soon as possible. As Autumn Dawn closed her eyes in exhaustion, Desire went to the fire and heated the shavings of the medicine root, making a healing tea that would insure that her friend did not take fever or birthing infection.

After Autumn Dawn drank the tea and was made comfortable, Desire took up the two small beaded objects she had made for the child's birth. Autumn Dawn, having neither mother nor grandmother in the village, had been happy when Desire had expressed her wish to make the little beaded turtle and sand lizard for the child's use.

Both small objects had been gracefully shaped, then trimmed with horsehair and breath feathers attached to the ends of the four legs. Desire enlisted both of these animals' protective powers because of the belief that they lived forever and were so difficult to kill; their power would ensure that the child lived a long life. Earlier, she had cut away a piece of the umbilical cord, and now, she placed this inside the turtle along with herbs with healing properties. The sand lizard would serve as a decoy to lure away malevolent forces that might wish to claim the child's life. The turtle was to remind the child that his existence was a precious gift from his parents, that he had the responsibility to join with a maiden and to pass the gift of birth and life on to his own children.

Desire fastened the sand lizard to the outside fur that
covered the infant; the turtle was secured inside, next to
his warm body. When the child would first begin to walk,
the amulet would then be fastened to his clothing, and
throughout his childhood it would be close as a reminder
of its purpose.

Desire took the child into her arms and smiled down at
his perfect features and feathering of dark, fine hair. He
was beautiful, and her heart began to skip with a breathless
beat as she marveled at the tiny perfection. For a time,
Desire sat next to Autumn Dawn and the two women admired the infant in companionable happiness.

It was Autumn Dawn who finally expressed her desire
that her friend show the infant to his father.

Desire willingly obliged. Proudly, she made her way
through the village to her own lodge, where she knew Spirit
Walker was waiting to receive word about his wife and child.
Pushing aside the entrance flap, she entered the lodge with
the little bundle held tightly in her arms. As she saw Spirit
Walker rise from his position next to Cetán beside the fire,
she drew away the fur that covered the infant's body.

Spirit Walker grinned widely, his dark eyes glittering with
happiness. "And my wife? She is well?" His eyes looked
into Desire's features as though he would measure not only
her words, but her expression when she answered.

Desire's grin was as wide as Spirit Walker's. "Autumn
Dawn is well. She is resting." Her golden gaze went to her
husband; her gaze had the power to draw him from his
backrest, to his friend's side.

"So, you have two fine sons now, my brother." Cetán
slapped Spirit Walker on the back, happy for him and his
wife.

"Isn't he wonderful, Cetán?" Desire wrapped the babe
in the fur, her own gaze unable to leave the perfect little
features.

"Perfect in every way," Cetán replied, believing the babe

in his wife's arms the most beautiful thing he had ever seen because Wacin herself was so happy with the little bundle.

Spirit Walker laughed aloud. "When you have your own child, brother, I hope I am there to share the moment with you." He recognized the true feelings that both his blood brother and his wife had for his child.

Cetán said nothing to Spirit Walker's comment because of the earlier discussion he and Wacin had about children, but as he looked back to his bride, he saw that a smile was still upon her lips, her head gently nodding in agreement with Spirit Walker's words.

Twenty

The birth of Autumn Dawn and Spirit Walker's child
became the focus of much celebrating over the next few
days. The morning following the birth of his son, Spirit
Walker gave away three of his finest ponies to the poorest
in the village. That same afternoon he arrived at Cetán's
lodge in a solemn mood, clutching a beautifully beaded
and fringed pipe-bag. The pipe inside was very old, and as
the two men sat beside Cetán's fire, Spirit Walker drew it
from the bag with reverent hands.

"I come this day to my brother's lodge to invite him to
perform the Aló Wanpi ceremony for my new son."

Desire's attention turned from her medicine plants toward the two men. Her eyes rested upon her husband; she
as well as Spirit Walker awaited Cetán's response to such
an honor.

"I am very honored that my brother would ask me to
sing over his new son," Cetán stated, his voice filled with
genuine gratitude. The Aló Wanpi ceremony was not taken
lightly; a warrior invited only a trusted member of the tribe
to make this pact with his child.

Spirit Walker filled the bowl of his pipe with kinnikinnick
and brought a twig from the fire to ignite the tobacco.
Drawing upon the stem, he exhaled the smoke, then
handed the pipe across the fire to his friend. "There is no
other that I would entrust with this honor, Cetán. My second son will be a great warrior one day. I wish him to have

you as his second father. You are the one I would have this son look to for instruction and guidance. I do not need your answer now. I will come back to your lodge this evening." This responsibility that he was asking of Cetán was a great one among his people, and Spirit Walker would not make his friend rush into something he was unsure of. In all the great ceremonies of the Sioux, there was not one that bound two together as closely as the Aló Wanpi. Spirit Walker's child and his blood-brother would be bound closer than father and son until one or the other died. This tie was stronger than any natural brotherhood, because the one that would sing over the Hunka, the child in the ceremony, would take his responsibility on with a willingness that was not imposed through birth.

The Aló Wanpi ceremony was seldom performed, and Cetán was well aware of the high esteem Spirit Walker demonstrated with his request. "There is no need to come back to my lodge this evening, brother. The moment I looked upon your child in my wife's arms, I knew he and I would grow close through the years to come. I am proud that you ask this of me. I will protect your son with my life, and see that he grows to adulthood with the knowledge of Wakán Tanka guiding his steps, and always holding the protection of the people in his heart." Cetán drew upon the pipe stem, then exhaled smoke that mingled with Spirit Walker's, wending its way upward through the smoke-hole. His words were a vow that was carried upward to The Great Spirit.

Desire felt tears fill her eyes as she listened to her husband's words. She also felt a bond with the child. Cetán's vow to protect the child and be his teacher throughout his life only increased her admiration for her husband.

"I will speak with Medicine Cloud about performing the ceremony as soon as Autumn Dawn has recovered." Spirit Walker's smile was broad. "I would also ask that you name my son during the ceremony, Cetán."

"I will think upon this matter very carefully, my friend."
Cetán promised; he was now doubly honored, and took
Spirit Walker's request very seriously.

The Aló Wanpi ceremony was similar to that held for
the Sun Dance, but on a much smaller scale. A special pipe
was used, decorated with woodpecker feathers because this
bird was a simple creature which stayed near his nest and
was seldom seen. A small tree was erected in the designated
area, and a buffalo skull altar set up. The ceremonial articles included an ear of corn, a tuft of white down signifying
the child's hair, and a bunch of shed buffalo hair.

The entire village turned out for the Aló Wanpi ceremony for Spirit Walker and Autumn Dawn's son. It was a
festive time for the villagers as the elders sat upon Mother
Earth and visited with their neighbors while the women
gossiped and ran after their children.

As Medicine Cloud, the ancient medicine man of the
Lakota village, entered the area, the medicine drums began to sound. The old shaman began to blow on his bone
whistle as he called forth the spirits that would oversee the
ceremony soon to take place.

Medicine Cloud made his way to the front of the altar.
Unwrapping the pipe bundle, he withdrew the pipe decorated with woodpecker feathers. Earlier, a fire had been
started at the front of the altar, and now the wicasa wakán,
or holy man, placed braided lengths of sweet grass on the
low-burning flames. As the sweet grass began to ignite, he
filled the bowl of the pipe with Indian tobacco and then
began to draw on the stem. As the smoke swirled around
him, Medicine Cloud took a medicine fan from his bundle
and began to fan the smoke over himself, the pipe, and
the articles in his medicine bundle.

As the drumbeat held a steady rhythm, Spirit Walker and
Autumn Dawn entered the sacred area with the Hunka

child. Cetán was the last to approach the altar; Desire watched from a distance, pride brimming her eyes.

As the small group stood near the altar, Medicine Cloud began to chant a prayer for the child in Autumn Dawn's arms. With the finish, he again drew upon the pipe, then fanned the smoke over the length of the baby.

Cetán entered the area with a large parfleche in hand. He pushed aside the leather flap and withdrew a white buffalo hide.

The villagers gasped in astonishment. An albino buffalo robe was so rare there had been only two others recorded in Sioux history. Many of the villagers recalled that Cetán had been the owner of such a magnificent robe; several years earlier, he had killed the large white tatanka. But few had ever seen the valuable hide until this moment.

"I give this robe to this child, who will be known from this day forth as White Buffalo," Cetán said loudly so all could hear his words clearly. He opened the buffalo robe and Spirit Walker lifted the infant out of the piece of fur that Autumn Dawn had wrapped him in and placed him upon the robe in Cetán's arms.

Handing the child back to his father, Medicine Cloud bent to his medicine bundle and picked up the paint that would be used in the ceremony. Giving the small horn vial to Cetán, the warrior began to paint the Hunka strips on the babe. In a singing tone he chanted the promises of protection and leadership that he would give unto White Buffalo, from this day forth.

The baby cried throughout much of the ceremony, and at the finish, Cetán took him from his father. "White Buffalo has strong lungs—this is good for a little warrior."

Spirit Walker drew Autumn Dawn tightly to his side. "It is good that my son has a second father as generous and wise as Cetán."

The villagers encircled the group near the altar, Desire among them, as they offered their congratulations and looked with awe at the sleeping child lying in Cetán's arms upon the white buffalo robe.

Desire could not take her eyes off her husband and the baby he cradled so lovingly in his arms. A trail of jealousy traced its fingers unwillingly down her spine, and with an effort, Desire banished such emotions. She had believed she would never want children, but looking at her husband this minute, she knew in her heart that she would suffer any pain to see Cetán looking down at their own child with such gentle love.

A tear escaped her eye, and she brushed at it with the back of her hand as she stepped to her husband's side, her arm slipping around his waist. She was welcomed into the happy group by Autumn Dawn's warm smile and Cetán's dark eyes, speaking silently of his feelings for her.

The rest of the afternoon and far into the night, the villagers celebrated. Feasting and dancing were always welcome activities to the Sioux, and the Aló Wanpi ceremony was reason enough for the participants to celebrate.

Full from eating the plentiful food that Cetán and Spirit Walker had provided, and exhausted from dancing, Desire and Cetán left the celebrating, seeking the quiet of their lodge as the evening drew on. Once inside, Cetán turned her around to face him; without hesitation, he pulled her into his arms, his mouth covering hers in a hungry kiss.

"I have wanted to do this all afternoon," he said and sighed softly against her cheek.

Desire wrapped her arms over his shoulders and interlocked her fingers behind his neck. "I was very proud of you today, Cetán," she confessed, keeping secret her own desires throughout the afternoon for her husband to do exactly as he now was.

"It is good that a wife is proud of her husband." Cetán grinned and nibbled lightly against the tender flesh beneath her ear.

"You truly love children, don't you?" She saw him once

again in her mind's vision, holding White Buffalo, and all those same emotions flooded through her.

"Mmmm," he murmured as he feathered kisses along the slender column of her throat. "I will love our children, second only to you," he whispered against the ties of Desire's hide dress.

"*Our children* . . . when I hear you speak like this, my fear of having children flees me." She knew she should guard her words, because she was still unsure of the feelings she harbored in her heart for her husband, and her fear that she could easily give him too much power over her. But at the moment these fears seemed groundless as she stood in her husband's embrace and listened to the husky tremor of his voice. Desire had watched Autumn Dawn give life to her son through pain, but also with happiness, knowing that Spirit Walker would love her for the gift she gave him, their love growing stronger because of this life they had created with their bodies. In her heart, she longed to experience these same feelings, even though a part of her consciousness knew that before she had joined with this man, her life had been all mapped out and she had been content with her fate.

Cetán led her closer to the fire, and with adoring hands, he began to undress her. "Is this fear you have born from watching other women bringing forth life?" As her dress slipped to the floor, Cetán drew her down upon his backrest next to him.

Desire nodded silently, the heat of his body drawing her against him like a bee to honey.

"Your gift of healing came to you at an early age. Perhaps you did not understand the suffering that a woman endures in order for a child to be born and walk in the light bestowed upon him by The One Above. It is hard to understand the reason for such things when one is detached."

"You think that I am detached from the suffering I witness?" Desire's naked limbs were stretched over Cetán, her elbows on his wide chest as she looked into his face, trying to understand his full meaning.

"Never would I believe you would not feel another's pain, mitá wicánte." Cetán ran a caressing hand down her back and over a rounded hip and buttock. "I believe that you feel the pain of these that you heal more than you should. You take the pain of those suffering into your heart, because you are tender of nature—that is what makes you a fine healer. But being young and not experiencing what takes place between a man and woman and how two hearts can build enough love to put aside the pain of bearing children, the suffering you witnessed turned to your inner fear—fear of having children of your own."

Desire knew he was right. She also knew she was slowly overcoming these inner fears because of this man. When she had seen Cetán holding White Buffalo, she had wanted the baby to be her own child. "Why did you name the baby White Buffalo, Cetán?" She absently stroked the curve of his shoulder and collarbone, her golden eyes alive with lights of liquid amber as she stared into his loving gaze.

"A child with the word *buffalo* in his name always strives to be strong and wise. The little one will always attempt to accomplish that which his name implies. The white robe I gave him will nurture this sense of belonging to tatanka and Mother Earth. White Buffalo will grow strong and love the things of the people."

This man was so strong and so wise, Desire wanted only to share some portion of him. Leaning over, she lightly brushed her lips against his, then pressed them fuller, the allure of his taste and scent evoking a stirring in her depths that would not be satisfied until they joined.

Cetán's mouth opened, welcoming the sweet, searching intrusion of her moist tongue as she sought out each hidden crevice, and then erotically drew his tongue into her mouth, an inch at a time, with a tantalizing sucking motion.

A flame ignited in Cetán's loins, and the hardness of his

shaft intensified as it pressed against his breechcloth, the leather material a barrier to her tender flesh.

Reaching down, he attempted to untie the leather binding, but Desire gently pushed his hand to his side.

"You have had a tiring day, Cetán. I will attend your needs." Her slender fingers brushed against the flesh of his belly, causing Cetán's breath to catch in his throat as he deftly brushed away the tie and tossed the breechcloth to the side of the fire. Desire's eyes widened as she beheld the magnificent, velvet-covered lance of steel.

Cetán's face was stark with passion, ravenous for the feel of her, his muscles tense as he watched her reach out, her head lowering, the petal softness of her slightly parted lips caressing the smooth tip of his manhood.

Desire felt her woman's power as she never had before. She heard a searing gasp of passion as her fingers enclosed the heated shaft. Slowly, she explored that which brought her so much pleasure. Then, as though it were a most natural thing, her lips pressed softly upon the sculpted head as her moist tongue swirled around the heart-soft apex. A little noise rose from the back of her throat to mingle softly with the low groan that escaped Cetán's parted lips. His masculine scent ensnared her senses, as she lavished attention over the velvet-soft tip.

Her silken black hair flowed across the lower portion of Cetán's body; one slender hand was lightly splayed over his inner thigh, the other encircled the base of his mighty shaft. Her moist tongue slowly licked and sampled the length of his vein-ribbed hardness, then roamed back up in a manner which held Cetán breathless.

Swirling depths of molten gold locked with darkest night as Cetán reached down, his fingers encircling her chin, their gazes clashing with understanding; there was no need for words.

Desire rose over him, her fine-spun hair a curtain closing out the outside world. Slowly, she lowered her body, the

moist portals of her woman's passion opening to receive
Cetán's manhood. With bated breath her hips lowered, taking the hard fullness into her depths, her tight sheath grip-
ping the entire length of him.

All of Cetán's senses were ensnared by her warm embrace. His hands settled over her hips as he began to set
the pace, bringing the shapely curve of her buttocks to rest
on his lap, then back upward, traveling the full length of
his shaft.

Uncontrollable quivers of deepest passion assailed Desire as Cetán's lance brushed against her womb, then slowly
withdrew to the very lips of her desire. She moaned his
name aloud, her head thrown back, eyes tightly shut,
caught up in the motion of their love-making. Her body
moved in rhythm to the pace set by her husband's body
and hands. Blinding rapture caught flame, then spun upward in a kaleidoscope of beckoning fulfillment.

Rising up to meet her passion, Cetán's shaft pressed
deeper, his mouth covering a full breast and sucking gently
upon the rose-crowned nipple. He lost himself fully to her
incredible need, the trembling tightness of her sheath
sending him headlong into the outer boundaries of total
satisfaction. Upon the slender pinnacle of ecstasy, their passions collided to erupt in a swirling climax. Cetán's name
burst from Desire's lips as his mouth caught hers in a deep,
delicious kiss.

It was much later in the evening before the couple re-
tired to their bed of furs. For now, they were satisfied to
lie upon the mat of the backrest, the warmth of the fire
against their naked flesh, each responding to the other's
words of love.

Twenty-one

The winter months passed, and with them, Desire found herself fitting into the routine of her husband's village. More and more, the villagers called upon her to help cure their illnesses. Some of the warriors even asked her counsel on different treatments for their horses.

Desire's friendship with Autumn Dawn also grew during this time of little activity throughout the village. Her grasp of the English language increased as the two women worked on their sewing together and watched over Autumn Dawn's children.

With the melting of the snows and the arrival of greenery throughout the forest and over the Lakota valley, Elkhunter spent more time away from the village. Some evenings, while the great wolf lay near the warmth of the center fire, Desire could sense his restlessness. A wolf call in the distance would send him through the entrance flap, and often he did not return for several days.

A few days earlier, a hunting party had left the village for the first trip since the end of winter. Cetán had eagerly joined this group, knowing the people were hungry for fresh meat. This morning, as Desire gathered wood and filled her water pouches, her mood was anxious with anticipation. Cetán would return this day—and she had missed his presence in their lodge; especially long had been the nights spent without his body pressed up tightly against her own. She had not realized how much she had come to depend on her husband for comfort and for company.

A small smile teased her lips as she placed a piece of wood in her willow basket. Her thoughts centered on the pleasure that she and Cetán would share this evening.

Her daydreaming was brought to an abrupt halt by the call of her name. A youth hurried in her direction. "Wacin, you are needed in your lodge," the boy called.

"Has something happened to Cetán?" Thoughts of her husband having been injured circled her heart and threatened to squeeze until life disappeared from her body.

Flying Squirrel shook his head hard. "One of the braves was riding in the forest this morning and found the great wolf. He is breathing . . . barely!"

"Elkhunter?" Desire's heartbeat lurched in relief that it was not her husband, but as quickly, she responded to the need to be at Elkhunter's side. Dropping the pile of wood, she hurried after Flying Squirrel, toward her lodge.

The boy had not exaggerated about the graveness of Elkhunter's condition. Black Beaver, the brave who had found the wolf, and another brave were leaning over the animal trying to determine the extent of his injuries when Desire hurried through the entrance flap.

"What happened to him?" she cried softly as she hurried to the side of the center-fire, where the braves had stretched the animal out.

"The great wolf must have fought a matóhota," Black Beaver spoke, his eyes resting on Desire. In their depths she read the seriousness of the canine's condition.

As Desire looked down and saw the deep, long gashes raked down Elkhunter's back and ribs, tears of anguish began to slip unbidden from her eyes. Elkhunter must have been lying wounded in the forest for at least a day, maybe two, she surmised. A great amount of blood was dried on his silver fur, and the gaping wounds were already festering with infection.

Laying her hand over his head, Desire received her first indication that Elkhunter recognized her. A faint groan escaped his throat and his eyes blinked open for only a second, but it was time enough for their glazed gold to look fully upon Desire.

Time was of the essence if Desire had any hope of saving her pet. Her hands reached for the water pouch near the fire. As she began to bathe the wounds, her mind worked furiously ahead, to the things she would need from her medicine bundle. The two braves silently left the lodge, leaving the medicine woman to her work.

Desire only had time to bathe the worst of the wounds before the entrance flap was pushed aside and Cetán stepped into the lodge. Desire's gaze filled with gladness, but she dared not take the time now to properly greet her husband.

Cetán had been told about the wolf's serious injuries. His features were grim as he squatted next to Desire. As she sprinkled a yellow powder over the ugly, gaping wounds, he spoke softly. "I am sorry, Wacin. I only wish I could help you."

"There is nothing you can do now, Cetán. I am afraid too much time has already passed. The wounds are fevered."

Cetán's own news was not good, and watching Desire finish sprinkling the wolf's wounds with the yellow powder, his hands reached out to capture hers. "I also come for your help as a healer, Wacin."

Desire saw the seriousness in his ebony eyes. "What is wrong, Cetán?" Her gaze broke away and hurriedly roamed over her husband's body, reassuring herself that he was well.

"It is Bird Rattler, Wacin. Two suns past, we came upon a small herd of tatanka. Bird Rattler was gored during the attack. He will die if you do not take your medicine to his lodge."

"But, Cetán, how can I leave Elkhunter?"

Cetán's hands tightened over hers. "How can you *not* take your medicine to Bird Rattler? His mother and sisters are even now weeping at his side. His wife chants out his death song."

Desire knew in her heart that she had no choice. "I have only enough of my medicine root for one." Her tawny-gold eyes turned back to the wolf lying still, his breathing shallow from fever.

Cetán knew that his wife was in the grip of indecision. The animal had been her pet since childhood. Bird Rattler was also a friend, and the brave had a large family that depended upon him. He knew what she would do, and his heart ached for the decision she would be forced to make. "Where is this medicine root that you need, Wacin? I will go now and get this medicine. Perhaps there will be time for Elkhunter to survive if I go quickly." He would help her make the decision, and in the process, he would ease the full burden from her shoulders. With The Great Spirit's help, perhaps she would be able to ease the great wolf's injuries until he returned with the medicine root.

"You would go to my father's village and get the medicine root I need to save Elkhunter's life?" Tears filled her eyes.

"I will not rest until I bring back the medicine, Wacin." Cetán's hand rose from hers to brush away a tendril of hair from her cheek. "I know how great your love is for the great wolf. I would do anything to keep sadness from your heart."

The huskiness of his tone left Desire trembling. Looking into his dark eyes, she knew he was speaking the truth. He was exhausted, having rested little to make sure that Bird Rattler made it to the village where he would have a chance to survive. Now, he pledged he would go to her father's village and return with the medicine root, even if there was only a slight chance to save Elkhunter's life! All the tender feelings she harbored for her husband, instantly rose to the surface. At that moment, she knew she loved him beyond anything in this life! "Cetán . . . I . . . I . . ." she began, unsure how to express the feelings swelling in her heart.

Cetán's head lowered, his lips parting over hers in a heartfelt kiss. "We will speak of this later, mitá wicánte. Now, you must go to Bird Rattler's lodge. I will speak to Curly Bear and have him stay here with Elkhunter while I go to your father's village."

The couple shared a parting kiss after Desire gave Cetán directions which would lead him through the forest near her father's village, and to the river, where he would dig down into the earth and find the medicine root the matóhota had shown her years before.

Doing all she could for Elkhunter, Desire left him to Curly Bear's watchful eye; clutching her medicine bundle, she hurried to Bird Rattler's lodge.

Pandemonium had broken out in Bird Rattler's lodge among the women. Prairie Flower, Bird Rattler's mother, and her three daughters were kneeling around the wounded brave, who was lying next to the lodge's center fire. Their loud weeping filled the lodge and clashed with the sounds made by White Swan, Bird Rattler's wife. The young woman chanted loudly for the Great Spirit to take her husband up to the star path, and there in the paradise hunting grounds, make him a great warrior among the sky people.

At first sight of the warrior, Desire believed he had already passed to the other side. Bending, she pressed her ear against the bandage wrapped tightly around his chest. A slight sound held her for an added moment. Finally, she looked around at the women and commanded sharply, "Silence! Bird Rattler still lives. Why do you fill his ears with the sounds of weeping?"

Mother and sisters instantly fell quiet, their eyes open

wide as they looked toward Desire. "Can you help my son, Wacin?" Prairie Flower brushed at the tears streaming down her plump cheeks. She looked at the medicine woman with the first breath of hope she had experienced since the warriors had brought her wounded son into his lodge and laid him out on the pallet next to the center-fire.

White Swan continued to chant her husband's death song, her grief already at a stage where she felt only the searing pain of her heart, heard only her own voice in her ears.

"If we all work together, perhaps there is a chance that Bird Rattler will live," Desire stated, hoping the mother-in-law would be able to calm her son's wife.

Within a few seconds, the lodge was entirely silent. Prairie Flower stood at her daughter-in-law's side, her hand gently but commandingly resting on the younger woman's forearm. Desire did not linger, but began to pull out the things she would need from her medicine bundle. She held the medicine bone whistle between her teeth and blew on the stem, evoking the presence of her spirit helper; every now and then, her fingers would touch the bear claw necklace around her neck, the cool stone pendant caressing the softness of her palm.

As she unwrapped the bandage on the brave's chest, the gaping wound was revealed for all to see. An audible gasp went through the women. The buffalo had gouged Bird Rattle below the ribs on his right side, the hole oozing yellow matter and blood. Drawing in a sharp breath, Desire began an exploration of the wound, assuring herself that no vital organ had been pierced and that the injury was free of any foreign matter.

Prairie Flower approached Desire and squatted down at her side. "What would you have us do, Wacin, to save my son?" Her dark eyes looked at the medicine woman, counting on her knowledge to save Bird Rattler's life.

"We will need plenty of water to wash the wound, and

the fire should be built up. I will make a special tea after I clean the wound, and I will need help making Bird Rattler drink."

Within minutes, the older woman sent the younger women for wood and water. She remained at Desire's side, helping to clean away the blood and grime from her son's body.

Desire worked laboriously over Bird Rattler, but she was not sure her efforts would be enough. The brave lay unconscious, unresponsive to anything that was said or done to him. Desire feared he had already started the journey toward the star path and that the small piece of medicine root she had left in her bundle might be wasted. Again and again, her thoughts went to Elkhunter lying wounded in Cetán's lodge.

"Wacin, I must confess I have spoken ill of you to some of the elder women of the tribe."

Desire looked up as she wrung out a piece of trade cloth into the bowl of water at her side. "Have I done something to make you speak out against me, Prairie Flower?"

Instant tears filled her dark eyes as the woman began to shake her head furiously. "No . . no, Wacin. It was I who did wrong. You are from another village, and I had hoped Cetán would find favor with one of my daughters. I was jealous. You are so young, and I could not understand how it could be true that you could be such a fine healer, as I have heard the people declare. I am sorry for the things I have said against you, Wacin."

"Why do you tell me this now?" Desire began to clean the inside of the wound with a mixture of yarrow and scarlet mallow.

"I see your skill for myself, Wacin. I do not want The One Above to punish me by taking away my only son. I am a foolish old woman, but Bird Rattler is all that I and his sisters have. My husband passed over four winters past, and without a son to hunt for us, I do not know what will become of my family."

"The Great Spirit is wise enough to understand why you did what you did, Prairie Flower." Even Desire could understand the woman's jealousy. Any mother would desire a warrior such as her husband to join with her daughter in order to provide for the rest of the family; it was the way of the people. She certainly did not resent Prairie Flower for the feelings she had harbored. "Let us not speak of this again. It is enough that we are working together to save Bird Rattler's life."

After cleansing the wound, Desire packed the gaping hole with the same mixture of yarrow and scarlet mallow, but in a paste form; after this, she sprinkled the same yellow powder over the wound as she had earlier done to Elkhunter's gashes. "I will need a soft piece of fur and rawhide to bind it as a cover over the wound," she instructed Prairie Flower.

As the young women entered the lodge carrying wood and water, Prairie Flower hurried to her own lodge to obtain the required items that the medicine woman had requested.

Desire burned sweet grass in the flames, then began to blow upon her medicine bone whistle. The fingers of one hand wrapped around the stone pendant of her bear claw necklace as she drew the spirit of the great matóhota to Bird Rattler's lodge.

Several minutes passed before Desire dropped the whistle from her lips, its leather tie around her neck allowing it to lie between her breasts. In a singsong tone she began to chant prayers for The Great Spirit to bless her efforts, to guide the power of the matóhota to her side and help her medicine, making it strong enough to heal the injured warrior.

Taking up the slender piece of medicine root, Desire began to shave slivers into her medicine bowl. As soon as the rocks resting in the fire were glowing with heat, she instructed one of Bird Rattler's sisters to place the rocks in the parfleche of water suspended by a deer antler next to the fire. Soon the water came to a boil, and a portion was poured into the medicine bowl. The fragrance of the steaming root filled the lodge, and Desire began to count the time before it would be poured down Bird Rattler's throat.

Returning to the lodge with the fur and rawhide, Prairie Flower helped Desire pull Bird Rattler into a sitting position, then forced the heated liquid into her son's mouth.

Setting the empty medicine bowl down beside the fire, Desire helped the older woman settle the brave comfortably on his pallet. As she began to cover the wound with the piece of fur, she spoke softly. "I have done all that I know. The medicine I have given Bird Rattler may not be enough. Cetán rides now to my father's village to bring back more, but I do not know if he will arrive in time. What I gave him will help to fight off the infection that fills his body. The wound is clean; all we can do is wait and pray to The Great Spirit." Desire was anxious to return to her own lodge to see how Elkhunter was doing. As she gathered her belongings and placed them back in her medicine pouch, the tinkling of her bells was the only sound in the lodge.

Looking at the group of women, she saw the worry on their faces. "Let him rest for now. I will return soon and check his condition." She hoped they would not commence with their wailing the minute she left the lodge. Their earlier noises were enough to make any warrior long for the peace of the afterlife!

Curly Bear did not speak when Desire entered the lodge, but as he rose to his feet, the sharp nod of his head indicated that there was no change in the great wolf's condition.

"Thank you for staying with him, Curly Bear," Desire called after the warrior as he bent to exit the lodge.

Throughout the rest of the afternoon and evening, Desire left Elkhunter's side only to go to Bird Rattler's lodge. The condition of the wolf and warrior appeared similar; both were only a breath away from leaving Mother Earth to go on to join the ones in the sky.

Early the following morning, Desire awoke to find Elkhunter's condition not much changed from the day before. Perhaps his breathing was somewhat eased, she thought as she again washed his wounds and sprinkled them with the healing powder. But she feared he would not survive much longer if the infection in his body was not treated with her special medicine root.

Going to Bird Rattler's lodge, she found the women still gathered around the wounded warrior's pallet, but they no longer wailed or sang his death song. The medicine root had helped the brave—he slept the natural sleep of one who is healing. The women were overjoyed and could not thank Desire enough.

Pleased that her efforts had not been wasted, Desire warned the women to watch over the brave lest he have a relapse. She showed Prairie Flower how to clean the wound and apply the paste of yarrow and scarlet mallow inside the injury, then sprinkle the yellow powder over the outside. If there was a change for the worse, she was to send someone for her immediately. She had no intention of letting Bird Rattler die! Because of the brave, Elkhunter's chances of surviving were very slim; she would not allow that portion of the medicine root to be wasted!

All that was left for Desire to do now was to watch over the great wolf, as best she was able, until Cetán's return to the village.

Twenty-two

The following afternoon Cetán returned to the Lakota village. Both he and Whirling-Warrior's-Ghost were exhausted. The trip to Gray Owl's village and back usually was made in four days; he'd cut the time in half. Dropping the gray stallion's reins outside his lodge, Cetán hurried inside. Worry etched his features as he sought out his wife, who was sitting next to the center fire.

"He still lives?" Cetán had feared that Wacin's beloved wolf would not survive, and since leaving Gray Owl's village with the medicine root, he had dreaded facing the pain that would greet him when he arrived.

Desire choked back a sob of relief at the sight of him. "He still lives, but barely," she whispered, her voice cracking with emotion.

Cetán hurried to her side. Bending, he unwrapped the piece of hide clutched in his hand. At the sight of the precious root, Desire allowed herself to give way to her emotions for the first time.

"I did not think you would return in time, Cetán." Tears fell down her cheeks as sobs overtook her.

Setting the medicine root down, Cetán's powerful arms lovingly pulled her into his embrace. "I know that much has been required of you, mitá wicánte. You have been very strong. Now, I have returned. I will help you get Elkhunter better." Even as he said the words, he doubted that their efforts would be enough to help the ailing wolf. Elkhunter lay where Cetán had seen him last, next to the fire, his breathing labored and rattling.

Allowing Desire a few minutes to regather her strength, he gently drew her away from his chest. "Tell me what is needed. I will help you administer the medicine root." Cetán was not a man to give up without a fight!

Desire brushed away the dampness on her face, and with a trembling smile, she kissed her husband's cheek. "Thank you so much, Cetán. I don't know what I would do without you."

"You will never have to find out, Wacin, for I will always be at your side." His hand reached up to lightly caress her jaw. Desire would have leaned into him for comfort except that she was aware of the need to work against time if she was to save Elkhunter's life.

"If you will boil water for a medicine tea, I will start the healing ceremony." Desire's medicine pouch was not far away and within seconds, she was pulling the required items from her medicine bundle. The quiet in the lodge was soon broken by the sound of her medicine bone whistle as she called forth her spirit helper.

Several times in the past two days, Desire had blown on the bone whistle and chanted her prayers to The Great Spirit on behalf of the great wolf. She believed this was the only reason Elkhunter had held on as long as he had. Clutching the stone pendant in her fist, she pulled forth the image of the mighty matóhota. She could envision the dark, penetrating stare of the beast as she had seen it that day in the forest, long ago. Silently, she began to shave off pieces of the root into her medicine bowl. After Cetán brought the parfleche of heated water and poured the required amount into the bowl with the shavings, Desire counted the time before she brought the bowl to the wolf's mouth.

Cetán helped Desire lift Elkhunter's head and pour the healing tea down his throat. After he was settled down once again near the warmth of the fire, she pulled forth the medicine rattle Medicine Woman had given her. Clutching the ermine-wrapped handle with its dangler of deer claws held only inches over the animal's prone body, Desire shook the gourd, her voice rising in prayer, evoking the powers to allow the medicine tea to do its work and allow Elkhunter to live. Tirelessly, she shook the rattle and chanted. With the finish of her prayers, she began to beat out an awakening call to the spirits with her medicine drum, her eyes never leaving Elkhunter, waiting for a sign that he would live.

Time had no meaning in Cetán's lodge; the constant sound of the medicine drum filled the space as the couple watched and waited. Finally, Desire's hand stilled upon the drum. Quiet filled the lodge. She turned to face her husband, a wide smile on her lips. "Do you hear that, Cetán?"

"I hear nothing, Wacin."

"I know. Isn't the sound of quiet wonderful? Elkhunter's breathing has eased. The rattling in his chest is gone." She felt like laughing aloud, her relief was so great.

Cetán looked closely at the animal, and indeed, his breathing appeared less strained, his chest moving up and down in a normal fashion. "He will be well, Wacin."

"Yes, he will be." Desire leaned back into the comfort of her husband's sturdy chest in relief. These past two days had been tense and tiring; this was the first time she had allowed herself the pleasure of relaxing for a few minutes.

"Elkhunter will need much rest," Cetán said and lightly ran his fingers through Desire's hair. "Why do we not also rest for a while, now that we know he will be well?" He knew that his wife had had little sleep in the last two days. Cetán's body was tired, too, but his worry was for his bride.

"You go and lie down, Cetán. You are tired, but I must go to Bird Rattler's lodge to give him the medicine tea one more time. He is recovering slowly, but the tea will make sure he regains his health without threat of a relapse."

Cetán had been told by a brave when he rode into the village that Bird Rattler lived, and was improving hourly. The warrior owed his life to Wacin, who had given him her precious medicine root. "Your mother and father will be very proud of you, Wacin, when they arrive in our village and are told of your healing powers and generous heart." He grinned at her look of surprise. He had wanted to make a gift of this news of her parents' visit.

"They are coming here, Cetán? When will they arrive? Did my father say when they would leave the village?" It had been a long winter without being able to see her parents, and as her excitement grew, she bombarded her husband with questions.

"They were to leave this morning—they should be here tomorrow." Cetán's grin widened as he saw his wife's happiness. "Go now, tend Bird Rattler. I will be waiting here for you. Then I will tell you all your mother and father had to say."

Desire did not linger, but gathered her medicine pouch and precious medicine root. Leaving her husband's lodge, she made her way to Bird Rattler's tepee. The warrior was recovering slowly. With his family ever-present, he lay on his pallet, watching the interaction all around him.

Desire was pleased that Bird Rattler was awake and was warmly greeted by the warrior as she went to his side. "My mother tells me you are the healer that beseeched the spirits to allow me to remain here on Mother Earth. I thank you, Wacin. My family needs me—it is good that I will live."

Desire nodded and laughed aloud. "Yes, it is good that you live, Bird Rattler." After administering the measured amount of medicine root and once again chanting her prayers to the spirits to watch over the wounded warrior, Desire hurried back to her own lodge.

Upon entering, her gaze circled the interior and instantly fell upon her husband lying on their sleeping couch. Before joining him, Desire made her way to the center fire.

For a few minutes, she stood over Elkhunter, watching his steady breathing to ensure herself that he was still on his way to recovery.

Pulling off her hide dress, leggings, and moccasins, Desire climbed beneath the furs and settled her slender frame beside her husband. Cetán was already sleeping, but even deep in slumber, his powerful arms encircled her and held her in a loving embrace. "I love you, Cetán," she softly whispered against the warmth of his chest. His heartbeat filled her ears, lulling her to sleep.

Desire could not remember when she had felt as happy with life as she did at this time. Her mother and father, as promised by Cetán, arrived in the Lakota village late the following afternoon. Gray Owl and Pretty Dove were welcomed warmly by the villagers. The first evening of their arrival there was a feast, which most of the villagers attended. Later in the evening, there was storytelling around the large fire in the center of the village.

Chanting Squirrel, an elder of the tribe and the best storyteller amongst the Lakota, entertained with stories of the people's past. He sat before the fire, claiming the full attention of children and adults with his lively version of the legend of the white buffalo woman—the sacred woman who, in days long past, had brought the people the peace pipe. Before the finish of the evening, Chanting Squirrel told the tale of the white buffalo robe given by the mighty war chief Cetán to the child he had named White Buffalo during the Aló Wanpi ceremony. The storyteller told the people the story of Cetán's killing the wakán tatanka, or sacred buffalo, for his valuable hide.

Desire smiled with pride as her sherry-gold gaze went to her husband, who sat beside her father and a group of men. Chanting Squirrel had added much detail to the story, and Desire knew that from this day forth, her hus-

band's killing the white buffalo would become legendary
throughout the plains tribes. It would be repeated many
times around the fires as the old men smoked their pipes.

Desire was just as surprised when Chanting Squirrel began to relate the story of the great wolf called Elkhunter
being attacked by a matóhota, and a strong warrior known
as Bird Rattler being gouged by a tatanka. Her own name
was called aloud, as the storyteller related how the medicine woman Wacin had only enough of her sacred medicine root to heal one, and had gone to Bird Rattler's lodge
to save his life in order that he might live to protect his
family.

Cetán's dark eyes met his wife's as Chanting Squirrel
related that it had been Cetán who had ridden without rest
to the Oglala village; deep in the forest, he found the sacred
medicine root and returned to the Lakota village in time
to save Elkhunter.

Sitting next to her daughter, Pretty Dove glimpsed the
looks passing between Wacin and Cetán. "Are you still un-
happy that you joined with Cetán, daughter?"

As the storytelling finished and the people began to talk
and visit, Desire clasped her mother's hand tightly within
her own. "I am very happy, Iná. I love Cetán very much."

Pretty Dove grinned. "Does your husband know these
feelings that you have for him, daughter?" She suspected
that her son-in-law was still unsure of his wife's feelings.
When he arrived in their village, he had remained only a
short time, but Pretty Dove had gotten the impression that
the relationship between Wacin and Cetán was still very
fragile.

"I have told him only one time, Iná."

"And was he pleased to hear your words, daughter?"

"He was sleeping," Desire admitted to her mother's surprise.

Pretty Dove was not as surprised at her daughter's confession as perhaps another mother would be. Her daughter

had always held strange ways. She was aware that Wacin feared giving anyone power over her. "Do you think that you will tell him again when he can respond to your words, daughter?"

Desire's laughter filled her mother's ears. "Yes, I will tell him. How can I not, when I am so happy to be his wife? He is strong and good, and he loves me so much. I only wait for the right time."

"You are a good daughter, Wacin. Now I can be happy for you, and not fall to sleep each night worrying about you here in this Lakota village."

There was no more time for such private conversation between the two women. Cetán and Gray Owl approached, and the small group made their way back to Cetán's lodge.

The morning that Gray Owl and Pretty Dove were to leave the village, four braves from Gray Owl's village arrived and offered to escort their chief and his wife. Panther Stalks was one of the braves who made up the small hunting party.

Panther Stalks had been one of the first of the group to arrive in the Lakota valley. He did not approach the encampment directly, but instead, circled around, traveling along the riverbank. His hope was to find Desire with the other women of the village, gathering wood and filling water skins.

Knowing that her parents were going to leave early, Desire awoke earlier than usual. She left her husband's lodge with the intention of gathering wood, then returning to fix the morning meal before her parents started the long trek back to their own village.

At this hour there were no other women along the path leading to the river. Desire took a few minutes to speak her morning prayers aloud as the first traces of Wi broke through the morning sky.

Just as she finished and turned away from the direction

of the morning star, she was suddenly greeted by Panther Stalks. "I see that you are well, Wacin." The warrior's dark eyes greedily feasted over her body; in his eyes she appeared even lovelier than the last time he had seen her.

Startled by the confrontation, Desire took a few steps back on the path, her gaze resting on the warrior sitting atop a pony. With a glance, she noticed the way his gaze swept over her in silent appraisal. "What are you doing here, Panther Stalks?" Her anger surfaced as Desire remembered the things Cetán had said this warrior had boldly expressed while they had fought.

"Wolf Plume and a few other braves and I are returning from a hunting trip. We knew your father was in this village and thought to offer our company for the return trip home."

"I am sure my parents will be grateful for your escort." Desire curbed her feelings toward this warrior, knowing it would be much safer for her parents to travel with a group of warriors, rather than alone. She did wonder, though, where the other braves were and why this warrior was at the river alone.

He must have read the concern on her features, for he said, "I had hoped I would find you here this morning, Wacin, so I could speak with you."

"I must get back to my husband's lodge, Panther Stalks. My parents and Cetán will wonder at my delay if I do not hurry." To prove her words, she bent and picked up a few pieces of wood. In her heart, she knew her husband would not be pleased if he found out she was alone at the river talking to the other warrior.

"Is he treating you well, Wacin?" Panther Stalks waited expectantly for her to renounce the man with whom she had been forced to join her life path.

Desire met the hard glint in Panther Stalks' eyes, and a slight shudder coursed over her back. She had never noticed how cold his eyes were. Her hands automatically tight-

ened upon the piece of wood. "I am treated very well in
my husband's village. There is no need for you to think
again on this matter, Panther Stalks." She told herself that
he only asked this question because of their past friendship.

Panther Stalks had not been able to put from his
thoughts the memory of Wacin, standing pale and frightened, the night she was joined with Cetán. "I know you
do not care for your husband, Wacin, and that you wish
to return to your village. Perhaps soon, you will be free.
Once you return to your father's village, you and I will
be able to join as we wished."

For a stunned moment, Desire stood in confusion. What
was he talking about? How could she be free of Cetán? She
had never wanted to join with Panther Stalks in the past;
had he believed that she did? She opened her mouth to
protest, to explain that she loved her husband and was
happy among his people, but before she could do so, the
rest of Panther Stalks' hunting party approached and drew
the couple's attention.

An hour later, Desire stood at her husband's side and
watched her parents leave the Lakota valley. As she
glimpsed Panther Stalks' among the group, the conversation that had passed between them repeated itself in
her mind. She had had no more time in which to speak
alone with the brave and explain her true feelings. She
now wished she had been able to question him about the
meaning of his words—what did he mean when he stated
that she might be free soon? It had seemed a strange
statement and it still had the power to disturb Desire's
peace of mind.

Twenty-three

It was during the moon of the grass appearing, April, that two attempts were made upon Cetán's life. The first had been when he had left the village with Spotted Pony. An unknown assailant shot at him with bow and arrow from the cover of underbrush. The arrow grazed the side of Cetán's cheek, doing little harm. While he and Spotted Pony dove for the cover of trees, the ambusher fled without leaving any sign.

The second attempt was made several days later with Desire at his side. The couple left the village early one morning, and as much as Desire had questioned her husband, he would not tell her their destination until they had left the village far behind.

"Why do you concern yourself so with where we are going, wife? Is it not enough that we are together?" Cetán's husky laughter threatened to erupt as he glimpsed Desire's stubborn chin.

"I should be gathering plants for my medicine pouch, Cetán. I don't understand why you won't tell me where we are going. What about Elkhunter? He is still not well enough to make a kill. What if he gets hungry while I am gone?" In truth, Desire was excited about having a worry-free day at her husband's side. It had been a long winter and she needed a few hours away from the village.

"Curly Bear will see to Elkhunter's needs."

"We will be gone long enough for you to have to ask

Curly Bear to watch over Elkhunter?" She wondered if they were going to her father's village, but if so, she didn't understand why Cetán would not have informed her. She had made her mother a beaded parfleche in which to carry meat, and Cetán knew she was anxious to give it to Pretty Dove and see her admiring look as she studied her daughter's handiwork.

"We will be gone throughout the day, Wacin. Why do you not relax and enjoy the ride through the forest? After we stop, I will help you gather some of your plants." Riding closely together along the forest path, Cetán was tempted to pull his bride off Star's back and settle her across his lap.

The temptation was far too great when she pursed her lips, once again seeking to know of their destination. The soft pursing of her berry-red lips was more than he could bear. Being a man with little resistance where his wife was concerned, he reached out a powerful arm to capture her by the waist. With a swift, sure movement Desire was soon sitting in front of her husband, her arms automatically rising as her hands clutched at his shoulders.

"You could have given me warning, Cetán!" Desire gasped, Star shying and sidestepping as Whirling-Warrior's-Ghost snorted, surprised by the added weight.

Cetán laughed aloud with happiness that this woman in his arms was his bride. "I could not resist doing this, Wacin." His dark head lowered, his mouth settling in a loving caress over her lips.

"Mmmmm, I think you might be right." Desire tightened her arms around his neck, pressing her breasts full against his naked chest in order to enjoy fully the powerful elixir of her husband's kisses.

As Cetán's head drew back and Desire settled herself more comfortably in his arms, she asked again, "Now, where are we going?"

"My woman is not one who enjoys surprises." Cetán

laughed, and feeling Desire's slender fist playfully striking his ribs, relented. "I wanted us to spend the day at a place I found when I was a young brave. I have taken no one there before. I would share this place with you, Wacin."

"Now, was that so hard to tell me?" Desire's laughter mingled with his as she traced a finger over the muscular curve of his forearm. "I will be delighted to see this place where no one, besides you, has ever been."

"I did not say that no other has ever been to this place, Wacin." Cetán's voice became serious. "I said, I have taken no other to this place that I now take you."

"Now, what is that supposed to mean?" Desire questioned, wondering at his play of words.

"You will see when we get there."

"Why don't you just tell me?"

"Can I have no surprises?"

"Of course not! A husband does not keep surprises from his wife!"

Cetán's grip on her waist tightened. Wacin was as curious as a squirrel, and he loved every questioning inch of her!

Cetán turned Whirling-Warrior's-Ghost along the forest trail before the sun centered in the sky. In this portion of the forest, there was no trail to follow. Whirling-Warrior's-Ghost had to pick his way carefully through the dense trees and underbrush, Star following closely on his heels.

Not long after turning off the trail, Cetán halted his mount, then with an easy movement, lowered Desire to the ground.

"Is this the place?" Desire looked around the area, trying to see what had drawn her husband to spend the afternoon here. "Is this where you came as a young brave? What were you doing here? Surely no wildlife would even dare to come into this overgrown portion of the forest!" Pines, cottonwoods, and oaks fought each other for survival, with an overabundance of vines and underbrush concealing a good portion of the leaf-and-pine-needle-strewn earth.

Cetán remained silent, knowing that any answer he gave would only bring forth more questions. Instead, he hobbled the horses with pieces of braided rawhide; then, taking hold of his wife's hand, he began to lead her deeper into the jungle of trees and plant life. "It is too dense here to bring the horses," he explained, pushing back vines and sidestepping the clutching fingers of prickly ferns.

"Whatever could have drawn you to such a place, Cetán?" Desire followed closely behind her husband's lead, swatting at overhanging branches that threatened to snarl in her hair.

"When I was fifteen summers, my father took me along on a hunt for fresh game. I saw a sign where an elk had recently stepped, and by the depth of his track, I knew he was very large. Thinking I would kill the elk and bring him back to my father's camp, I left the hunting party and trailed after it. I was soon lost in the forest."

"I don't doubt that. As dense as this portion of the forest is, anyone could get lost!"

"If I had not followed the elk and gotten lost, I would never have discovered this secret spot." The couple had come upon a mountain, as densely covered as the forest they had been traversing.

"Now what?" Desire questioned, her gaze traveling upward to the towering mountain.

"We go in through here." Cetán pulled back foliage and vines, revealing a hidden hole in the side of the mountain that led into a long, winding cavern.

Desire's honey-gold eyes widened in disbelief. "There is a cave in there?" She hesitated only a moment as Cetán parted the plants concealing the opening.

"For a youth of only fifteen summers, I thought I had discovered the most wonderful place on Mother Earth," Cetán said as he stepped in after her. "Over the years, I have returned here many times, especially when I desire peace and wish to draw closer to The Great Spirit."

The interior was dark, and Desire stayed near her husband's side. "Over here is a torch that I left the last time I was here." Cetán struck his flint to the dry torch and light instantly filled the wide frontal chamber.

Desire's gaze swept over every portion of the cave. "You made that fire pit?" she asked, glancing toward the back of the cave where a dug-out portion of earth was circled by smooth stones.

"The pit was here when I found the cave." Cetán took her hand and began to lead her through the first chamber, then into a long passageway that led deeper into the heart of the mountain.

It was cool and strangely eerie and Desire was hesitant to follow Cetán's lead. "Is it safe for us to come in here?" she asked. Halfway through the passageway, Desire noticed drawings on the walls, their presence illuminated by Cetán's torch.

"Do you doubt that I can protect you?" Cetán softly questioned, knowing he would receive no answer. As Cetán had done that first day when he entered the cave and traveled down this passageway, Desire's full attention was centered upon the artwork so boldly displayed on the timeless, cold stone walls.

"What are these creatures, Cetán?" Desire paused to stare at the great, shaggy beasts with tusks jutting upward from their mouths. The pictograph showed two men with long lances fighting one of the great beasts.

"I have studied these pictures, and believe that they were drawn during the time when the people lived within the heart of Mother Earth. Perhaps these two warriors ventured out into the unknown and were attacked by the great beast."

Desire realized that the prehistoric pictographs portrayed a lifestyle much earlier than that which the people now lived. Many of the sketches revealed the ceremonial aspects of their earlier culture, displaying weapons, decorated shields, headgear, and other ceremonial regalia. The artist had paid close attention to the daily life of the people who had lived in the cave, portraying a hard-working community of no more than a dozen. Their household implements were crude in shape compared to the tools that the people now owned. There were a variety of animals sketched over the passageway walls, verifying the spiritual relationship between the artist and animal spirits.

Desire could have spent more time in the passageway studying the drawings, but Cetán was anxious for her to see the rest of the cavern. Clutching her hand, he led her through the rest of the passageway, then into another chamber.

The sound of rushing water instantly filled their ears; an opening on the far wall revealed a shimmering shower of water. "A waterfall!" Desire gasped in surprise. Cetán no longer had to pull her along; she was anxious to look down from this position in the very heart of the mountain, to view the waterfall gushing over the side of the mountain, forming a glistening pond at its base.

Cetán enjoyed her excitement as he followed her across the chamber. The couple stood on the ledge, watching the cascading water rush downward. The sun filtered through the opening, revealing a bounty of swirling colors.

"This is a wonderful place, Cetán," Desire said, mesmerized by the incredible beauty. "Do you think when the people lived here in the cave, there was a couple like you and I who stood upon this same ledge and gazed on this sight?" It was pleasant to imagine another couple long ago, standing where they were standing, holding hands and viewing this same breathtaking scene.

Cetán did not speak, but instead pointed to the wall near the ledge. On the smoothly weathered surface were two perfect handprints, one smaller than the other. Cetán stretched out his hand and placed it in the largest imprint. Desire was surprised at the fit of her husband's hand with the mark made hundreds of years previously. Stretching out her hand, she placed it within the smaller handprint, and to her utter amazement, her hand fit perfectly. She looked in question at Cetán.

He smiled as his dark head nodded slightly. "Even before man left the security of Mother Earth's womb, you and I were one in heart and spirit. These marks were left to remind us that from the beginning, even before the people heard the mighty thundering of tatanka as he ran in vast herds and the sounds of their hoofbeats became one with the pumping of the people's hearts, even then it was known that our love would exist."

His words were true . . . Desire knew it in the very depth of her heart . . . in the long-past memories of other lives, other times. Without further conversation, she leaned toward him. Her husband's arms embraced her as their lips joined in communion with the feelings filling their hearts. This man was all to Desire . . . her husband . . . her heart . . . her love through every door of the future and past.

"Cetán," she sighed softly, her body trembling with awakening desire.

Cetán's large hands unlaced the leather binding securing Desire's dress, his dark eyes heatedly devouring the soft, creamy flesh which was slowly being revealed. "Feel the power you have over this warrior, Wacin." Cetán drew her hand up to press the palm against the center of his chest. "Until I heard the sigh of my name on your lips, there was no sound within my chest. I give unto you freely this power that no other has ever claimed, and ask only that you look on me tomorrow with the same loving warmth that I now see reflected in your eyes."

This man had given her so much and asked so little in return. A crystal tear fell unbidden from Desire's eye as the emotions in her heart threatened to overwhelm her. "Oh, Cetán, don't you know that I will always look on you

with the same feelings of affection in my heart? I love you."
With the confession, Desire felt the leaping of Cetán's heart
beneath her hand.

Cetán gloried in the words that blessed his ears. He had
waited a lifetime to hear them. As the hide dress fell to the
stone surface of the ledge, Cetán lovingly lowered his bride,
and with one movement he spread her thighs and slowly
eased the hard, long length of his man-root deep into the
warm haven of her woman's bounty. "Your love is a gift I
will forever cherish, mitá wicánte."

The husky tremor of his voice, combined with the things
he was doing to her body, set off an instant quickening
deep within Desire's womb. She clutched his shoulders,
her body meeting his every touch, her slender legs tightly
drawn around his hips.

"As our hearts beat as one, our bodies fit together perfectly," Cetán whispered into her ear. "Open your eyes,
Wacin, and look at the beauty of our bodies joined as one."

Desire's eyes slowly opened, and as bid, she glanced
down the length of their twined limbs. The sight of their
clasped, naked forms evoked an overwhelming response.
Desire began to tremble, her sheath shuddering and tightening in erotic anticipation.

Capturing her hand, Cetán began a slow, downward caress of their joined bodies. "Your skin is soft where mine
is hard, pale where mine is dark." Cetán knew they com-
plemented each other, and wanted to share his feelings.
As their hands traced the outline of her full breast pressed
tightly to his chest, the husky spell of his voice ensnared
Desire's senses as her gaze followed the movement of their
joined hands.

"Feast upon my body, Wacin, not only with your eyes,
but with your body and your lips. Take all that I am, knowing that each small measure which you receive, I gladly
share. You are my reason, Wacin."

A moan of rapture escaped Desire's parted lips, but was

instantly smothered by Cetán's hungry kiss. She was surrounded and filled by the presence of this man that she
loved. There was no holding back—she gave all that was
demanded of her. With the offering, she was lifted to a
loftier place . . . a place that only she and Cetán could
share . . . where their bodies came together in a clash of
passionate oneness which broke all restraints and boundaries. For a time, their passions spun wildly out of control
as they were pulled into the raging center of an all-encom-
passing climax.

The lingering aftermath of their passion was sweet and
sensual. Cetán showered Desire's face and neck with little
kisses. His words of love filled her ears as his hands roamed
over the tempting contours of her soft flesh. "Tell me once
again those words that I have ached to hear from your lips
from the first time I looked upon you, Wacin."

"I love you, Cetán, I love you." Desire laughed aloud
with joy. She kissed his firm chin and the tempting spot
beneath his cheek. She had at last come to grips with the
power struggle that had raged in her heart since she had
joined her life-path with this man's. Why had she not realized long ago that her heart had always belonged to
Cetán?

It was not until the couple left the cavern to return to
the village that the second attack on Cetán's life took place.
Cetán rode in the lead, Desire following on Star, when the
forest-sounds were shattered by a shrill battle cry, which
was soon followed by another. Within seconds, two fierce-
looking warriors leaped from the cover of the trees.

Desire screamed in terror, trying to pull Star off the trail
and out of immediate danger. The warriors were embla-
zoned with paint and brandishing weapons of war. Their
attack was made even before Cetán had a chance to draw
his own weapon from his shoulder.

The attackers were seasoned warriors, and were not lacking in the skill it took to attack and overpower their opponent. Even before Cetán had his weapon ready, one of the warriors was boldly striking out at him with his war-club.

The blow caught Cetán on the shoulder, and for a second, he was overcome by searing pain. Whirling-Warrior's-Ghost instantly rose up on his hind legs, sharp teeth bared as he charged the attacker.

Watching from a few feet away, Desire screamed her husband's name as she watched in horror. Her cry, as much as the efforts of his mighty war-horse, revived Cetán enough for him to clutch his deadly weapon. Whirling the dangerous rifle-stock and blade overhead, Cetán brought the mighty weapon down fully noon the warrior's shoulders.

No longer feeling the pain inflicted by the enemy's war-club, Cetán dropped his weapon. Wrapping his fist around the bone handle of his hunting knife, he leaped from Whirling-Warrior's-Ghost's back, landing atop the remaining warrior.

The fight lasted several minutes. Both warriors lashed out with deadly knives, but Cetán was craftier and better trained than his opponent. As the warrior fell beneath Cetán's blade, Desire dismounted and ran to her husband's side. Cetán caught her close, his hand tightening around her waist, as though her touch had the power to bring him back to full reality.

"Let me look at your shoulder, Cetán." Desire reached up to push away the hide shirt, which was soaked with blood.

Cetán sucked in deep breaths as he attempted to steady himself. Looking over the warrior lying at his feet, he was surprised to see articles of clothing that belonged to the Sioux. The weapons looked like those belonging to his enemy, the Crow, but both warriors were dressed to appear like his own people. He remembered the attack that he and Spotted Pony had suffered in the forest. The arrow had only grazed him that day; this attack, with Wacin at his side, had been much worse.

"Cetán, come and sit down. Let me stop the bleeding," Desire said, tugging at her husband's sleeve.

Cetán complied, hearing the worry in her tone. Before sitting down on a log, he pulled off his shirt, and then allowed Wacin to work her medicine on him. For a few minutes, he forgot about the fight as he enjoyed his wife's attentions. Seeing concern in her sherry-gold eyes, he pulled her head toward him and lightly kissed her lips. "I am fine, Wacin. I have suffered much worse wounds than this."

"What did the warriors want?" Desire cleansed the wound, deciding she would stitch the gaping flesh together as soon as they returned to their lodge. It was unusual that two warriors would don war paint to attack travelers in the forest. War parties usually consisted of several braves, each depending on the others' abilities and strengths.

"We will never know what they wanted, now." A feeling came over Cetán that this attack, like the one in the forest with Spotted Pony, had not been mere chance. Someone wanted him dead . . . but why?

Twenty-four

With the passing of the spring days, Desire thought less and less about the attack against her and her husband. Cetán's shoulder wound healed quickly and without complication, and as Cetán planned a hunting trip with a group of braves, Desire busied herself with plans to go to her parents' village with Looking Hawk and his wife, Willow. The older couple's granddaughter had joined with a brave from Desire's parents' village three summers past and this winter she had given birth to her first son. The couple was anxious to make the trip to visit with their only grandchild and her new family. Desire would travel with them, and on his return from his hunting trip, Cetán would go to her father's village and he and Desire would travel back to the Lakota village together.

Desire had been planning the trip for two weeks, and now that the morning to depart had arrived, Cetán helped her load the gifts she would take to her family and friends on the back of the packhorse.

"I only wish that Elkhunter was well enough to go along with you," Cetán said as he brushed aside a stray strand of fine hair from Desire's cheek. His dark eyes glowed with love for his bride as he looked at the happiness on her features.

"He still needs a little more time to heal, Cetán. Perhaps, when you return from your hunting trip, Elkhunter will be strong enough to come with you to bring me home." De-

sire had made arrangements with Curly Bear to take care
of her pet until her return. The great wolf needed only a
week or two before he would be fit to travel, as he had in
the past.

"I will miss you, mitá wicánte," Cetán confessed softly as
he pulled Desire into his arms. Several women were going
along on his hunting trip, and at first Cetán had hoped
Wacin would go along. He had been disappointed when
Looking Hawk and Willow had invited his wife to travel
with them to Gray Owl's village, but he could not deprive
her of the opportunity to spend time with her family.

"I will miss you, too, Cetán. This will be the longest time
that we have been apart." Several times over the past two
weeks, Desire had almost changed her mind and decided
to go along with the hunting party. But if she did not go
with Looking Hawk and Willow, it might be some time before she would have an opportunity to go to her parents'
village again. "You will not forget that I love you with all
my heart?" she asked shyly, still self-conscious about speaking aloud the feelings that filled her heart.

"Never!" Cetán swore as his head descended and his lips
covered Desire's in a heartfelt kiss.

Looking Hawk and his small party left the Lakota valley
an hour before Cetán's hunting party departed. Desire's
spirits were high as she rode Star, the reins of her packhorse
tied to her saddle, the pony following up the rear of the
group.

Throughout the morning travel, Desire rode alongside
Willow and the two women spoke of everyday matters of
the village. Often, Desire slowed Star when she spied
plants along the trail which she wished to add to her
medicine pouch. As the older couple rode ahead, she
used her stick to work the plants loose from the ground,
then placed them in her parfleche. Once she arrived in
her father's village, she would dry the plants and add
them to the others.

Now that spring had arrived, the forest was vibrant with new growth, and Desire looked around greedily, hoping to replenish her medicinal supply. It was early in the afternoon when Looking Hawk halted for a break. While Willow and Looking Hawk relaxed and ate pemmican, Desire gathered green moss and lichens from beneath a decayed log.

It was only a short time later, after the group resumed travel, that Desire's attention was drawn to a small bunch of cone-shaped yellow flowers, known among her people as napostan, or thimbles. Desire halted Star near the plants, and with her stick carefully uprooted each delicate coneflower. The napostans were a great find, as Desire's small supply of the medicine plant had been greatly depleted during the winter months. This plant was given to horses who had problems with urination, and the cone-shaped tops were made into a tea which treated headaches and bellyaches.

Desire's attention was totally absorbed with her work, so she did not hear the rider and horse that approached. The warrior sat silently, his dark gaze fully centered on the young woman digging the napostan plants.

Placing the plants in her parfleche, a small noise behind her drew Desire's attention. Surprise registered on her features as she straightened to face the warrior. "What are you doing here, Panther Stalks? Is there some kind of trouble in the village?" He was alone, so she discounted the idea that he was with a hunting party. The serious intent in his cool gaze made her wonder if he had been on his way to meet up with her party. Reason told her he could not possibly have known that she was on her way to visit her parents. No word had been sent in advance, because she had wished to surprise them.

Panther Stalks was as surprised as Desire to come upon her here in the forest. He and the three warriors he rode with had heard the approach of Looking Hawk and his wife on the trail. Panther Stalks had circled around to come up behind the riders and horses. Not believing his good fortune, he had silently allowed his gaze to feast on Desire's delicate beauty as she dug up her plants. He had been watching and waiting for just such an opportunity! As Desire faced him with her questions, Panther Stalks did not hesitate to speak the words that would make her leave the trail and travel at his side. "You are right, Wacin, there has been trouble in the village. Your father has been wounded and has sent me to bring you to his side."

"My father?" Desire clasped her slender fingers in worry. "Wounded?" In her concern for her father, she forgot about the parfleche lying on the ground next to the plants. "What happened to him, Panther Stalks? Is the wound serious? Is my mother all right?" She started for her horse, her concern evident by the trembling of her hands as she reached for Star's reins.

"It is serious, but he will live if we hurry and leave this place." Panther Stalks knew his friends would take care of Looking Hawk and Willow. There would be no evidence that he had a part in Desire's disappearance. "I know of a quicker way through the forest. Follow me, Wacin." Panther Stalks turned his horse in a northwest direction. Waiting only long enough to be sure that Desire was willing to follow him, he kicked his pony into movement.

Desire wished she had given her packhorse over to Looking Hawk so they could travel at a quicker pace. Mentioning this to Panther Stalks, she was more than a little surprised by his immediate reaction.

Turning his mount without disturbing the hurried pace that he had set through the forest, Panther Stalks pulled his hunting knife from its sheath and with a downward motion of his wrist, cut the leather lead rope tied to Desire's saddle.

"What are you doing?" She pulled back on Star's reins as she watched the packhorse slow behind her.

"I told you, Wacin, we must hurry if you are to help Gray

Owl." Panther Stalks and his pony blocked Desire from turning Star around in order to retrieve the packhorse.

"We can't just leave the pony! I have supplies and gifts in those packs!" For the first time, Desire realized that she had left her parfleche of medicine plants back on the trail. For a second, she thought to insist on turning around and going back for it, but she knew that would only delay them further. Panther Stalks was acting as though time was of the essence if there was a chance for her to help her father, so she could not risk even a small delay.

"Do you concern yourself with supplies and gifts when your father could be, this very minute, dying as he waits for you?"

His words instantly ordered Desire's chaotic thoughts. "Yes, of course, you are right. We must hurry and get to the village." Desire felt tears gather in her eyes, spurred on by the helplessness she was feeling. If only Cetán were here with her, she thought, as Panther Stalks once again took the lead. Cetán's strength would have offered her hope. She would not feel such an inner desperation to get to her parents' village if her husband were here at her side instead of Panther Stalks. She would trust in Cetán's judgement, believing that no matter the odds, her husband would get her to her father's side before he passed on to join the ancestors in the sky.

Travel through the forest was rough going, their pace hurried, as Panther Stalks did not linger to rest or drink water. Desire wondered at their direction, feeling they were going too far west to reach her father's village. She did not reveal her fears to Panther Stalks, knowing the warrior had her father's best interests at heart, and telling herself that he would surely know the shortcut he was taking better than she.

By the time Panther Stalks did break the hectic pace, Desire felt as though they were fleeing from someone, instead of riding to the Oglala village.

"We'll take a few minutes to let the horses drink," Panther Stalks said as he dismounted, allowing his pony to drink from the swiftly running stream nearby.

Desire did the same. Reaching for her water bag secured on Star's saddle, she drank thirstily. "What about Looking Hawk and Willow? They will wonder at my disappearance." For the first time, Desire thought about the elderly couple she had been traveling with, and could imagine their upset at finding her gone from the forest trail.

"Don't worry about them." Panther Stalks' tone was sharp.

Desire had never seen Panther Stalks act so harsh, but putting his behavior down to his concern for her father, she added, "I guess they will understand when they reach the village and find me already there tending my father."

"Where is Cetán, Wacin? Why is he not with you?" Panther Stalks ignored her talk. Her companions were no longer of any importance, but Cetán might well be.

"He went with a hunting party. Buffalo were sighted, and a large party was assembled. They left the village this morning. When he returns, he will come for me at my father's village." In the back of Desire's mind were thoughts of trying to get her husband and Panther Stalks to forget what had taken place in the past, and to at least be civil to one another. After all, Panther Stalks had come to escort her to her father.

Panther Stalks was tempted to reveal to her that she would never see Cetán again, but he stifled the impulse. It was better to have Desire a willing traveler as long as possible. It might take him some time to convince her that she belonged to him. For now, he would let her believe they were heading toward her father's village. Soon enough, she would realize the truth. When she did, he expected her to rebel at first. No matter how much she disliked her husband and had refused to join with him, it was in her nature to be faithful and honor the ceremony that bound her and

Cetán together. It would take time for Panther Stalks to convince her that he was the only man whom she belonged to, and from this day forth, she would never leave his side!

"We should get moving." Panther Stalks took his pony's reins and mounted while Desire tied her water bag back on her saddle.

"Are you sure we are heading in the right direction, Panther Stalks?" Desire mounted Star, but received no answer from Panther Stalks, who kicked his pony's sides to set a hurried pace once again.

By early evening, Desire was truly confused. They still had not turned from the northwesterly course Panther Stalks had originally set. Desire was beginning to worry that Panther Stalks had made a mistake.

Some time later, hunger and thirst forced Desire to call out, "Are we going to keep up this fast pace, Panther Stalks?" The forest was growing darker; there was no doubt that if they did not slow their pace, the trek could become dangerous for their animals as well as for themselves.

Panther Stalks ignored Desire. After a few more minutes, she pulled up on Star's reins. No matter what, she could not endanger her horse! Surely her father's life was not so threatened that they had to risk their own in order to arrive at the village. She had not even asked Panther Stalks what kind of injury her father had sustained, nor had she thought to question if Medicine Woman had been called to his lodge to treat him.

Realizing that Desire was no longer following, Panther Stalks turned back on the trail. They had been making good time, and he hoped to put an even greater distance between where he had found Desire and themselves before someone discovered that she had disappeared.

"What is wrong?" he questioned when he reached Desire's side.

"I'm hungry and thirsty, and Star needs a rest."

"We'll rest later," Panther Stalks declared as he reached out to grab hold of the mare's reins.

"What are you doing?" she cried as Star shyly side-stepped away from the warrior's hand and Desire was forced to clutch the pommel of her saddle.

"We don't have time for such foolishness, Wacin! If you can't follow my lead, I'll hold your horse's reins!"

"But why are you acting like this, Panther Stalks? Why are you pushing so hard, not even allowing a break for food and water? Is my father in such bad condition that we must go at such a fast pace, even in the dark?" Desire felt the first trembling fingers of fear as she looked into Panther Stalks' hard features. In the past, he had always been kind in his dealings with her. She saw no such kindness in the dark eyes glaring at her now.

"You aren't taking me to my father, are you?" As if awakening from some terrible dream, Desire was shocked to her senses, even as she voiced the question. She should never have left the forest trail with this man! She should never have allowed herself to be betrayed into believing that something had happened to her father, without even asking questions. She had trusted Panther Stalks; now, too late, she realized her terrible mistake!

"If we return to your father's village, Wacin, I will be forced to give you back to Cetán." Panther Stalks' words were hollow, with no trace of warmth.

"You can't mean that you are going to keep me from my husband?" Desire was stunned, incredulous that this man would dare to take her away from her husband and family. "Cetán will come after me, Panther Stalks. You must take me back to my father's village before it is too late!"

"It is already too late, Wacin. I will never release you!"

"But Cetán will kill you when he finds us!"

"He will never know what happened to you. We will go far away where we can live together as it has always been meant to be." Panther Stalks knew Desire would resist at first, but he was confident that given time, she would understand that what he was doing was best for both of them—for their future!

"My father will come for me! When Looking Hawk and Willow arrive in the village and tell them I disappeared from the trail, he will come with a war party!" Desire's only hope was to convince Panther Stalks that there was still time to return her to her father's village.

"Your father will never know what happened to you until it is too late for anyone to find us."

"But Looking Hawk and Willow . . . ?"

"Will never arrive at the village. They were taken care of by my friends, just like Cetán should have been, but the fates always seem to be on his side!"

"You had them killed?" Anger and fear combined to overwhelm Desire as she listened to the warrior's confession. "Was it you who had the warriors attempt to kill Cetán?" He did not have to answer; she already knew it had been Panther Stalks who had set the two warriors on her husband that day in the forest. "But why, Panther Stalks? Why would you kill innocent people, and try to harm Cetán?" She shook her head as though to clear her thoughts, to make sense of what he was revealing.

"For you, Wacin. Always for you!" Panther Stalks' grip on Star's reins tightened. Slowly he pulled on them, kicking his own mount's sides until the two horses were drawn closely together. "You should have been mine! Cetán stole you, and that evening when I watched you being forced to join with him, I made a vow that I would one day claim you as my own!"

His face was inches away from her own, and with the closeness, Desire saw the hidden lights of insanity in the dark depths of his eyes. "I love Cetán. He is my husband, Panther Stalks," she whispered as fear gripped her heart.

His reaction was instant. Without any warning, Panther Stalks' free hand shot out and grabbed Desire's chin in a firm grip. "Never again will you speak Cetán's name! I am your husband now, Wacin! You are mine, and no other will ever take you from me!"

Twenty-five

The fierce pace set by Panther Stalks was never-ending. Over the next few days he pushed their horses through forest, prairie, and rough, hilly terrain. They broke only for short intervals, and not until the moon rose high in the night sky did Panther Stalks allow a few hours needed rest.

By the fourth day, Desire was so exhausted, Panther Stalks had to help her mount Star. "Once we reach my cousin's people, we will be able to rest for a day or two before we start back on the trail," Panther Stalks said, attempting to lighten Desire's spirits. He knew that she was weary from the days of hard travel, but told himself that with just a few more days' distance between them and Gray Owl's village, they would be able to rest. Once they reached the Cheyenne village where his cousin Otter Hand lived with his wife's family, they would be safe; then he could take time to plan their next step. In the back of Panther Stalks' mind was the ever-present threat that somehow Cetán would pick up their trail. At such thoughts, Panther Stalks' anger surfaced and once again he pushed his pony and Star harder toward their destination.

After that first day, when Panther Stalks had confessed his intent to keep Desire with him and not return her to her father or husband, Desire attempted to escape twice. Both times, Panther Stalks had caught her before she could get far enough away to hide in the cover of the forest. After the second attempt, he tied Star's reins to his own saddle, and threatened to tie Desire to her mount if she tried to jump from the mare's back. Desire was totally at the warrior's mercy!

This day, as the one before, seemed to pass in an endless blur of movement as Desire clung to the pommel of her saddle. Telling herself to hold on, to survive until Cetán could find her, was the only thread of hope that kept her from giving in to total madness.

In the early afternoon, when Panther Stalks halted the animals for a short break, Desire tried to sway her abductor from his course. "I can't go on any longer like this, Panther Stalks! Please, can't we rest for a few hours?" If she could convince him to ease the pace, there might be a better chance for her to be rescued by her father or Cetán. The outlook for rescue, she knew, was slim at best. Cetán might still be with the hunting party, and her father, as far as she knew, was not even aware of her abduction. But there was always a slim chance that someone would be looking for her. She had to believe this . . . it was her only hope!

"We will rest when we reach Otter Hand's village." Panther Stalks handed Desire a piece of pemmican. When she hesitated, he shoved it into her hand. "Eat, or you will grow weak. A weak woman is good for no one." His dark gaze took in her unkempt appearance. The press of the hard ride was already taking its toll. He hoped his harsh words would force strength into her limbs.

Desire would have attempted to plead with him to return her, but there was nothing she could say that would change his mind. Her only hope was that someone was looking for her. Once they reached the Cheyenne village somehow she would have to find the chance to escape! The second Panther Stalks was out of sight, she would make her break and find someplace to hide until she had the opportunity to find her way back to her husband! Panther Stalks' harsh words did have the desired effect on his captive. Desire swore she would not weaken on the trail. Her back stiffened with renewed resolve, and taking the pemmican, she knew that her only hope lay in her strength!

"Soon, I will show you how a real man can make your body sing with complete happiness. I have never forgotten the joining of our lips that day by the river. When we reach my cousin's village, Otter Hand will see that we have a lodge to lie in. I will teach you the many ways that a woman can pleasure a man." Panther Stalks had no doubt that Wacin had been intimate with Cetán. But believing his sexual prowess to be unequaled, he boasted to this woman who he believed in his heart had always belonged to him. Once Wacin joined her body with his, she would forget Cetán, and they would live together as fate intended.

Desire had not forgotten that kiss, and sudden revulsion flushed her features. She would have loudly protested his promise to bed her, but wisely kept those thoughts to herself. Lowering her eyes and turning her head, she thought of her plans to flee as soon as they reached the Cheyenne village. If she appeared docile and seemed to welcome Panther Stalks' words, she might be able to keep him off guard. Once in his cousin's village, she might be able to steal a horse. Hoping that her voice did not waver, she looked squarely into his hard features. "I will be happy to arrive in this village that you speak of, Panther Stalks."

For the first time since her abduction, Desire saw Panther Stalks smile. "You will not regret that I have taken you away from that other life, Wacin." Panther Stalks would not say Cetán's name aloud for fear that anger would overcome him and he might strike out at this woman he had betrayed his people to claim as his own. His inner thoughts plagued him: it was as much Desire's fault that she had joined with another warrior as it had been her father's. If Desire had protested louder, Gray Owl would have given in to her desires to join her life-path with his own.

That other life was all Desire had ever wanted! Her heart

cried silently for Cetán even as she appeared to agree with
Panther Stalks.

Pleased with her response, Panther Stalks did not tie
Star's reins to his saddle. Instead, he allowed Desire to take
the reins, but keeping her in his sight at all times, they
started back on the trail that would eventually lead them
to the Cheyenne village.

Occupied with thoughts of Desire—and the need that
gripped him to make it to his cousin's village and put an
end to the madness eating at him to make this woman his
own—Panther Stalks did not realize that they were being
followed. When the attack came, it was a complete surprise!

Desire was the first to notice the four warriors boldly
sitting atop their ponies directly ahead of them. A tight
knot of fear instantly gripped her belly, and with a cry, she
warned Panther Stalks.

Panther Stalks' first reaction was to turn away from a
direct confrontation in order to assure that Desire was safe.
Reaching out, he grabbed her reins and turned the horses
sharply to the right. There, too, were warriors, and as Panther Stalks turned around, he saw more warriors approaching from the rear! Loosening Star's reins, he looked at
Desire once before pulling forth his war-axe and shield in
one hand, his tomahawk in the other. "They are Pawnee,
Wacin." Panther Stalks' tone was chilled. "I will ride for
the first group—follow me. When I·make a path, ride as
hard as you can!" Panther Stalks had no second thoughts
about giving up his own life for this woman whom he desired.

There was no time to argue over his plan, nor was there
time to humor the fates. The Pawnee warriors were warily
closing in on their prey. Desire clutched Star's reins tightly.
When Panther Stalks turned his pony and started back the
way they had come, she was close on his heels.

Panther Stalks' fierce battle cry erupted from his throat.
Raised high overhead, his tomahawk was brought down in

a deadly arch as he converged on the four warriors, his weapon striking the nearest man with deadly intent.

Desire did not wait to see the outcome of the fighting; she urged Star around the group converging on Panther Stalks. With a cry, she kicked Star's flanks, rushing head-long through the belly-high prairie grass in the direction of a stand of trees several hundred yards away.

"Don't look back . . . don't look back," she whispered over and over. "Make it to the trees, and you'll be safe! You can find a place to hide!" These were the only thoughts in Desire's head. Her heart hammered wildly in her chest and she could taste her own blood where she was biting down on her lower lip. "Run, Star . . . run!" Hearing the screams from the fighting behind her, Desire was goaded on, the fleet-footed mare stretching out her long legs as she felt her mistress's panic. The cover of trees was just ahead—the only chance to escape! Panther Stalks would not survive the assault; there were too many warriors for one man to fight off.

She dared not breathe deeply. She dared not think of anything except making it to the trees! She was only a few yards away from the copse when she felt something grab her from behind and pull her from Star's back. Desire screamed, striking out at the Pawnee warrior who pulled her up in front of him onto his pony.

Kicking, hitting, and attempting to squirm out of the warrior's arms, Desire fought madly. Her frantic efforts brought her release as she was thrown to the ground. Jumping to her feet without a thought to the punishment her body had just received, Desire turned sharply, trying to run back toward the trees.

There was no escape! A dozen warriors surrounded her. A few bore bloody gashes over their upper bodies where Panther Stalks had valiantly fought. But now, all of them focused their attention upon this singular victim.

All the warriors, except the one who had caught Desire,

wore breechcloths. Their hair had been shaved at the top of their heads and over their ears; scalplocks hung from their crowns to the back of their necks. Each warrior's scalplock was decorated differently, with assorted feathers and strings of colorful beads. A gold disk hung from one, and in the leader's scalplock there was an arrow; his costume was made from owl skin and strips of ermine.

Desire's terror was a viable thing. She felt fear in every portion of her body; her mouth was dry as she stared with wide eyes at the horses and riders surrounding her.

"Let us vent our lust on this woman before we continue with our mission!" A warrior's voice broke the quiet that had settled about the group.

"I say we satisfy ourselves with her body, then take her to the trading post upriver. We can trade her for whiskey," another muttered.

"Forget the Sioux bitch! Kill her as we did her man— then we can go on to the village of our enemy!" another stated cruelly.

Desire could not understand the words the warriors spoke, but with each statement, all glances followed the man who had pulled her front Star's back. Lifting her gaze, she looked at the leader of this band of Pawnee. If she was going to die, she would face death now. She did not waste any sympathy on Panther Stalks. His death did not fill her with satisfaction, nor did she feel remorse for the man once considered a friend. He was the reason she was in this situation. Panther Stalks had stolen her from the man she loved, and as she faced death, she held thoughts of Cetán in her heart. Desire resigned herself to her fate. Her life would end this very day!

The Skidi Pawnee leader, Scar Hand, ignored the words of the warriors. With the young woman looking directly at him, his dark gaze roamed over her with a keener sense of interest. Her appearance was haggard, dark hair snarled and unkempt, hide dress wrinkled and torn in spots. But what caught Scar Hand's full attention were the golden eyes that stared boldly back at him. Without looking at his men, he silently dismounted, then walked the few steps that brought him to the woman's side.

Desire's breath clutched in her chest, but she forced herself to stand still before the warrior's approach. She prayed he would bring death to her quickly. Holding the image of Cetán in her mind, she kept her eyes tightly shut.

"Opirikuts—holy, for the Morning Star!" Scar Hand spoke the Pawnee word loudly in reverence. He placed one of his ocher-painted hands on the woman's arm; the painting of both hands indicated hand-to-hand combat in which Scar Hand had been victorious.

"This woman cannot be Opirikuts! We have not held the Morning Star Ceremony!" one of the warriors spoke out in direct opposition to the leader's declaration. "We must kill the woman, then go on to our enemies' village, as is the custom!"

The minute the warrior set hands upon Desire, her eyes flew open. She had no idea what Opirikuts meant, and was surprised that her arm was being held so gently.

"Look at the woman's eyes!" cried Scar Hand as the rest of the warriors began to agree with White Bull, the warrior who had spoken out. "Her eyes are a sign! She is the one who must be returned to our village and placed on the scaffold to greet the Morning Star with her life-offering!"

One of the youngest warriors in the group spoke out in support of Scar Hand, after looking closely into Desire's face and studying her eyes. "This woman's eyes will send their golden light directly to Cupirittaka—female white star, the Evening Star." The first god placed in the heavens by Tirawahat, the Skidi Pawnee all-powerful god, was Opirikata of the eastern sky, the god of light, fire, and war, a mighty god-warrior who drove all other stars before him across the sky. Opirikata was considered the most powerful of the stars, and it was believed that Skidi Pawnee warriors obtained their powers from him. It was the union between Morning Star and Evening Star from which sprang the girl who was the first human to be placed on earth. Legend held that as Morning Star rose, he sent a beam into the entry of the earth lodge, symbolically lighting the fire in an act of procreation, and it was to Morning Star that the Skidi Pawnee offered a human sacrifice. This band of warriors had been singled out by the keeper of the Morning Star Bundle to approach the camp of their enemy and bring back a female captive to offer as a sacrifice to appease Opirikata. There had not been a sacrifice in several years, but the signs were now right in the sky.

"We can conduct the Morning Star Ceremony after we have rested this night. We will keep a portion of today's meat for an offering," the young brave offered, hoping to sway the rest of the warriors to Scar Hand's decision.

Several heads began to nod in agreement, but there were still a few who were not convinced. White Bull once again voiced his objections, "Silver Wolf, the keeper of the Morning Star Bundle, will not be pleased that we stray away from our instructions. Opirikata may not honor this girl as a sacrifice because we did not honor all of our traditions."

"Our people are going hungry, we are losing our land to the white-eyes, and White Bull would tell us to turn away from the power of the woman with the golden eyes to make sure that we do not stray from the old ways?" Scar Hand spoke out in anger, his hard glare fastened directly upon White Bull. "Have the people ever viewed the path of the red star in the morning sky, dimming as it travels toward the west? And has there ever been seen such a brilliant Morning Star, which seems to grow brighter and brighter? The people have never seen such signs in the sky before! I tell you that this woman with the golden eyes is also a sign. She will be the means for the people to regain all that they have lost! Opirikata will be pleased with this woman, as he has never been with another!"

None dared to openly oppose such a declaration from their leader. White Bull sat sullen and silent on his horse as the rest of the warriors spoke in low tones about the woman with the golden eyes.

Having absolutely no idea what they were saying, Desire was surprised when a pony was brought forth and the leader of the group motioned that she was to mount. Star had been so frightened, she had not returned from the stand of trees. Believing that the warriors had decided to take her captive instead of murdering her on the spot, Desire did as she was bid, telling herself, if given the slightest chance, she would find a means to escape and somehow make her way back to Cetán!

Twenty-six

Desire slept soundly for the first time since Panther Stalks had abducted her. Shortly after dusk, the Pawnee band made camp and the leader helped her to dismount. After making sure that his captive was well fed, Scar Hand placed a pallet of furs not far from the campfire, signaling that this was where she was to sleep. Desire had attempted to stay awake, determined that once the encampment settled down for the evening, she would sneak away and hide until the band had gone on without her.

Her need for sleep chased away all such plans. Within a short period of time, Desire was sleeping soundly, and did not awaken until the early hours of the morning, when she was pulled from slumber by the strong voices of her captors as they sang their prayerful songs.

The fire near her pallet had dimmed to embers, but Desire remained where she was as she observed the ritual being performed at the edge of camp.

A small spot had been cleared away, and a central fireplace excavated, a portion of yesterday's meat was laid out in offering to the Morning Star. Carrying the sacred objects from the Morning Star Bundle, Scar Hand stood silent among the group as the smoke from the fire was offered to the sky gods, and songs about the union of the Morning and Evening Stars, from when the first human was born, were sung by the warriors. With the first of the singing, Scar Hand loudly spoke the words that had been passed down from each generation. He instructed the warriors that they were sitting in a sacred place dedicated to the Morning Star. He told them that they went in search of Opirikuts, instructing that no hand must touch the captured woman except he, who called her Opirikuts and took hold of her first. Death was the punishment for any who disregarded this tradition. At the end, he instructed everyone to dance around the fire and show their bravery.

Though the band of Skidi Pawnee had already captured their female captive, the warriors danced around the fire and sang loudly to the Morning Star, as was their religious custom. Desire watched their actions, believing this ceremony to be the manner in which the Pawnee prayed to their gods. Her own people prayed in their own fashion each morning, to Wakán Tanka. She imagined that these warriors were now addressing their own gods, but in a different manner.

Again, it was Scar Hand who brought Desire food to break the morning fast, then in a manner that appeared cool and withdrawn, he offered her wash water and a porcupine quill comb for her hair.

After a full night's rest, plenty of food, washing her face and hands, and combing her hair, Desire felt much revived. As she received the surprised looks from her captors, she knew her appearance had greatly improved. She felt the curious stares as the morning progressed, but none but Scar Hand approached her or tried to converse with her in hand-signing. Desire hoped that once they reached their village, she would be able to convince someone to help her return to Cetán. If not, she would somehow escape and return to her husband, no matter the risks she'd be forced to take!

The afternoon of the third day, the Pawnee band, which had been instructed to bring back a female captive, arrived at their earthen-lodge village. The lodges had been erected with the use of heavy posts, cross-beams, brush, and earth. They were structured in a circle clustered around a large, central plaza surfaced by stone worn smooth with age.

Having dreaded the moment when she would be brought into her captors' village, Desire was taken by surprise by the lack of animosity directed her way by the villagers. She had expected outbursts of abuse for being an outsider, the same as she had witnessed in her own village. Surprised by the treatment bestowed on her by her captors during the trek to their village, she was totally confused by the smiles and calls of greeting directed at her by the villagers.

Scar Hand helped her to dismount. Taking her elbow, he led her to the center of the plaza, which had two groups of steps leading upward. The entire population of the village stood back from the steps, watching as Scar Hand slowly turned Desire around so everyone could see her features. Then in a loud voice he cried, "Opirikuts!"

Again, the warrior called her that strange name, and afterward, the villagers shouted praise and thanksgiving. Desire had no idea what was taking place, or who Opirikuts was! She had expected to be treated as a lowly slave in the Pawnee village, but apparently these people thought differently.

In total confusion, Desire watched the approach of two elders. As the villagers quieted, Scar Hand stepped aside and the two men stood beside her.

Silver Wolf, keeper of the Morning Star Bundle, looked the captive over with a critical eye. He had already heard that the young woman had not been taken captive in the usual way. As her tawny-gold eyes looked into his own, Silver Wolf's lips pulled back into a rare smile. Surely this woman would appease the Morning Star, ensure the renewal of life in their village, and help prevent the destruction of their world by sun-fire. His gray head nodded agreement; this female captive was indeed Opirikuts!

It was to the high priest of the Skidi Pawnee, Yellow Plume, that Desire's fate was handed. Like Silver Wolf, Yellow Plume's piercing jet eyes scanned every inch of the captive woman. Dressed in his ceremonial robe of dyed black elk hide with embellishments of the Morning Star painted over front and back, the frail figure of the ancient priest seemed lost within the garment's folds. His hand rose upward, gnarled fingers twisted, yellow nails long and curling downward; then his hand was brought down on the head of the captive. "You are to be honored as our daughter." He stated the Pawnee words in a gravelly voice. "Opirikata, the Morning Star, will shower his pleasure on us, for the gift of the one with the golden eyes!"

The people cried out in agreement to the aged priest's words. Having no idea what was happening, Desire endured the touch of the old man with the lank, gray hair and foul breath.

"Wolf Ghost and his family will see to our daughter's needs until the stars reveal a sign for the start of the Morning Star Ceremony to commence." Yellow Plume removed his hand. A middle-aged warrior stepped up onto the stone plaza; Yellow Plume's gnarled fingers clasped hold of Desire's, setting her hand in the man's known as Wolf Ghost.

Thusly, the female captive for the Morning Star Ceremony was placed in the care of one who represented the Wolf Star, wolf in Pawnee mythology being blamed for bringing death into the world. This ceremonial transfer of the captive sealed Desire's fate.

Wolf Ghost was pleased that this duty of caring for the female captive had been entrusted to him and his family. With a great show of affection before the villagers, he patted Desire's shoulder and called her *daughter.*

Desire wondered if she were being given over as a slave to this kindly, smiling warrior who was patting her shoulder in a paternal fashion. Instant terror assaulted her again and set her limbs to trembling when the warrior placed his arm over her shoulder and began to walk across the plaza. Unanswered questions raced through her mind. Where was this man taking her? What was he going to do with her? Would he force himself upon her the minute the villagers were out of sight? Was this the reason she had been brought to this village and so carefully tended while on the trail? Had she been brought here to be a slave . . . or more, to this man whose strong arm held her against him as he led her where he would?

As she was led down the steps of the plaza, Desire attempted to draw away from the warrior, but the effort was wasted. The arm draped over her shoulder drew her tighter to the man's side. As the villagers followed behind in a long procession, Wolf Ghost took her to a small, earthen lodge in the center of the village.

Smiling in the same affectionate manner, Wolf Ghost hand-signed that Desire was to enter the lodge. At her hesitation, husky laughter filled her ears and his hand reached out to pat her shoulder, once again. As caretaker for the female captive, part of Wolf Ghost's obligation was to make every effort to conceal the ordained ritual from the young woman in his charge. Not wishing to frighten her any more than she already was, he lightly nudged her through the entryway.

Though there were many among the Skidi Pawnee who objected to the Morning Star Ceremony, none dared to openly object or interfere with the treatment of the female captive; legend held that to do so would result in the offender's instant death. Many of the villagers turned away from the lodge as the young woman entered. In the minds of some, it would be far better to kill the young woman outright than to allow her to live until the star signs would deem it time for her to give her life on the Morning Star scaffold. Others, though, rejoiced with the arrival of the female captive into their midst. The old traditions lived in their hearts. With the depletion of their lands and the hard toll of survival, there was renewed hope that the appeasement given to the Morning Star would restore the lifestyle once belonging to the Pawnee.

Desire was gently pushed inside the lodge. Standing within the entrance, it took her a few seconds to adjust her eyes to the dim interior. In the center of the earthen floor there was a shallow pit fire, the glowing flames the only light inside the surprisingly roomy lodge.

Wolf Ghost did not enter, but instead he motioned for his eldest daughter, who had been standing among the crowd of villagers. "You, Night Lilly, will see to the captive's needs. Your brother, Horned Elk, will keep guard outside the captive's lodge."

"Why must I see to the young woman's needs, Father? Why do you not give this task to Little Waters, my sister?" The young woman called Night Lilly did not appreciate being signaled out for the job of catering to the captive's needs. In fact, Night Lilly strongly objected to the entire idea of the Morning Star Ceremony.

"Little Waters will help when she is needed, as will the rest of my family," Wolf Ghost admonished his daughter. "Though you now have your own lodge and husband, you cannot forget the traditions of your people, Night Lilly. It is an important part of the Morning Star Ceremony that the captive be happy with her surroundings. You will be blessed by Opirikata for your efforts."

Night Lilly knew that her wish to stay at a distance from the preparations for the ceremony would not be respected. She had been raised in a family that was proud to represent the Wolf Star. As Wolf Ghost's daughter, her father believed it Night Lilly's duty to serve the captive female. There would be no getting out of this duty. Silently nodding her dark head, Night Lilly bent to enter the lodge.

Desire spun around to face the person who had followed

her through the entryway. Though the one who entered the lodge was a very beautiful young woman, her unease did not lessen.

As Night Lilly glimpsed the wide-eyed fear that crossed the captive's features, sympathy for the young woman touched her heart. Forcing a smile, she looked in each direction of the lodge, then, pointing to Desire, indicated that this would be her new home.

The interior had been decorated regally so the captive of the Morning Star would have every available comfort. The earthen walls were covered with bleached-white buffalo robes, and drawings of animals had been artfully arranged from top to bottom. Near the center fire was a beautifully beaded backrest, which boasted downy eagle-breath feathers along the edges. To one side was a large sleeping couch piled high with silver wolf and fox furs. Desire watched the other woman's movements and understood her meaning, but fear of the unknown could not be set aside. "Who are you? Why have I been brought here?" she questioned in the Sioux tongue.

Night Lilly shook her head, indicating that she did not understand the other woman's words.

Desire desperately wanted to communicate with someone. She needed to understand what was happening in this Pawnee village. Communication might be the only way that she would win her freedom! Pointing to herself, she repeated her name over and over. "Wacin . . . Wacin."

The young woman stared at her with a blank expression. Night Lilly had never been exposed to the Sioux dialect, and she had no understanding of what the woman was trying to say.

In frustration, Desire stated louder, in the wasichu tongue, which Autumn Dawn had been teaching her, "My name is Desire!"

Surprise lit up Night Lilly's features. "You speak the white-eyes' tongue?"

Desire nodded in grateful disbelief. It had only been chance that she had spoken out in English. Frustration at wanting to communicate had forced her to try anything!

"I too speak the tongue of the white-eyes," Night Lilly stated proudly. "My mother's sister, Little Dawn, joined with a trapper called John Smith, many winters past. He stayed in our village for a long time and taught many of the children, including me and my brother, his words."

Night Lilly spoke the wasichu words much better than Desire, but much of what she said, Desire understood. Trying to calm her racing pulse, she formed words in her mind before saying them. Desire slowly questioned, "What is your name?"

"I am called Night Lilly. My father, Wolf Ghost, sent me here to tend to your needs."

"Wolf Ghost? Was he the warrior who led me to this lodge?"

Night Lilly smiled warmly, nodding her head. "My family will see to all your needs; whatever you desire, you have but to tell me." It would be much easier now that the two women could communicate, Night Lilly told herself.

Desire was more confused than ever. What did the young woman mean when she said that her family would see to all her needs? "Why am I here in this lodge? Have I been brought here to be a slave?" She could not force herself to ask the most dreaded question of all: was her purpose here to become either Wolf Ghost's or another warrior's woman?

Night Lilly smiled fully before trying to reassure the captive. "Do you not like this lodge?"

"It is fine, but I don't understand my purpose here in your village."

"Why do you not rest for a while on the sleeping couch? I will bring you clean clothes and something to eat."

"But you haven't explained anything! Why am I here? Am I going to be a slave?" When outsiders had been brought into her own village, it had always been for the purpose of lightening the workload.

"You will not be slave to any in this village, Desire."

"Then, why was I brought here?" Desire feared the answer, but she longed to know her fate.

"If you badger me with such questions, I will no longer speak the tongue of the white-eyes with you." Night Lilly could not tell the young woman her purpose here in the Pawnee village, and she felt uncomfortable with the questions being asked of her.

"But . . ."

"Rest now. I will return later." Night Lilly turned back toward the lodge's entryway.

"Can you not at least tell me if I will have to share this lodge with another?" Desire could not let the other woman leave without knowing if, while she was resting, someone would join her on the sleeping couch.

Night Lilly laughed softly. "Rest easy, Desire. You will share this lodge with no other."

"Then, why am I here?" Desire cried out, her head throbbing in her confusion.

"No more questions." Night Lilly's tone instantly hardened. "If you need anything before I return, Horned Elk will be outside. He will see that you get what is needed." Night Lilly did not linger any longer, but was relieved to get away from the young woman's questions.

Desire started to follow Night Lilly through the entryway, but was halted by the presence of a young man standing guard outside the lodge. The solid bulk of his body barred her from leaving the lodge, and was a harsh reminder that she was a Pawnee captive. Choking back bitter sobs, Desire turned back into her prison.

The only relief for Desire was Night Lilly's assurance that she would not be forced to endure the attentions of any Pawnee brave. For the first time since Panther Stalks had abducted her, she gave full vent to the anguish that filled her heart. Without understanding her purpose in this village, and tormented because of the separation forced upon her and Cetán, the tears that flowed down her cheeks were not halted. In the isolation of this decorated prison, Desire wept out her unhappiness.

Later, as she fell in sheer exhaustion upon the pallet of silver furs, she cried her husband's name aloud. "Cetán, I fear I will never see you again . . . my heart aches in misery!"

Twenty-seven

Early in the morning, the hunting party had come on the herd of buffalo they had been seeking. Cetán rode ahead with the braves, and at the first charge, he and Whirling-Warrior's-Ghost crested the rise that separated the great shaggy beasts from the Sioux encampment that had been set up the afternoon before. The first shot of Cetán's bow brought down the first kill. With shouts and whoops from the rest of the braves, the warriors attacked, killing as many animals as possible.

Throughout the rest of the day, warriors and women worked side by side. Great hunks of buffalo meat were stacked on travois and carried back to camp. The hides, bones, vital organs, hooves, and brains were set aside for the use of the people. It was hard, dirty work, but it meant the survival of the Sioux, and there were no complaints until the work was finished.

That afternoon, while Cetán washed himself and Whirling-Warrior's-Ghost stood in the rushing stream drinking his fill, Cetán's thoughts turned to Wacin. The image that he held in his mind of his bride usually brought him peace, but this day, he could not set aside the feeling that something was not right. Wading further into the cool water, he splashed water over his head and chest, hoping that the uneasiness that gripped him would somehow vanish.

Standing silent in the knee-deep water, Cetán tried to

fight off his mounting anxiety. There was no relief to be found. The rustling of the overhead trees, bending with the slight afternoon breeze, seemed to call out his heart's name. The rush of the swirling water formed an ominous background to his dark thoughts. The need to act pressed in on him. "Wacin," he called aloud. He turned sharply, thinking that someone was playing tricks on him. He was alone . . . alone with his nameless fears, and the terrifying image in his mind of his wife crying out to him.

Desire was unsure how long she slept, but on waking, she found the center fire built up and a bowl of savory stew warming next to the coals. Her sleep had been troubled; she had gotten little rest, her dreams plagued by disturbing visions of her Pawnee captors, Panther Stalks, and Cetán. Taking up the wooden bowl and spoon, Desire knew she would have to endure her fate until she could escape, or her husband could somehow miraculously rescue her.

It was not until the next morning that Night Lilly returned to the lodge. Over her arm she carried a gown that, except for the occasion when the female captive of the Morning Star wore it, remained in the Morning Star Bundle. The dress was made of soft, bleached elk hide, taken from the underbelly of the animal. Delicate beadwork decorated both sleeves, the neck and chest area, and the hemline. As Night Lilly held up the gown, Desire's attention was fully captured; she had never seen such a beautiful dress.

"I will take you to the river so you can bathe," Night Lilly stated in the white-eyes' tongue.

Desire was more than willing to follow the other woman to the river to wash away the days of travel from her body. She had only been able to remove the visible dirt picked up on the trail since her abduction, and she longed to submerge her body in the refreshing depths of a cool, clear river. "Thank you for the stew you brought last night, Night

Lilly. It was very good." Desire had awakened early this morning and had lain abed, making plans to escape from this village. By befriending this young woman, perhaps she would be able to get aid. The first step would be to win Night Lilly's trust.

"My sister brought you your food last night. My mother will bring food this morning while we are at the river." Night Lilly was pleased to find the captive in a responsive mood. "I have brought you a fine robe and slippers." These also had been taken from the Morning Star Bundle, and Night Lilly set the articles of clothing on the sleeping couch. Keeping the robe over her arm, she led Desire from the lodge.

As the young women made their way through the village, Desire noticed that the young man who had stood guard outside the lodge last night was following, but kept his distance. "Who is that following us?" Desire questioned. When the young woman had informed her that she would be taking her to the river, a wild thought went through Desire's mind; perhaps she would be able to overpower Night Lilly and make her escape. She now knew she would not get such a chance.

"That is my brother, Horned Elk. Do not pay any attention to him." Night Lilly tried to put the captive's mind at ease, but did not offer to send her brother away.

At the river, Horned Elk went down the bank and sat with his back propped against a tree. He appeared to pay the two women little attention, but Desire was fully aware of his presence. Sensing that the young man would react swiftly to any disturbance made by the two women, she knew she would not get the chance to escape this morning.

"I have brought along a cream that will aid in washing your hair and body. It is pleasant to the senses. My mother makes it, and my sisters and myself find it very refreshing."

Desire distrustingly held out her hand for the horn vial the young woman held up for inspection.

Night Lilly ignored her hand. "I will help you wash, Desire. You have had a long ordeal on the trail; you must still be tired. I am here to help you with any task." The young woman set down the vial and, without hesitation, lifted her dress over her head and kicked off her moccasins. Stepping to Desire's side, she began to lift the hem of her hide dress in order to help her remove her clothing.

"I am quite capable." Desire tried to pull away, but the young woman was relentless.

"I am here to help you." Night Lilly tugged harder until Desire's grip on the side of her dress lessened.

Within seconds, both young women were standing naked along the riverbank. Desire cast a hurried glance toward Horned Elk, but found him gazing off in the opposite direction. Without waiting for Night Lilly to retrieve the horn vial, she dove into the swirling, cool depths of the river.

Desire had no say in the matter as Night Lilly took over her bathing. She spread the fragrant-smelling, white-colored lotion through her long, dark hair, and over her entire body. Talking about inconsequential matters that did not concern Desire, Night Lilly lathered the captive female's body and hair and then allowed her to rinse the creamy, smooth substance from her body.

Desire's bathing was completed quickly, and after climbing back up the riverbank, Night Lilly wrapped the robe around her and led her back to the lodge. Horned Elk followed, once again at a short distance.

Once inside the lodge, Night Lilly dried Desire's body and led her nearer the warmth of the center fire. As Desire reached out to draw the robe around herself, Night Lilly's hands stilled her. "Come and relax on the sleeping couch, Desire. I will rub a soothing lotion over your body. It will ease your tired muscles."

What captive was ever pampered in such a lavish manner? Desire wondered as she was drawn toward the sleeping couch and coaxed into lying down.

Pouring small amounts of the soothing balm into her palm and massaging Desire's body, Night Lilly put her full attention to the task at hand and did not speak until she finished. Then she held up a bowl of red ocher mixed with a small amount of buffalo fat. "It is our custom, Desire, that you are painted each morning."

"Painted? It is your custom? For what purpose, Night Lilly? Please, won't you tell me why I am here?"

"I am told that the paint put on after the lotion is pleasant on the flesh. You will feel no discomfort." Night Lilly pointedly ignored the other woman's questions.

Desire was beginning to understand; the other woman would answer none of her questions relating to her purpose in the Pawnee village!

"While you are being painted, you can eat the meal that my mother left by the fire for you while we were at the river," Night Lilly offered. Before she began the painting procedure, Night Lilly retrieved the wooden bowl and spoon that had been brought from the Morning Star Bundle and left in the lodge for the captive's use. Her mother had filled the bowl with the choicest pieces of meat from her family's morning meal. Night Lilly entreated Desire to lie upon her stomach and eat the food while she rubbed the mixture of red ocher and buffalo fat over her backside.

After the body painting, Night Lilly helped Desire to dress in the elk gown and matching moccasins. "Let us sit near the fire, Desire. I will comb out your hair," Night Lilly offered.

"I can at least comb my hair myself." Desire had never been one to sit still and let someone pamper her, and she had taken about as much of Night Lilly's ministrations as she could suffer.

"It is the custom that this duty be performed for you each day," Night Lilly interjected before Desire had the chance to take up the comb lying near the beaded backrest. "Sit down and enjoy this attention, Desire."

Confused, and in no position to protest, Desire obeyed. Her body felt refreshed as never before. Her flesh tingled in a strangely pleasant way, due to the massage and the body painting. And now, Night Lilly was tending to her hair as she sat before the warmth of the center fire. One would think she was an honored guest among the Pawnee instead of a captive, Desire reflected. But before she became too complacent, the image of Cetán boldly swept to the forefront of her mind. "Are you joined with a warrior from this village, Night Lilly?" Desire asked the other woman.

As Night Lilly braided Desire's hair in a plump length down the center of her back, she bound eagle-breath feathers across the crown before answering. "My husband is known as White Bull. He was one of the warriors with the hunting party which brought you back to the village."

Desire wondered which of the warriors was Night Lilly's husband and hoped, for the young woman's sake, that it was not the one who had been the leader. She had sensed a cruelness about the warrior, and though Night Lilly was her enemy, the young woman had been kind to her, even though she refused to answer all of her questions.

"Are you in love with this White Bull, Night Lilly?" Desire was not sure if the young woman would think she was prying, but she hoped that conversation might help her gain her release, through friendship.

"White Bull and I have always loved one another. Even as children, we played together as we joined the other children of the village. As the years passed, White Bull and I sought each other out more often, and three summers past, we joined our life-paths. All in our village knew that we belonged to each other and were not surprised that we joined." Night Lilly's soft laughter filled the lodge.

"I also am joined with a warrior, and like you and your husband, Cetán and I love each other very much." Desire tried to keep her tone as light as possible, but she had to use much effort. Thoughts of Cetán brought sharp tears into her eyes.

"Do you wish to keep your bells in your hair?" Night Lilly did not wish to hear any more about Desire's past life. Knowing the young woman's eventual fate was bad enough without hearing about the one she loved, and would never see again.

"I would feel naked without them," Desire responded as Night Lilly twined the bells, secured to the strips of trade-cloth, through the single braid. Drawing a deep breath, she broached the subject, once again, of her being captive in this Pawnee village. "Night Lilly, you are not at fault for my being held here in your village, but you must know how much I wish to return to my husband. Cetán would reward you with any gift you wish if you would help me escape." Desire turned and looked at the other woman, her tears now flowing without let-up as the ache in her heart intensified.

For a few minutes silence filled the lodge, and as the tension mounted, Night Lilly could only stare into the damp, golden eyes. She was unable to help this woman. She was powerless! There was no helping the captive of the Morning Star! Once again, Night Lilly wished that her father had given her sister this job of tending to the female captive's needs. She did not wish to hear about the captive's husband and the love she had for him. Her own love for White Bull made her vulnerable to Desire's pleas for release!

That evening, Night Lilly left her husband's lodge to take a portion of their evening meal to Desire. Before arriving at the female captive's lodge, she was approached by Scar Hand.

"How is our little Morning Star captive, Night Lilly?" Scar Hand's fingers lightly caressing Night Lilly's upper arm, where the tender flesh was revealed beneath the pale moon-light.

Pulling her arm out of his reach, Night Lilly struggled to hide the fear she felt whenever she was in Scar Hand's presence. "The captive is well, Scar Hand. There is no cause for worry. She does not know her fate, and is being pampered and feted by my family, as is our custom." Night Lilly had caught Scar Hand watching her upon occasion as she went about her work in the village with the other women, and this evening the usual feelings of revulsion nearly overwhelmed her. Keeping a tight grip on her emotions, she told herself that the only reason Scar Hand approached her was because he had been the leader of the hunting party that had brought the female captive back to the village.

"I do not worry, Night Lilly. Wolf Ghost will see that his part of the ceremony is carried out in the manner that is called for."

"Then, why do you stop me in the dark? Is it my husband that you wish to speak with? White Bull is in our lodge. I am sure he would enjoy your company, Scar Hand." Night Lilly hoped that talk of her husband would remind this warrior that she was joined with another and it was not proper for her to be alone in the dark with him. She feared and disliked Scar Hand because of his reputation for cruelty, and the stories she had heard about the mistreatment inflicted on his past two wives. There was much talk among the village women about Scar Hand, and none of it was favorable.

"It is not White Bull that I seek, but you, Night Lilly." Scar Hand reached out to feel her tender flesh, but this time, he did not allow her to draw her arm away. His fingers pressed into the soft skin of her forearm as his dark eyes sought out the traces of fear he knew were hidden in the depths of her eyes.

"What is it that you want from me?" Night Lilly gasped,

not wishing to call out for help for fear that White Bull would hurry to her rescue and a fight would ensue. Night Lilly was practical and did not delude herself that her husband could best Scar Hand, nor did she want her brother, Horned Elk, to be forced into facing this warrior over his sister's honor.

"I have just left Silver Wolf's lodge. As keeper of the medicine bundle, it is up to him to say when the star signs read that it is time to commence with the Morning Star ceremony. In the passing of three suns, Silver Wolf will announce that on the fourth day, the ceremony will begin."

"What has that to do with me?" Night Lilly would be glad to have the ceremony over so her life could get back to normal!

The slight pressure on her arm increased. "On the first day of the ceremony, Yellow Plume will gather the people. At that time, he will inform the village women that if any warrior desires her and approaches her, she is expected to go with him so the tribe might increase."

Night Lilly's features paled beneath the moonlight. Her body began to tremble as she looked into the dark eyes staring down at her. She had known this portion of the ceremony would eventually come, but she had not allowed it to affect her, telling herself that she was joined with White Bull; he would take no other woman during the ceremony, and she had given no thought to any man approaching her with expectations of lying with her.

"When that day comes, Night Lilly, I will seek you out." Scar Hand had been waiting for the time when he would be able to taste the tender flesh of the beautiful Night Lilly. Soon that day would be at hand, and his waiting would be at a finish!

"No!" Night Lilly gasped, jerking her arm free. "I will never willingly . . ."

"You will have no choice!"

"But White Bull . . ."

"Will wait alone in his lodge for you to leave my lodge, after I have finished with you!"

The horror stories that Night Lilly had heard about Scar Hand and his abuse of women came starkly to mind. It was said that his manhood was the size of a full-grown pony's, one woman swearing that there was a great knob on the head. Both of Scar Hand's wives had died from severe hemorrhaging. Many evenings, the women's cries had been heard throughout the village as he hammered at them without mercy! Not only did he inflict his wrath upon women sexually, but often his wives had visible marks from his disabuse.

Night Lilly knew that her slender body would not be able to sustain such abuse! She looked at the warrior, proudly declaring his intention to use her as cruelly as he had his wives. There was nothing she could do or say that could change his mind! It was the custom of the people, a part of the Morning Star ceremony! For her to deny him her body would be the same as hindering the joining of the Morning Star with the Evening Star.

"In four days, I will enter the paradise of your body, Night Lilly. Then, you will know the worth of a real man!" Scar Hand grinned widely before he turned to walk away, leaving the beautiful Night Lilly shakingly pale as she followed his retreating back. He had waited for this opportunity, even volunteering to become the leader of the hunting party sent out to capture a female for the Morning Star ceremony. Throughout the seven days of the ceremonial rites, Scar Hand could seek Night Lily out as often as his body's needs demanded, and there would be nothing White Bull could do about it!

Not only would he indulge himself in the pleasure of Night Lilly's body, but he would also get his revenge against White Bull! The other warrior would think better of openly defying him in front of the other warriors again!

Twenty-eight

The same day of the buffalo hunt, Cetán gathered his belongings and started back to the village alone. He could not quell his uneasy feelings about his wife, and so he pushed Whirling-Warrior's-Ghost harder than in past days on the trail. Cetán arrived in the village in less than half the time it had taken the hunting party to find the buffalo.

In the Sioux valley, Cetán found things as he had left them. There was no indication that Looking Hawk, Willow, and Desire had not arrived safely at Gray Owl's village.

Finding Elkhunter healed and rested and ready to travel, Cetán dismissed Spirit Walker's advice to remain and rest throughout the day and night before setting back out on the trail.

There was no sign of life in his lodge, the interior cold and uninviting without Wacin there to greet him. His thoughts centered on getting to Gray Owl's village. He would not rest until he could see and feel Wacin, and know that all was well.

Gathering a few fresh supplies, with Elkhunter running ahead, Cetán started Whirling-Warrior's-Ghost upon the forest trail that would lead them to the Oglala village.

A few hours later, Elkhunter began to run back and forth, howling and barking as he sniffed at the ground and kicked up dirt with his hind legs.

"Settle down!" Cetán commanded, wondering if the wolf had lost his senses, but remaining cautious in case this was

Elkhunter's way of giving a warning. He was not as familiar
with the great beast as was Wacin, but as he watched the
animal once again dashing ahead of Whirling-Warrior's-
Ghost's sharp hooves and then running back up the trail,
his free hand tightened on the wood portion of his rifle-
stock weapon. He would be prepared if there was an attack—even Whirling-Warrior's-Ghost appeared to be
listening and watching for signs of an enemy.

What Cetán found up ahead on the trail was not the
enemy, but the dead bodies of Looking Hawk and Willow.
The couple had been cruelly murdered and left where they
had fallen from their horses.

Cautiously, Cetán dismounted. Whirling-Warrior's-
Ghost snorted warily at the scent of death. Going to the
bodies, Cetán determined that the couple had been taken
by surprise and attacked from behind; they had never had
a chance!

"Wacin!" The name of Cetán's beloved erupted from
his lips. Dismounting, his dark gaze circled the area for
any sign of his wife.

Elkhunter came to Cetán's side, his large yellow eyes
studying the man who had called out his mistress's name.
Sensing Cetán's anguish, the great wolf turned and ran
back the way they had just come. The sharp sound of the
animal's barking brought Cetán out of the sorrowful stupor
that suddenly surrounded his heart.

Mounting the stallion, Cetán knew there had to be some
sign that he had missed. Wacin had not been murdered as
had her companions! He would have felt her departure
from Mother Earth—his heart would have been crushed
the instant she drew her last breath. Wacin was that part
of him that kept his path straight upon Mother Earth. If
she were gone, he would bend as the mighty tree before a
crushing storm!

Turning Whirling-Warrior's-Ghost back down the trail,
Cetán tried to remain calm. He would have to use all of

his knowledge of trails and forest signs to discern any disturbance along the path. The bodies had been lying there for several days. The attack had come the same day the small party had left the Lakota village. Much time had passed, but thankfully it had not rained in the past few weeks. Cetán's sharp eyes took in everything along the trail; if there was a sign to pick up, he would not miss it!

Suddenly Elkhunter's sharp nose scented his mistress's parfleche. Running back to the trail and then into the forest for several yards, he barked sharply for attention.

Following the wolf off the trail, Cetán inhaled sharply as he glimpsed the hide satchel lying on the ground. Wacin's plant-stick was lying next to the parfleche; it was apparent that she had been here digging her medicine plants. "Still!" Cetán commanded as the wolf pawed and whined at the bag.

Elkhunter immediately obeyed. Cetán's dark eyes studied the surroundings. Dismounting, he brushed away the dried leaves around the parfleche and plant-stick, easily discerning the imprints of his wife's moccasined feet. The earth was dry beneath the canopy of trees, and as Cetán searched out his wife's prints, he noticed another set; it was obvious by the size that these were made by a warrior.

Brushing away more leaves, he discovered the hoof markings of two ponies. Cetán knew one set belonged to Star, the other . . . he did not wish to admit that his wife had been taken captive, but Cetán was not a man who could ignore the truth when it was right in front of him! And the truth was, Wacin had been taken away by a warrior who had come upon her here in the forest.

Straightening, Cetán's fingers caressed the fringed edging of his wife's parfleche. Some small sense of relief filled his heart. For a second he closed his eyes as he savored this feeling. Wacin had not been murdered, as had her companions! His wife still lived . . . and somehow he would find her!

Once again Elkhunter began to whine; racing back toward the forest trail, he barked loudly for Cetán to follow. Mounting Whirling-Warrior's-Ghost, Cetán followed the great wolf. Crossing the forest path, his nose pressed to the earth, Elkhunter headed in a south-westerly direction.

I will find you, Wacin! Hold on, my heart! We will not be parted forever! Cetán's inner being cried for his wife to have courage, and not give up. He would find her, no matter how long it took!

Over the next two days, Desire was bathed and massaged, her body painted, her hair combed and trimmed with eagle breath feathers. Food was continually brought before her in the Morning Star bowl. She was pampered and entertained, her slightest wish fulfilled—except the one thing she desired above all else . . . her freedom!

On the third afternoon, shortly after the midday meal, Night Lilly placed the Morning Star buffalo robe over Desire's shoulders and asked that she sit on the beaded backrest before the center fire.

It was not long before Silver Wolf, keeper of the Morning Star Bundle, Yellow Plume, the Pawnee high priest, and Star Chief, the Skidi Pawnee high chief, entered the captive's lodge. Silver Wolf held an aged, smooth piece of hide with a drawing of the star chart on its surface. Looking at the chart, the keeper of the Morning Star Bundle instructed the higher-ups of the village about where they were to sit in the female captive's lodge.

Silver Wolf sat at the captive's right, and as the interior of the lodge filled with the warriors, Wolf Ghost, representing the Wolf Star, sat directly behind the high priest.

Desire sat on the beaded backrest as beautifully bedecked as a queen, but beneath the buffalo robe her limbs were shaking uncontrollably. She had no idea what was taking place. Her fear intensified as the lodge filled with warriors, but no village women. Her appearance was pale, her golden eyes large as she looked from Silver Wolf to Yellow Plume.

Wishing to put her at ease, Silver Wolf reached out and lightly patted her hand. "You are honored, you are honored," he softly assured her in the Pawnee tongue.

Yellow Plume placed sweet grass in the center fire after the warriors were all seated. Standing, he began chanting a prayer, evoking the presence of Tirawahat, the Pawnee high god.

Desire tried to understand what was taking place, and reasoned that the one speaking must be the village holy man.

With the finish of the prayer, Yellow Plume sat back down and Silver Wolf rose. "The star signs have been read, my brothers, and they tell us that the time is right for the Morning Star Ceremony to commence. Tomorrow, the anima powers will begin their four-day ritual of being set aside. With these powers reduced, the captive will be vulnerable. On the fourth day, the designated warriors will go to the sacred place and erect the scaffold of elm and cottonwood for the uprights, willow and box elder for the cross-pieces. With this done, the animal powers will be retained here on Mother Earth and the upright posts will hold up the sky."

The warriors shouted out their agreement. Desire cringed against the backrest. Having no understanding of the Pawnee tongue, she was unaware of the plans that these men were making for her death.

As was the custom, the keeper of the Morning Star Bundle recited the days of the Morning Star Ceremony aloud to the village men. Such a ceremony had not been performed here in many years, and it was Silver Wolf's duty to instruct everyone in the manner that had been passed down from generation to generation. "On the seventh day the captive will be dressed in a black robe and moccasins, her body will be painted black on one side, red on the other; these colors will signify night and the Evening Star and day, the time of the Morning Star. Her head will be embellished with eagle feathers and a hawk skin, which will signify the messenger bird of the Morning Star."

"The captive will believe this a ceremony held in her honor. She will be led to the scaffold before dawn, shortly before the Morning Star rises in the sky. Being coaxed, the captive will climb the scaffold, where her hands and legs will be tied with the thongs made from the skins of the sacred animals. She will be facing east, greeting the Morning Star."

Silver Wolf drew in a deep breath before continuing. "This is a crucial time, my brothers, and we must make sure all goes well. As the Morning Star appears, two warriors will step out of hiding and approach the captive with firebrands. They will touch her lightly on her loins and arms in order to overcome all obstacles in the path of the Morning Star. I, the keeper of the Morning Star Bundle," Silver Wolf added as his chest puffed out, "will step from behind the designated tree of hiding with a bow and arrow from the sacred Skull Bundle; my arrow will be blessed by Tirawahat, and will pierce the captive's heart. Star Chief will then go forward with the club from the Skull Bundle and strike the captive on the head. The captive's soul will go straight to Tirawahat, who will then direct her to the Morning Star, from whom she will receive clothing of glowing flint, and she shall be placed in the great vault of the heavens, where the people for whom she gave her life will always see her. When her body is taken down from the scaffold, it will be placed facedown upon the earth, in order to enrich our lands. There will be rejoicing in our village; crops and game will be abundant again, and warriors will be successful in war!"

The men in the captive female's lodge shouted their approval. The people's spirit in the Pawnee village had been low, their crops had been lacking, their lands intruded upon, and game scarce. The Morning Star Ceremony would ensure that they would survive and live in plenty once again!

"We will find favor in our father's sight once again!" Silver Wolf shouted. "We will be reminded of the struggles of the great male star in subduing the female white star in order that life might be renewed here among our people!"

The shouts turned to an uproar. Yellow Plume, noticing the stark fear on the female captive's face, quieted the men. "Save your rejoicing for outside, away from the Morning Star captive. She is the holy one of Opirikuts, and is not to be frightened."

The noise in the lodge immediately calmed as the males of the village made their way back through the entryway. Before passing by the center fire and the captive female sitting on the backrest, each village man, in turn, held his hand to his chest, giving honor to Desire.

When the last warrior filed out, Night Lilly reentered. "What was that all about?" Desire questioned the other woman.

Over the past few days, Night Lilly had grown fond of the captive female, and because of this, and the fact that lying never came easy to her, she felt some shame when she gave her reply. "The warriors of the village wished to pay you great honor. It is the custom of the Pawnee to do so in this fashion."

Desire could not fathom the reason why her captives would honor her in any fashion, and said this aloud to Night Lilly. Stepping away from the center fire and backrest, she began to pace around the interior of the lodge. "I cannot imagine any custom that forces its captors to honor their enemy! I know you are not telling me the truth, Night Lilly." Desire turned and fully faced the other young woman. "Please tell me what is going on!"

Night Lilly could not look the captive in the face, and

as those golden eyes settled on her, she turned her head away. "I have given you no reason to distrust me, Desire. Why would I wish to lie to you?"

"I am not sure," Desire confessed. "But, if I am to be so honored, why don't your people just let me leave this village and go back to my husband?" Tears stung Desire's eyes, but for the moment, she ignored them.

"This is not for me to say. As I have told you before, I cannot talk to you about these matters. I will leave you now, to get you some of the ripe berries my mother picked this morning." Night Lilly was anxious to get out of the lodge, and away from the young woman's questions.

"I am tired of being fed and pampered! I want to know why I am being kept isolated here!" This meeting of the warriors and the manner in which they had acted had given Desire more reason to be concerned. There was more happening in this village than they were letting her be aware of, and she was sure their actions were not, as she was being told, in her honor!

Night Lilly did not linger to answer any more questions. Instead, she hurried through the village, not stopping until she was safely inside her own lodge. White Bull met her at the entryway, his features filled with concern.

"What is the matter, wife? Has something happened to the female captive?" White Bull had been among the warriors in the lodge, and had noticed the captured one's pale, trembling state.

"No, White Bull, it is not the captive. Just hold me, please." Night Lilly pressed herself against her husband's chest, seeking the security of his embrace. Her own plight at the hands of Scar Hand seemed interwound with the fate of the captive, and Night Lilly was frightened of what tomorrow would hold for all of them, when the first day of the Morning Star Ceremony would commence!

Twenty-nine

The morning of the first day of the Morning Star Ceremony found Desire and Night Lilly performing the ritual of the female captive's toilet. This morning, Night Lilly paid special attention to every detail, readying Desire for the day ahead. Taking a step backward, Night Lilly admired her handiwork. The captive had never looked more beautiful. Desire glowed with natural health and beauty. As thoughts filled Night Lilly's inner consciousness of what this day might hold for her, she made her way to the center fire and retrieved the bowl of food her mother had brought to the lodge for the captive. *If only Scar Hand had not brought Desire back to the village as the captive for the Morning Star Ceremony! If only there was no ceremony!*

"You haven't told me why I must go to the chief's lodge this morning Night Lilly." The Pawnee woman had told Desire that when she finished the morning meal, she was to go to Star Chief's lodge. Desire was nervous about going to another meeting with the warriors of the village!

"All that is taking place is done in your honor, Desire." Night Lilly did not find the lie easy to get out of her mouth.

"I don't understand—why would anyone wish to honor me? What purpose is there for your people to honor one from a different tribe than their own?" Desire hoped that this morning the other woman would reveal more than she had in the past.

"Do not worry yourself, Desire. Just be pleased that you

are being honored among women." Some of what Night
Lilly stated, she truly believed. She had been raised with
the belief that it was an honor for a captive to be brought
into their village and be sacrificed to the Morning Star.
But, deep in another part of her reason, she told herself
that this tradition was cruel and inhuman. With her own
fear of Scar Hand and what the warrior intended to force
on her, she wanted to shout to Desire to take her chances
and escape by any means possible!

Night Lilly restrained the insane impulse that swept over
her. She could not encourage the captive to flee! With the
finish of the morning meal, the young Pawnee woman led
Desire out to the entryway of Star Chief's earthen lodge.

By this mid-morning hour, the men of the village were
already sitting in their designated positions. The interior
of the lodge had been totally cleared of furnishings. The
villagers sat on the earth around the center fire, and after
being prodded through the entryway by Night Lilly, Desire
was greeted warmly by the inhabitants.

Night Lilly did not remain at Desire's side, but exited
the lodge, returning to her own home and the duties that
awaited her there. Standing nervously before the group of
men, Desire cried out in alarm when Scar Hand stepped
to her side and took hold of her arm.

Scar Hand wore a costume from the Morning Star Bundle: leggings and moccasins made from black buckskin and
a headdress with twelve eagle feathers that stood upright
over the crown of his head. These indicated that he was
the personification of the Morning Star deity; in the
Pawnee legend, it was said that this is how that deity appeared in visions or dreams.

Scar Hand's lips turned back into a sneer as he pulled
the frightened captive closer to the center fire. Desire tried
to pull back, but her strength was lacking. Upon trembling
limbs, she stared at the men who encircled her.

"Opirikuts . . . Opirikuts!" Over and over, Scar Hand

shouted the word that meant *holy* for the Morning Star, and each time he did, the men shouted out their agreement. Never had there been such a beautiful captive sacrificed to the Morning Star! The gold of Desire's wide eyes gleamed as she glanced around in desperation, her skin shining from the red ochre that Night Lilly had rubbed so generously into her flesh. In the dim interior, the captive appeared to glow with a radiance that any deity would surely welcome with abundant pleasure!

Scar Hand released Desire, and for several minutes, he danced around the captive and the licking flames in the center pit. His voice was loud as he proclaimed to all how he and his band of hunters had come across the female captive. "She was guarded by a brave warrior!" he cried aloud in a boastful manner. "This Sioux warrior fought valiantly, but he could not save the female from being delivered into our midst and becoming the prize of Opirikata, the Morning Star!"

With the finish of Scar Hand's recital, the keeper of the Morning Star Bundle rose. In a loud voice, Silver Wolf instructed the high priest to take the three young men being instructed by Yellow Plume—who would one day themselves become Pawnee priests—to go outside the lodge and gather the four twelve-foot poles to be used in the opening portion of the ceremony.

As Yellow Plume and his apprentices exited, Silver Wolf began to speak to the gathering, his words having been taught to him years before by the previous keeper of the Morning Star Bundle. His speech was replete with symbolic statements, which made reference to the earth and animals as well as the sky powers; every now and then, Silver Wolf directed his full stare at the captive, as though relishing the power he had over the female.

It was during a lull in the speech that Yellow Plume and his priests brought the requested logs into the chief's lodge. The twelve-foot poles were placed with their ends resting in the fire, forming a cross with the ends pointing in a semi-cardinal direction, which resembled a four-pointed star, the fire glowing at the center. One of the four poles was of elm, which represented the bear and the northeast. The second was box elder, representing the mountain lion and the southwest. The third was cotton-wood, representing the wildcat and the northwest. The last was a willow pole, which represented the wolf and south-east. These poles represented the four star beasts which in Pawnee mythology were believed to have opposed the Morning Star as he sought union with the Evening Star. These poles were large enough to last through the four days of this part of the ceremony, and as they were gradually consumed, they would be pushed into the fire, but kept in the shape of the cross as they were eaten away by the flames. Thus, the Pawnee believed that the opposing star beasts were progressively destroyed.

Desire watched the men place the poles across the fire, and as ever, was at a loss to understand the meaning of what was taking place around her. The circling warriors appeared not to hold her any ill will; even as they whooped out their agreement with whatever the speaker was saying, no malice appeared to be directed at her.

With the conclusion of the ceremony, Silver Wolf instructed a group of men to go to a designated area, a mile east of the village, to begin construction of the sacrificial scaffold. After their departure, Star Chief instructed the apprentice priests to go out and call the villagers to gather before his lodge.

Throughout the entire four-day period, and also for three days after the actual sacrifice, the ordinary social rules of conduct in the Skidi Pawnee village were ignored. As the people gathered before Star Chief's lodge, Yellow Plume stood before the populace. He announced to all that beginning with the rising of the Morning Star on the following morning, if any man desired a particular woman and approached her, she was expected to go with him and do what he would desire of her so that the tribe might increase in population.

Night Lilly stood silent and pale among the village women as these instructions were announced. Her worst fears were beginning to be realized! She knew that Scar Hand had not made his threats without every intention of carrying them out! She would be forced to suffer his assault on her body, and there would be nothing her husband or father could do to save her!

"You must not seek Scar Hand out!" Night Lilly wept as she clutched the front of her husband's hide shirt. "He will kill you! He only waits for you to oppose him in order to have reason to destroy you, White Bull!" Night Lilly had worried over the matter of Scar Hand the entire day, and unable to bear the misery any longer, had confessed everything to her husband.

White Bull had gone into an immediate rage. How dare the other warrior approach his bride and declare his intent to use the Morning Star Ceremony as an excuse to take her to his sleeping pallet! He, like the rest of the villagers, knew about Scar Hand's sadistic behavior toward women. White Bull's first inclination was to call Scar Hand out!

"What will happen to me if you are killed, and I am left alone to the mercy of Scar Hand?" Tears fell from Night Lilly's exotic eyes, and White Bull felt the twist of a knife in his heart as he saw her misery. "I will let no one harm you, Night Lilly!" he swore as he held her tightly in his embrace.

For a few silent minutes, the couple stood in the middle of their lodge. They had loved each other since childhood, and now someone threatened to destroy all that they had built up over the years.

"What would you have me do, Night Lilly? If I do not

challenge Scar Hand, he will seek you out again when I am not around to protect you. I cannot sit by and wait for the time when he will try to use you as cruelly as he has other women in his past!" White Bull could not control his mounting anger as he thought of another man taking his beautiful Night Lilly to his mat and using her body to sate his madman's passions!

"I don't know what to do, White Bull," Night Lilly confessed. "I have tried to come up with a plan, but the ceremony has already commenced! There is nothing we can do now!"

"There is, perhaps, something you have not considered." White Bull brushed away the moisture on his wife's cheeks.

"I have considered everything. There is nothing we can do that will save me from Scar Hand!" Night Lilly was so caught up in her own fear and misery, she failed to notice the calm which had settled over her husband's features.

Taking Night Lilly's chilled hands within his own, White Bull led her over to the lodge fire and gently encouraged her to sit with him on his backrest. "If necessary, we can leave the village until the ceremony is finished, Night Lilly." His voice was strong and sure; feeling her body tremble, he gathered his wife tightly in his embrace.

"We cannot leave the village, White Bull! My father would be disgraced before the entire tribe if it were known that we left because of Scar Hand!" Night Lilly attempted to calm her emotions, knowing her husband was in as much pain as she was.

"Then I will take the captive away from the village! Without a captive, there will be no ceremony!"

White Bull's declaration hung in the air for a few moments as Night Lilly considered the outcome of such a proposal. "Elk Bull will help you take Desire to Bent's Fort, where you can trade her to the white men!" Night Lilly herself had considered encouraging the captive to flee, but

not until she heard her husband say these words had she
realized the full merit of such an idea. She knew that her
brother, once told of Scar Hand's threats to her, would be
more than willing to help White Bull take the captive to
the fort on the north side of the Arkansas River. Elk Bull
stood guard outside the captive's lodge; it would be believed that he went in search of the captive once she made
good an escape. If anyone asked about White Bull's where-
abouts during this time, Night Lilly would claim that her
husband went with Elk Bull in search of the captive!

Desire had fallen asleep upon the luxurious furs, and
like so many nights since her abduction by Panther Stalks,
her dreams were of Cetán. At times, she reviewed the happy
moments she and her husband had shared during the short
time they had been allowed. Other times, she wept softly
in her sleep over the loss of Cetán's strong arms holding
her tight. This evening in the depths of her mind's inner
workings, she lost all reason beneath Cetán's flaming kisses.
Their naked bodies came together in a spellbinding union
that left Desire calling her husband's name aloud.

"Hush, mitá wicánte, I am here at your side." The husky
tremor of his voice filled her with the security she longed
for.

"Cetán . . . I thought I was being held captive in a
Pawnee village! It was horrible! I didn't think I would ever
see you again!" Desire pressed herself tightly against her
husband's body, her face buried in the hollow of his throat
as she cried out in anguish.

"I am with you—I am always with you, Wacin. You are
my heart. I am nothing without you!"

"Wake up, Desire!" An urgent voice tried to intrude on
Desire's dream-world.

"No . . . no! Cetán, don't leave me!" Desire clung to the
night vision that was slowly fading.

"You cannot be stolen from my heart, Wacin! I am coming! I will find you!" Cetán slowly disappeared, his arms held out to her in parting.

Desire jerked upright, crying as she remembered the nightmare she was being forced to live out! As her dream disappeared and reality dawned, she saw Night Lilly standing over her. "You? What do you want at this hour? Am I not even allowed my dreams?" Tears of anguish glistened in the golden eyes and slipped down Desire's cheeks.

"You must get up and dress, Desire." Night Lilly spoke in urgent, hushed tones as she leaned over the captive's bed, her silhouette cloaked in a dark robe.

"Go away, Night Lilly. I am not up to any more of your strange ceremonies! You will have to wait until morning!" Desire's fear of being forced to face the tribal warriors again made her clutch the furs to her chest like a barrier of protection.

"No, you must listen! There are no more ceremonies, Desire. You must get away from the village tonight! There will be no other chance to escape!" Night Lilly was desperate to make the young woman get up and dress before she was discovered here in the captive's lodge at this late hour.

The urgency in Night Lilly's tone finally made its way into Desire's slumber-laden thoughts. Pulling herself upright to her elbows, she stared at the dark figure standing next to the sleeping couch. "Why do you want me to leave?" Instant alertness swept over Desire. She remembered the countless times she had begged Night Lilly to let her escape, and how many times the other woman had refused to speak to her when the subject came up. *This could be some kind of trap,* her mind warned. *Have a care where you place your trust!*

Night Lilly reached out and took hold of Desire's wrist. "My husband and brother await you on the outskirts of the village, with horses. If you do not go with them tonight, you will be sacrificed to the Morning Star with the passing of three suns. If you remain, I will also become a sacrifice, but to Scar Hand, the warrior who captured you and brought you to our village!" Night Lilly felt her desperation keenly as she tried to make Desire understand. At any moment one of the villagers could pass by the captive's lodge and notice that Elk Bull was not standing guard. Time was precious if they were going to get Desire away from the village!

Desire sensed that Night Lilly was not setting a trap. With that realization, she pulled herself from beneath the covers.

"I brought you a dress and moccasins." So much of the Pawnee culture was instilled in Night Lilly, she could not bear the thought of Desire fleeing the village wearing the clothes from the Morning Star Bundle.

Pulling the dark robe from her shoulders, Night Lilly wrapped it around Desire. "Keep yourself covered. White Bull and my brother are waiting for you at the entrance to the village. They will take you away, and I will claim that you escaped! Stop for no one if you value your life!"

"Thank you, Night Lilly." Desire did not have long to ponder this benevolent gesture; she looked back at the young woman one last time before hurrying through the entryway and walking as quickly as possible in the direction Night Lilly had indicated.

"Be careful, and hurry!" Night Lilly's words of warning were lost on the evening breeze as she watched the captive disappear in the dark. Hardly daring to draw a full breath, Night Lilly hurried to her own home. Tomorrow morning, she would go early to the captive's lodge, then report to her father that the young woman had escaped—and her brother and husband had gone in search of her. This night she would spend praying to Tirawahat, that he keep White Bull and Elk Bull safe and allow them to deliver the captive to Bent's Fort without being discovered.

The image of Scar Hand stole into Night Lilly's thoughts.

Sighing softly, she placed a few more twigs on the lodge-fire. Scar Hand would not be pleased that he had been cheated out of his passion, but without the female captive for the Morning Star Ceremony, he would not dare approach her again! Her family was too important here in the Pawnee village. It was not the usual manner of the people that a warrior could approach another man's wife; she was safe!

Thirty

Cetán came upon the spot where Desire and Panther Stalks had been attacked by the Pawnee. What he saw filled him with a cold dread. For several minutes, Cetán sat atop Whirling-Warrior's-Ghost, his dark gaze taking in the scene. Slowly his mind put together what had taken place. Staring down at the prone body of a warrior, his face turned toward Mother Earth, Cetán knew by his Sioux trappings who the dead man was.

Elkhunter whined as he sniffed at the ground around the prostrate body. Before Cetán dismounted, the great wolf's attention was suddenly diverted; springing into action, the canine raced through the prairie grass, heading toward a copse of trees in the distance.

Dismounting, Cetán pushed the lifeless form over with a moccasined foot. His dark gaze intently studied the tomahawk handle, its blade buried deep in the fallen warrior's chest. He gauged the amount of time which had passed since Panther Stalks had been killed, and also deduced that his attackers had been Pawnee. There was other evidence which made him draw this conclusion: a spear and two Pawnee arrows lay next to the body.

Cetán's eyes sharply scanned the area, searching for any sign of Wacin. Relief filled his soul with the fact that her body was nowhere in sight. Breathing deeply, Cetán whispered aloud, "She still lives!" Perhaps Wacin had gotten away while Panther Stalks fought off the Pawnee attackers; this was all Cetán had to cling to at the moment!

Remounting Whirling-Warrior's-Ghost, Cetán followed Elkhunter through the belly-high prairie grass. From a distance, he glimpsed a horse near the stand of trees. Drawing nearer, he recognized Star. Hope began to fade slowly as Cetán drew closer to the mare.

Elkhunter circled the area, his excited yips indicating that he had picked up some sign of his mistress.

The excited actions of the wolf, and the approaching horse and rider, caused Star to shy away nervously as Cetán approached. With some effort, Cetán began to calm the mare with soothing tones. As her trembling began to subside, he was able to go over the mare's sleek flanks, checking for wounds.

Tieing Star's reins to his saddle, Cetán went to Elkhunter as the wolf excitedly circled and sniffed the ground. The signs left by several ponies and moccasined warriors were easily discerned. There was only one print made by a woman, and Cetán knew it was made by Wacin!

His bride had been captured by the Pawnee! A chill raced through Cetán's blood, slowly turning to boiling rage. If any harm had befallen Wacin, everyone in this group which had captured her would be made to pay!

As he turned Whirling-Warrior's'-Ghost in the direction in which the sign pointed, Cetán looked up into the early morning sky. Raising a mighty fist heavenward, he swore loudly, "Those who have stolen my woman will know the taste of death! These Pawnee will now know why they fear the dark!"

The ride to Bent's Fort with White Bull and his brother-in-law was a desperate flight. Desire and her two Pawnee escorts were well aware of their fate if they were caught. That first night, their pace never slowed. The three traveled by moonlight, the two warriors keeping careful watch for any sign of approach from behind.

The next morning, the small group stopped only long enough to water and feed their mounts and themselves. It was at this hour that Desire made her first attempt to speak with her escorts. The previous night she had been too frightened to speak out or slow the pace. But this morning, with no indication that they were being followed, she attempted to communicate with the two warriors, requesting that they allow her to travel on alone. She was sure that even now, she could somehow find her way back to her husband's village. The direction they were heading in was even farther north, and she feared each additional mile that separated her from Cetán.

Hand-signing that she wished the two warriors to return to the Pawnee village and allow her to go on alone, Desire was surprised at White Bull's negative reaction. He shook his head adamantly and pointed up ahead on the trail, indicating that they were taking her on to Bent's Fort.

Desire tried for some time to convince White Bull that this was not necessary. The two warriors could go back to their village before anyone was the wiser, and she could go back where she belonged. She knew it would be dangerous to travel alone without weapons or supplies, but she was determined that somehow she would make her way back to her own people!

White Bull had other plans for the young woman! He and Night Lilly had discussed trading the captive for blankets and other supplies; perhaps he would even be able to obtain some of the white man's sugar that he was so fond of. His family had been put through too much because of this woman coming into their lives, and White Bull was loath to allow her to slip away without some form of compensation. Elk Bull stayed out of the interchange, but Desire could tell that he would agree to whatever his brother-in-law decided.

White Bull would not bend in this matter, and a little
later the three were back on the trail. Their pace was now
more of a steady gait, which did not push their mounts
unnecessarily, but kept them traveling throughout the rest
of the day and long into the night.

The following morning, after traveling only two hours,
Bent's Fort stood out boldly along the mountain branch
of the Santa Fe Trail. Desire stared in total amazement at
the Fort and the activity taking place around it. Bent's Fort
had an unusual appearance here in the mountains-plains
region, due to the fact that it had been constructed of
adobe, sun-dried mud bricks, revealing a Spanish-Mexican
influence which was totally alien to anything Desire had
ever seen.

On the outside grounds, to the right of the fort, there
were several Indian lodges, creating the appearance of a
small village; Desire could see that the lodges belonged to
a small band of Crow. Drawing closer, the threesome passed
two trappers on horseback leaving the open entrance of
the fort. At the same time an oxen-drawn, open-flatbed
wagon was entering the gates, the vehicle driven by a grizzled trapper with a Flathead Indian woman sitting at his
side.

The interior of Bent's Fort was similar in appearance to
many of the trading posts being built along the Missouri
River and throughout the plains regions. Along the inner
walls, there were housing barracks, a smoke house, black-
smith shop, wash-house, animal pens, and a couple of canvas tents which housed occupants, desiring for reasons of
their own, to remain behind the towering walls of the fort.
Upon entering the front gates, the most imposing building
in the fort was directly ahead; the trade store, which flew
the United States flag overhead.

A wooden sign swung over the front door of the establishment, boasting the founders' names; BENT, ST. VRAIN
COMPANY. The traffic coming and going through the open

double doors testified to the brisk business taking place inside.

White Bull was first to dismount and secure his pony's reins to the railing post. Apprehensively, Desire did the same after Elk Bull dismounted, and followed the two warriors to the wooden walkway in front of the trading post.

Having never entered a building made from the giant trees nurtured by Mother Earth, Desire's tawny-gold eyes grew large as she followed the men inside. Her glance quickly traveled upward as she went through the portal, insuring herself that the structure would not collapse upon her head.

She breathed easier after a quick glance around. She looked at the wealth of goods lined on the walls of the establishment, stacked into corners and displayed for easy reach in the middle of the floor. Never had Desire seen such an abundance! There were shelves of trade blankets, trade pots and pans of every description, bolts of cloth, crates of trade beads, shovels, picks, axes, knives, rolls of pigtail tobacco, and rifles and ammunition lined against the wall behind the long counter. There were barrels, crates, and sacks of food supplies, as well as an assortment of smoked meats hanging from ties overhead on the rafters.

Desire stumbled along behind White Bull and Elk Bull, the warriors going directly to the counter at the back of the building. A large man greeted White Bull in the Pawnee tongue as White Bull waited his turn to conduct business. Looking behind the counter, through an open doorway, Desire glimpsed a storeroom and piles of tied and sorted pelts and hides.

"What can I be doing for you today, White Bull? I'm hoping you've brought some more of those fine pelts like you did the last time you came to my post." William Bent was a good-natured man who got on well with Indians and trappers alike. Having taken a Cheyenne woman as wife, he was trusted and well liked by most who came to Bent's Fort.

White Bull shook his head at the white man's words. "I have not brought furs this time, William Bent. I bring woman to trade for blankets and sweet sand white man call sugar."

"A woman, you say?" Bent looked more closely at the warrior and his small group. It was not unheard of for Indian women to be traded upon occasion, and Bent himself had gotten a few good workers by indenturing. His wife could always use an extra pair of hands in the wash-house or back in the supply room. Looking the young woman over, Bent frowned with lack of interest. The woman did not have the appearance of a hard worker. She stood with head lowered, seemingly shy or embarrassed. "She 'pears a mite young and thin, White Bull! I can't be taking on trouble here at the fort. I could use a few more workers, but this one would be having every buck entering the fort trailing her skirts!"

"She is strong! William Bent can trade her to one of the white men who hunts the mountains. She keep a man warm in his blankets!" White Bull reached out a long arm and pushed Desire's chin upward, making it easier for the white man to fully appreciate her beauty. "She work hard for William Bent! Worth three blankets and sack of white man's sand!"

There was no doubt in Desire's mind what was taking place between White Bull and the large man behind the counter. She keenly felt her embarrassment. As her chin was pushed upward, she closed her eyes tightly, not wanting to see the scorn on the white man's face. She had been stolen from her husband, captured by the Pawnee and almost murdered, and now she was being traded like a pony or a weapon! Silent tears made a path down her smooth cheeks, her anger and helplessness overwhelming.

Looking at the young Indian woman, for some reason

William Bent was touched by her tears. He loved his own Indian wife, and perhaps this was the reason he felt pity for the young woman's plight. But, business was business! And, he told himself, he could not be expected to help every helpless creature that made its way to his door. The woman was too frail to work here at the fort, and that was that! White Bull could try to trade her, himself, here at the Fort. The warrior could do what he would with her. It was none of William Bent's worry! Although the logical portion of his brain made his decision, the gentler side of his nature wished to console the young woman, if only for a brief minute. Reaching out a beefy hand, he gently wiped away the tears that stained her cheeks.

At the white man's touch, Desire's eyes flew wide.

Bent's features instantly registered surprise. He stared across the counter at eyes the color of brushed gold. One glance, and he knew she was not an Indian. His fist tightened as he lowered his hand. "Where did you get this woman, White Bull?"

"She was with a Sioux warrior. I was with a small hunting party when we came on them. The warrior died bravely. She was taken to my village, and was held as the captive female for the Morning Star Ceremony. Elk Bull and I brought her to Bent's Fort to trade for blankets and white man's sand." White Bull saw no reason to lie about how he had obtained the woman. It was a part of Indian life that women and children were captured in raids. The woman was in his company, and now belonged to him. He could do what he wished with her!

William Bent was incredulous. Having heard many of the details about the Morning Star Ceremony, he knew that the young woman was lucky to be alive!

"She speak Sioux tongue, not understand Pawnee." White Bull noticed that Bent's interest had been sparked.

Ignoring White Bull, Bent questioned the woman in the Sioux dialect. "What is the name you are known by?"

Desire's eyes sparkled with renewed tears. These were the first words in her own tongue that she had heard in weeks. Perhaps . . . just perhaps, this large man would help her rejoin her people! "I am called Wacin," she replied.

William Bent's dark gaze studied the young woman for another minute before his gaze returned to White Bull. "I will give you two blankets and five pounds of sugar."

"Woman worth three blankets!" White Bull stood firm on his end of the trade. He and Night Lilly would have two new blankets for next winter, and Elk Bull would have one.

Bent knew he would give White Bull what he demanded. It was the trader in him that made him attempt to better the bargain. "You've got a trade, White Bull. The girl will stay here. You go and pick out the blankets on that shelf over there." Bent pointed to the upper shelf lining the right wall of the building. "I'll bag you up some sugar." Bent wasn't surprised that the Indian had demanded sugar. In the past, the warrior always traded for sugar. Like many of the plains Indians, White Bull had a sweet tooth.

White Bull and Elk Bull did not bother to look Desire's way again. They had gotten what they wanted, and as soon as possible, they would return to their village.

Desire stood nervously, eyeing the large man as he came around the counter to go to a large barrel. He scooped out the white sand and poured it into a small burlap bag.

Before Bent made his way back around the counter, three trappers approached, their arms stacked high with beaver pelts. Two of the men wore fox-head fur caps, the other, a beaver cap. With much grunting and groaning, they placed their cache atop the counter. "We've got more out yonder on our pack-horses, Bent," the largest of the three commented.

"Yeah, we be needing supplies and such before heading on back into the mountains." A different trapper spoke up before his glance fell upon Desire. "Now jest what ye gots here, Bent? Me and me boyos been aiming to find us a squaw to take along with us a'trapping. Maybe this little ole Injun gal be liking to hitch on up with us?"

Desire visibly cringed from the three men. As the largest of the group reached out a hand and caught her by the forearm, she jerked herself free from his touch. "C'mon, gally, there ain't no need fer ye to be shy with ole Simon. If'n ye come along with me, McDougal, and Sammy, we'll buy ye some pretty ribbons fer yer hair."

"She's not for trade." William Bent caught the trappers' attention as he rounded the counter, and glimpsed the fear on Desire's face. "I'll take your pelts, but leave the girl alone!"

"C'mon, Bent, ye've got yer own squaw. Ye ain't needing another. Me and me boyos stay as randy as rutting goats up there in the mountains! Why, the gal won't have to lift a finger if'n she don't be a'wanting to. All she gots to do is keep us warm in our blankets."

"I said, she is not for trade!" Bent's voice hardened. Turning to Desire, his features softened. "Wacin, go on back there into the supply room until I finish up here." He spoke Sioux, and was instantly rewarded by the sight of the young woman hurrying to do as directed.

"Now, Bent, that ain't no way fer ye to be doing business!" the large trapper who had grabbed hold of Desire's arm interjected.

"The fact is, gentlemen, I don't need your business! You can take your pelts off my counter and go do your trading up river, if you like."

"Naw, there ain't no need fer ye to get testy over an Injun squaw." Ben McDougal had remained quiet until now. "The boys here ferget, once and a'while, that they're among civilized folks when they see a pretty woman. They'll be minding themselves from here on out, Bent. Ye jest give us the worth of our hides, and we'll get our supplies."

William Bent had dealt with McDougal before and found him a reasonable enough man. For this reason, he did not order the three out of his establishment. It was known that William Bent was a fair man, and his trading post thrived for that reason. Bent didn't want trouble with any of the trappers But, by the same token, he wanted them to know he wouldn't allow any bullying here at Bent's Fort.

Before Bent tallied up the pelts on the counter, White Bull approached with the blankets. Obtaining the bag of sugar, he noticed the Sioux woman was nowhere in sight. Bent could do whatever he liked with the young woman—White Bull and his people were well rid of her. Night Lilly would be safe from Scar Hand, and his family would remain happy as they had been in the past.

Finishing with the trappers, William Bent called Avery Mockler, the lanky, tow-headed teen who worked for him in the post, to work the counter until his return. Entering the supply room, Bent immediately spied Desire sitting on a pile of burlap bags in a corner. "You can use this chair over here, Desire." He pointed out a wood rocker near a pile of hides across the room.

Desire glanced from the chair to Bent. Now that she was alone with the large man, she did not know if she should be frightened or not. He appeared kindly enough, but she knew that looks could be deceiving.

"Can you speak English?" Bent questioned in the Sioux tongue.

Desire nodded her head. "I can speak the white man's tongue." Her response was spoken with caution.

Bent sighed with relief. It was always easier to communicate in his own language. Though, he spoke many of the plains tribes languages, he always feared that something would be missed in the interchange. "Can you tell me anything about your folks?"

"Folks?" Desire was unsure of the meaning of this wasichu word.

"Your people . . . your family?" Bent drew closer to her,

and from where she sat on the bags, he was reminded how beautiful her golden eyes were.

"My people are Lakota. My husband is Cetán." Desire hoped this man would help her reunite with her tribe.

"No . . . no . . . I mean your white family?" William Bent corrected. In the back of his mind, he thought he recognized the name Cetán. He was sure he had heard about a Sioux warrior called the Hawk. He would think about this later.

"My *wasichu* family?" For a minute Desire did not know what he was talking about, but then some of his meaning registered. "You speak of those who lived in the Pahá Sápa? They were killed by Gray Owl, my father, and his band of warriors. I have no *wasichu* family. I am Sioux. My husband and people are Sioux!"

William Bent knew he had not misjudged. This young woman was not an Indian. If her people had been killed by this Gray Owl, perhaps there would be some record of their death. "Do you remember how old you were when these people you say lived in the Black Hills were killed by this Gray Owl and his warriors?" Any information this young woman might be able to give might aid him in finding out if she had any family still living.

Desire did not wish to speak of the wasichus who had lived in the Pahá Sápa. She rarely thought about this part of her past. She had been raised Sioux. In her heart she was Sioux. Her father had explained long ago that the only reason she had been born to the wasichu was in order for Wakán Tanka to bring her to Gray Owl and Pretty Dove. "I wish to return to my husband—will you help me?" She forced herself to appear brave, but her heart was hammering a wild tattoo. She knew nothing about this man. Was this William Bent kind of heart, and would he be willing to help her return to her family? Or would he only be another obstacle hindering her from returning to Cetán?

William Bent would not answer her question about returning to her husband at this moment. It would be impossible for him to agree to get her back to the very people who had more than likely killed her parents and stolen her to raise as their own. "First, you must answer my questions, Desire, before I can promise to help you get back to this Cetán." Bent was a trader, and it was easy for him to swap information. "Now, tell me how long you lived with the Sioux. Were you a child when this Gray Owl took you away from your family?"

Desire searched her mind for the bits and pieces of information she had heard over the years about the raid Gray Owl and his warriors had made in the Pahá Sápa. This portion of her history had never seemed important to her parents or her people, so she had not asked questions. She believed her father when he told her she had been a gift from The One Above. "I was an infant. My father took me from the wasichu's wooden box and brought me to my mother's breasts. Their baby had joined the sky people."

William Bent stared in wonder at the young woman as she recounted the little she knew of her history. Surely there must be some record of this family that had lived in the Black Hills. Silently, he marveled at what this young woman's life had become since her infancy. Perhaps he would find some documentation in the archives that Ceran St. Vrain, his and his brother's partner, had brought to the fort from Fort Union, a trading post erected near the confluence of the Yellowstone and Missouri Rivers. "Do you know how old you are now, Desire?" If he had an idea of how long ago it had been since this Gray Owl had attacked her family, he would be better able to find some information.

"How old?" Desire wished to answer the large man's questions in order to return to Cetán, but she was unsure of what he meant by these words.

"How many summers or winters passed while you lived with the Sioux?"

Desire smiled in remembrance of the beaded leather sash her mother wore upon occasion. Each summer, during the moon when the ponies shed, Pretty Dove added another bead to her vermillion-dyed ornamental sash. "I can show you the number of summers that have passed with these bags." Desire began to place bags in a small pile on the floor.

When she finished, William Dent counted out each burlap bag. Straightening, he smiled at her as he stated, "Twenty years. You are twenty years old, Desire. It should be possible to find out who your real parents were, and if you have any family still living."

None of this meant anything to Desire. The large man appeared happy with her answers; now, she hoped, he would return her to her family. "Will you help me return to Cetán?" she questioned softly.

"I'll take care of everything. Don't you worry yourself about this Cetán—don't you worry about a thing." William Bent had a lead, and he had every intention of following it up!

Thirty-one

Cetán's mind was one with his heart. He hobbled Whirling-Warrior's-Ghost a short distance from the Pawnee village. In his silent attempt to study the strategic locations of the village, he was aided by a moon-bright night. Staying hidden among the encroaching shadows caused by the trees encircling the village, Cetán, with Elk-hunter at his side, came within several feet of the sentries keeping their nightly vigil against surprise attacks.

It would have been so easy for Cetán to step out of the shadows and attack the three warriors huddled near their small campfire. His need for vengeance so overwhelmed him, it was all he could do to control the deadly impulse. Caution and his wish to overtake the Pawnee with an element of surprise stayed his hand, which absently caressed the sharp blade of his rifle-stock weapon.

With the rising of the morning star, Cetán would make his presence known among the Pawnee, not before. Once he had found the village and contented himself with the knowledge of the sentries' position, he had prayed to The One Above, seeking guidance in his mission to recover his bride. Throughout the long night, Cetán awaited a sign. It came through the sharp cry of a hawk. Cetán did not see the bird that circled the dark sky. The wing-spirited creature spoke to his heart, giving out instruction that would aid him in his quest to defeat his enemy and recapture that which belonged to him.

Returning to the spot where he had hobbled the gray stallion, Cetán pulled out his paints from a hide parfleche. After smearing a small amount of bear grease over his face, arms, legs, and chest, he carefully dipped his fingers into a leather pouch of black paint, rubbing the stain evenly over his body. The color black was used for the fires of vengeance that burned hotly within his soul. With the completion of his own body painting, Cetán carefully painted Whirling-Warrior's-Ghost's head black, and down the length of each leg, he drew zigzag lines indicating lightning, which would impart speed and power. After tying the stallion's sacred medicine pouch around his neck and Cetán's own pouch was laid against his heart, the warrior whispered plans of approaching the Pawnee village into the mighty stallion's ear.

Whirling-Warrior's-Ghost's excited response indicated full understanding. Man and horse were setting out on a venture that would gain them that which they sought—or they would meet their deaths!

Elkhunter pushed against Cetán's hand with his nose, not allowing the warrior to leave him out of the enterprise. Cetán bent to the wolf, and as he had painted his horse, he now painted the silver wolf's face with the black rage that filled his own heart.

As the first traces of daylight stole through the Pawnee village, cries of alarm awakened those who lingered abed. Somehow, without any warning from the sentries, an enemy, bearing the signs of oncoming death, had stolen into the center of the village!

Whirling-Warrior's-Ghost sensed the impending fight and carnage. In high-strung expectation, he pranced in a tight circle, his head thrown back, eyes enlarged as he snorted loudly.

Cetán did not curb the stallion's movements, knowing his sense of excitement was as great as his own. Elkhunter growled low in his throat, his glittering eyes challenging

each newcomer that peered out from one of the entrance-
ways of the earthen lodges. The villagers were terrified at
the sight of the bold and vengeful painted warrior sitting
atop the prancing stallion, the vicious wolf at their side.

Some of the villagers whispered that the warrior and his
animal had been sent by the Wolf Star to demand vengeance for allowing the female captive to escape, thus depriv-
ing the Morning Star of appeasement. Others were sure
that the warrior and animals were from the dark side, having traveled through the galaxy to find their village in order
to wreak his cunning knowledge as a fighting warrior upon
their own Skidi Pawnee warriors.

At first sight of the painted warrior, Scar Hand knew
what had brought him to the Pawnee village. He was
Sioux—their female captive had also been Sioux. The warrior came in search of his woman. He hoped to claim that
which belonged to him.

Cetán waited, his knees tightly clutching Whirling-
Warrior's-Ghost's back, one hand on his war shield, which
had also been painted black, the other laid against the
smooth, well-worn wood of the stock of his weapon. His
dark gaze took in every movement, his heart pumping
adrenaline through every inch of his body. His presence
bespoke power as he awaited those he knew would come
against him.

Three of the bravest warriors amongst the Skidi Pawnee,
riding atop their war ponies, parted the crowd at the opposite end of the center of the village. Each of the warriors
clutched their weapons of war. Scar Hand, riding in the
center, held a war axe and tomahawk, his scorn for the
Sioux's daring display obvious on his hard features.

Cetán would extend no mercy to the three warriors, neither would he expect any! "Find Wacin!" he shouted to
Elkhunter, only a second before he raised his war shield
and shook it at the morning sun, then, as his war cry broke
his lips, he kicked Whirling-Warrior's-Ghost's flanks, set-

ting the great stallion into motion. At the same time, he bent, brushing his shield upon Mother Earth, invoking medicine-power which would turn away the assault of the enemy.

The gray stallion, which many of the villagers claimed was a ghost horse, and the painted warrior raced headlong through the center of the village, Cetán's weapon whirling expertly overhead. The singing blade whistled upon the morning air, as though in welcome of the coming taste of death. The villagers trembled as they raced for cover, the sight of the charging warrior evoking fear in all. The three set their ponies into motion, charging their challenger as their own war cries filled the brittle morning air.

The steel of Cetán's weapon was but a flash as he caught the warrior on his far right side, full in the chest. Whirling-Warrior's-Ghost turned toward the center warrior, his sharp teeth snapping at the war pony as the mighty steed pressed his great weight, overwhelming the much smaller animal. At the same moment, Cetán brought up his shield to cover Scar Hand's vicious attack. With a whip of his hand, far swifter than the eye, Cetán deftly deflected the war axe coming at his head and turned the rifle-stock weapon upon the warrior.

Scar Hand and the remaining warrior kicked out at their mounts, avoiding full contact with the dangerous blade, then readied themselves for another charge. Scar Hand glanced down at his midsection as he drew in great gulps of air, and noticed the stream of blood flowing from side to side. He had not been lucky enough to avoid the sting of the Sioux warrior's weapon, but the wound was not deep enough to be fatal. The sight of his own blood only increased his anger, and reinforced his determination to overcome this enemy! Scar Hand's war cry was more of a scream for blood lust! The two Pawnee warriors surged forward with their combined attack!

Cetán did not linger, but gave Whirling-Warrior's-Ghost

a free head, knowing from past experience the love of a good fight that filled the stallion's heart. Again, his deadly weapon circled overhead. As he passed between the two warriors, fighting off their dual attack, his blade pierced deeply into one warrior's back. With a practiced motion of the wrist, Cetán freed the steel. With little pressure on his sides, Whirling-Warrior's-Ghost turned and charged the remaining warrior and pony.

As the mighty gray stallion's deadly teeth bit the pony's neck in a death-grip, the fighting was too close for Cetán to use his weapon effectively. With a practiced motion of his hand, he slipped the beaded hand-strap of the rifle-stock weapon over one wrist, then drew forth his bone-handled hunting knife from the sheath at his side as his other hand held his war shield out to fend off Scar Hand's attack.

All the fury raging in Cetán's heart was suddenly unleashed on the remaining Pawnee warrior. Cetán lunged from Whirling-Warrior's-Ghost's back, his physical strength upsetting Scar Hand's seat on his pony and hurling him to the ground. Cetán boldly straddled the warrior, his war shield taking the full brunt of the brutal force of Scar Hand's war axe. Again, Cetán's battle cry spilled from his lips, his sharp-bladed knife slipping between his own war shield and the Pawnee's ribs. With a twist of his wrist and an upright thrust, Cetán felt his opponent sag back against the ground.

Wasting no time to savor the taste of victory, Cetán leaped to his feet. Whirling-Warrior's-Ghost turned away from his attack on the pony and raced to his master's side. Turning around in the center of the Pawnee village, Cetán's piercing cry filled the silent area: "Wacin!"

There was only silence. With one glance at Elkhunter, Cetán knew that his wife was not in the Pawnee village. His heartbeat thundered heavily in his chest, not from the exertion but from his inner fear that he was too late to save Wacin. In those few seconds, Cetán silently swore he would destroy this village, lodge by lodge, to extrac his full vengeance!

Like the rest of the villagers, Night Lilly had watchec from her hiding place as the fierce warrior had overcome Scar Hand and the two Pawnee braves. There was no regre in her heart for the fate Scar Hand had suffered. But now as she watched the storm of passion on the Sioux warrior' features and heard the cry that rose from his lips, she braved what none other in the village would.

"Do you speak the tongue of the white eyes?" she ques tioned, her limbs weak with fear as she stepped out intc the open. Night Lilly could only hope the warrior spoke the tongue that had enabled her to communicate with De sire.

It took a few seconds for Cetán to clear the black rage from his mind. He forced himself to focus on the word the woman was asking. "I speak the wasichu tongue," he admitted, the stock of his weapon slipping back into his palm as he cautiously watched for an attack by more Pawnee warriors. The woman could be a ruse to catch him off guard.

The large wolf growled low in warning, and Night Lilly dared not step any closer. From several yards away she ques tioned, "You come in search of Desire?"

Cetán's piercing, dark eyes centered on the woman as he attempted to comprehend her reason for approaching him.

"I do not wish any more of my people to suffer as these have." Night Lilly read his questioning look, and as she pointed to Scar Hand and the two warriors, she hoped the one standing before her would mete out no further de struction.

"Where is my wife?" Cetán had no mercy in his heart a the moment. He wanted only to look upon his beloved and know that she was unharmed!

"Desire is no longer here in the village. My husband and my brother took her to Bent's Fort."

"Where is your husband and brother? I would have words with the men!" Cetán's full anger had not, as yet, been appeased. He would take out more of his fury upon those that this woman said had taken his wife further out of his reach!

"You will not kill my husband, nor my brother!" Night Lilly refused to allow this war-trained warrior to attack her family. "My husband and brother saved Desire's life! She is at Bent's Fort. If you travel upriver, you will reach the fort and find your woman there. There has been enough killing this morning to satisfy even one such as you!"

"Such as I?" Cetán's lips twisted back in scorn at the woman's accusation. "Any warrior who has had a portion of his heart torn from his chest does what he must to retrieve that one that allows the very life to renew in his body!"

Night Lilly had never seen such raw passion in a man's face, nor had she witnessed such profound pain in a warrior's eyes. She could look into this man's very soul and see his anguish. "Desire told me about you. She told me of her great love for her husband, for the one known as Cetán. My family freed her from sure death. You have destroyed the one that brought her here. Your vengeance is no longer needed here among the Pawnee. You have done what was needed."

No further conversation was necessary. Cetán believed the young woman, and knew that she had had a part in saving his wife's life. Mounting Whirling-Warrior's-Ghost, he turned and left the Pawnee village without a backward glance.

Thirty-two

By the evening of the day of Desire's arrival at Bent's Fort, Charles and William Bent had searched the archives and found information about a McCray family living in the Black Hills around the time the two men figured Desire had been born. According to the few details available, a trapper called Buz French reported to Jonathan Baxley, the trader at Fort Union, that he had visited a family of three men, one woman, and a newborn child in the summer of 1811. Benjamin McCray, his wife Sarah, and his brothers Armstrong and Samuel had come from St. Louis to set up farming in the Black Hills. French had taken a meal with the family, and warned them to keep a wary eye out for Indians. A month later, passing by the farm, French had found the McCray family wiped out by the Sioux. What remains could be found, the trapper had buried. French also recalled that the infant girl's body was never found. By French's recollection, the child had been named Paula Carri McCray and had eyes the color of Black Hills gold.

Neither of the Bent brothers had any doubt that Desire was Paula Carri McCray. The significance of their find was monumental to both men, who now considered it their Christian duty to make sure the young woman was told the details of her white heritage.

That same evening the brothers came to an agreement. Charles Bent would leave the fort in two days, since he handled the shipping and buying for the fort in St. Louis.

He would take the young woman back to St. Louis, and press a search for any of the McCray family who might still be living in the area.

Desire's reaction to the news about her family was not what either brother had anticipated. There was no eagerness about her as they explained the news made about the McCray family. She listened silently to what had been reported by Buz French, then looked directly at William Bent. "These words mean nothing to me. I wish to return to my people, and my husband."

"But you're a white woman, for God's sake!" Charles gasped out, surprised at the young woman's response.

"I am Sioux. I am a healer among my people." This had been Desire's identity for the last twenty years. It did not matter that these men had found marks on paper, saying that her name was Paula Carri McCray. In her heart she was the daughter of Gray Owl and Pretty Dove. All that mattered was that she be returned to Cetán!

"But, girl, don't you understand? You've been deprived of the life you should have lived! You might still have kin in St. Louis—they would be pleased to know that you're still alive!"

"I have family among the Sioux. Why would I want to know these other people?" Desire did not understand these wasichu. They insisted she sit in their white man's chair and eat their strange food. Now, they wanted her to react to their words in a way she didn't feel. Her father told her, long ago, that the wasichu were strange. Now, she believed all that Gray Owl had told her.

"She's been brainwashed by them heathens!" Charles turned to his brother, William. "I know you get on with the Indians, and all, William. I'm not saying anything against Owl Woman, but what the Sioux did, killing her people and stealing her away to raise as one of their own, just wasn't right!"

Owl Woman was William Bent's wife, and he was aware

that his brother meant her no disrespect. Charles had a big heart, and hated to see anyone mistreated. He had a fine sense of right and wrong, and deplored injustice. In this respect, Charles Bent was like his grandfather, Silas Bent, who had led the bogus Indians in the Boston Tea Party incident during the American Revolution.

William gave his brother a reassuring smile, before turning back to the young woman. "Listen, Desire, for the time being, why don't we call you Paula Carri? Why don't you just try and consider everything we've told you tonight over a good night's sleep? In the morning we'll talk some more about this, and maybe you'll want to meet someone from the McCray family." William wasn't so sure it would be a good idea to tell this young woman that he and his brother had already made plans for her to travel to St. Louis. There was no sense stirring up trouble before it was necessary, he always said. Maybe in the morning she would think differently.

"My name is Wacin, and my family are the people of the Sioux. I do not need to think about what you say, William Bent. Tomorrow, I will still wish to return to Cetán!" Desire had had hope that this large man would return her to her husband, but now she was unsure. Though she did not believe her life was in danger here, as it had been in the Pawnee village, she was aware that these men posed a different kind of threat, one which would enforce the separation between herself and her husband.

Desire was shown to a room adjacent to William Bent's. With a last cautionary warning that the fort's gates were closed nightly and there was no way in or out, the brothers left Desire alone.

Desire turned around in the small room, curiosity in her gaze. Her eyes touched on the single bed with its lacy coverlet and the rocker resting to its left, with a flowered embroidered throw rug on the floor. She could not help but admire the strangeness of the white man's world.

Before she had time to look around thoroughly, the door reopened and Owl Woman stepped into the chamber. "I have brought you a gown to sleep in, Paula Carri." The Cheyenne woman placed the cotton gown across the back of the rocker.

It was obvious to Desire that Owl Woman's husband had told her about the brothers' belief that she was this Paula Carri McCray. Desire did not respond to the other woman's greeting, but eyed her warily as she turned down the covers on the bed.

When Owl Woman faced the young woman once again, there was sympathy in her expression. "It is a hard thing to find that one has lived a life that does not belong to one. The life of the white-eyes is easier than that of the Indian. In time, you will be glad that you are this Paula Carri. The white-eyes have wooden houses that do not leak when it rains, and it is warm inside during the winter months. You will not go hungry or lack for clothes. You will see—it is better to be a white woman than an Indian."

"I am Sioux," Desire stated softly.

Owl Woman shook her head sadly. Her husband had told her that the young woman was resisting her fate and that it would be easier if she would accept the truth and find her white family. William and his brother did not give up a project easily once they made up their minds. Both men were determined that this young woman regain some of what had been lost to her these last twenty years. "It would be better if you would accept yourself as Paula Carri McCray and forget the life you have lived with the people. I have gone with William into the white man's town. There are more white-eyes than the people have ever imagined. Many of them are determined they will live on the peoples' land. There will be no turning the white-eyes away. It will be hard on the people in the future. One day there will be no more buffalo, and the people will not survive without the white man. Their land will no longer belong to the

Mother which gave it to them. The white man will not be happy until he owns everything!" Owl Woman was practical, and repeated those things she had heard as well as those she had figured out for herself. She wished this young woman would listen to her and choose the road that would allow her a better future. It was not often that one of the people could turn aside their past and become one of the white-eyes. Even as wife to William Bent, Owl Woman knew she was not accepted by her husband's people.

Desire listened to the Cheyenne woman, but her words had no meaning. She had no desire to become one of the white-eyes. All she wanted was to be returned to her husband and people. What Owl Woman told her may be true, but she would stand with the people while they went through their suffering.

"Blow out the candle before you go to bed." Owl Woman knew the young woman would need time to adjust. Everything was happening too fast. Tomorrow things might seem clearer.

The minute Owl Woman left the room, Desire's thoughts turned to escape. Remembering William Bent's warning that the fort's gates were closed at night, she knew any effort on her part would be wasted. She certainly could not scale the stout mud-and-brick walls. No, she would rest tonight, and tomorrow she would await her opportunity. The gates would be reopened, and while everyone was busy, she would simply slip outside and hide in the forest until she was sure it was safe to start the long trek back to her village.

Ignoring the nightgown Owl Woman had left, Desire slipped naked beneath the soft coverlet. The mattress was harder than the soft pallet of furs she had shared with her husband, but it was much better than the hard wood floor, where she had first considered sleeping.

Though exhaustion overcame Desire quickly, her sleep was restless because of her dreams about a group of faceless people calling out to Paula Carri. The *wasichu* clutched at her as she fought them off. Cetán's image twined in the inner sphere of her thoughts—his husky voice, the thin precipice she clung to as she fought off the white men and women who wished to claim her as one of their own.

The following morning, Desire awoke to find her Pawnee clothing gone. In their place was a cream-colored gown sprigged with peach flowers and a pair of black leather walking shoes.

Desire's first reaction was to charge out of the room and demand her property. Reaching the door, she realized she was naked. Searching the room for anything to wear besides the thin nightgown, she found only the lacy coverlet, and she certainly could not drape that around her body to confront the Bent family! The trading post was far too busy to dare such a thing. She would only embarrass herself!

Wrapped in her mutinous thoughts, she put the white lady's dress on. Thank goodness she had been too tired to unbind her hair, or her bells would have been stolen with her dress and moccasins!

Ignoring the shoes, Desire straightened her hair as best she was able before leaving the chamber in search of Owl Woman. She would demand her clothing back; then she would demand her release! No matter who these people believed her to be, she would not give up. In her heart, she knew who she was!

Making her way downstairs, she was greeted by the young boy, Avery Mockler. "Mr. Bent said when you woke to send you out to the kitchen for some breakfast." The trade store was empty of patrons at this early hour. The boy was keeping himself busy with a broom in one hand and a dust rag in the other. "The kitchen's that a'way," he said and pointed to a closed door at the back of the building.

Drawing in a deep breath, Desire braced herself for the confrontation. She felt stronger this morning. Though her sleep had been troubled by strange dreams, she was ready to demand that the Bent brothers help her return to her people. If they would not willingly agree, then she would insist that they not attempt to hinder her.

Stepping through the door that led to a dog-trot leading out into the building that had been set up for the kitchen, Desire's senses were assailed by the smells of fresh-baked bread, roasting meat, and corn chowder bubbling in the blackened trade pot hanging over a great open hearth.

"Come in, come in. Take a seat over here next to Charles, Paula Carri," William Bent's loud voice urged from the doorway. His beefy hand waved her into the large kitchen, directing her to the empty chair next to his brother.

Thinking it best for the minute to comply to the invitation, Desire warily made her way around the end of the table and took the seat at Charles's right.

"You look mighty fetching this morning, Miss Paula Carri." Charles Bent smiled as he stood and pushed in her chair.

Desire smoothed her skirts nervously. She would have reminded them that her name was Desire, but she was sure her objection to being called by the wasicun winyan name mattered little to these brothers. "I would like my clothes back." She kept her tone low, not wishing to put the Bent brothers on the defensive. She still hoped she could persuade them to help her return home.

Wearing a typical Cheyenne costume, Owl Woman set a cup of coffee down in front of Desire. "You are not pleased with the dress and shoes?" Her dark gaze had already noticed the young woman was barefooted.

"I am comfortable in my own clothes, as you are." Desire observed the woman's buckskin dress with its beadwork across the shoulders, the upper and lower portion stained with yellow earth paint. Her heavily beaded leggings were embellished on the sides with German silver buttons, and she wore a dentalium shell necklace around her throat.

Owl Woman ignored the other woman's remark and went back to the wood stove, where another Indian woman stood frying bread.

"Your clothes will be returned to you when you leave the fort." William was quick to realize that a night's sleep had done little to change the young woman's attitude; she was still as determined as ever to remain Wacin of the Sioux!

"When can I leave Bent's Fort, William Bent?" Desire's question was direct. "If I can borrow a horse and supplies to travel to my people, my husband will return what is owed." She hoped that William would offer to take her home or have one of the people at the fort guide her, but she would not ask for that. It would be enough if she had a horse and supplies. She would find her way back to Cetán. She knew in her heart she could overcome every obstacle between herself and her husband!

William did not respond quickly. The group remained silent as the two Indian women set plates of food down in front of the Bent brothers and Desire. At last William replied, "Charles and I have made the decision that you will accompany him to St. Louis, tomorrow." There, he had informed her of their plans. He expected her to be upset, but reasoned that she would rally quickly enough. After all, she was a white woman. Having been raised by the Sioux, she could not know her own mind!

For a full minute Desire stared at the man across from her, believing she must have misunderstood. Slowly, as the full meaning of his words registered, bright spots of heat appeared on her cheeks, the lights in her tawny eyes glittered, and her hand tightened in the folds of her skirts. "I will not go with your brother to this place called St. Louis, William Bent." Her voice was hard, her tone low.

Taken aback by her vehemence, William stared at the

young woman. There was certainly no denying Paula Carri McCray was a rare beauty, but for all that, he was finding the young woman had a stubborn streak in her a mile long. "You have no choice in the matter, Paula Carri. The decision has already been made. Charles will help you find some member of your family." William turned his attention back to the plate of food before him, but unfortunately, he found that he had lost his appetite.

"You'll see, girl. In no time at all, you'll fit right into white society. As soon as we find some of your family, you'll forget all about this Cetán you keep talking on about." Charles tried to be reassuring, but it seemed that his effort was wasted. The young woman was determined to get back to the Sioux.

Realizing there was nothing she could say that would change the brothers' minds, Desire sat quietly until after breakfast. In her heart, she was just as determined to return to Cetán as these two men were that she be introduced into white society.

Throughout the rest of the day, wherever Desire went, she found Avery Mockler not far from her heels. It soon became apparent that the youth had been sent to keep watch over her, making sure she did not walk through the front gates of the fort.

That evening, Desire was again shown to the small room, and again, her dreams were a never-ending fight between the faceless white family that pulled at her relentlessly, and Cetán, whose husky voice permeated the inner foundations of her mind, imparting to her the agony of loss that filled his soul.

On waking, Desire found her hide dress, leggings, and moccasins resting on the chair next to the cream-and-peach gown. Ignoring the wasicun winyan clothes, she dressed in the comfortable Indian apparel. As she dressed she remembered that William Bent had stated that she would be given back her clothes when it was time for her to leave. Desire was smart enough to realize that the only reason she was granted this small favor was because it would be impossible for her to ride a horse with the wasicun winyan clothes on; her Indian attire afforded her the ability to ride astride.

Once again, she joined the Bent family for breakfast out in the kitchen. But this morning, there were two trappers sitting at the table with the brothers.

"Ah, here she is now, gentlemen." William rose as Desire entered the room, as did the rest of the men at the table. "This is Paula Carri McCray. She will be traveling to St. Louis with you and Charles."

The trappers had already been advised about Desire's circumstances, so were not totally unprepared for the sight of a young white woman dressed in Pawnee clothing. "It's a right big pleasure to meet ye, mam," said the largest of the pair of trappers. "I be known around these here parts as Hambone Wilcox. Me partner here is Sage Galloway. We be looking forward to traveling with ye and Mr. Bent, mam."

Hambone Wilcox was a larger-than-life, good-natured woodsman hired by the Bent brothers to travel with Charles into St. Louis and help haul supplies back to Bent's Fort. Hambone and his partner certainly had no objection to having a pretty woman traveling along with them.

Desire did not respond to the trapper's introduction. Looking at William Bent, she appealed to him one last time. "I do not wish to go to this place called St. Louis, William Bent. I wish to return to my people."

"We've been over this already, Paula Carri. I feel it's my responsibility to see you are reunited with your family. Let's eat our food now, before it grows cold." William tried to change the subject before a full-blown argument broke out at his table.

Desire's desperation was readable in the telltale depths
of her golden eyes. She glanced around the kitchen as
though expecting some help; seeing none, she said, "I am
not hungry, William Bent. I will wait outside until your
brother is ready to leave the fort." Once away from Bent's
Fort, there would be no stopping her from escaping the
three men and eluding them in the forest.

As soon as Desire closed the kitchen door behind her,
William turned to Charles. "I thought I recognized the
name Cetán when she first claimed she was married to
the Sioux warrior. Last night, I remembered a story I
heard about a Cetán. If it's the same buck she's wanting
to get back to, you'd better hope you don't run into him.
It was some time back, if I recall, when a couple of trappers told me they had joined up with some buffalo hunters and were attacked by a small band of Sioux. They
swore one of the warriors rode a ghost horse, and he
alone killed four of their group. The trappers claimed to
have only gotten away by crawling off into the forest while
the buffalo hunters fought off the attack. They lost the
fight. One of the trappers said the leader of the band,
the one riding the ghost horse, was called Cetán, and he
used a wicked-looking rifle-stock weapon."

"I'm sure there are plenty of Sioux braves with the name
of Cetán," Charles said, making light of the story. "Anyway,
this Cetán the girl keeps talking about is probably a long
way from Bent's Fort and will never even know that she
was taken to St. Louis. Once the girl finds some kin, she'll
be able to forget this whole part of her life."

From where Cetán sat atop Whirling-Warrior's-Ghost, he
could watch the fort from the cover of the forest and study
the activity at this early hour of the morning. The gates
had been thrown wide a short time ago. For some intuitive
reason, Cetán waited, his steady tone reassuring Elkhunter.

Cetán's patience was soon rewarded. Watching the three men and a woman passing through the fort's gates, he instinctively knew, even from a distance, that the woman was Wacin. His first reaction was to race to her side, but caution made him grip his stallion's reins in a tight hold.

Whirling-Warrior's-Ghost sidestepped, his head thrown back, sensing his master's agitation. Star also seemed to sense the tension in the air, nudging closer to the stallion, as though following his lead.

Calming himself with deep breaths, Cetán's gaze followed the small group as they began to head in an easterly direction, toward the forest he was using as cover. They were riding some distance ahead. For the time being, Cetán was content to follow. He could not endanger Wacin. He would choose the moment carefully to show himself.

As though preplanned, the two trappers rode at Desire's sides, Charles Bent leading the group at an easy pace. He had traveled this same route many times in the past, and enjoyed this part of the trading business. Once they arrived in St. Louis, Charles would gather supplies from the Bent, St. Vrain Company warehouse on the waterfront. What was not on hand from his suppliers, he would purchase himself. The two men traveling with him would be in charge of the freight wagons on the return trip to Bent's Fort. Charles would remain in St. Louis for the time it would take to see Miss McCray safely embraced by family. He and William had deemed it their responsibility to make sure Paula Carri McCray found some portion of her family, no matter the cost or the time involved. This wrong had been forced on the young woman, and it was their Christian duty to set it aright.

Throughout the long morning and afternoon, Desire awaited her chance to get away. She attempted to lag behind, hoping to ease off the trail, but she was not to be so lucky. Slowing her mount, she found Hambone Wilcox doing the same, his generous smile widening as he explained that he found her company quite enjoyable.

Desire was not fooled by his friendly manner. The trappers had been ordered to keep a sharp eye on her, and it was obvious they took their work seriously. They would have to sleep at night, though, she told herself. She would find a way after the men had fallen asleep. She would slip off into the forest, even if she to go on foot.

There was still an hour or so before dusk when Charles called out that they would set up camp a quarter of a mile ahead. The trail turned off, and he remembered from past experience that there was a spot along the river that was just right.

The trappers' mood seemed to become more jovial with Bent's announcement. The two men were being paid handsomely for their escort, and Bent appeared to be a man who traveled at a leisurely pace and brought along plenty of supplies. What more could a couple of mates be needing out of life?

"I heard tell about this fella down South a ways that ran into a grizzly one day while he was out a'trapping. Ran smack into that old griz without his rifle or a knife."

Sage Galloway was used to listening to his partner's yarns, and took the appropriate cue to ask, "What'd this fella do, Hambone?"

"Well, I'll tell ye what this fella did, ole son. He started running, and the griz took off after him. But this fella was right smart. He ran that ole griz round and round in circles until he had him dizzy enough where he didn't know if he was coming or going."

Another prolonged silence on Hambone's part, and Sage questioned with feigned interest, "How'd this fella get out of it, Hambone?"

"Why, at the right minute, the fella just stepped aside, and that ole griz jest kept on a'going in circles."

"What happened then, Hambone?"

"Why, I reckon as how that old griz is still going in circles somewhere down South, Sage." Hambone's gruff laughter erupted; his partner and Charles Bent joined in and Desire smiled also, the silly story lightening the tension that had been building all day.

Not only was the area up ahead the perfect spot for a campsite, it was also the right spot for an ambush. When Cetán appeared, it was so swift, there was little time for reaction. One minute Charles Bent was leading his small party, the next minute, a large, war-painted body hurled itself out of a tree and landed astride him, the cold steel of a large hunting knife pressed against his throat.

"Tell your men to throw down their weapons!" Cetán hissed against Bent's ear.

"Cetán!" Desire cried, and kicked out at her horse's sides.

Her attempt to reach her husband's side was swiftly halted by Hambone as the trapper grabbed hold of her mount's reins.

Sage Galloway drew his rifle out of the sheath at the side of his saddle.

"Don't shoot!" Charles Bent cried to his men, seeing from the corner of his eye the rifle pointed toward him and the Indian.

"I can plug him, Hambone!" Sage looked down the bead of the rifle, sighting the Indian straddling Bent.

Desire lunged from her saddle and grabbed hold of Galloway's rifle barrel.

"What the hell ya doing, missy?" Hambone attempted to pull her away from his partner, and at the same time Galloway was fighting to keep a grip on his weapon.

"Throw your weapons down! He'll kill me. He's dead serious!" Charles Bent looked directly into the Indian's eyes and knew that if his men did not do exactly as he ordered, he would not live to see another day.

"Throw the rifle down, Sage," Wilcox ordered his partner.

"This ain't right, Hambone. There could be more of them savages hiding in the woods." Galloway clutched the butt of his rifle, Desire's fingers still wrapped around the barrel in an unbreakable grip.

"There ain't no more Injuns, or we'd already be missing our scalps. Do what the boss says, or we might not get paid."

"Get to your feet, wasichu." Cetán jerked the man beneath him to his feet, the blade of his knife never leaving Bent's throat.

Bent obliged, having no other recourse. His eyes bulged as he looked over at his men, knowing their actions could well affect his life.

"Let Wacin go!" Cetán hissed.

"Let the woman go, Wilcox," Bent ordered without hesitation.

For a few seconds, the trappers remained undecided. "Ye really want us to turn her over?" Wilcox demanded.

Bent could only nod slowly as he swallowed hard, feeling the chill of the steel blade against his throat.

In the next minute, Desire was loosed by the trapper clutching her forearm. Jumping from her horse's back, she ran straight into the embrace of her husband's free arm.

"Cetán . . . Cetán!" Desire could barely get her husband's name out as tears overwhelmed her. Her hands roamed over his chest, reaffirming the fact that he was really here next to her.

The pressure on Cetán's knife increased slightly with his emotions. "Mitá wicánte, I have searched for that portion of my heart that was stolen, and now I reclaim that which belongs to me." For a second nothing existed except the feel of his bride in his arms.

Charles Bent attempted to pull back, bringing his attacker back to the moment. "I guess this means you won't be going along with us to St. Louis, Paula Carri."

Desire shook her head, knowing the wasichu was not serious. She placed her hand over the hand holding the knife at Bent's throat. "I will go with my husband, Charles Bent."

"It's your decision." Bent knew he had no choice in the matter.

Cetán's hand loosened its grip on the white man as he listened to the exchange. "Who is this Paula Carri you speak of?"

"It is the wasichu name that was given to me by the wasichu in the Pahá Sápa, long ago. Charles Bent was taking me to the wasichu town to find some of these people that are my wasichu family." Desire did not wish harm to come to Charles Bent. Both Bent brothers had been kind to her. She knew that they had done only what they believed to be right.

"Do you wish to go to this wasichu town, Wacin?" Cetán had been taken by surprise by her response, but knew that if she wanted to go to this place with these men, he would not stop her. He loved her too much to stand in her way.

"No, Cetán, no. I have always wanted to return to you. I want nothing more than to share your lodge, and your life."

Though this interchange was spoken in the Sioux dialect, Charles Bent understood most of what was being said and realized he and his brother had been about to make a terrible mistake. This woman's blood was white, but, as she had told them repeatedly, she was Sioux. "She's right, Cetán. She loves you, and all the time she was at Bent's Fort, she only wanted to return to you and her people."

Desire looked at Charles Bent with gratitude. At last he understood. She never really was this Paula Carri McCray.

Cetán lowered his knife. "Then we will leave, Charles Bent. I have regained that which I sought. My heart is found."

Charles Bent would not attempt to stop the warrior from

taking the woman, nor would he allow his men to interfere. It was not often that an outsider was given the privilege of witnessing such great love.

The couple disappeared into the forest. Cetán led his bride to the place where he had hobbled the horses, and had instructed Elkhunter to remain. Desire's reunion with Star and the great wolf was one of overwhelming happiness; even Whirling-Warrior's-Ghost appeared happy to see her, nudging her in greeting.

"I feared I would never see you again, Cetán," Desire softly confessed against his chest as she sat before him on Whirling-Warrior's-Ghost.

Cetán's strong arm tightened around her, his lips descending to meet hers in a breathtaking kiss. "I never would have given up, Wacin. No matter where my search would have taken me, I would have followed you to this wasichu town, and still I would have searched for you. How can a man live without his heart? How can one endure, knowing that a portion of his soul has been stolen from his body? I would have searched until I found you, Wacin."

Desire did not doubt he spoke the truth. "I love you with all my heart, Cetán." There was no longer any trace of doubt that her feelings for this man were meant to be. He had taught her to love, and to feel the inner tremblings of her heart. She would never regret being Cetán's wife.

"We will make camp shortly, Wacin. I wish to show you how much I have missed you, and how deeply my love burns for you."

Turning in his embrace, Desire whispered softly, "Love me, Cetán."

"Always, my heart."

Epilogue

The moon of the black cherries (August), 1838
The Lakota summer valley

Talking Woodpecker finished telling his tale. Many of the smaller children had fallen asleep in their mothers' arms, but his audience remained attentive to the last word.

Talking Woodpecker had repeated this story, which was called "Legend of Desire," many times over the past few years. His audience never tired of hearing such a tale of love and adventure.

Looking beyond the villagers, the ancient storyteller's dark eyes fell upon a man and woman sitting in back. The couple sat side by side, a boy child of two winters on his father's lap.

For a moment, Talking Woodpecker's eyes locked with the woman's of glittering gold, his head nodding in acknowledgment. The woman smiled, her hand reaching out, her fingers interlacing with the man's. Their bond was unbreakable; the child born of their love sat between them, attesting to the depth and beauty of their union. Their story would live on throughout all time!

YOU WON'T WANT TO READ
JUST ONE—KATHERINE STONE

ROOMMATES   (0-8217-5206-5, $6.99/$7.99)
No one could have prepared Carrie for the monumental changes she would face when she met her new circle of friends at Stanford University. Once their lives intertwined and became woven into the tapestry of the times, they would never be the same.

TWINS   (0-8217-5207-3, $6.99/$7.99)
Brook and Melanie Chandler were so different, it was hard to believe they were sisters. One was a dark, serious, ambitious New York attorney; the other, a golden, glamourous, sophisticated supermodel. But they were more than sisters—they were twins and more alike than even they knew . . .

THE CARLTON CLUB   (0-8217-5204-9, $6.99/$7.99)
It was the place to see and be seen, the only place to be. And for those who frequented the playground of the very rich, it was a way of life. Mark, Kathleen, Leslie and Janet—they worked together, played together, and loved together, all behind exclusive gates of the *Carlton Club*.

Available wherever paperbacks are sold, or order direct from the Publisher. Send cover price plus 50¢ per copy for mailing and handling to Kensington Publishing Corp., Consumer Orders, or call (toll free) 888-345-BOOK, to place your order using Mastercard or Visa. Residents of New York and Tennessee must include sales tax. DO NOT SEND CASH.

TALES OF LOVE FROM MEAGAN MCKINNEY

ROMANCE FROM JANELLE TAYLOR

ANYTHING FOR LOVE   (0-8217-4992-7, $5.99)

DESTINY MINE   (0-8217-5185-9, $5.99)

CHASE THE WIND   (0-8217-4740-1, $5.99)

MIDNIGHT SECRETS   (0-8217-5280-4, $5.99)

MOONBEAMS AND MAGIC   (0-8217-0184-4, $5.99)

SWEET SAVAGE HEART   (0-8217-5276-6, $5.99)